GAMES OF ASTRAEUS

Also by Jeramy Goble

Science-fiction/space opera:

<u>The Akallian Tales Trilogy</u>:

Souls of Astraeus (fall 2013)
Games of Astraeus (summer 2015)
Fates of Astraeus (spring 2016)

Dark fantasy:

The Coven Queen (fall 2016)

Games of Astraeus

of

The Myalllian Tales, Book Two

Jeramy Goble

Noachian Books
North Carolina

Noachian Books
North Carolina
Noachian noachian-books.com
Books
Noachian Books and the portrayal of a flooded Martian silhouette with stone tablet insets are trademarks of Noachian Books

Edited by Jeramy Goble
Printed in the United States of America

jeramygoble.com
facebook.com/JeramyGoble
twitter.com/JeramyGoble

Book design by Jeramy Goble
Jacket design by Jeramy Goble

Cover art by Jonathan Powell
jonathanpowell.daportfolio.com

Publisher's Cataloging-in-Publication Data

Goble, Jeramy.
    Games of Astraeus / Jeramy Goble.
        pages cm. – (The Akallian tales, bk. 2)
    ISBN: 978-0-9898841-3-6 (hardcover)
    ISBN: 978-0-9898841-4-3 (pbk.)
    ISBN: 978-0-9898841-5-0 (e-book)
    1. Extraterrestrial beings—Fiction. 2. Reincarnation—Fiction. 3. Interpersonal relations—Fiction. 4. Science fiction, American. 5. Adventure fiction.   I. Title.
PS3607.O26 G36 2015
813—dc23   2015910552

First Edition

10 9 8 7 6 5 4 3 2 1

This one is for Mary Cole.

Games
of
Astraeus
The Akallian Tales: Book Two

Jeramy
Goble

This one is for Mary Cole.

Games of
Astraeus

The Akallian Tales: Book Two

Jeramy Goble

Chapter I
The Lost Wind

WHEN AZLI OBLITERATED AKAL, the news spread in hundreds of different ways, and within only a few seconds. There were hand gestures, growls, howls, shouts, and displays of exotic contortions of body language. Beeps, honks and sorrowful bellows, both audible and telepathic, dispersed awareness of the horrific event. Combined with the merciless decimation of the defending Astraeans, the word of Akal's death commanded the attention of his fellow Astraeans. The fighting slowed, then lessened, and finally, stopped. The Astraeans began to look towards Akal's last known location. Countless other Astraeans had been butchered, and many of their deaths heightened the shared sorrow, but Akal had grown to be the close friend of many Astraeans. The amount of rapport he had with everyone, arguably rivaled Elcyd's.

The attackers didn't just sit there and allow the

Astraeans to pause. They seized the opportunity to take their leave. They had suffered only moderate losses, but most notably, the destruction of their primary ship that was suppressing the repairs being done to the ribbon mechanisms. As more and more ribbons came back online now that the attacking ship was destroyed, and as more Astraeans were able to return to the Harbor, it seemed the attackers had no desire to press their luck. They were satisfied with what they had accomplished in Akal's death. They weren't retreating and were grotesquely in no hurry. They could have stayed if they had wished, and murdered more.

Daebaugh, Azli, and their fellow aggressors, began to bark between themselves.

"Remember, don't leave any of these behind!" Azli yelled in her vicinity, referring to the machine she used to destroy Akal. "They cannot have them!"

"Azli, it's time to go!" Daebaugh shouted at her, over the sound of their ship settling in its own flames. "Get everyone out of here. They're restoring the ribbons quicker than we thought they would!"

Many of the Astraeans heard their urgent need to take the machines with them and began a final counter-offensive to try and capture one of them. Only moments had passed since Akal was killed, and while many Astraeans took part in the counter-offensive, Lannya didn't. She couldn't. She had no control over what entered her mind. She had no say, no input, and no choice. There was no delay or hesitation. Having just seen Akal snuffed out of existence, she was pierced with a memory. The moment the recollection breached her thoughts, her soul ached for absolutely anything else to think of, due to the pain and anger it generated. As soon as she saw Akal jump towards her, and it registered that he was intercepting the shot from Azli's weapon, Lannya summoned a hate and anger she never knew she was capable of. Lannya retreated into her memory of laying in bed with Akal after the last time they had made love in the Habitat.

In conjunction with the beginnings of her stimulating memory, without hesitation, she whipped her neck around to locate the nearest turret. After the primary enemy ship was destroyed, many of the turret gunners had abandoned their position to join the fight on the roof. Lannya ran to the nearest one.

She jumped up and strapped herself into the turret harness. Like coldly executing a perfectly coded program, she trained her sights on Azli, Daebaugh, and the remnants of the command module near the wreckage of their ship. She unleashed the powerful energy bolts from the turret with complete focus and precision. Her forehead began to sweat, but it was only from the physical energy she had been exerting since she, Akal and the Trio ascended to the roof. It wasn't sweat from fear or anger. She simply knew right then what needed to be done. Azli and Daebaugh needed to die.

Her aim was true, but her initial turret bolts struck the ground too late. Daebaugh and Azli quickly escaped to some of their smaller evacuating ships. The other attackers followed their lead on other ships, transports, and fighters, or by creatures and beings. In under a minute, the attackers sprinted up ramps or jumped onto platforms of ships racing by, which slowed down just enough to pick up their comrades. Other fleeing attackers poofed into energy which was then siphoned onto spacecraft, or became part of whatever other ship or creature they were escaping with. They were gone.

Lannya jerked her head out of the turret's targeting mechanism and scanned the roof of the harbor with her own sight. Her memories took back over as she did so.

The next image to pop into her mind from her past, was that of a small speck of dust riding the meager currents of the sterile air, as it approached the air filtration vent, above the bed in their living quarters. The speck was only barely noticeable in the bright artificial light of the Habitat. Akal rested his head on her chest. His breathing had almost returned to normal. While Lannya played with his earlobe, she became fixated on the speck of dust. She knew that there would always be dust, dead skin, dander and the like, to clean up after, but it represented so much more. It was a symbol of the dirt and grime that came with life. The types of things that came with the territory of living. Necessary evils. *Why hide from them?* She thought at the time. *If they were necessary, then how could they be evil? Why try to hide or eliminate the dust?* It was a byproduct of their lives. Their flesh. Their ecstasy. Their love, passion, and joy.

The Habitats and their Councils tried to pretend there wasn't any dust of any kind. They had become obsessed with minimizing and eliminating the literal and figurative dust, and encouraged others to look down upon the leftovers of life. But Lannya knew better. She could see through the mind games and propaganda that came in the form of the P.E.N's Declaration.

Her mind continued to remember long-gone moments as her eyes scanned the present. She felt her hand slide down the turret's harness to the release mechanism. Her thumb pressed the button on the release and she felt the harness slide up and across her chest. She looked down just as the harness slid out of place. The gentle but quick sensation made her snap back to her memory.

Akal gently but quickly slid his arm across Lannya's naked chest. She continued to watch the lonely dust float in the air. The speck grew closer, and then, it was abducted by the air vent. Gone to who knows where, to become who knows what. Lannya smiled internally but remained physically expressionless. She amused herself in contemplating the idea of the countless individual specks being inhaled through a series of air ducts, and finally collecting in some dark chamber, deep below the Habitat. There, they may accumulate, grow, and mutate. They would eventually gain sentience and destroy the evil air filtration system. Lannya audibly giggled at considering herself the dust, and the Habitats, the filtration system.

Akal stirred slightly when he heard her giggle and moaned slightly as if to ask what she was giggling at. He had almost fallen asleep and Lannya didn't wish to disturb him, so she offered no reply. She smiled externally this time, both at Akal, but also at her epiphany.

She and Akal had discussed her frustrations with the Habitat, the Declaration and the bureaucracy, countless times, and the discussions usually ended up sounding the same. Lannya would list her frustrations, and Akal would always try to make excuses for them. Previously, she thought Akal was just acting submissively, but he realized now, that even in his pre-Astraean form, he was simply looking out for her. When he jumped to take the shot from Azli's weapon, he was doing the same thing.

Lannya's memory was once again interrupted. This time, Rigella was shouting at her from the base of the turret.

"Lannya!" Rigella shouted, trying to get her attention. She quickly repeated herself after not getting an answer. "Lannya! Are you ok?"

Rigella was slightly worried, but calmly re-positioned herself to try and get a better view of the turret seat. Finally, she saw Lannya stand up and shake her head with reality. She turned slowly and looked down at Rigella. She nodded a few times. There was no urgency in her nods, and nothing was spoken.

After acknowledging Rigella, Lannya turned back around and prepared to jump down and out of the turret, but before doing so, she started punching the back of the seat with her left fist. She punched it as furiously and angrily as she could. It felt to her as if she had punched it for hours. After running out of energy, she fell back into the turret seat and cradled her gridlocked mind, and swallowed, to try and alleviate the pain in her throat that had accumulated from the pain of losing Akal.

She struggled and yearned to return to her memory. The pain made her wish she could temporarily rid herself of it somehow. Akal's legs shifted and slid in the sheets. They were intertwined with Lannya's, and she loved that feeling. She felt his leg hair bristle against her own legs as they moved. When one of his legs came to rest on one of her shins, it quickly became uncomfortable. It was right in the middle of the shin, where the least skin was. She didn't care, though. She let his leg stay, without doing any shifting of her own. She did, however, lightly squeeze Akal's back in a horizontal hug of sorts. He responded by squeezing her around her side and slowly lifting his head to kiss her in the center of her exposed chest. While laying flat, her skin presented a perfect landing pad for his kisses. She was his world, and she wanted to give the world to him. There was no inequality in their relationship. They simply approached the outside world around them differently, but they had no higher individual priority, than the other.

Lannya knew this better than ever now. She had, she felt, regretfully taken a long time to realize it, but she realized it. There was no longer any ambiguity in how she felt about everything that happened back then. She knew Akal was doing what he thought was best for them. But, another repetitive flash of Akal jumping to protect her from Azli's weapon stole her inner eye. She was once again stabbed with anger, spawned from the fresh batch of fear that she wouldn't be able to tell him her tomes of realizations. She was ripped out of her memory, once more. Painfully, and yet, thankfully.

Akal took the hit and was gone. Lannya shivered as she replayed it in her mind. On top of their daughter, Azli, being one of the attackers, and the confusion from the unexplained assault, Akal was gone.

Dead. Gone. Millions of lives worth of Akal. Erased.

* * *

At the moment Akal was struck by Azli's weapon, Lannya flinched slightly out of instinct, when she thought she was going to get hit. But once Akal disappeared, she ducked behind some nearby debris and attempted to locate the Trio. They all saw what happened to Akal. And if they hadn't already looked for Lannya, they quickly did to confirm her safety. Once she caught everyone's eyes, she shouted with passionate hate, "Azli killed Akal!"

By the time the Trio had begun sprinting to meet up with Lannya and make their way towards Azli and Daebaugh, Router and Hergie had already joined the rest of the turret gunners in attacking the remaining enemies on the roof. While Lannya waited for the Trio to make it to her position, she quickly looked out towards the beacons. She saw what she believed to be flickers of ribbon energy flashing on and off a few times, at various positions, as she realized some of the ribbon paths to the Harbor were being re-established. Even though the enemy ship had been destroyed, receiving reinforcements to make quick work of the remaining attackers was imperative and most welcomed.

Chapter II
Triage

The time it took for a ribbon to be restored decreased with each repair. The engineers rapidly developed a way to eject a hook, of sorts, from the portion of the ribbon connected with the Harbor, to the matching portion of ribbon adrift out in space. Once the hook latched on and made a temporary, new connection, the line of the hook then quickly regenerated the remaining gap in the ribbon and restored the connection to full capacity and strength.

While the speed of the repairs was admirable, it didn't make much of a difference. The attackers had already come and gone on their own schedule. They weren't there to destroy the Harbor, or kill as many Astraeans as they could. Once Akal was dead, they quickly began to withdraw. By the time the majority of the ribbons had been repaired, all attackers were gone.

The roof of the Harbor was littered with smoking,

glowing, and settling chunks of debris of various materials from countless different types of spacecraft. Corpses of those from all over the multiverse created a haphazard grid of connect-the-dots between heaps of rubble. Those who had only lost a single regular life during the battle began to return in different forms.

Astraeans, if still conscious after sustaining what would eventually be a fatal wound, could sometimes do something similar to rewinding time, but only to the moment just before they sustained the fatal wound, in order to preserve that form. It required a great deal of spiritual focus and energy. It could obviously not be done if that life's death was instantaneous, or if the Astraean was too weak.

Most of those new to the Astraean existence didn't have enough control over, or experience with their soul to do it, either. But that's exactly what Carthal was able to do during the initial assault on the Harbor. He rewound his usual form's life to just before it was killed.

At some point between the beginning and end of the attack, however, Astraeans began to discover that they could no longer do that. They could no longer rewind time, to any degree. Something had started suppressing that ability.

Others who had been hit by the same mysterious weapons that claimed all of Akal's lives, were also noticeably absent from groups expecting their return. Everyone had a face warped by the shock of destruction, death and confusion. No one knew why this war had come to them. No one knew who would have this level of malice towards the Astraeans.

Those who had, for now, escaped a death of any kind, were quickly being tended to. Shrieks and screams from the wounded, and those who saw the wounds, began to creep out into the air. People and creatures from throughout the multiverse began to run to and fro, back and forth between terminals, scrambling to generate emergency supplies appropriate for different types of organisms. The vast majority of survivors however, continued to stand, frozen, looking around in disbelief at what had transpired. No attack on the Astraeans as a whole, had ever come to the Harbor like this.

The Trio, Lannya, Thyra, Router and Hergie, who were favoring wounds of their own and limping in various gaits, began to make their way towards each other. After stopping here and there to help some of their fellow Astraeans, they reached each other. The Trio exchanged hugs and tears in the mutual realization that they had lost Akal. They had traveled with him for thousands and thousands of years. They had saved each other thousands of times, told each other as many stories, and done countless other things for each other, more times than anyone could count. Thyra and Router looked at each other with eyes of silent despair before retreating their gaze to the ground. Hergie stood expressionless, but silent. Being absolutely quiet was the only way an Oreis can show their sadness.

As everyone comforted each other or took solace in reuniting with the remainder of their group, they all silently began looking to Lannya. Even with Router and Hergie nearby, she was still the newest addition, if she was an addition at all. They felt awkward not knowing how to read her feelings, and not knowing how to talk to her in the wake of Akal's death. Feet shuffled and gazes began to wander. Lannya's eyes had been trained to the ground the whole time after exiting the turret and meeting up with the group, but after what felt like an eternity to everyone else, she raised her head. No one knew what to expect to leave her lips.

"I'm sorry," Lannya said sincerely and strongly. Her voice wasn't weak. She meant it. She said it slowly and thoroughly.

The Trio, Thyra, Router and Hergie didn't know how to take her apology. No one replied, but their previously wandering gazes came back to Lannya after she spoke. They were puzzled. Carthal's head tilted compassionately as if silently asking who she was apologizing to, and what she was apologizing for.

Rigella couldn't stay focused on Lannya. She turned slightly away from the group as her eyes couldn't take it anymore. Rigella never cried. She just didn't, and didn't ever need to. She was the definition of strength. She didn't hide from emotion or expression, but she just didn't cry. She did now, though. She missed her friend that had been ripped away from them all.

Heersan offered the first consolation as he put his hand on Lannya's shoulder. No one else had spoken yet. Lannya's open-ended apology was still floating among the group without addition or response. Lannya's face remained pointed to the ground, but there was no indication from her that she was waiting for anyone to acknowledge her apology, and if she was expecting an acknowledgment, she knew it wouldn't come from any of them. She just needed to say it.

To Akal.

No comment ever came, and one didn't need to. After a time, it was all silently understood who Lannya was talking to, so they all let the apology go to whom she intended it to go to, without any input from them.

The silence between them was left undisturbed until the large door leading down to the upper dome stairs flew open and slammed against the wall. Everyone turned to look at the commotion. Everyone but Rigella. She was still stubbornly and needlessly trying to maintain her strength in front of the group.

"Let's tend to the wounded first," Elcyd shouted, at some of his fellow Helpers as they poured through the doors. He continued speaking as he pointed and planned with some engineers, "If you would, work on getting the turrets repaired and if needed, replaced."

Elcyd caught a glimpse of the Trio, Router, Hergie, Lannya and Thyra. He nodded quickly and gestured with one hand at the group that he would come over to them shortly. Afterward, he began tapping a nearby console with one hand. A small, semi-transparent blue globe popped out of the console's artificial ribbon energy panel, and flew up to just within an inch of Elcyd's mouth. It followed the movements of his head and stayed just in front of his mouth as he spoke. As he did, what he said was amplified and transmitted to all those within hearing distance on the roof. Translations of what Elcyd said also appeared in some of the other more common communication methods on projected banners of energy towards the bottom of the artificial atmosphere that encompassed the dome's roof.

"Everyone, this is lead Helper, Elcyd. We will get

what information we have to you all as soon as possible. But for now, we are working on tending to the wounded and restoring our defensive turrets. We have restored most of the ribbons and should complete repairs to the remaining ribbons, and all ribbon energy systems, shortly. If you are wounded, we will get help to you. Please everyone, stay calm and focus on helping each other."

Hergie spoke up for the first time since the end of the battle.

"I must go ASSIST WITH REPAIR," he said, not giving anyone time to respond. His desire to help was too strong. The lead engineer nodded at Hergie as he joined up, then turned to address his team.

Elcyd then tapped a final command into the nearby console at which point the small globe he used to transmit his statement, evaporated. He then pointed and gestured to Helpers and engineers who had stopped to ask him questions as he bent over slightly to grab his leg, which had a huge rip in it. No one, including Elcyd, had paid it much attention. While partially bandaged, there was still an exposed area that was bleeding profusely. Even so, he started limping his way towards the Trio.

Rigella, who had turned and wiped her eyes as Elcyd began his statement, now proceeded to march towards him to help alleviate his wounded gait. She marched with purpose, much like she paced. She wasn't angry, and even if she was, it wouldn't haven't been at Elcyd, but she wanted information so she could take action.

Elcyd anticipated their meeting as they approached each other and began to speak.

"Rigella, we don't know..."

"No, Elcyd," she interrupted. "I need to know everything you know," she continued, while sliding up under his arm on the side of his injured leg.

The rest of the Trio and the others had followed Rigella and gathered around. Rigella helped him to a recess in the nearby railing, and motioned for Elcyd to sit down so she could better wrap and tend to his leg.

"Here, sit up against the rail here and move your leg as little as possible," Rigella ordered. She then shouted to the group and anyone nearby, "Anyone have any ribbon pouches?"

No one in the vicinity had one. She stood up and ran to the terminal that Elcyd had used previously. After tapping a few commands to specifically request a medical pouch, the terminal dispensed one. These pouches contain a more gelatinous form of the artificial ribbon energy used throughout the Harbor. After running back to Elcyd, Rigella got back down on her knees, ripped the pouch open and squeezed its contents onto, and into, the huge gash in Elcyd's leg. It ran from the inside of his leg, down to his ankle. Once she had squeezed the contents of the pouch into the wound, she then tore the empty pouch lengthwise and placed the packaging over the wound, covering it. Lastly, she pressed a button on the pouch that wirelessly synced with the console and received the command to quickly heat up, and cauterize the wound.

Elcyd choked down a rushed breath through his teeth and followed it up with a furious, but muffled grunt as the wound cauterized.

"There," Rigella said, as she began to dress the area with bandages.

Having caught his breath after the shock of finally paying attention to his wound, Elcyd forced a few more deep breaths to compose himself.

"They killed Akal, Elcyd," Rigella blurted out. Elcyd took a break from his heavy breathing and looked around at the group in disbelief.

"A regular?" Elcyd began to ask before being interrupted.

"No. Everything. All of his lives," Rigella answered quickly. Her voice was starting to buckle from her throat's swollen and failed denial.

Elcyd began involuntarily breathing heavily again as he continued to look around at the faces of the group. Heersan, Carthal, Rigella, Lannya, Thyra and Router were devastated. Melted faces of loneliness, emptiness, and stolen companionship, completely communicated their dark sadness.

Rigella began with her questions. "What happened after we left to meet up with Akal?"

"It was so sudden and coordinated," Elcyd began. "We had been trying to question Azli and the others you brought back from Lenmeteq for hours. They didn't say a word. They didn't give us anything. Didn't answer anything. I guess they were just waiting."

"Waiting for what?" Rigella prompted.

"For us to give them access to our internal ribbon systems, I guess," Elcyd assumed. "We were going to take a break from interrogating them and move them from the temporary holding room, to a more secure area in the bottom dome, when we brought in a ribbon reader to scan them, positively identify them, and record their actions.

We wanted to find out where they had been, and what they were doing."

Rigella had an idea of what was coming and let her head drop.

"It happened so fast. After initially refusing to, we grabbed Azli's hand and forced her to slide it into the reader. She made no sound or gesture. She just stared at her hand in the ribbon energy, waiting for it to happen. The ribbon reader picked up some kind of malicious information from her body's ribbon energy. After a few seconds, alarms went off from all over the Harbor, for all systems. The beacon security systems went offline. The turrets went offline. Communications went down. A few seconds later, we were all fighting in the room. I killed one of her friends. She killed a few of our Helpers. I lost consciousness at some point and woke up on the floor with this gash in my leg. I heard the fighting from all over the Harbor, and up on the roof. I gathered what engineers I could and worked to restore what ribbon systems and turrets we could. And here we are."

Everyone looked at each other, posing additional questions silently. While being caught up on how they had arrived at that point was helpful, it didn't shed any light on who did this, or why they did it. Router then spoke for the first time.

"It sounds like something that happens all the time on my home planet," Router started to surmise. "Malicious data packages get sent back and forth constantly. She must have inserted something into your ribbon traffic to take control and set the stage for this ambush."

Router looked around at the group as he posed his

next question to everyone.

"Do you not have some kind of mechanism to check for, or prevent that kind of activity?"

"No," Elcyd offered softly.

Rigella came to her feet angrily as she shouted down at Elcyd.

"How can the Harbor not have any kind of defense against something like that? Are you serious? How could this have been allowed to happen?"

For the first time since her apology to Akal, Lannya took part in the discussion.

"I don't think any of us knew something like this would be, or could be possible, Rigella," Lannya proposed calmly and rationally.

Rigella slowly turned her body around to face Lannya completely before replying. With each degree as she turned, she was formulating her reply.

"What would you know about what any of us knew or not?" Rigella challenged. "We've only heard stories about you. We've never seen you before until I crashed the fighter into the library."

Lannya was surprised at Rigella's snarky bite. She knew she was the new to the group, but she also knew she didn't deserve the attitude.

"I've been an Astraean for quite a long time as well, Rigella," Lannya confidently replied, as she took a few steps towards Rigella. She took the steps not to intimidate, but to reclaim the portion of ground that was rightfully hers.

"And I know this," Lannya continued. "None of us knew we were so vulnerable, so at the same time, we are all responsible."

Lannya and Rigella continued their steadfast standoff, but not out of competition or hate. They both simply had contempt for the fact that the Harbor, and all of the Astraeans got caught off guard.

Heersan attempted to break or weaken the tension.

"Hey, we don't need to do this. Regardless if we all share the fault, or if no one could have anticipated this, it's a wash. Either none of us saw it coming, or we all should have seen it coming. It's the same thing. Let's help the wounded, help repair, and work on getting information. After that, we can make sure nothing like this ever happens again."

Both Lannya and Rigella relaxed their posture and with their faces, noticeably redefined their priorities in a silent consensus.

Chapter III
A Late Arrival

The smothering tidal wave of screaming and groaning from the wounded soon transitioned into the drone of machinery. As a wounded Astraean was stabilized or taken down from the roof, an engineer would take their place, repairing the turrets and other systems on and around the scene of the battle. Blood, plasma, water, oil, rock, and other debris from the injured of the multiverse was cleaned up as quickly as feasible. There was no humor in any conversations, and nothing was said that wasn't directly pertinent to the restoration of defenses or caring of the wounded.

The roof quickly became crowded. Those who weren't tending to the wounded below, or directly involved in the repair of ribbon systems and Harbor defenses, made their way up to the roof. They didn't know where else to go or what else to do. Within a very short amount of time after the battle, large numbers of Astraeans began to form groups and loiter, speaking softly between themselves.

The entire Astraean awareness had been disrupted. Conversations between the countless Astraeans on the roof of the Harbor all dwindled to awkward silence as no one could make any sense of what had transpired. Confusion bred questions with no answers. The lack of information spawned anger that began as passionate exclamations, but then morphed into unfinished and rhetorical outbursts. Each cluster of Astraeans took on something akin to the oblivious beauty of a sea anemone, wavering gently in the sea of space, silently, with no clue as to how it had come to where it was, or what to do with itself.

A ribbon strike flashed, which was fairly common in and around the Harbor. If one were looking out across the expanse of the Harbor roof with all of the gathered Astraeans, one wouldn't have given it a second thought. But, the once individual groups of Astraean anemones began to cluster together. Their attention began to focus around where this particular ribbon flash landed. The sea of Astraeans on the roof had now become compacted and were throbbing around their center of attention. The nauseous silence was beginning to be replaced by the innocent whispers of awe.

The Trio, along with Elcyd, Hergie, Router, Lannya, and Thyra, hadn't escaped the accumulating curiosity. As they began making their way from the outer perimeter of the roof near the turrets, towards the focus of attention, the noise level began to rise. Everyone was looking back and forth at each other with no idea as to what was going on. Within quick succession, each member of the group broke through to the inner circle that had formed around...

Mamdod.

Mamdod had come to the Harbor. Each face that saw him arrive was twisted in concentrated confusion. Mamdod had never left the ribbon island. Mamdod was always, *on the island.* No Astraean had ever heard of any rumor or tale that indicated that he, at any time, could leave the island, over the course of billions of years. But, that was no longer true. Until this moment, during the lifespan of any Astraean anyway, Mamdod had always been confined to the ribbon island. Each soul that now looked upon him, took a second to recall what he had told each and every one of them at some point. He couldn't leave. There were never any ribbons available to him. Until now, apparently.

Everyone was mumbling, whispering, gawking and pointing. No one had addressed Mamdod directly yet. A few had begun to stumble aimlessly towards him, but that was it. Everyone knew Mamdod as a comforting guide and companion throughout all of their deaths and ribbon travels, but seeing him here, at the Harbor kept everyone at a distance.

Mamdod slowly looked down at his feet, or more accurately, looked at what his bare feet were standing on. It wasn't the dirt and grasses of the ribbon island. He looked back up and took his time with soaking in each face that met his vision. He knew each face. He remembered each conversation he'd had with each face, individually. The emotion of seeing so many of them at once started to strike his face like the beginnings of a meteor shower. One face caught his eye, then dozens, hundreds, and thousands.

For the first time since time was a child, Mamdod

was no longer alone. He was surrounded by almost countless souls, each one he had grown to care for as a father might. He had given advice to each of the Astraeans around him and relished every moment of conversation with them. These Astraeans were no longer temporary memories for him, but now, constant realities. His eyes began to blur and hurt from the pressure of his building tears. He cupped his forehead and looked down. He didn't know what to think, where to start, or what to say. As he released his forehead and looked up, someone addressed him.

"Mamdod?" One of the gathered Astraeans blurted. "How? How have you come here?" The inquisitive Astraean shared in the confusion on the faces of all who had witnessed his arrival.

The Trio, and their new friends, breathed heavily after running from the back of the crowd. They panted and heaved while waiting for Mamdod to answer the question that he had been asked. There was a foreboding silence. A silence that went unbroken for a time as Mamdod searched the crowd for some kind of hint as to where he should begin his story. The reason he was there and the method in which he arrived. The uneasy silence continued to linger. The entire throng of Astraeans condensed among themselves, but kept their distance while patiently waiting. There were no repetitions of the question. No one left the roof.

"For the first time in billions of years," Mamdod began, "I am able to travel again."

His statement did little to alleviate any curiosity or questions.

"I know," he continued. "That doesn't explain how I have come to you now."

Elcyd took a few steps closer to Mamdod. He was the first one to noticeably move closer to Mamdod since his arrival. Elcyd wore a smile that then melted into a titled face of admiring confusion.

"Mamdod," Elcyd began softly. "You've been on that island since any of us first existed. I don't understand."

"This has all come to pass as a result of a game, old friend." Mamdod didn't move as he spoke, but merely shuffled his feet as he chuckled quickly. "Hmm! I'm not used to having much room to move around on."

Mamdod returned his attention to Elcyd before quickly addressing the entire crowd.

"I'm very sorry to say my friends, that what all you have experienced today has been one consequence, of an incredibly ancient game," Mamdod revealed, visibly doubting his choice of words. "A naive game that was conceived long ago. A game, whose creator could have never predicted the amount of pain it would bring."

"Whose game?" Another Astraean questioned somewhat pointedly.

"Whose naiveté?" Asked Rigella with an even more elevated tone. She propped her arms up on her hips as she asked.

"Mine, and mine," replied Mamdod. His voice was firm, only to make sure there was no mistaking his admission. More than a proud exclamation, it was a regretful confession.

The crowd began to shift and voices began to mumble.

"Mamdod," Elcyd quickly responded. "We don't know what you're referring to."

Elcyd quickly walked to Mamdod within arm's

reach this time. His approach wasn't aggressive, but urgent. Elcyd quickly tapped a portable input terminal to instruct one of the nearby panels to eject another small globe of ribbon energy. It shot out from the panel and flew on a perfect trajectory to the space between Elcyd and Mamdod.

After the ball of energy arrived, Elcyd addressed Mamdod once more.

"Will you please explain what's going on?"

Mamdod nodded immediately.

Afterwards, Elcyd tapped another quick command into his portable input terminal, sending the ball of blue energy to just in front of Mamdod's mouth, at chin level.

"The entire Harbor can hear you now," Elcyd advised. He then stepped back, giving Mamdod some room as he began his address.

Mamdod shifted his eyes aimlessly as he collected his thoughts. He licked his lips as he did so. His face remained firm and confident as he formed his next words. Once he began speaking, his words were clear, supported, and articulate.

"Astraeans, and friends of the Astraeans. My name is Mamdod. The Astraeans should know of me as the one who dwells on the ribbon island, and who has, as far as you all have ever known, been confined there for an unknown reason, to help reveal to each of you, your spirit's next available destinations. If you are wondering how I am addressing you, or where I am addressing you from, I am addressing you from the roof of the Harbor, where I have just arrived. Obviously the circumstances surrounding my ability to travel have changed, and I will explain those to you now."

Everyone who was already on the roof remained

where they were, still stunned by Mamdod's arrival. There was no way any Astraean would want to miss what Mamdod had to say. And as the seconds sped by, the crowd grew steadily, yet calmly, as the Astraeans from the lower levels and outer docks began trickling up to the roof.

"For as long as you all have known, I have only been a ribbon guide and adviser. None of us have had any information regarding my origin. None of us knew why I had been bound only to the island, and restricted to only the knowledge needed for temporary moments, to help guide each of you on your next ribbon path. I am here today to tell you, that I am much more than that. I am no longer bound. My memories and knowledge are no longer restricted."

Mamdod forcibly inhaled and sighed twice to gather his thoughts as he paced a quick circle. He continued.

"You see. I am the multiverse's oldest, sentient inhabitant. I existed in various forms of random energy and material, long before I was aware of being aware. I think back to those times and realize that was when existence began existing, and time began growing. This wasn't during the beginning of an individual universe, but the beginnings of the multiverse. It was the beginning, or resumption, or rebirth of the multiverse. Before any individual universe began, I existed within the entirety of multispace, the void between individual universes. I witnessed the beginnings of separate universes and eventually condensed into a singular mass of energy which then came to rest at what is now, the ribbon island. As I accumulated awareness and knowledge, I began traveling and experiencing the universes, galaxies, and worlds of the multiverse. I grew in my knowledge of the ribbon energy which I had been produced from. I used it, nurtured it, grew in it, and protected it. I lived across the span of countless pockets of time, to the point that my soul became fatigued. Not from any negative connotation, but due to the shear wealth of experiences it had, over the course of more time than can be expressed. It was at this point, that I decided to retire to the ribbon island, rest, and work on a way to share my knowledge."

Though Mamdod was broadcasting his comments to the entire Harbor, the people around him began to encroach on him. They wanted to be closer to him as he spoke.

"It was at this point, before any of you existed, that I decided to create two companions," Mamdod continued. "Well, more accurately, I *requested* companionship from the ribbons. I communed with the ribbon energy at the island and beseeched it. I asked for company. Pupils. Children. Students. There is really no term to appropriately describe what I requested."

An older, wounded Astraean named Bick, tightly holding his bleeding but wrapped arm, interrupted.

"With all due respect, Mamdod, look around. There is a lot of pain, death, and destruction around you. Could you practice some of your god-like powers and fix some of this before you finish this history lesson?"

As he was interrupted by Bick, Mamdod turned immediately to face him in order to give him all of his attention. But as Bick finished his brazen question, Mamdod's body went from relaxed and loose, to rigid and defensive.

"Being the multiverse's oldest resident does not make me its master," Mamdod educated sharply. His eyes made sure Bick understood. "I am no god."

As Mamdod corrected Bick, the ribbons around the Harbor, and all the terminals and machinery that use ribbon energy, seemingly very sensitive to Mamdod's emotions, faded from the normal neon blue, to a deep and vibrant orange.

No Astraean had ever seen the ribbon energy change color like this, or at all, perhaps because no one was as attuned to the ribbons as Mamdod was. A momentary flood of panic washed over the crowds of the Harbor, which was quickly alleviated as Bick apologized.

"I was out of line, Mamdod," Bick quickly offered. "I'm sorry."

Mamdod legitimately and sincerely relaxed his anger. The ribbons returned to their normal color.

"It's alright, Bick. I understand your frustration, concern and worry," Mamdod reassured him.

The exchange between Bick and Mamdod had been heard by everyone at the Harbor, and Mamdod resumed his statements and explanation.

"I truly do understand, everyone. I understand your confusion, questions and need for answers. I'm trying to provide all of the information that I can, and answer all questions that I can. And I promise you, I will work with you all to answer any questions none of us yet have any answers to."

Mamdod walked over to Bick and placed his hand gently on his shoulder. He then continued to reassure everyone.

"As I was saying, I wanted someone to share my experiences with. I wanted help in cultivating the relationship I had with the ribbons. Someone to whom I could pass on the ultimate privilege of a relationship with the ribbons like I had. That's what I hoped for. And the ribbons answered my request. The ribbons generated two new lifeforms from their energy. These two energies started existence out just as I had, as numerous other types of non-sentient life. And just as I had done while maturing alongside the ribbons, I nurtured these two new energies as well. I taught them, cultivated them, and in a sense, raised them. They grew, learned, traveled, experienced things on their own, and developed their sentience and intelligence. They grew to become the two who are now known as Daebaugh, and Akal."

The crowd bristled and heated shouting began. Pointing. Doubting. There was no purpose, intent, or focus in the arguments. People just didn't understand, and across the crowd, onlookers began roaring with their confusion. "What does that mean?" or, "How is that possible?" and, "Where did Akal go?

"Akal was and Daebaugh is, simply, a child of the ribbons, as I am, and as you all are," Mamdod continued. "They are the oldest sentient residents of the multiverse, second only to me. As they grew in their experience with the multiverse, I decided to develop a game to decide who would take over my responsibilities at the ribbon island. A necessarily objective and unbiased game, given that we three at the time, were the only sentient beings capable of taking part. The only instruction I gave them was to learn and love. Together, we built the Harbor for them to call home, and I left them with the message inscribed in the floor of the lobby. The ribbons would bring them to worlds full of danger, and the ribbons may bring danger to the Harbor, but I wanted them to bring love to as many places as they could. Before I actually set the game in motion, I told them that after one of them had lived out all of their Astraean lives, which would take almost as much time as had already passed through existence, I would hand over my responsibilities to the surviving brother. While they were out in the multiverse learning, loving, and doing the work I had commanded them to do, I told them I would put a block on my memory, so as not to influence their lives, or their work in the multiverse. I also made them aware that their memory of being my sons, and their memory of being connected to the ribbons in the way they were, would be suppressed, so they wouldn't contaminate their new experiences in the multiverse. Lastly, I told them that once one of them had outlived the other, my memory would be restored, and the process of passing on my responsibilities would begin. In other words, my intention was to make them earn the right to take over for me, and to learn all that they could of the multiverse."

Rigella spoke up. Her questions were pointed, but they needed answering.

"That's it? Daebaugh is now the ribbon guide? Will he pose a threat to us and the multiverse? He's going to take your place? How can that be allowed? Can't you just not follow through?"

"No," Mamdod replied, without hesitation. "I am bound to those conditions. I developed them and swore to them within the confines of the ribbons. Though I want to disregard the rules I established, I cannot. Unfortunately, I did not know Daebaugh would deceive me, and I don't know what will he will be capable of if he takes over as ribbon guide. I would imagine that he may be capable of anything, given enough time to commune with the ribbons. But now that my memory and awareness has been restored, I know how I was deceived. As I was explaining the rules of the game to them, Daebaugh somehow channeled the restrictions on him, to a leaf from the tree on the ribbon island. The same tree that represents my role as ribbon guide. Now that the rules of the game have been realized, and Daebaugh has outlived Akal, the leaves on the tree will begin to fall. Once the last leaf has fallen, Daebaugh will replace me as ribbon guide. Any bond I have with the ribbons will be severed, and I will be forced to take the final ribbon."

Lannya stepped up next to Rigella, as if silently taking her side in their frustration with Mamdod's explanation, and started to speak up as well.

"Friends," Elcyd respectfully began. "Please allow us to stop the broadcast momentarily while we organize some of this information and get it to you in the most efficient and beneficial way. More information will follow soon. Thank you."

Lannya didn't relinquish her desire to ask her follow-up.

"You're telling us that Daebaugh has known for billions and billions of years that he only needed to kill Akal to take over control over the ribbons? How could you not have seen that deception like that was possible?"

For the first time, Mamdod had no immediate reply. His eyes didn't leave Lannya as his closed mouth twitched as if going through withdrawal. A withdrawal, not from drugs, but from answers.

"I... I don't know, Lannya. All that time ago, I had no idea, inclination or expectation of such malice or deception. And for billions of years, Daebaugh took advantage of that through the cloak of my self-imposed blocked memory."

A long silence followed. A few Astraeans left the immediate area surrounding Mamdod in disgust. Not so much with Mamdod, but with the helplessness of the situation. Others returned to helping the wounded or to repairs around the Harbor. Most Astraeans stood where they had been, looking aimlessly at the ground, frightened of the unknowns that were on the horizon. The unknowns surrounding Daebaugh's impending ascension to master of the ribbon island struck many with a cold and helpless fear.

"What's going on with souls that arrive at the island in your absence, Mamdod?" A curious and wise voice asked from deep in the crowd.

"Right now," Mamdod began to explain, "any incoming souls to the island are essentially halted at the end of the ribbon that leads them to the island. I will be making return trips frequently to receive them onto the island and assist them with their next ribbon options."

Nonchalantly, and with an innocent curiosity, Carthal then posed a question to Mamdod who had suddenly faced a familiar sense of loneliness, despite being surrounded by a large number of Astraeans.

"How long until all of the leaves fall from the tree?" Carthal asked. "How long do we have?"

The slight disruptions in the focus on the topic ceased immediately. All attention returned back to Mamdod and the conversation.

Mamdod's face tightened as his expression reflected a frenzy of thought.

Chapter IV
The Bleeding Stops

Mamdod looked up at Elcyd, then back at Carthal before replying.

"I planted that seedling on the island after returning from a planet very similar to Earth. I would say we have a time frame of about three earth months before the tree loses all of its leaves. But something I hadn't considered when I established the original rules, was what would happen if the surviving brother lost all of his lives before the leaves fell."

Elcyd and the surrounding Astraeans remained silent as Mamdod followed his train of thought.

"As it is now, Daebaugh would take my place when the last leaf falls, but if he has already taken the final ribbon by the time that falls..."

Mamdod shrugged from being puzzled. "I established no condition for that scenario," he continued. He looked around at everyone before reaching the end of his thoughts.

"I don't know what would happen."

"Even if we were to somehow generate that scenario," Heersan began. "We're talking about somehow destroying the billions of lives of your only surviving son." Mamdod's eyes weakened.

"I asked the ribbons for companions to show the multiverse to. I was given two and one killed the other."

Mamdod's eyes twitched and collapsed even more as he noticeably struggled with his emotion.

"I will do what I can to make sure that evil is not rewarded."

Elcyd motioned to some of the senior Harbor engineers, beckoning them over. At the same time, he gestured to Rigella and her group.

As Mamdod continued to ponder the situation with Daebaugh, Elcyd addressed the assembled group, but made no effort to stifle his comments to any other Astraean listening. In fact, he tapped a command into an input terminal, confirming the conversation was once again being broadcast to the entire harbor.

"Everyone, this is Elcyd once again. I want to make sure every Astraean understands the situation. Mamdod is no longer bound to the ribbon island and has joined us here at the Harbor for the time being. Akal and Daebaugh were brothers, and more or less sons to Mamdod. Daebaugh deceived Mamdod to gain control over the ribbon island when Akal died, but we have until the tree at the ribbon island loses its leaves before that transition takes place. We are going to develop a plan to defeat Daebaugh to prevent that from happening. At the same time, we will be continuing to tend to the wounded, while working to restore the Harbor defenses, bolster them, and seek to counteract the advantages Daebaugh has over us. The specifics aren't quite clear, but among other things, he seems to be able to intercept ribbon data, manipulate it, and influence what we here at the Harbor know, or do not know."

Elcyd then turned from specifically addressing the public address module, and focused his gaze on the group assembled next to him as he continued.

"I believe we should also begin developing some form of proactive and offensive team focused primarily on the immediate dangers posed to the Astraeans and the multiverse's continued safe use of the ribbons. If you wish to lend to these initiatives or have any questions, please reach out to me or any other Helper, or Harbor official. I only ask that you please be patient as we begin to work on these numerous tasks. Thank you."

With that, Elcyd closed the communication channel opened to the entire Harbor, and posed a question only to Mamdod, Rigella and the rest of the group.

"What do you all think about that?"

"I think those are sound beginnings," Mamdod replied, quickly. "If there is no objection, I would like to remain here at the Harbor and help where I can with the work being done on our understanding of the ribbons."

"That would be perfect," Elcyd agreed. "We would be honored to have your help, Mamdod. Now that your memory has returned, there is no one with an older or deeper experience with the ribbons."

"REMAIN also I WILL," Hergie blurted. "I ALREADY HAVE MANYS IDEA on how to strengthen HARBOR DEFENSES AND WEAPONS."

No one jumped or showed any sign of being caught off guard by Hergie's voice. Everyone had long become used to him.

Carthal, who had remained in the same form for longer than anyone could remember, suggested the Trio's next move.

"I'd like to try and find out where Daebaugh's group went and bring the fight to them," he suggested.

Heersan quickly retorted.

"Wouldn't they be expecting that? If I followed what Mamdod said correctly, then Daebaugh only needs to wait out the leaves on the tree. They're sure to have a major defense centered on him."

Mamdod nodded, agreeing with Heersan's assumption.

Router, who had remained close to the group for the duration of this conversation added to it.

"So, it sounds to me as if a fight needs to be brought to Daebaugh, but not just yet."

"Exactly," Elcyd replied with a single and sharp nod of the chin. He pointed quickly at Router as he continued.

"Exactly. We have a rough idea of how long we have until all the leaves fall at the island. We need to scout and gather information, and then launch an attack. Until that time comes, we need to secure the Harbor, grow our knowledge of the ribbons, build an offensive force of some kind, and equip them properly."

"Don't forget," Lannya began. "We need to remember during all of this that Daebaugh has had billions of years to prepare for any reaction to his actions, and to consider all contingencies."

Everyone nodded in agreement.

"Right," Elcyd resumed. "As for an offensive force, how should we go about that? We need to harness all Astraean knowledge and shift some of our focus from peacekeeping and defense to offense and martial combat. Who should we ask to head that up?"

There was a slight silence among the group. It wasn't awkward or aimless. Everyone was carefully considering possible nominees.

"Rigella. I think," Lannya said, and then paused, as Rigella spun her head to look at Lannya in astonishment.

"I think Rigella would be perfect," Lannya finished. Her voice was kind and sincere.

"I agree!" Thyra said with quick enthusiasm.

Rigella's eyes were still focused on Lannya. She was taken by complete surprise at Lannya's suggestion and was temporarily confused by considering all of Lannya's possible motives.

"Me?" Rigella asked. Her face conveyed a puzzled amusement, not from being nominated, but from being nominated, by Lannya.

Lannya let her eyes drop from Elcyd, to whom she had made the suggestion, down to the ground as she had thoughts of Akal.

"Yes," Lannya said, as she began to qualify her suggestion. "You are extremely capable in all types of combat, are very level-headed, and fought alongside Heersan, Carthal…" Lannya's voice got slightly weak before finishing. "And, Akal, for an extremely long time."

Lannya's eyes lifted once again, but this time, to Rigella. Given their earlier argument, Lannya wanted

Rigella to know she was sincere.

"I can't think of a more pure warrior than you, or anyone nearly as familiar with what Daebaugh may have in store, by way of fighting alongside Akal for so long."

Mamdod, who had been soaking in Elcyd's proposals and the ensuing discussion, absentmindedly caressed the temple of his head before speaking again.

"I think that is a wonderful idea, Lannya," Mamdod said with heartfelt support. "What does everyone else think?"

There was no argument from anyone or awkward silence to make anyone think they were hesitant.

Carthal placed his hand on Rigella's shoulder as a sign of support and affection. Everyone else nodded, and Elcyd said, "Definitely."

After determining everyone's position by looking at each person in the discussion, Elcyd turned his focus back to Rigella. Lannya was already looking at her, respectfully, as if silently making amends for their disagreement earlier. Rigella softly blinked and bowed her head slightly to return the sentiment.

"Ok, then. It's settled," Elcyd said, while reaching to the input terminal once more. He initiated a new Harbor-wide communication.

"Attention everyone. Please be aware that Mamdod and I have assembled a preliminary reaction team to address the initiatives I mentioned a short while ago. Mamdod and I will work with engineers to deepen our ability to interact with the ribbons. That includes our ribbon capabilities, but also hopefully identifying how Daebaugh is able to manipulate information being transmitted through the ribbons. Hergie will be leading his team in the repair of Harbor defenses and construction of new defensive systems. Finally, Rigella will be leading the effort to assemble an offensive force. More information will follow. Thank you."

Elcyd closed the communication channel and addressed those in the immediate group who were not leading one of the initiatives.

"Lannya, Carthal, Heersan, and Thyra. Were you planning on working with Rigella's initiative? And our new friend, Router, were you wanting to return home to Lenmeteq?"

Heersan had begun to reply in the affirmative, but was interrupted by Carthal who eagerly responded.

"I was hoping to take part in some form of scouting effort," Carthal proposed, after confidently taking a step forward.

Heersan reached for Carthal and lightly grabbed his arm, prompting Carthal to turn around.

"I thought we would stay with Rigella and work on forming the army or whatever it will be," Heersan asked, reminding Carthal with his eyebrows that the Trio rarely operated separately.

Rigella had no immediate comment and simply watched the discussion unfold.

"Normally, I would agree," Carthal replied calmly, "but one of us needs to be out there gathering information and trying to locate Daebaugh. We don't have enough time to stick together."

There was no anger, but merely an exchange of tactics.

Heersan let his arm drop from Carthal's as he

weighed and considered the options.

While Heersan was thinking, Lannya supplied her decision on what she wanted to do.

"I'd like to accompany whatever group goes scouting. I'm very eager, you could say, to find out anything we can."

Heersan then turned to Rigella.

"Do you need any of us to help you? If you want any of us to stay, just say the word."

"No," Rigella quickly answered. "I don't believe so, and like Carthal said, we can't be afforded the luxury of staying together right now. If you want to go with Lannya and Carthal, I should be fine here. We can always reach out to each other if we need something. And actually, if Thyra wouldn't mind helping me, I could definitely take advantage of her knowledge of the history of military and warfare since she works in the library, to help me with planning."

"Sure, I'm happy to help wherever I can and wherever I'm needed," Thyra acknowledged with appreciation.

"Alright," Heersan confirmed with a weighted and deliberate voice.

"And if it's alright with Hergie, I'd be glad to stay and help with any fabrication or technological needs," Router offered.

"I would MUCH APPRECIATE this, router," Hergie replied in his usual monotone, fluctuating between volume extremes.

Elcyd looked around at the group one by one. Everyone knew the plan and everyone had a job.

"Alright, my friends," Elcyd began to conclude. "We all know what to do. Let's get to work, and please, let's all remain in as much contact as possible."

As everyone was about to break to begin taking action on their various assignments, Lannya spoke up again.

"Elcyd, I'm sorry to delay, but I had one last thought."

"Of course," Elcyd obliged respectfully. Everyone else turned back to Lannya.

"In the event of another attack, or, another catastrophic battle that may send us scattering, should we have some form of fallback location? A safe location to regroup?"

Mamdod turned to Elcyd, and came short of answering for him.

"That is an absolutely perfect suggestion," Mamdod stressed, with a weighted agreement.

"Yes, definitely," Elcyd quickly agreed, which was followed genuinely by an echoed "Yes" from Rigella.

Elcyd posed his next question to Lannya initially, but turned to each face in the group as he finished the sentence.

"Where would be a good place, and when would be a good time? What criteria for this location would there need to be?"

"Well, we've never been in a position like this before," began Heersan. "We have the advantage of precedent."

"That's true," added Elcyd. "And I would think it would need to be something somewhat remote to the Harbor, but easily accessible from multiple locations."

"Well then, anywhere in the basement should work," offered Thyra.

Carthal's eyebrows jumped up as he realized where Thyra was going with her suggestion.

Mamdod didn't understand what she was referring to.

"The basement? What is that?" Mamdod asked of Elcyd.

"Ah, yes. The basement is what many Astraeans refer to as the bottom section of the multiverse. Most of the universes and planets within that section..."

Mamdod realized what they referring to and completed Elcyd's thought.

"...have more ribbon sections and hubs than other areas of the multiverse. Right! That's an excellent idea. I just didn't realize that area had a nickname."

"Caecus. Caecus might be a suitable option," suggested Rigella. "It's in, um, universe 37-B, I believe... not even a dozen hubs out from the Harbor, two hops from 30,000 inhabited planets, and four hops from over a million star systems."

Elcyd looked around to see if anyone had any expressions of dissent, and didn't find any.

"Let's look into Caecus, then," decided Elcyd. "Keep this decision among yourselves only for now, and I'll work on a secure way to communicate that to all Astraeans once we've established that relationship. Speaking of communication, we need to come up with a plan on how to begin communicating with non-Astraean allies, bring them up to speed on the situation, and see who we may be able to rely on, should the need arise."

"Ok, as soon as you want to act on that, let us know," requested Heersan. "We can start on reaching out from wherever we're at once we hear from you."

"Ok. Will do," acknowledged Elcyd. "Alright, my friends. Let's get to work. Be safe, and please keep in contact with each other. Watch out for communicating too much sensitive information, though. We'll reach out to everyone once we've established some new, more secure communications methods."

Lannya walked closer to Rigella, reached out and squeezed her shoulder with a slightly distant respect, but appropriate level of affection. She nodded at her, turned and began to walk away. Rigella was then rushed by Heersan and Carthal who gave their own extremely affectionate embraces in the form of hugs. After Carthal and Heersan reiterated Elcyd's plea to keep in touch, Rigella approached Lannya this time.

"Lannya," Rigella began.

Lannya turned around, slightly surprised by being addressed once more by Rigella.

"Since I'm staying behind at the Harbor," Rigella continued, "you three should take Paige. Get Hergie to have the fighter repaired, and I'll be sure to send you the command codes."

Lannya was stunned, and surprised by the amount of emotion she felt from Rigella's gesture. This was Akal's ship she was being offered part control of. The ship that Rigella, Carthal and Heersan felt as nearly bonded to as Akal did. Rigella offering shared command control of Paige was an extraordinary olive branch, and Lannya was overwhelmed and thankful for the humility she was dealt by Rigella's offer.

"That's not necessary, Rigella. I won't need it.

Heersan and Carthal can..." Lannya attempted, before being interrupted.

"No, Lannya," Rigella insisted. "If things get hairy, all three of you will need all of Paige's capabilities at your disposal."

"Thank you, Rigella. We will take care of her," conceded Lannya, with an appreciative smile.

As Rigella nodded, Carthal tapped Lannya's shoulder and tilted his head, quietly signaling the time had come to leave.

"Hergie's already gone back down. I'll go ask about getting the fighter repaired," added Heersan.

Chapter V
Doubts and Challenges

The mood around the Harbor had noticeably stabilized in the short amount of time since the attack. Repairs were well underway, the wounded had been treated, and the majority of the Astraeans were moving along deliberately. No longer were faces filled with despair and defeat, but now, brows were compressed with the welcomed burden of focus, and paces were quickened by determination. Whether it was Daebaugh or any other enemy of the Astraeans, they would not be caught off-guard again.

After Heersan had left to check on the repairs of Paige's fighter, the remainder of the group had broken off to tend to their work or their preparations to leave. Only Rigella remained on the roof, continuing the conversation with Elcyd and Mamdod about the formation of the

Astraean army. The intimidating and unprecedented scope of the task at hand chiseled sharply on the expressions of those discussing it.

"Well, we have a bit of work ahead of us," Elcyd huffed with fatigue. "How do you want to begin, Rigella? What can we do for you?"

Rigella looked past Elcyd, into space, to silently prioritize her thoughts before responding.

"The first thing I'd like to do," as she focused her attention on Mamdod, "is to find out exactly what ribbon capabilities we have at our disposal now that Mamdod is here."

Mamdod listened intently and nodded quickly, as a long-absent father might after recently returning to the care of his children.

"I have a deeper and older relationship with the ribbons than any other. I will do everything I can to make use of that relationship," Mamdod confirmed.

"As for the actual army, military, paradigm we end up developing, or whatever we end up classifying and identifying it as," started Rigella, "we need to establish an organizational structure, supply infrastructure, and..."

An obscure, ancient, and powerful bellow, native to a distant universe, interrupted the conversation and startled the group in an initially unrecognized tongue. Rigella couldn't place the language at first, but the creature, who resembled a large and complex, geometric entanglement of thick, red vegetation, shook the ground with its volume, and reminded Rigella that it was the language of the Cuedils of the 59th universe. Along with their imposing size and sound, the Cuedils were sometimes known for missing parts of speech when compared with other races across the multiverse. Their lack of pronouns was especially confusing at times.

"...question," Verdius thundered with an edgy sharpness. Rigella missed the beginning, but caught on afterwards. Those around Verdius were initially startled along with Rigella, Elcyd and Mamdod, but the Astraeans nearby continued about their business soon after Verdius began speaking because they knew Cuedils rarely spoke out of anger. They were simply startling in their volume and sharp articulation.

"Why are no alternatives permit to be leader of army? Many Cuedils should qualification. Many strong and smart. Opportunity is desir..."

In an attempt to reassure Verdius, and to also silence his agonizing voice, which was much louder than the playful annoyance of Hergie's voice, Elcyd politely jumped in.

"I completely understand your concern, Verdius. We unfortunately do not have the luxury of time and felt this was the best way to proceed."

Verdius stood in place, shuffling slightly, with no discernible face to measure the expression of, and he did not speak before Rigella replied.

"No, Elcyd, I think Verdius had a good point," Rigella countered. "We may want to consider opening up the position for applications of some kind. If we were a conventional race with a conventional army, I might not agree, but being Astraean, I think any of us should have the opportunity to lead."

Elcyd puckered his face while pondering the notion

and soon turned to Mamdod for his input.

"I agree with Verdius and Rigella," Mamdod offered. "I think any army we form will be more united and inspired if being led by someone who won the position after a selection of some kind."

"How should we go about this selection?" Elcyd asked of the group.

Verdius erupted an enthusiastic suggestion.

"There should be battle tournament! Leader of army should be able to win combat of many kinds in many races!"

Rigella smiled slightly and nodded at the simplicity of Verdius' proposal. Mamdod and Elcyd looked at each other. Mamdod humorously gestured and deferred to Elcyd.

"Well," Elcyd said, giving in. "In that case, we should begin planning this tournament right away. Do we all agree that we must make this as fair, yet efficient a process as possible? We do not have a lot of time to waste."

Verdius barked a Cuedilian grunt in the affirmative to match Mamdod's nod and Rigella's, "Definitely."

"I think it goes without question that there will absolutely never be any element of this tournament that is to the death, correct?"

Another rapid and unanimous agreement from everyone but Verdius who sighed slightly in disappointment.

Elcyd shot Verdius a disapproving but affectionate squint of his eyes. He then began to pace slowly while brainstorming out loud to the group.

"A bracketed tournament system of some kind? Transformations allowed? Where will it be held? We should probably put a time limit on each match along with a point system of some kind."

Elcyd, Rigella, Mamdod and Verdius rushed through no more than an hour of additional ideas. All manners of details had been discussed and mostly settled. How the tournament would be announced, how the brackets would be formed, qualifications to enter, various rules. It was also decided how all of these decisions and rules would be reviewed in the future, in the event the tournament method was to be used again for selecting future leaders of the Astraean military. By the end of the discussion, they were all extremely proud of ensuring the selection was fair to all Astraeans.

* * *

Once the discussion was completed, Elcyd wasted no time in announcing the tournament to the Harbor. The tournament was announced not only to the Harbor, but to most Astraeans abroad as well, via the recently repaired ribbon communications system. In an effort to secure the communications going forward, Harbor engineers had embedded a new security feature in communications originating from the Harbor. Only those recognized as being friendly Astraeans would be able to properly receive and decipher communications from the Harbor. Erroneous communications of various kinds were also dispatched without encryption, at regular intervals, to throw off any unfriendly ears.

Within only two hours from when the process had been decided on, the brackets for interested and eligible competitors in the tournament to decide a leader of the Astraean military were mostly crafted. Within six hours, most competitors had converged on the Harbor. By the twelfth hour following the announcement, all contenders had arrived, and a large population of non-competing Astraeans had arrived to witness the competition. The urgency in the process needing to take place rapidly, but fairly, was stressed heavily in every announcement, communication and posting.

While there was still a heavy sense of shock across the whole of the Astraeans, at being so overwhelmed by Daebaugh and his forces, a steady pulse of excitement quickly grew in and around the Harbor, in anticipation of the selection of their military's leader. The leader that would lead them to a victory over Daebaugh.

The cavernous expanse of the lower dome would be the site of the tournament, with each match beginning on the floor of the lower dome. Each competitor was able to begin their match in any form of their choosing, as long as they started the match in a form that was subject to gravity, with their feet, or the equivalent of feet, on the floor. After the match began, each competitor was then able to assume any form they had access to, as long as the form, or the process of assuming the form, would not harm themselves, their opponent, or any spectators. Also, for the ease of officiating, the competitors and match must begin and remain in the confines of the lower dome. Lastly, and most importantly of the main set of rules, no match would ever be to the death. If a submission or living incapacitation could not be obtained by a competitor in a match, the winner of the match would be the one with the most points awarded at the end of a five minute match.

The setting of the tournament was especially gritty, primal and exhilarating. Normally the lower dome is tame and sterile, with the routine and automated docking and releasing of Astraean ships and transports, but that wasn't the case for the tournament. Astraeans had assembled impromptu bleachers, markets and shops. Artisans had crafted clothing and toys to feature various competitors in the tournament. Food vendors and stands sprung up. There were Astraeans assuming a myriad of forms from throughout the multiverse with the clothing, sights, sounds and smells from as many places. More so than ever before, the diversity of the Astraeans was trumpeted and their love for their collective diversity was heralded. And while the entire spectating operation rapidly blossomed with the assistance of the ribbon technologies of the Harbor, it was extremely friendly and clean, and impressed most at the Harbor by how quickly it all came together.

The epochs-old walls of the lower dome, previously plain and boring were now peppered with holes of various sizes from Daebaugh's attack—many of them smaller than they initially were, now that repairs had begun. The temporary large portholes into space, along with the increased noise, hustle and bustle of traffic coming and going from inside the docking slots of the lower dome, made for a thriving, lively and optimistic environment to hold the tournament.

While Rigella agreed that the leadership of the new army should be opened to all interested Astraeans, she still heavily desired the position, and felt confident she could do it best, and would be competing. Mamdod, Elcyd and three other judges would be officiating the tournament. The other three judges were non-Astraean military leaders from different areas of the multiverse. The extra three judges would never repeat, and would change from year to year.

The first judge, Dullow, was from Spherb in the 40th universe, where all disagreements and conflict are resolved by a method most would associate with defensive or deflective martial arts. They are remarkable diplomats and highly respectful of individuals. They value consensus and resolution above all selfish motives or desires. The most amiable result is always the most cherished. Seeking to become an expert at finding the most beneficial outcome for all involved parties is the life goal of all Spherbans.

The second judge was Ehwilda from the planet of Jorvik in the 17th universe. Jorvik's citizens are notorious for their mastery of all types of offensive combat and weapon efficacy. The inhabitants of Jorvik value the most efficient way to arrive at someone's death, whether within the context of battle, or as something as trivial as a simple challenge to the death, for fun. The purpose was not for honor or glory, but to simply be known as the best killer. Ending another life was not an activity anywhere on their moral spectrum. They lived to kill and kill better than the next, but were obviously aware that this passion for killing was not shared or thought of by everyone else in the multiverse. Ehwilda was sought purposely as a compliment to the judging criteria of Dullow. Between the two, defensive and offensive tactics would be expertly reviewed.

The third non-Astraean judge was brought in to judge combat tactics, ingenuity and improvisation. The judge's name was Bokvinnit, from the planet Stannton in the 32nd universe. The three non-Astraean judges were an amazing first judge panel, and would assist the Astraeans with finding a well-rounded and deserving first leader for their army. Mamdod and Elcyd would score for special criteria and manage the scores for successful attacks and blocks of various types, as well as monitor the official match clock.

The spectators grew louder in their anticipation of the beginning of the tournament. The area of the floor of the lower dome that wasn't sectioned off for the tournament grew more and more crowded. Room became scarce. Onlookers started to pull their ships and transports out of storage and hover them high above the seated spectator sections. Astraeans of all kinds were draping from ships, docking areas, windows, ship decks, sitting on the debris from the holes blown into the wall of the dome, and countless other makeshift seating. The excitement was palpable.

Elcyd requested the assistance of a fellow Astraean to act as Ceremony Announcer. His job was to reiterate to the crowd the most important rules of the tournament as well as educate anyone who hadn't already heard, where they can locate all of the documented rules and how they will be reviewed in the future. After that, the Announcer revealed the first round pairs. Match one was minutes away.

Rigella was in the first round, and she was glad. If she were to make it through all the rounds and if she were to win, she wanted there be no question as to her legitimacy. But it wasn't an issue of ego or personal pride. She would have the same thought about the winner, regardless of who won. She wanted the leader to at least be involved with the tournament from the first round, having worked their way through every round. She wanted the entire Astraean population to rally and support the winner. She was very pleased with how the process was proceeding so far, and was very eager to win, or see who ended up winning, if not her. She was ready to fight Daebaugh, no matter the rank or position she did it in.

She paced slowly with her head up as she waited for her first round match to be announced. Those not fighting at the moment were informally separated from a section of nearby spectators. She exchanged short chit-chat with competitors that offered it, and reciprocated nods and gestures of respect. Finally, it was time. Through the noise of the crowd and traffic above, she heard the impending start of the match announced. The Announcer's comments reverberated throughout the lower dome.

"And now, one of our most anticipated first round matches, we have Rigella and Verdius!"

The Announcer paused, to let the explosion of anticipating applause rise and fall.

"Word has it," the Announcer continued, "that Verdius challenged the automatic appointment of Rigella to the position this tournament is auditioning for. This should be an exciting match! Fighters, you have five minutes until the match ends, unless you are able to win by submission or incapacitation, first. Please. Take your places at the marks on the tournament floor."

Rigella felt like running to her spot, but she forced herself to retain control over her adrenaline, excitement and energy. She began walking toward her spot. Her legs overtook each other with a brisk but reserved gait. She looked around and took in the controlled chaos around her. Her blood rushed through her veins in excitement. She let the adrenaline have the best of her for just a moment as she waved to the crowd.

Portions of the crowd started to bellow friendly chants in favor of Verdius, just as he began making for the other spot on the floor. Despite those cheering for him, Verdius knew Rigella was well respected, and he respected her as well. They both had similar desires for the army and for the position of leader. He simply thought he could do it better. He thought he could do it more justice and bring more success to the responsibility, and to the Astraeans.

The cheering and chants of "Verdius!" and "Rigella!" quickly leveled out and sounded equal in the moments before the match started. Rigella had given into the excitement of the moment long enough. She mentally flipped that indulgence off and began shutting everything else out but her objective. It was time to focus and to win. While the Announcer was giving the crowd another quick reminder of some in-match rules, Verdius surprised Rigella with a last minute question. The combatants had amplification spheres floating just below their chins, or in Verdius' case, where his sound emitted from, and the exchange was heard by all.

"Rigella is sure want to stay in current form at beginning? Fight might not take long," he condescendingly teased, doubting the abilities of her human female form.

Rigella knew right away that while he didn't have as much knowledge of the various politics, ideologies, genders, races and species from across the multiverse as she did, he was still trying to get under her skin and in her mind before the match started.

"Verdius," Rigella quickly retorted. "I have men and

beasts in my soul. Creatures and energies from across the multiverse. I've wielded their bodies, powers and ambitions. With those and millions of other options available to me, I've easily chosen to fight as a woman."

The crowd erupted in a unanimous roar of approval over the perfection of her answer. For a moment, Verdius had no supporters.

She smiled provocatively and devilishly after finishing her reply. Verdius made no other comment but shifted the weight of his rear half so as to anchor his center of gravity. Rigella bent her knees slightly and held her arms up slightly, and loosely out from her sides. Her hands were open. She was ready.

"Contestants," the Announcer spit into the microphone. "Fight your match on three! Two!"

The sound used to signal the release of a ship from a dock in the lower dome was amplified to signal the beginning of a match. *BEEEYOOOOOONNNGGGGGGGGGGGGGGGG.*

The amplified dock buzzer called all spectators to attention.

"One!" Completed the Announcer. The match had begun.

Before the buzzer had even been released, Verdius ejected extensions of his red vegetation in almost every direction. Within seconds, the majority of the open tournament space within the entire lower dome was made up of a web of Verdius' vegetation. The crowd moaned and swooned in wonder at the confusing spectacle.

At the same moment Verdius had shot extensions of himself throughout the lower dome to confuse Rigella, she began running towards his original position. She darted in, out, and around various extensions of the vegetation. She double-backed on some of her path. If she was being stalked or chased by Verdius, she hadn't seen him yet and at the very least, knew not to stay stationary while she developed a plan.

She had it. She knew what to do. Seamlessly, Rigella went from sprinting throughout Verdius' confusing sprouts to climbing up them. While moving vertically now, she still maintained a random pattern. The higher she climbed, the louder the crowd became. After a short moment, Rigella could see movement out of her peripheral vision, not associated with her climbing.

She smiled.

While increasing her height to improve her advantage, she knew that sooner or later Verdius would have to act to stop her or slow her down. A separate, perfectly camouflaged segment of Verdius was on the move. He had come to her, and that was exactly what she wanted.

The vegetation that makes up the geometric body of a typical Cuedil is extremely sensitive to the ultraviolet light of their planet's sun. As such, when the star of their homeworld's solar system is in the sky, Cuedils retreat deep enough into the ground to shield themselves from the ultraviolet light. They then emerge each time the star sets on their horizon. Most of their activity is nocturnal.

Rigella could hear Verdius. He was gaining on her. She had to strain less and less to hear his movements.

Now!

Rigella transformed into a cell of overwhelming ultraviolet light. Most of the crowd instinctively turned away from the light, but some were able to maintain their attention. Within moments the single cell of light split into hundreds. A cell for each cube created by the intersections of Verdius' vegetation extensions. Involuntarily, Verdius' extensions began to recoil and shrink. The extremely high lattice Rigella had climbed in her first form became unstable. She returned to her form as Rigella and began to free-fall down to the floor of the lower dome.

As Rigella was falling, she thought of what form to assume next. She saw that Verdius' extensions were still constricting in on themselves and knew it was time to go on the offensive.

She summoned a strike of ribbon energy and well before hitting the ground, transformed into a Zanfult. She was now roughly twice as large as Verdius before he extended himself, which was still quite enormous. Having a significant size advantage over Verdius now, her bipedal and somewhat reptilian form was now hurling sharp, bony discs at Verdius in an attempt to slice his shriveled extensions. These discs of Rigella's were attached to her Zanfult body externally, via long, sinewy, yet extremely durable tendons. The Zanfult's four arms were constantly throwing, catching and returning these extremely deadly weapons.

At this point, Verdius' appendages had retracted as much as they could go. His face and body writhed and jerked with each toss of Rigella's discs. They were getting closer and closer to various points of his body. He was panicked and Rigella knew it.

A ribbon stream flashed.

Verdius' Cuedil form was gone. Rigella's Zanfult face smiled, but didn't have the time to fully form before she began looking feverishly for him. As soon as Rigella registered the thought that she had to begin looking for Verdius, she was impaled in the upper back by a Sugamite bolt. Before Rigella could reach for it and pull it out, it exploded, leaving a moderately critical wound in her upper back. She began running to avoid additional bolts while grimacing and holding her wound. Verdius had taken the form of numerous pockets of atmosphere from the Hazijuv planet, which has its surface constantly bombarded with various hazardous and explosive elements from high in the sky.

Rigella regained her composure quickly as she darted in and out of Verdius' sights, narrowly dodging additional Sugamite bolts. Just as she was about to be struck once more with another bolt, she jumped and dove back towards the floor of the lower dome. While still in the air, her form liquefied. The form of this puddle increased exponentially as it splashed to the ground. The bright white liquid of Rigella's new form intercepted each Sugamite bolt and absorbed them, causing her no harm. As the liquid grew and spread, it began to reach toward the heights of the ceiling where Verdius was spread out across in his various pockets of Hazijuv atmosphere.

Rigella's liquid form grew and reached up at various points towards the pieces of Verdius. Each tower of Rigella's rich liquid grew vertically in simple appearance and practical engineering. One by one, a branch reached a piece of Verdius and encompassed him. There was a struggle from each piece of Verdius as it was swarmed by Rigella. As each piece was overwhelmed, Verdius tried to call a ribbon to change forms, but the projectiles could not pierce Rigella from the inside, nor could the ribbons pierce the liquid from the outside. Verdius was effectively stifled, and he had no ability to change forms to continue the match.

The crowd started to gasp and Verdius' supporters shouted words of encouragement while Rigella's supporters started chanting her name. Slowly but surely, the flood of Rigella's liquid overtook Verdius more and more. Her fluid bubbled and burped with Verdius' increasingly weaker attempts to break free. For a moment, the lightning flashes of ribbon strikes Verdius was attempting to summon, rapidly increased before quickly slowing down and stopping. Allowing just a few moments to confirm that he had stopped resisting once becoming completely enveloped by Rigella, and after no more ribbon strike attempts were made, Dullow began a five second countdown to end the match due to incapacitation.

Dullow counted the five seconds down. The spectators supporting Verdius held on to hope and rallied with a quick but extremely loud chant. But it was no use. There were still no signs of a struggling Verdius, no remaining sections of him that were visible. She did it. The countdown ended, and Rigella defeated Verdius.

* * *

When Dullow finished his countdown, Rigella immediately recalled her expanded and fluid mass into a pop of a ribbon. Returning to her usual form, she then walked over to a regenerated, but extremely weak and defeated Verdius in his Cuedil form. She stopped just before him and looked up. She repeated the same confident smile she had given him earlier. Verdius said nothing.

After Rigella turned to the crowd, she shot her hands

up in victory, as high as they would go, and savored every sound coming from the spectators. She then headed for the judges table for a quick post-match health and fairness review, to confirm she was safe and not harmed, and that there were no blatant signs of cheating. She passed with flying colors and then settled into a section of stands for the contestants. She watched with enthusiasm and pride in her fellow Astraeans as the tournament progressed. Bracket after bracket ended, and Rigella defeated each opponent she faced, handily, all the way through to the final bracket.

She was tested more than she ever had been, and she performed as she never had before. She was victorious. She had won the tournament and had the respect from her fellow Astraeans reaffirmed. It was public knowledge that she had initially been offered the position, but that she then suggested that it be opened to all the way it was. There was no doubting her strength and integrity, and there was no doubt who the leader of their military should be, and now was.

Chapter VI
What's Old is New

The celebrations to mark the end of the tournament were short-lived, but what they lacked in length, was more than made up for in intensity. Species, numbered as many as the stars, sang, drank, ate, displayed, danced and relished, only as Astraeans joyfully and inclusively could. Recognizing Rigella as the first Central Commander of the newly established Astraean Defense Force, (ADF), was a rallying call that every Astraean believed in. There was unconditional support for Rigella. The entire Astraean culture knew that the tournament was fair and just and that the new ADF would be properly developed and led by Rigella.

The celebration of the end of the tournament was not just for Rigella's victory, but was a powerfully unspoken addition to the definition of what an Astraean was. United under Rigella to defeat Daebaugh, the Astraeans were now, more than ever, a partner to the multiverse. Their existence pulsated with a fresh infusion of purpose. They would go anywhere they were needed to provide assistance, wherever it was requested, in the name of preserving peace. No longer would they passively wait for issues to arise, but would, along with the coordination and planning with indigenous cultures and local species, actively seek out threats to peace across the multiverse, and end them as quickly as possible.

In the immediate days following Rigella's victory while she began to organize the ADF, Hergie and Router had already crafted new prototypes of offensive and defensive weapons, and tools, in coordination with Mamdod and Elcyd. They wasted no time in getting to work and had already started working on various projects before the tournament had even finished. They understood the need for the main populace to spectate and celebrate, with the devastating attack still fresh in their memories, but Hergie, Router, Elcyd, and Mamdod knew their individual time would be better spent on their work.

That's exactly what they did. Despite the fact that Astraean ribbon technology far surpassed the next most advanced technology outside of the Harbor, the Astraeans very often had to make less capable or less efficient weapons and technologies, so that they would be practical and effective out in the multiverse. As a result, it was safe to assume that any Astraean-crafted item was the best example of its kind. But that wasn't the case with these new Harbor improvements. These were some of the best executions of Astraean concepts. Only a few days after the tournament ended, Hergie and Router presented the following items for Mamdod and Elcyd's consideration:

-An advanced Harbor radar. With Mamdod's

assistance, this new radar would build upon the current technology at the Harbor which previously only sent out occasional ribbon energy probes to collect data. Now, there would be an active and frequent radar that would be engineered using ribbon energy and monitored by Astraean staff. The radar transmissions would collect real-time data on locations in the multiverse. Things such as space and weather conditions local to a planet, and temporal anomalies, (if present), would be collected.

-Increased and improved Harbor beacons. The existing beacons would be physically reinforced and given defensive weaponry, increased monitoring capabilities, and the ability to establish protection barriers between them. The existing beacon perimeters would have additional beacons added, and there would be more beacon perimeters added outside of the current outer-most beacon perimeter.

-Improved and increased defensive turrets. The existing turrets would be improved upon in regards to projectile type and maneuverability. New turrets would also be added not only to the roof of the top dome, but along the bottom dome and throughout various other locations at the Harbor. All turrets would also be converted to remote automation in order to be monitored and operated from a more secure location within the Harbor. Many of these new turrets would have extended range options as well.

-Improved communications between Astraeans and the Harbor. Another advancement made with Mamdod's assistance was the manipulation of the constantly flowing ribbon energy to allow immediate communications between Astraeans and the Harbor. It would now be possible for an Astraean to dispatch a thought and/or data, via ribbon, to another Astraean and/or the Harbor.

Almost a combination of the new radar technology and method of spiritual travel, this type of communication would be virtually instantaneous. While an Astraean would previously need to leave a location to return to a vessel or building where they can access ribbon energy, they would eventually be able to carry devices, available in a manner of configurations, to interface with and communicate. The device would then establish a wireless connection with the main ribbon energy threads in the local galaxy, and initially, transmit only tiny bits of data. While the devices were still in development and limited in their capabilities, the hope was that they could eventually transmit much more.

When the initial presentation of some of the new technologies was made to Elcyd and other senior Astraeans, he was beyond impressed.

"Absolutely phenomenal work, my friends!" Elcyd fawned, while twisting and turning a prototype communications device in front of his eyes.

Hergie, Router, and a few nearby engineers beamed proudly but remained silent while Elcyd continued to inspect the device.

"I never thought any of the ribbon technologies could be so mobile like this," Elcyd said with a glaze on his voice, still impressed and focused on the small device.

"It was actually very simple to develop," Mamdod offered, dryly. His arms were crossed as he stood away from the rest of the group. "I recalled that Daebaugh and Akal were as closely attuned to the ribbons as anyone ever could be, save myself, and that before Akal was killed, someone told me they saw him changing through various forms without having to actively summon and connect to the ribbons. He had essentially become seamless with them, part of them, via the surrounding elements and matter of the multiverse between him and the ribbons. While I would assume that level of connection can eventually be harnessed by any Astraean through study and experience, we studied how to apply that concept to these small devices, which for now, can at least connect with the ribbons and transmit thoughts and small chunks of data at a time."

Mamdod's comments ended and were followed by a silence that broke Elcyd's concentration. He knew something was bothering Mamdod.

"What's the matter, Mamdod?" Elcyd let his hands fall to the middle of his chest before holding it back up in Mamdod's direction. "This is a great new tool!"

"No, no, I'm sorry." Mamdod waved the group off, letting them know he wasn't angry at them. "I just had no idea we would need to develop some of the things we've come up with recently. I never knew the warning I etched into the floor of the lobby those eons ago would be a warning against my own... son. I would have done so much more and worked hard to prevent this. Because of my own silly game, I never had a chance to warn Akal. I didn't know I would need to plan for deception from Dae..."

"Mamdod," Elcyd interrupted with stern respect. "No one blames you for hindsight. No one blames you for Daebaugh's actions. Optimism, and excitement for altruism, are defining characteristics of Astraeans, and you should never feel like you need to apologize for that. If either of those traits lend to others manipulating us or taking advantage of us, then shame on them! Shame on them! We will not be surprised like this ever again. We've said it a million times since Daebaugh's attacks, and we'll say it a million more times or as long as it takes to defeat him. We will not be surprised ever again. Nihilism may encourage the motives of others, but not ours. Ultimate power and control may be what others strive for, but not us. How dare they think they have a right to any of that? They will not have it!"

Elcyd, an Astraean not usually prone to showing overt amounts of emotion had snagged the attention of numerous engineers and Astraeans within hearing distance as his volume increased. They drew nearer and nearer as he spoke. Some became noticeably emotional. Some dropped to a knee to focus on what was being said. Others' eyes began watering. Some silently connected with coworkers by placing their hands on coworkers' shoulders. Mamdod, who was in a state of borderline defeat and disappointment in himself, let his arms fall as Elcyd spoke. He became more rigid and confident. Mamdod's pride was returning. It was quickly evident that it was more than just his pride. It was indeed, as Elcyd suggested, Mamdod's optimism. By the end of Elcyd's speech, Mamdod had placed his hand on Elcyd's shoulder.

"Thank you," Mamdod whispered to Elcyd, with a strength not weakened by the delicate volume he used. "Thank you for that!"

Elcyd, who had slightly surprised himself by the volume of, and emotion in his comments, nodded to acknowledge Mamdod. But, for a moment, he nodded through Mamdod's stare, as if he were repeating his comments silently to persuade himself. There was of course a doubt over whether or not they could defeat Daebaugh in time in the minds of all Astraeans, but Elcyd would absolutely not let himself, or any other Astraean, succumb to any level of defeatism.

The faces of the engineers and crowd that had gathered, tightened with renewed purpose and hope. Demonstrations of prototypes, plans, and displays of new systems were resumed with fresh excitement and gusto. An engineer rushed through screens on a display terminal to give a demonstration of the new radar system. He was stuttering and repeating himself, not out of being nervous, but because of the excitement he had for the new technology. Elcyd weaved in and out of the team with an ear-to-ear grin as they gave their demonstrations, appreciative and proud of the work that had been done. Every so often, he would look back to Mamdod. Mamdod was also grinning.

Hergie was particularly proud of the work he did with improving the turrets. Everyone else had been so rallied by Elcyd's comments that from the start of Hergie's explanation, no one showed any sign of being startled by Hergie's voice, and stood stoically and attentive for Hergie's presentation.

"We have not only DOUBLED TOP DOME TURRETS," Hergie began, while using many of his appendages to point at a map of the improved turret locations, "but duplicated amount OF TURRETS FOR BOTTOM DOME. ASSORTED turrets are placed strategically throughout OTHER AREAS OF HARBOR ALSO. TURRETS have new projectile generators that will generate various TYPES OF PROJECTILES TO ADAPT to targets when necessary. SOME new turrets are hiding AND SOME HAVE HAD RANGE EXTENDED."

The demonstrations and presentations continued. More plans and maps were unfurled and pointed to. Equations were written out to explain processes and technologies. Ribbon terminals were used to access this diagram and that schematic. Ideas were being applauded and lauded. Others were being questioned, tweaked, and refined. Ideas and prototypes evolved and improved. Never had the Astraean engineering community been more inspired and empowered, or produced so much technology at once.

The individual groups that were engaged in multiple, smaller discussions regarding the various technologies and developments, slowly began to fade as one topic started gaining more and more attention. Router was speaking, and he was attracting more listeners with each sentence as he commanded more of their curiosity.

"Hergie and I spent most of our time fleshing out this idea with Rigella, and she is very anxious to get this up and running as soon as possible."

The entire group of engineers had now descended upon Router's and Hergie's table, where the duo was leaning over a scaled down, three-dimensional projection of the Harbor.

"She would like the new fabrication section placed here," Router continued. As he spoke, an addition to the projection of the Harbor grew into place. "Here, between the two main exterior dock sections for easy deployment of vessels and loading of cargo."

A lead engineer that had just joined in around the table spoke up.

"I'm sorry, Router. New fabrication section?"

"That's right," Router confirmed, with a flat and elongated face. He didn't realize how quickly his demonstration's audience had increased. His following silence indicated that he had become shy in the company of so many Astraeans. After all, he was fairly new to the Harbor.

One of Hergie's appendages whipped out and harmlessly stabbed Router in the side to break his shyness.

"Yes, yes," Router resumed. "It's a new imaging and fabrication facility independent of the one that Hergie currently manages. Its primary and only function will be to supply the ADF with weapons, vessels and tools. Anything needed to combat Daebaugh and defend Astraeans and allies throughout the multiverse."

"Just to clarify," interjected Elcyd. "Can you tell us why this has to be separate from Hergie's facility?"

"Of course," obliged Router. "Hergie proposed, and Rigella heartily agreed, that any new militaristic production should be entirely separate from the current production facility, not only for practical reasons, but philosophical and safety reasons. We didn't want any military production to endanger, change or delay any normal, civilian production, and vice versa. And philosophically, we wanted to separate the functions as to not equate their importance."

There were only barely audible murmurs and slight movement in the crowd as everyone considered Router's comments.

"It's already been brought up, but..." Mamdod said calmly. "Does anyone have any additional concerns about this shift in Astraean focus? I want to make sure there is no hesitation with how we proceed. Like Elcyd alluded to earlier, none of us should feel like we need to compromise who we are as an Astraean culture to counter this threat."

There was more thoughtful silence. It was a short-lived silence as another lead engineer responded to Mamdod's question.

"I don't believe so," the engineer offered. "We are proceeding carefully and considerately. We are being mindful of our history and culture. We are being deliberate in our planning and execution. I, for one, feel very good with the way we are responding."

Mamdod and Elcyd scanned the faces of the gathered engineers and concerned Astraeans, for any signs of hesitation or concern. Router and Hergie scanned as well. The crowd looked each other over, and then returned the favor to their leaders. There seemed to be no disagreement. They would proceed with the construction of the new ADF imaging and fabrication facility.

"GOOD!" Hergie spouted. "I will coordinate once again with Router and RIGELLA TO ASSEMBLE TEAM TO CREATE NEW imaging and fabrication facility."

"Yes, that would be perfect, Hergie," Router obliged, before turning back to the entire audience. "This will be a tremendous way to quickly counter some of the time we've lost because of Daebaugh's deception. We will be working with Rigella to design command vessels and fighters, weapons and defensive items of all kinds, and I believe Thyra will be working to research, and build active military relationships with various contacts throughout the multiverse, to make sure our military is as equipped, trained and well-rounded as possible."

"Ah, that reminds me," Elcyd broke in. "How is the planning for the ADF coming along?"

Chapter VII
Confirming Caecus

Heersan and Carthal stomped across Paige's gangplank, brushing against each other's arms while feverishly whispering as they discussed the best approach to Caecus. They were about to get underway to confirm its viability as a safe planet for the Astraeans. Together with Lannya, they were planning for a quick visit and discussion with local governments to establish a mutually beneficial military agreement. Afterwards, they would be off to scout and search for any additional information they could find on Daebaugh.

Heersan and Carthal posed a question to Lannya but stopped in their tracks soon after and looked back at her. She hadn't answered. They hadn't realized she had fallen behind and stopped just short of the gangplank.

"Lannya? What's wrong?" Heersan questioned softly.

She quickly blinked twice and slowly turned her head, as if trying to look away from Paige, but didn't manage it. Her eyes remained focused on the ship.

Heersan and Carthal walked back slowly to Lannya. She licked her lips in an effort to speak.

"I just miss him," Lannya finally said. Her voice was steady, but the melodic lifetimes of affection as she spoke became dissonant from regret. Heersan and Carthal detected the regret and acted upon it.

"We miss him, too, Lannya," Heersan reciprocated as he collected her wrists in his hands. He bobbed his head down and around for a moment, trying to catch her eyes.

"We're going to avenge him," Carthal added. "Him, and every other Astraean we lost. And we're going to stop this."

Lannya shuffled her feet to reclaim the ground gained temporarily by her sadness. She reached for one of Heersan's hands as he still held her wrists, and patted one of them. He let go of her. She nodded at the two of them and let them know she was ready.

"I want to meet Paige," Lannya said as she began to walk towards the ship.

Heersan and Carthal looked at each other, thrilled, and flashing wicked grins.

"She looks great!" Carthal excitedly hollered.

Heersan's curiosity about the status of the fighter flashed across his face. He sprinted across the remaining length of the gangplank and ran up the stairs towards Paige's bow. He jumped onto the top of the rails and plopped his chest against the hull while extending himself even more to look up into the fighter hold.

"It looks good as new!" Heersan shouted down to Carthal and Lannya. He was thrilled beyond relief as he hopped back down onto the platform. "We'll have to make sure to let Rigella know."

As Heersan hopped down and disappeared through the exterior bow hatch, Carthal turned to Lannya and winked.

"Come on," he teasingly beckoned. "I guess you're Paige's part-owner now. Let me give you the tour."

Carthal led Lannya up the ladder to the main hatch on Paige's secondary sail, between the primary sail and the clear top of the tactical fighter bay, below. She handled the ladder quickly and expertly, as any other Astraean might. Each time Carthal looked back out of courtesy, to check on Lannya's progress, she was right there, ready with raised eyebrows, informing him silently that he didn't need to wait on her. It only took a few of the silent exchanges for Carthal to smile and to stop checking.

When Carthal and Lannya reached the command deck, Carthal watched the same expression of amazement and excitement wash over Lannya's face that had washed over his and Heersan's each time they stepped on board Paige. It was close to the same expression Akal had when Hergie first presented the ship to him.

As Carthal began showing Lannya some of Paige's more obscure features, she felt a sense of unexpected relaxation brewing within her. She didn't zone out and quit listening to Carthal's explanations, however. She was listening sharply and making sure to lock eyes on the location of things he was explaining at the time. The feeling of relaxation however continued to brew and spill over into her entire body. It was a feeling of being sincerely welcome aboard Paige by Heersan and Carthal, despite the gap that had grown between her and Akal. The feeling of being welcome, in addition to the simple fact of being part of something that Akal was so close to for so long, reminded her of their mission.

As Carthal was wrapping up the last bit of his initial tour of Paige's sections and features, Heersan sprung onto the command deck.

"Yep, the fighter looks great," Heersan confirmed. "Most of it has been largely rebuilt from what I can tell. I ran a quick systems diagnostics check and everything is perfect."

Heersan's attention shifted.

"Oh. We've got a message waiting."

Heersan walked over to the flashing message indicator at one of the control panels and flicked it quickly with his knuckle. A recorded video message from Hergie popped up on all near-by command deck terminals.

"Ah, it's Hergie!" Carthal exclaimed with friendly admiration. The video quickly buffered and began playing. "Yeah, when I went to check on the repairs, Hergie said he had to run to a meeting about the new imaging and fabrication facility and would leave us a message," Heersan informed.

"FRIENDS SO SORRY CAN NOT be in person to discuss repairs and improveMENTS BUT HERE IS QUICK VIDEO TO TALK ABOUT."

Carthal shifted his eyes playfully as he tapped the volume indicator on the nearest terminal down a few notches.

Hergie's video continued.

"FIGHTER IS OF COURSE repaired fully. Structural integrity and performance is RETURNED TO LIKE NEW STATUS. Fighter and host ship have been modified with recently developed TECHNOLOGIES TO ALLOW FOR BETTER WEAPONS projectile adaptations and changes. Main ship also has improved radar and COMMUNICATIONS CAPABILITIES IN CONJUNCTION with developments made AT HARBOR."

While Lannya and Carthal continued listening to Hergie about the various repairs, improvements and additions to Paige, Heersan innocently waved his fingers to catch their attention without interrupting the video. He was plugging in the coordinates for Caecus. As Hergie's recorded message ended, the locks on Paige released and the automated departure sequence began. Just before Paige floated through the automated exit ribbons and shot off towards Caecus, Lannya looked back at the Harbor. Most of the damage from Daebaugh's attack had already been repaired, or was in the process of being repaired. Old and new life was starting to seep back into the streets, docks and buildings of the Harbor.

* * *

The conversations on the way to Caecus were plenty and practical. The mission was being discussed constantly not only between the three aboard Paige, but also with contacts back at the Harbor. A few of the discussions were with Rigella, but most were with her newly appointed immediate subordinates, as well as with Mamdod and Elcyd.

The goals were simple. Visit Caecus. Reaffirm

the diplomatic relationship the Astraeans have with the planet. Ask to use a portion of the planet as a safe area for emergencies, which included unannounced and unplanned visits from Astraeans. If permitted, Astraeans arriving would have an encrypted way of announcing their arrival. The Astraeans would also in no way seek to involve the planet in any military actions, (whether offensive or defensive), without the express acknowledgment and agreement of Caecus.

"Do you two remember Caecus at all?" Carthal asked, while chewing on a snack as Paige surfed the stars.

"I don't," Lannya blurted, while squinting her eyes, trying to confirm mentally. "I don't believe I've ever been there." Her eyes narrowed even more. "I don't think I've ever been a Caecusi, now that I think about it."

Heersan's gaze didn't avert from the ribbon path in front of the ship as he spoke up.

"I do, barely, but it's been ages since I've been there or used one of their skins. I just remember it being dark. Very dark."

"That's right!" Carthal splattered through his mouth full of food. He grimaced as he forced himself to swallow so he could continue speaking comfortably.

"It's a gorgeous planet! It's not just dark though," Carthal began to explain. "It orbits what is now a neutron star or brown dwarf, I can't remember. Anyway, the star it orbits has long-since stopped giving off meaningful light, so the Caecusi, and the native wildlife and flora evolved with some form of bioluminescence. Every living thing on Caecus has these extremely ornate light patterns emitting from them. They've only become more ornate over time as they evolved to be a means of attracting partners like humans might with hair or muscles. The planet's life is the only source of light. It's a great place!"

"Oh yeah, I remember now," Heersan picked up, having broken his attention from space. "All of the life on the planet has that light pulsing through their veins and cells. It's beautiful."

"Exactly," resumed Carthal, turning to Lannya. "The primary sentient species on Caecus look like, I don't know, shadows, whose forms are defined only by their veins, pulsing with this bright green light. There isn't really any other species like them."

Carthal then slammed another handful of snacks into his mouth before continuing.

"I haven't visited in forever and can't wait to see it again. They engineered an artificial version of the light which decorates their homes and buildings too, if I'm remembering correctly. It's amazing, but really soft and ambient. They evolved in such low light that any light brighter than what the buildings and life give off, can harm them. It's a very ethereal planet."

Lannya had developed a slight grin in anticipation of reaching Caecus. She let her focus drift up to the main sail as she daydreamed of the planet. Though Heersan's and Carthal's description seemed thorough and magical, Lannya had a suspicion it didn't quite do Caecus justice.

"Destination: Caecus in 30 seconds," Paige announced.

"Ah, here we go!" Carthal shouted as he jumped up from his seat. As he stood, he unknowingly dumped crumbs from his shirt onto the floor of the command deck. Paige's incorporated vacuum system under the seats, along the rail, made quick work of them.

"I wouldn't worry about changing skins," Heersan advised. "The Caecusi know the Astraeans and are friendly."

"I hope that..." Lannya started, before being moderately slung into a nearby support column by Paige's rapid deceleration.

The last time Paige had any kind of unplanned deceleration was when she was catastrophically attacked by Daebaugh's forces at the Harbor. Heersan and Carthal's faces were painted with a fresh coat of fear, confused as to why they stopped so suddenly.

"Propulsion ceased. Ribbon path blocked by unknown obstacle," Paige calmly announced.

"What the..." Carthal attempted to ask.

Lannya quickly recovered from being slung against the support column and looked to Heersan.

Heersan initiated the quickest of system checks.

"Paige: Diagnostics test 1."

As Paige replied that all systems were functional and that the ship had sustained no damage, an immensely large and circular field of blackness overtook the view ahead of Paige. To the sides of Paige and behind, the view remained unobstructed.

Before leaving the Harbor, the ship had been outfitted with the means to eject itself, intentionally and safely, from one ribbon to another nearby ribbon. Heersan thought it would be a beneficial safety measure to answer attacks on ribbons like the one they sustained with Akal. Just before Heersan was about to start emergency procedures to begin looking for an alternate ribbon, and to retreat from the large black mass ahead of the ship, the mass began to change.

Within the solid blackness, extremely bright and perfectly symmetrical paths of neon green light began to glow. As these organized paths of light began to brighten, additional paths of green light began to appear. These were fewer and fainter. It seemed to be some form of Caecusi vessel, Lannya assumed, judging from the descriptions she had just heard from Heersan and Carthal. She assumed the stronger and symmetrical paths of light were artificial, and that the fewer and fainter light was natural.

Lastly, a shade or window of sorts receded, and a large blotch of solid light appeared high at the top of the black mass. Silhouettes of what resembled leaves and various foliage appeared at the window.

Paige's crew was extremely concerned and still somewhat shocked at having been so abruptly stopped, but took no offensive actions yet. The ship had not been harmed, there were no injuries, and they were not yet under attack. They were further stunned where they stood by the extremely imposing vessel ahead of them. Within seconds, after the vessel had fully revealed itself, Paige's loudspeakers broke their silence.

Sssswwwwiissssssshhhhhh sshhhhh shhhwwwiiss, the three heard over the speakers, sounding like wind blowing through branches and leaves.

No one moved, but their suspicions were correct.

"It's the Caecusi," Heersan confirmed. "That's their native language."

"That's right, right. These ships must be new, though." Carthal nervously sputtered. "Paige," he directed.

"Auto-translate."

"Confirmed," answered Paige.

"Caecusi vessel," Lannya began with gentle respect. "There are only three of us aboard our ship. We are Astraeans and as always, come in peace. We were under the impression we were not required to announce our visits and seek only to speak with your leadership."

There was no immediate reply. There was no movement except for the slow pulsing of the light from the Caecusi vessel.

Just before the silence got worrisome, there was a reply.

"Hold."

There was slight movement high above in what seemed to be the cockpit or cabin of the Caecusi vessel.

Carthal quickly but softly tapped a button on a nearby console, muting Paige's microphones.

"I guess they're checking?" Carthal rhetorically asked of Heersan and Lannya.

Lannya eyes were stuck wide open. Not out of fear, but from the instinctual desire to take in as much visual information as possible during a tense situation. That, and being slightly alarmed but humored by her first experience with sailing alongside Heersan and Carthal.

"You are permitted to land," the Caecusi vessel declared. "You will be escorted into our atmosphere and then to your docking area. Once you dock and disembark, you will then be met by Caecusi security. Your vessel will be monitored until you dock."

Heersan unmuted the microphones.

"Understood," he replied. "We need only to detach

from our ribbon connection."

"Very well," replied the Caecusi vessel.

Heersan gave the command to Paige to detach from the ribbon at which point Paige's recently modified local space propulsion system engaged. As Paige adapted for non-ribbon space flight, the immense and singular Caecusi vessel could be seen to split and crack. They were clean and organized splits. The single large vessel, which had been created by hundreds of smaller, linked Caecusi ships, disassembled. Most then flew off into other areas of the atmosphere, or to the other side of the planet, but many remained to escort Paige and her crew down to the Caecusi surface.

"Following you, Caecusi ships," Carthal announced. Heersan followed with commands to Paige to follow their escorts and dock at the provided coordinates.

"I thought we would have a more," Lannya said, just above a whisper. "Well, different reception."

Heersan looked quickly over to Lannya and Carthal and then back to the lead escort.

"Yeah, I'm not sure what this is all about."

* * *

Before the Caecusi docking mechanisms had even finished securing Paige, Heersan, Carthal, and Lannya could see the movement of hundreds of clusters of light in the darkness, marching in quickstep across a bridge to their location. It was hard for them to make out additional details because it was so dark, but the clusters of light seemed to be holding separate items. Weapons, the three of them assumed, with light patterns of their own. While Carthal and Heersan discussed what they should do, if anything,

Lannya quickly scanned the surrounding area and what she could see into the distance.

Nothing could be seen, and depth perception was hard to define with their human eyes, because the planet was pitch black, except for the light coming from the patterns in the structures, the plants and trees, and the Caecusi themselves. Lannya had never been a Caecusi before, but even if she had been, she doubted that she would have assumed the form of a Caecusi for fear of startling the native Caecusi. She thought Heersan and Carthal felt the same way, since they had Caecusi forms available to them, but didn't transform.

While the oddities of the situation made Lannya feel uneasy, the location and what she saw did not. The light coming from the bodies of the Caecusi, their clothes, weapons, buildings, decorations and vehicles, was warm and inviting. Even the artificial light threaded throughout the buildings and roads was comforting. None of it seemed mechanical, electrical or arbitrary. It was beautiful, energetic and full of life. Almost like the clearest of greens coming from the most vibrant of leaves on the brightest days on Earth, the patterns in their skins were unique to each Caecusi. They twisted and turned in the most ornate ways, and the mix of natural light paths in the skins of the Caecusi and artificial light paths in everything else, contrasted the darkness and brought a great deal of light to any given area. The longer Lannya looked out to the horizon, the easier it became for her to define distances between herself, the Caecusi, and their buildings. As she became more comfortable with what she was seeing, she saw that the Caecusi that were approaching were doing just that, approaching, and not attacking.

After the three of them had a moment to take in what they were seeing and what was happening, Heersan turned to the other two.

"Well, let's go see what this is all about."

After taking various flights of steps through Paige's interior to exit, they emerged from a hatch that had been attached to by a small platform just large enough for a single creature to stand on. There was no immediate way for them to reach the Caecusi shore. Completely surrounding Paige and the little platform, was only a sea of black. No light of any kind. Only darkness of an undefinable consistency and depth.

"Oh, I remember," Carthal said softly, but loud enough for Heersan and Lannya to hear him.

Carthal stepped out from the threshold of the hatch onto the small platform. The platform then flashed a bright pulse of the same green light that pulsed within the bodies and infrastructure of Caecus. Much like wind may carry pollen from plant to plant, a small disc then raised up from the platform and carried Carthal over the few hundred feet over to where the Caecusi were waiting to receive the three Astraeans.

Heersan and then Lannya followed. They stood there on the shore quietly, and weren't fearful as much as they were confused. The three of them continued scanning the horizon without moving their heads and reviewed the assembly of Caecusi more closely. After a moment, the gathering of armed Caecusi began to ruffle, until another Caecusi emerged from the group and approached them.

"Astraeans here, eh? Already? But just three of you?

Ha!"

The wide-open eyes belonged to Heersan this time. They had no idea what he was referring to.

The assertive Caecusi spoke directly and forcefully without a need to translate since the three had announced themselves as Astraeans. He spoke in their language, but still with a hint of the native Caecusi, windy whooshes, as he spoke.

"Sir," Carthal tried to get out.

"Sir? I am not a sir. I am Caecusi Vefly Dionaea." Dionaea corrected.

"Oh, I'm sorry, that's right," Carthal acknowledged. Carthal then bent his head in the direction of Lannya and attempted to further clarify.

"Vefly is his military rank. Dionaea is his name."

"I know who and what I am, Astraean!" Dionaea admonished, making Carthal snap to attention without really thinking about it. "And surely, I would imagine that any attacking forces would know who and what we are, as well as our command structure!"

"Vefly Dionaea," Lannya squeezed in, equally assertive, yet respectfully. "We are not attackers, and are not here to engage in any violence. We came simply with the hopes of speaking to the Caecusi leadership. The Astraeans are friendly and known to the Caecusi and we are not sure why we have been met this way."

Lannya got out all of the important points and questions and ended with clasped hands before Dionaea responded.

"You are not sure why you have been met this way?" Dionaea mockingly repeated. "This is without a doubt the most peaceful, albeit smallest and ignorant, group of invaders I have ever had the misfortune of intercepting! You three are lucky to be alive! I do not know what this little group's intentions are, but Caecus is in a complete state of readiness and will counter anything you Astraeans wish to throw at us!"

The three Astraeans were at a complete loss.

Dionaea was mere inches from Lannya's face as he completed his threat and seemed poised to snap off Lannya's head at any second.

Heersan spoke up quickly.

"Vefly Dionaea, we completely apologize for any of our behavior that may have been offensive, but we have absolutely no idea what you're referring to. We are allies to the Caecusi. We seek no violence, and no Astraean threat is behind us, or on its way in any form. Please, we wish only to speak with your leadership if that is at all possible. There must be a misunderstanding somewhere."

Dionaea's proximity to Lannya remained unchanged, but he did turn his head to Heersan as he spoke. After Heersan's comments, Dionaea turned back to Lannya, and backed away, extremely slowly. Dionaea turned to one of his junior commanders, Lepidium, with the rank of Brassica, and ordered him to come over by bending the spikes on the top of his head inward, as a human may curl their fingers. Lepidium approached as instructed. Dionaea addressed him, but what was said couldn't be heard by the Astraeans. Lepidium then ran off, for an unknown purpose, and was quickly lost behind the group of assembled Caecusi.

Dionaea then turned to another subordinate, Brassica Erysimum, and made no attempt this time to hide what he was saying.

"Erysimum!" He shouted, without moving his focus away from the three Astraeans. "Report all contacts in local or in the immediate, surrounding space."

A Caecusi reached with a branch of their body and made contact with a terminal that was previously unseen to the Astraeans. It lit up as the Caecusi the Astraeans assumed was Erysimum interfaced with it. The light that had come to an end at Erysimum's branch continued on into the terminal. The terminal then started to fill with bright pathways of light of its own.

"There are no new contacts, Vefly," reported Brassica Erysimum.

"Very well," replied Dionaea.

He began to pace contemplatively, back and forth in front of the Astraeans. "I am looking into something, but in the meantime, you three will stay right here while Caecus maintains its currently level of readiness."

The three Astraeans had no choice but to remain where they stood.

* * *

After an amount of time had passed, that went well beyond the comfortable range, Brassica Lepidium, the subordinate that Dionaea had sent off for whatever reason, could be seen running back into view, eventually returning to the assembled group of Caecusi, and approaching Dionaea once more. He was fatigued, but had no signs of labored respiration. He did however appear wilted and droopy.

Lepidium struggled to straighten himself and raise his gaze to Dionaea so that he could speak softly. He did so, and the Astraeans could once again not hear what was said.

After taking a few moments to exchange comments and questions with Lepidium, Dionaea turned back to the three Astraeans. This time, he leaned closely into Heersan's face.

"There is by no means an unconditional or complete acceptance of your comments by my superiors." Dionaea barked at the three. "And we will maintain our military readiness, but at their request, and despite my stern disapproval, you will be escorted to meet with our leadership."

Heersan attempted to reply with an expression of thanks but was ignored and immediately interrupted.

"Chitin!" Dionaea shouted to another one of his lower subordinates, "You and your sporlings will take these three to the Lumiveil. Stay in absolute perpetual contact in the event of any issues."

"Right away, Vefly!" Chitin replied.

Chapter VIII
Piling On

At Dionaea's order, the three Astraeans were marched briskly through the assembled Caecusi soldiers. After passing through various military vehicles and fortifications protecting the shore, they were put into a large, open-air transport. Along with a few dozen heavily armed guards, the three Astraeans shot off towards the center of the largest Caecus city, their capital, Lumiveil.

The three Astraeans were never all too concerned about their safety. They of course had a multitude of ways to escape their captors or overwhelm them, disappear, and so on, but they had a mission and had to accomplish it. Going on the offensive in any way would jeopardize that and give incredibly valuable time to Daebaugh. They collectively decided, between a few grunts, expressions, gestures and body language that they would go along with the ride for now. There was no desire to deceive or lie, only to remain calm and talk with the leadership. They didn't fault Dionaea or any Caecusi military for their actions. They were simply following their orders in the name of protecting their planet.

Instead of planning an escape or worrying, each Astraean took time to admire what the multiverse had brought to them at that moment, and reveled in the Caecusi landscape as the transport sprinted along. The trees and plants of varying degrees of size and shape flickered in the camouflaged winds. The organic patterns of light pulsing through the Caecusi life waved at them in the unseen current. The light of the buildings shot up and fell down, ebbed and flowed. Everything seemed to be moving.

Nothing was stationary, and there was a purposeful orchestration to it. Whether it was the natural bioluminescence in the blood and cells of all life on Caecus, or the artificial light in the streets and walls, everything around them seemed to be connected by the same network of living arteries and majestic veins. It was the type of sight that made each of the Astraeans wish they had the time to linger and soak up the wonder.

But they couldn't just sit and watch. The transport zipping into and stopping at a small platform reminded them of that. The site of what appeared to be a major capital structure far back from the platform, and high into the sky at the horizon, brought their awareness home. The building was immense and imposing, but simultaneously striking as only the most beautiful and inspired of things can be. It was adorned and decorated with bands of light of varied sizes, widths, lengths and patterns. The intricacies of the structure's actual shape, that were normally, partially hidden by the darkness, were almost completely visible from the amount of bright green filigree and scroll-work in the columns, steps, and terraces. Flanked around it were the highlights of trees, streams, parks, and plants, etched and flowing in even more complex examples of glowing emerald.

The Astraeans would have to come back to admire the area later, however. They had business to take care of. In one visit, they needed not only to secure their release, but re-establish their ages-old friendship with the Caecusi *and* ask them to use a part of their planet as a safe area.

A portion of the armed guards that accompanied them for the trip hopped off the transport and formed a barrier around the exit of the Astraeans' transport. Lannya, Carthal, and Heersan were led off and stopped while the remainder of the guards exited and joined them. Once the entire guard compliment had exited, the transport zipped off and blended into the distance. The guards then led the Astraeans up towards the building, across a massive expanse of flickering walkways, through a park and grid of gardens, to the steps that led up to the entrance of the Lumiveil capital building.

Once inside, the Astraeans saw that the general ambiance of the inside of the building matched that of the exterior, and countryside they saw on their way in. It was warm and inviting. Everything was designed towards harmony and beauty. Lawfulness and order. Strength and kindness. And while everything surrounding them appeared to be on the good side of morality, Heersan, Carthal and Lannya knew they were on their way to see the Caecusi leadership, and that their behavior and actions in the next few moments would heavily influence the Astraeans' future relationship with Caecus.

The guards led the Astraeans up a centralized set of tall and narrow steps to the second level where the leadership chambers were. As they climbed the steps, Heersan was struck by how simple and plain the steps were. It would be a stretch to fit two humans side by side on one step, and there were no rails or banisters. As the stairs rose, they did so at mundane right angles. They were smooth and uninteresting, and had minimal light incorporated into them, which was unlike everything else they saw. It seemed that the more practical the item was, the less ornamentation it had. The designers of this building clearly didn't want the steps to take away from the designs and lights in the floors, walls, doors and ceilings. Ironically, their lack of decoration and little light, made the steps stand out and draw attention.

When they reached the second floor landing, one of the guards sprinted ahead and connected with a terminal next to a sealed door. The guard extended a bouquet of tangled twigs, limbs, and leaves, and inserted it into holes that accommodated the jumble, perfectly. The previously dormant panel lit up, which triggered the pattern of light on the door to change to a new pattern. A mechanism behind the wall began to move, indicated by a sound that resembled substantial rustling and crackling forest noises, which opened the door.

When the Astraeans were led into the Veridi, or leadership chamber, by the guards, they were met with a room large enough only to compliment the nine Caecusi Clade seats, arranged in a semi-circle. Each individual leadership member had the title of Clade.

The height of the room's ceiling was nebulous due to the darkness, partially definable only by a high and sparse canopy of dangling Caecusi lights which resembled that of a forest canopy. The three Astraeans felt claustrophobic and slightly compacted by the ceiling, but were more focused on the Caecusi Clades. Their chairs were shiny and reflective, which contrasted with the matte finish of the majority of other structures and furniture.

Each Clade chair was in a group of three, with three groups in total. Three Clades on each side with three in the center of the semi-circle. Each group of three was set apart from the other. Just before Lannya could address the leadership, the Caecusi Clade in the very center, spoke. The voice was breathy and windy like the other Caecusi, but this Clade's voice was drastically louder and in no way friendly. The crisp bite of the windy voice, high in frequency, scratched at the Astraeans' eardrums.

"You are alive," the frightening Clade voice began, "only because your ship was by itself and because the sentry vessels checked with their leadership before firing on you. We are fully prepared to eliminate each of you, but will allow you to speak. Choose your words carefully, for we know of your intentions towards us."

Heersan, Carthal and Lannya were all breathing deeply and quickly. They were in a state of fearful readiness to be attacked and killed. They looked at each other, trying to determine if they should attempt to escape. Finally, and quickly, Heersan spoke before any of them attempted anything.

"Respected Clades," Heersan nervously rushed. "I cannot speak for the entire Astraean race at this very second, but I will speak for the three of us before you. We beg you to hear us when we say that we do not know why you think we are planning to attack, or are intending to threaten you in any way. Please. We have submitted unconditionally to how we have been received, and have no other forces nearby. Your military has confirmed that. We sought to come here to speak to you in peace, make a request, and maintain our very old friendship. Again, we do not know what has instigated this change in relations, but I swear I will do everything I can to assist in resolving the situation."

The Clade who had spoken first launched up out of the chair. He seemed to be the largest of the nine with his frightening structure that resembled an uprooted and upside-down tree. The energy of his natural green light rippled rapidly up into what appeared to be roots, with slower, throbbing pulses going down into his branches, and even further to the tips where there were leaves and flowers.

The sound of his voice, the only one the Astraeans had heard up to this point, grew louder, and then seemed to multiply. The Astraeans could tell that all of the Caecusi Clades had begun conversing with each other. Initially only a few others were speaking. But quickly, the entire group, made up of various plant-like creatures with unique light patterns, began talking and arguing at once. The sound had become excruciating.

The three Astraeans fell to their knees and covered

their ears while their eyes were clinched shut. They couldn't take it. A Clade from one of the side groups, trudged its piles of branches over to Heersan, Carthal, and Lannya, while the remainder of the Clades argued. The Clade that had approached the Astraeans made a very specific gesture to a nearby guard.

The guard immediately turned to the other guard and signaled him. With a coordinated movement, the two guards knelt down and allowed part of their personal, natural light to interact with the floor. Their bright green essence started to stream quickly into a thin circle, recessed into the floor that was previously not visible. It increasingly filled with light the longer the guards were connected with it, and once one end of the light met the other and completed the circle, the radiant beam then shot up to connect with a matching ring in the ceiling.

The distrusting Clade then grabbed Carthal by the head, and dragged him to the semi-transparent, circular curtain of streaming green light. Heersan and Lannya were able to crack their eyes open just long enough to see him being dragged, but were so crippled by pain that they couldn't act. The voices of the arguing Clades got louder and was made worse by the confined area of the Veridi. Some of the other Clades seemed to be cheering on what was happening with Carthal. Others were screaming with anger at those cheering. There was obviously a heated disagreement going on between the Clades, but it was about to be too late for the Astraeans to understand what it was about, or why they were met with such hostility from the start.

The Elder Clade, who had initially been undecided

on how to deal with the three Astraeans, stood up from his seat, located in the grouping on the right. After seeing Carthal being dragged to the wall of energy, the Elder finally decided on which side of the internal argument he fell.

The Elder turned towards Carthal and noticeably planted himself firmly on the floor of the Veridi. His head, made up of a wealth of illuminated roots, started to grow, and reached to the ceiling where the light from his roots then infiltrated the ceiling, activating intricate paths and patterns to the edges of the ceilings, down the walls, and down to the floor. When the Elder's light reached the floor, the curtain of energy collapsed and receded back to the guards. At the same time, the Elder's light continued winding through patterns in the floor on its way to the center.

Once the Elder's light reached the center of the floor, and then reached the other Caecusi Clades, the light penetrated the bottoms of the other Clades, and dramatically supplanted their individual light patterns, which were then replaced by the Elder's patterns. The hostile commotion from the argument stopped as he temporarily took control of them, and allowed the Astraeans to take a full breath and open their eyes. The other Clades were now silent and effectively frozen under the control of the Caecusi Elder. He stood there, in control of the entire room.

His entire body was rigid and full of potential energy. He was angry and in no mood for any additional chaos. The entire room pulsed with his power while the others were frozen, but they could hear him. The Elder took advantage.

"We only kill those we fight," he said, burning a

blister into the other Clades' insolence. "And we are not yet fighting the Astraeans."

The leader turned back to Heersan.

"Not YET!" The Elder furiously repeated with obvious emphasis.

There was no sound and no movement. The Astraeans silently clawed for solace or hope in the confines of their minds, but found none. The chilling flow of the Elder's light throughout the entire room, and the temporarily lifeless forms of the other Clades, filled each Astraean with terror. After allowing plenty of opportunity for the Astraeans to understand how his patience had been depleted, he had a question for them.

"What can you do to resolve this situation?" He sharply asked of Heersan. The Elder's voice was still agitated and loud, but his question was not rhetorical. He was giving Heersan a chance.

The Elder began to relax his body and energy, just enough to release control of his fellow Clades. Without addressing them verbally, the other Clades were slow to begin moving again, and as they did, they submissively took their seats. They had overstepped their bounds, but had been put back in their place.

Heersan's body rocked as he slowly started to get up. He massaged behind his ears and scalp as he came to his feet. Lannya did the same and slowly shuffled over to Carthal to help him up, mere inches from the outline of the circle on the floor that would have killed him if he had been dragged into the wall of light.

"Would you agree," Heersan started, through grunts and further massaging, "to let me to reach out to our leadership?"

"How do we know that isn't part of a plan?" the Elder barked back. "A signal to them to let them know you've gained access to our capital?"

Lannya had grown impatient with the Caecusi's unfounded hostility and startled Carthal when she joined in the argument.

"We are alone!" She shouted.

The Elder violently rustled over to her position. Lannya was beyond being intimidated.

"We attacked no one! There is no history of hostility between our people! We are allies! Whatever information you have to make you think we mean you harm, is wrong! Precedent demands we be given the benefit of the doubt!"

Lannya stood her ground and was overcome with anger and frustration. The amount they had been pushed around, had for now, trumped the temporary fear they had succumbed to.

The sound in the Veridi once again dropped to nothing. But in this silence, something entirely different, than what happened last between the Clades, began to take place. The individual light patterns from the other Clades, began to flow down through their bodies, into the chairs, to the floors, and then made their way to the Elder. When their individual energy reached the Elder, you could see that he was accepting it, but where they were controlled by his energy, he was merely receiving their energy. They were communicating with him and giving him feedback on what had been said so far. It was much more peaceful and civil. The Astraeans remained silent, for their part, and waited for a response to Lannya's angry, yet true observations.

"More than a majority of my fellow Clades," the Elder said, slightly softer, and while gesturing back towards the other leaders, "now actively believe you do indeed deserve the benefit of the doubt, in light of your lady Astraean's comments just now."

The Astraeans remained silent and attentive as the Elder spoke.

"I also agree," he said.

Lannya's body folded in and slumped slightly in a less confrontational posture.

The Elder's body reacted similarly.

Heersan calmly pleaded. "What was it that made you think we were planning to attack?"

There was no immediate answer, but the atmosphere had lightened, and the patterns and speed of the light throughout the Veridi, and through the bodies of the Clades, had softened and slowed. The Elder turned his back to the three Astraeans, only to return to his chair. The guards, who had approached the three outsiders, retracted back to their posts near the entryway.

The Elder sat down slowly. His gaze returned to the Astraeans. His body heaved and then relaxed.

Bursts of confined energy began to flow from a branch of the Elder into one of the arms of his chair. Within a few seconds, the energy had finished flowing, and a pool of light appeared inside the circle on the floor. Almost as soon as it appeared, it began to rise and step up at increasingly intricate levels until it formed a representation of Elcyd's face. The Caecusi Elder had made contact with the Harbor.

At the Harbor, a terminal had initiated a

communications and video channel with Caecus. Elcyd saw it almost immediately and was glad to see the Caecusi Elder, who had not revealed his name to the three visiting Astraeans.

"Roson!" Elcyd greeted quickly, with a burst of friendship. "So great to see you! I take it Carthal, Heersan and Lannya have arrived?"

"We are indeed in possession of those three Astraeans, yes," Roson replied, dryly, picking each word carefully. Elcyd's bright green likeness reflected his real-time confusion in the darkness of the Caecusi Veridi.

Elcyd's tone flat-lined.

"In possession of? I don't understand. Is there a problem?"

"We have been led to believe you mean to attack us," Roson replied, showing no signs of intimidation.

"Roson... Caecusi Clades. There is absolutely no plan to attack Caecus," Elcyd replied with a heavy concern. "We were seeking a diplomatic discussion with you, the details of which I'm hesitant to discuss over this communications medium. That is why we sent the three before you now, to meet with you. Has there been an incident? Has anyone been harmed?"

Roson's visual receptors glanced at Carthal quickly, who had returned to his feet and was not injured, and then back to Elcyd's image.

"No," Roson snapped. "Not yet."

"Roson, you have not been attacked, and you have not been harmed. Your people are not in danger," Elcyd said with a flowing and confident lilt. "And, we have absolutely no malicious intent towards Caecus, as we never have. In the name of our ages-old friendship, I must request an explanation. Why do you think we mean your people harm?"

As Elcyd brought Roson to task, Roson shot back up out of his chair and came face to face with Elcyd's projection. Roson could be seen barreling up with ferocity, ready to escalate the situation even more. Only when Elcyd brought up the old friendship between the Astraeans and the Caecusi, did Roson finally seem disarmed. He stepped back, but left his visual receptors on Elcyd. A bit of energy could be seen to be silently exchanged between Roson and the other Clades once more.

"Tell him!" One of the Clades shouted to Roson.

Before the energy transfer was over, Roson shot a separate ray of energy through the floor and back to his chair. A second display shot up from the floor. Roson began to read the text from it to Elcyd.

"While our identity must remain anonymous for our own safety, we wish to send word to you, your entire planet, and all your allies, that you are in danger. Those known as the Astraeans are coordinating a massive assault on various species throughout the multiverse in the name of ultimate domination. Their attacks are imminent! Defend yourselves at all costs and if at all possible, prepare for any feasible preemptive attack upon them. Look at the enclosed images of their carnage. We hope to be in contact again, soon."

As Roson began reading the last sentence, he sent a signal to close the display and immediately addressed Elcyd again.

"As the message said, it was anonymous, with no

signature," Roson continued. "Look at these attached images. Look! How else could any responsible leader and protector of a people respond to such a message, Elcyd?"

Roson was shouting, but it was clear he wasn't shouting at Elcyd, as much as expressing his frustration with the threat. The images included were scenes of the dead on the roof of the Harbor during the attack where Akal was killed. But, instead of the background being of the Harbor and the surrounding space, the images had been edited to show backgrounds of various locations throughout the multi-verse.

"Those images are scenes from the attack on the Harbor, Roson! They have been manipulated to manipulate you! Why didn't you make an attempt to confirm the message?" Elcyd shouted back. He made no effort to further restrain himself against the false accusations and threats of war.

"You should have confirmed with allies, and neighbors, reached out to us, or tried to trace the message somehow!"

Roson had stepped back into Elcyd's virtual face.

"We did try to trace the message! We couldn't! Reaching out to you didn't make strategic sense if the threat was true, and we did indeed verify that many of our allies have received the same message!"

Elcyd's mouth dropped to angrily gasp for more air at the shock of what Roson had said. His eyes danced all around as his brain scrambled with thought. Mamdod, who had been next to Elcyd during the transmission and heard everything, placed his hand on his shoulder.

"Daebaugh's trying to turn the entire multiverse

against us," Mamdod whispered to Elcyd, with a thud of finality. "To help them annihilate us."

There was nothing said for a moment. Elcyd shrunk in on himself even more as he contemplated the implications of what he had just learned. While staring blankly into the distance, and without turning his attention back to the Caecus video transmission, Elcyd wet his lips and swallowed, then spoke once more to Roson.

"Roson... Please do not harm my people. I do not know who has sent that message, but it is absolutely false. As I said, we were the ones who have already been attacked here at the Harbor. We've lost... so, many, of our people." Elcyd's voice broke before swallowing again, and continuing.

"Whoever may be lying to you and setting the multiverse against us, may be monitoring us and relishing this conversation."

Elcyd's focus, which had been floating out into the distance, snapped back, directly into the camera transmitting his signal to Caecus.

"I beg you to take my word that we are still proud to call the Caecusi friends, and mean you no harm of any kind. Please allow Carthal, Heersan and Lannya to share with you the specifics that I can't over this transmission. Should you wish to speak with me after they bring you up to speed, they will inform you of some new, more secure methods we have recently developed. In fact, I hope you do contact me again soon."

Elcyd's face continued to glow and light up the entire Veridi. The frozen definition in his face, silently hoping for compliance from Roson was easily distinguishable.

Roson, who had remained defensively furious while

almost mashed up against the image of Elcyd's transmission, stepped back slightly and slowly as he replied.

"Very well... my old friend."

Elcyd's face bobbed as it was obvious he was taking a large breath. He sighed in relief as a thankful smile came across his face. He then nodded to Roson in acknowledgment of helping rescue their friendship, and ended the transmission.

Roson continued peering through the blackness where Elcyd's transmission had just been. All of the green lifeblood of the Caecusi, in the room, from Roson, the other Caecusi Clades, their chairs, the floor, walls, and ceiling, drained out of the majority of the paths in the room and their bodies. For the first time since the three Astraeans arrived, there was an actual sense of calm.

Roson no longer looked to be threatened or angered by the visiting Astraeans. He turned around and addressed them softly.

"My friends. Please accept my apologies. Not for the prudent protection of my people, but definitely for not confirming the message more thoroughly. I alone am responsible for that. I rushed our people into a state of fear and unfounded paranoia."

Heersan quickly looked to Carthal and Lannya and back to Roson.

"I don't think any of us would have done much differently, if our roles had been reversed, Roson." Heersan offered, respectfully and wisely.

Roson made a movement that sent energy throughout the room which increased the light moderately. An ambient sense of warmth and welcoming had come to the room. Roson and the rest of the Clades began properly introducing themselves to the three Astraeans, while attendants came in with refreshments. Roson signaled for comfortable seating to come up from recesses in the floor, to accommodate the Astraeans.

"Please, do not let me delay your mission any further," Roson insisted kindly.

Though the Caecusi never felt obligated to translate their native communications to outsiders, Roson let the Astraeans know what he was transmitting to the planet at that moment, in a rare example of Caecusi transparency. He ordered his people to stand down and informed them that more information would follow to clarify and confirm the threat upon their people. The Astraeans were to be regarded once more as ancient allies who had no ill intentions against Caecus.

"Please, tell me everything you can," implored Roson to the Astraeans, with regretful urgency. "Let me know how we can assist."

Chapter IX
The New Help

Thyra stood and tapped her foot while looking out across her wrecked library. It was of course not only hers, but she loved it more than anything else. Her skin tingled with an uncomfortable itch at the sight of its cluttered and damaged state. The gash in the wall, where Rigella had crashed the fighter through it, was repaired soon after the attack, but a good portion of the books, artifacts, shelves, and cases, were still in various collected jumbles across the floor of the library. There had been some restored sections, but disarray was still the rule, and not the exception. Thyra hated that.

Despite their advanced technology and abilities, Thyra and the rest of the library staff had to be deliberate and careful with restoring what they could of the library. Many of the artifacts were originals that required meticulous attention and delicate handling. It was a slow process, but one filled with love and respect. Each library staff member was taking their time and getting help from Thyra when she could provide it. She was extremely busy meeting with allied leaders, conducting research, and reporting to Rigella on military history, organization and tactics. Much of the information was known to Astraeans, but it was especially important to Rigella during the early days of the ADF, that she have at her disposal, as much organized data, history, and information, as possible.

But for the moment, Thyra had taken a break from that research. After wandering out from her office and around to the front of the main desk to measure the progress being made on the library's restoration, she huffed at the mess. But, that was as far as she got. She was quickly startled by a small electrical pop, followed by a quickly diminishing buzz. She snapped her head towards the direction of the sound, and found down below and to her side, an engineer working on replacing the ribbon interface terminal that had been damaged.

She didn't allow being startled get in the way of her manners.

"Thank you for replacing that," Thyra extended kindly to the engineer. She bent down to take a closer look. "I still can't believe how much damage the Harbor sustained."

The engineer eagerly obliged her in conversation while maintaining his focus on his work.

"I know," he said with a low groan. "I can't either. We'll have it back to normal soon, though."

"You're all doing amazingly," Thyra returned, kindly.

"Thank you, Thyra. We'll get there," he said confidently.

Thyra started to bend and stand up.

"I'll let you get back to it. Thank you again," she offered a last time.

"My pleasure," the engineer replied, taking a break from the ribbon interface. He then dipped his hand into an unpretentious pouch held together by seams of ribbon energy. As he passed his hand through the top of it, the bag scanned the engineer's ribbon energy and discovered what he needed. It then generated inside, whichever tool he was thinking of.

After Thyra stood back up, she leaned against the counter and focused her attention away from the piles of debris and materials, and towards the dozen or so engineers she could see from her point of view. They were working feverishly on the ribbon interfaces, the ribbon transit carpet system, displays, and terminals. She was very thankful for them and their work. She knew it would get back to where it was supposed to be. She just had to be patient, and help where she could, when she wasn't working on the project for Rigella.

"Alright," Thyra said softly to herself. "Time to get back to it."

Just as she was about to turn to disappear behind the counter and return to her office, she heard a warm tenor voice address her.

"Excuse me, do you have a moment?" The man's voice requested respectfully.

Thyra stopped and spun around. Her hair, which she had let grow recently, was thicker at the moment, and contained more of the predominantly red, gold, and orange, leaf-shaped strands than usual. The thin metal edges and glassy interior of the leaves, tapped and clinked bluntly against each other as she turned. In addition to her hair's added length and bulk, there were also new, natural highlights of dark and rich violets appearing in Thyra's hair. Much like certain types of plants or trees, Thyra's hair went through subtle changes every so often, similar to season cycles.

"Hello! Yes? How can I help?" she offered pleasantly. Her preoccupied face still managed an enchanting sincerity and curiosity, as her eyebrows lifted and brought with them, a smile.

The library patron was caught off guard as Thyra turned to greet him. He felt his chest wash with warmth and his eyes freeze in a stare. He had become overwhelmed with an exquisite rush of confusion, but it was the absolute best kind of confusion. His train of thought had been completely derailed by Thyra's gentle greeting and stunningly rare appearance. Hers was the kind of beauty that was authentic and natural. Too stunning to require modification. A kind of beauty that is only accentuated by the experience and humility of an Astraean, which was in turn, amplified by her true goodness.

While it was a subjective notion, very few across the breadth of the multiverse would argue that Thyra was not the epitome of beauty, inward or outward. It was this beauty that commanded every molecule of the visitor's existence to attention. An attention not of lust, but of respect and fascinated bashfulness. Thyra's demeanor, voice, and appearance, made the visitor temporarily forget what lust even was. Lust was too simple. The library patron was feeling something far more complex at that moment.

He felt as if something had been revealed to him. A secret and powerful something. Only he knew about it, and only he would ever know about it. Looking into her eyes, he felt an intoxicating honor and obligation to protect that something. He had no word or definition for it. It was just, it. He was stunned with awe, in the awareness that whatever he was feeling for Thyra right then, was probably his best estimate at the reason for the entire multiverse's existence.

Thyra jokingly extended her eyebrows and turned her head, waiting for a reply. The visitor just stood there, without blinking. He breathed heavily but slowly, as his mouth, previously closed, started to slide open. He wasn't aware of it, and outwardly, he probably appeared as if he was trying to speak. It was just another one of his symptoms of being caught up in Thyra. He wasn't aware of anything but her at that moment.

Thyra opened her mouth and chuckled. She then playfully mocked him by rapidly lifting and lowering her jaw, hoping to inspire a response.

The patron started to come out of his trance with a blink. He then wet his lips and closed his mouth. After clearing his throat, he finally spoke.

"Yes, I'm sorry! I, um," he started, still attempting to wrestle his focus back. "I was trying to remember what I came here for."

Thyra tilted her head with a humorous pity.

"Are you ok?" she asked with dry, but jesting concern. "Do I need to call medical?"

"No, no" the patron said, shaking the fogginess out

of his head. "I just have a lot on my mind."

"You and me, both!" Thyra affirmed. She then walked around the back of the counter to begin picking through one of the piles of collected debris.

Now that he was no longer frozen in awe or thought, like plugging in the rest of a puzzle, the patron glanced at Thyra's entire figure as she walked around the counter. His following thoughts centered on his admiration of the refined strength in her steps.

Thyra began reaching down to sort through some display pads. While making two stacks, one for pads that were functional and those that weren't, she tried again to assist the patron.

"So, what was it that I can do for you? Have you remembered yet?" Thyra chuckled as she bent down for another pad.

Just about mentally back on the ground, he finally responded. But first, he laughed at himself and exhaled a burst of embarrassment.

"I, I'm sorry. I'm exhausted," he poorly provided as the reason for his distraction.

As Thyra looked up from her stacks, she played along and agreed with him that he did in fact look exhausted. His face did however, droop with a sleepless, but temporary burden and days-old beard stubble. Despite this, Thyra instantly recognized a handsome foundation below the weariness that he seemed to have no immediate power over. As they spoke, Thyra noticed his frequent favoring and rubbing of his sufficient muscles that she assumed to be sore or injured.

She found conversational and social comfort

in seeing that he was apparently not concerned with impressing her, and he found similar comfort in her lack of a facade. Often times, regardless of location or species, the opposite mating gender(s) felt compelled to put on some form of show for Thyra, simply because she was assuming a female human form. That grew old quickly with her, and was relieved this wasn't one of those times. She began to give second and third glances at him, and devoted more of her attention to what he was saying.

"I'm here at Rigella's suggestion, actually," the patron submitted. "My name is Siguren."

Thyra straightened up with heightened intrigue, and slid the display pads she was holding down the counter a bit. She leaned in on the counter and concentrated more on Siguren.

"Rigella sent you here?" Thyra attempted to confirm with an emphasis on Rigella's name. She was somewhat impressed that Rigella had sent someone directly.

"Yeah, well," Siguren quickly sought to clarify. "I ran into her in the lobby and introduced myself. I told her that I was interested in helping the Harbor get back on its feet. We talked a little bit. She told me about some opportunities in the ADF, and places that needed help at the Harbor, so, I thought on it a bit and, this is where I decided to try and help out."

By the time he finished, Thyra had assumed the position of a barkeep waiting on their customer's drink order. But she was only propping and listening. She enjoyed learning things about new acquaintances, and she was enjoying listening to Siguren.

"Ah, I see," Thyra responded. "What kind of help

did Rigella say the library needed, out of curiosity?"

"Oh, just that it saw a heavy bit of fighting during the attack." Siguren provided immediately before continuing. "She said there was a bunch of clean up to do, and repairs, but also that you were working on some research on military topics for her. Between helping restore the Harbor's hub of knowledge and doing what I can to help with the research, I just thought I would enjoy it."

"Hmm," Thyra hummed without particular meaning. "Well, that sounds great. We could use all the help we can get. Are you an Astraean? A visitor?"

"Oh, I'm an Astraean," Siguren clarified gently while stretching and rubbing his neck for relief. I was actually involved in the uh, fight."

Thyra's head leaned in slightly. Her normally warm demeanor got even a bit more compassionate and concerned.

"Daebaugh's attack?" Thyra attempted to clarify.

"Yeah." Siguren let his eyes drop from hers for the first time since he arrived at the library.

"Well, I'm very glad you made it out of that mess," Thyra said with a comforting tone.

Siguren's eyes were still diverted to the ground.

"Thanks," he said, before a single and awkward laugh. "I just wish my parents, brother and sister had made it."

Thyra's mouth dropped and her eyes constricted from dark sadness. She craved something to say but the lump in her throat starved her. The smack of empathetic pain slapped Thyra without warning. She couldn't and didn't want to imagine losing four family members in one setting, or what that might feel like to Siguren.

"One of those permanent soul-killing things was sweeping a wide path in the area we were all fighting." Siguren was obviously replaying the event in his head as he described it, and Thyra noticed his eyes were remarkably calm, but more than that, seized and barren. She knew he never wanted to remember what he was describing again, but also, that he would never forget it.

"I was fighting with my back to it," he resumed, "and I turned around just in time to see it take them all out. I couldn't do anything about it. They were just... just, gone by the time I registered what had happened. And right when I thought I was going down, too, one of our guys took the operator out."

Thyra was struggling to contain her feelings. She let her head fall as her eyes instantly welled up. She quickly picked it back up however, to try and force some kind of reply through her broken heart and lumped throat. He deserved and needed a reply from her, and she was doing everything she could to provide one. But at the same time, Siguren didn't need one, and he didn't want her to think he needed one. It was just one of those terrible moments that inevitably come up in these types of conversations. Those involved can only help the other push through to its completion.

Thyra was still struggling. She was still trying to steal her voice back from the pain she was sharing with Siguren. Instead, she did something probably better, and placed her hand on his.

He looked back up at her, lost in pain. He had no intention of burdening her with it, but he never really had complete control to begin with.

"I'm sorry, Thyra," his quiet and gritty voice offered. "I didn't come here to spill my guts or dump this on you, or anyone. I know plenty of us that lost far more than I did."

Thyra squeezed his hand as she responded.

"That's not how it works," she said. "There's not a threshold for approved mourning. And even if there was, you would have crossed it. That's far more loss than anyone deserves."

She squeezed his hand again and then let go, only to give Siguren a chance to take a break from his pain. He recognized that and took advantage.

He looked away and sniffed forcefully. He wasn't ashamed or trying to hide as he looked away. It was just a reflex. In his mind, he was simply trying to set that heartbroken part of himself down temporarily, and for now, pick up the hopeful part of himself. The part that looked to the future. He then wiped his eyes and turned back to Thyra.

"You're not like any other librarian I've ever met," Siguren suggested sweetly.

Thyra grinned in appreciation, as their eyes sat with each other quietly, on the bench between their minds.

* * *

They spent the next few minutes making the necessary transition in conversation from pain and uncertainty, back to forward thinking and lighter talk. Repairs. Lending to the new Astraean effort. Catching each other up on the tidbits of their past that were relevant to the conversation. But not one twitch of body language, glance or word shared between them, lacked in unspoken gratitude or appreciation for that powerful moment of pain they had shared.

The bond developing between Thyra and Siguren already had a substantial foundation poured for it. Most Astraeans are so old, in so many ways, that their ability to unconditionally care for someone is unrivaled when compared with almost every other being in the multiverse. Bonds were common. Foundations were common. But this was already establishing a stronger bond, with a deeper foundation.

After the humidity of Siguren's painful recollection had begun to dry, and the subsequent small talk had passed, they started to trade more involved stories about their regular lives and experiences after first becoming Astraeans. They were pouring their hearts and souls out to each other, and neither of them realized how much they needed what they were receiving from the other at that moment. Perhaps they both had needed to form a bond like this for some time, but only now were they able to. They laughed and remembered, and became more relaxed and trusting with each other. After a great deal of time, the topic of conversation finally returned back to Siguren's original motivation for visiting the library.

"So, what can we have you help with, hmm, Siguren?"

He forced his mind to flip through the possibilities.

"Uhh, hmm," he mumbled while considering. "What about helping with the work you told me you're doing on a portable imaging system? The technology you used to help stall Daebaugh's forces with when they attacked? I'd love to help with that."

Thyra nodded and pondered.

"Well then, that's what we'll do," she accepted with enthusiasm. "That's been taking up a lot of my time recently. Trying to reverse engineer an extremely old system and modernize it so that it can be incorporated into other areas, ships, and other places that aren't necessarily always in contact with the ribbons..." She forced an intimidated sigh through her lips before finishing her thought. "It's been tough."

* * *

The engineers that were around the library repairing various systems eventually started to trickle out. They would just wave or say, "See you tomorrow," to Thyra and Siguren as they passed by the counter. But the two new friends weren't planning on going anywhere for some time. For Siguren, there was too much to learn, and for Thyra, there was too much to catch him up on. And the fact that they were enjoying each other's company shielded them from fatigue. They were having fun.

Over the course of many hours, Thyra brought Siguren up to speed on the library's imaging system, how it worked, when it had been developed, how it currently functioned, as well as its limitations. Thyra also took Siguren out into the library floor to one of the few functioning terminals with a still-operable link to the imaging system, to demonstrate it for him.

Tap after tap on the screen, Thyra brought up warriors, artists, scaled down ships, galaxies, trees and ancient structures from all over the multiverse. Siguren was itching to try it out for himself. His eyes were glued to the display that Thyra was whizzing her fingers back and forth on. He'd laugh with wide eyes as Thyra would change out the hair styles or personalities on historical figures, with those that didn't match.

When he thought he had a handle on it, he felt comfortable enough to ask to give it a try. He put his hand on Thyra's to softly stop her. She looked up to Siguren who was looking at her with a wild grin.

"Can I try?" he asked.

"Sure!" Thyra obliged. "Have at it!"

She took a step to the side and Siguren slid into place. He clapped his hands together and devilishly giggled as he rubbed them together.

"Let's see..." he began, while skimming the lists of categories and options. "So, not only can this thing reproduce historical figures, beings and objects, but fictional entities and items from a culture's literature and things like that?"

"Right," she confirmed. "There's a bit of ambiguity and guesswork in reproducing things that existed millions of years ago, for example, so it was fairly easy to extend the algorithms and functionality to also incorporate fictional things."

His grin grew into one of a truant delinquent.

"Let's see if we can do something like this," Siguren said, as his fingers began to fly. "Oh, wait. Ok. Let me go back here. There it is."

Thyra took a few steps back in an effort to remain surprised once Siguren had settled on whatever it was that he was creating.

"Do you know which category has the," Siguren attempted before stopping himself. "No, never mind. No help!" He said with a smile and a raised index finger. Thyra flashed her palms to let him know this production was all his.

Thyra watched as Siguren's eyes drowned in the fun, and as his head jerked while his hands moved to tap different parts of the display.

At last, Siguren made a few theatrical and exaggerated flails and taps as he seemed to finish with his creation. His finger hovered over the "Generate" button.

"Are you ready?" He asked Thyra with humorously rabid eyes.

She giggled heartily and threw open her arms.

"Let's see what you've come up with!"

After an extra second of hesitation over the button for added drama, Siguren quickly pressed it.

Thyra and Siguren then watched as numerous banks of small ribbon energy emitters slid out from the walls and ceilings, high above. Some of the emitters shot out beams of physical ribbon energy, while others only ejected light. As Siguren's creation began to take shape ahead of them, he pressed the "Hide Terminal" button on the display. The terminal then quickly contracted down onto itself into a compact and flat square, and then folded flush into a hidden compartment in the floor.

Something large was forming. The emitters started at one section of whatever was being generated, which was quickly growing, as the emitters added more and more to its shape. The bright light from the reflections of various beams flashed and danced across their faces. The library was ablaze in the mysterious creation's energy and light. Thyra was lost in the spectacle. For the first time in a long while, she was able to let her stress subside and enjoy the powerful technology of the imaging system.

Siguren didn't really care all that much about watching his imagination come to life. His motive from the start was to create something for Thyra to enjoy. He watched the joy and suspense on her face. That was his show. He found all sorts of solace and warmth from looking at Thyra over the past several hours, but there was something just a bit more magical about looking at her when she wasn't aware.

The fruit of the imaging system's labor grew, and began to take a recognizable shape, as Thyra laughed and shook her head in an impressed and approving appreciation. She looked to Siguren quickly and then back. She wanted him to know she was excited to see the completed object, but mostly, that she was simply appreciating the moment.

Though the imaging system's creations were not sentient and only behaved in whatever way they were programmed to at the terminal, they were by every other measure, lifelike and physical, and could of course have an impact on their surroundings, just as the creations that defended against Daebaugh's attack had. Because of this, whatever was generated at any given time could inspire legitimate reactions and emotions in those that were nearby. That was especially true right now as Siguren's spawn emanated into being.

The ribbon and light beams flicked, whipped, and intertwined. Within just a pinch of time, a large portion of the recuperating and cavernous library was brimming with a perfectly petrifying sight. Whatever doubts or questions Siguren might have had about the capabilities of the imaging system, had been extinguished. Before their eyes, stood a frightening vision long forgotten in the ancient Sumerian mythology of Earth.

It was Kur.

The first dragon ever conceived, by one of Earth's oldest civilizations. A beast of such significant power that species and cultures across the multiverse were inspired to conjure or duplicate that which began with Kur. Kur was not a secondary conception with a superior example. Kur was the first of its kind, and a symbol whose genesis summoned the pride and wonder of time itself. This most ancient and intimidating dragon from all existence, now stood before Siguren and Thyra.

As soon as the imaging emitters completed their work, the first gulp of breath and formulated life was charged into Kur. As Siguren proceeded through the selection screens, he had selected the "Historical Estimation" option for personality, and didn't put much more stock into that particular selection. But now that Kur was before them, he started to moderately regret his option.

He turned his head to Thyra. She seemed to be unnerved with a combined fear and stupefaction. The two of them were rooted by extraordinary horror.

They weren't sure of how to proceed. In truth, proceeding wasn't even mentally an option right then. Siguren eventually looked to the floor, thinking he should immediately call the terminal back up and end the projection, but he hesitated. His curiosity for how Kur would behave subconsciously trumped his fear.

With every fiber of Thyra's being, she wanted to end the projection herself or quickly request Siguren do so. But she also paused. The sight of Kur was just too amazing to immediately bring to an end.

Kur's body was, at first, tightly compacted as he began to wake up. His thin and nimble tail, at least as long as his body, began to twitch and curl. The last three quarters of the tail were adorned with bulbous, bony spikes of varying lengths. At the end, rested a single rattle, short, wide and blunt. As Kur's muscles began to flex and more drastic movement came to his body, the rattle would occasionally sound a slow, low and horrific hiss.

His body, shielded by plates of onyx and emerald scales were noticeably worn. They weren't worn in the sense that they had been weakened, but only that they had seen a lot of carnage and war. They were dull and rough. Each plate of scales had numerous black hairs protruding from them, but not so many that they decreased the strength or integrity of their protection.

As Kur exhaled his first breath, he sat on his hind quarters while absentmindedly puffing out his considerable chest, which was also shielded by the same scales as the rest of his body. Thyra and Siguren let their attention get stolen next by Kur's massive claws at the end of his sturdy front legs. To each toe, belonged a curled, ivory spike. The apex of each claw was as tall as Siguren.

Thyra and Siguren were beginning to pass the awe phase, and had started growing closer towards the cliff of primal fear. What happened next would shove them over the edge.

Kur's eyelids popped open for the first time to reveal two, solid black orbs with slim yellow pupils, which instantly locked upon the two Astraeans, now cowering before him.

At the same time, Kur unfurled his wings and let them crash like waves onto the open reaches of the cluttered library. After loosening his wings, he then extended them to their maximum in a momentary stretch of comfort. Their span was easily four times Kur's body length and almost reached from one side of the library, to the other.

Siguren was upset with himself, but mostly with his decision to naively bring this dragon to life at all, much less in the library. He didn't know what to do. He was sure that any attempt to grab Thyra and run would only result in them being chased and killed, with additional damage being done to the library and Harbor as a whole. Recalling the terminal from the floor crossed his mind again, but his uncertainty about how intelligent Kur was kept him from doing that as well. Kur would probably have other plans.

After Kur's wings finished stretching, and returning to rest along Kur's back, the dragon stood up, extended his neck, but then resumed his dark stare on Thyra and Siguren.

Siguren, while trying to otherwise remain as motionless as possible, started to slowly scoot his foot towards the plate that would recall the terminal.

Thyra whispered to Siguren with her mouth open, but while holding her lips still. Her eyes never left Kur.

"What hhare hyou dohing?" she nervously huffed through a breathy whisper.

Everything they said was partially obscured by the crisp gusts from their open mouths.

Siguren replied as his foot continued to slide slowly, millimeters at a time, towards the plate. His mouth was also hanging open wide as he spoke, so as to provoke Kur as little as possible.

"I'm tryhing... to ghet the terhninhal hback hup," Siguren ridiculously moaned.

If not for the ancient abomination taking up the bulk of the center of the library at the moment, watching and listening to Thyra and Siguren try to communicate with fear-frozen bodies and gaping mouths could have almost been construed as humorous.

"Please... dhon't.. dooh thhat," Thyra pleaded softly.

"They'hre haren't reallhy manhy other hoptions," he said, frustrated with himself.

His foot grew closer to the plate.

"Wait, hwait!" Thyra growled, almost resembling a shout.

It was too late. Siguren kicked the plate.

With a heavy mechanical thud, the door hiding the terminal thundered open. The compacted terminal unfolded upwards with thick and powerful clicks, and then snapped up into place.

Kur did not care for that.

His tail thrashed and circled far above his head like a lasso before whipping to a firm readiness behind him. His large rattle hissed and rumbled in an ominous drone. Kur's yellow pupils became constricted, and taller, as he focused on the aggravating movement and sound. His mammoth torso started to recoil in an effort to summon as much kinetic energy as possible, while the dragon's mouth began to part. Revealing his split tongue, Kur also displayed his hundreds of spiky teeth across five rows. He then lifted his head, which was framed by a dozen horns that flared out before curving back in.

Lastly, he tested his weapon. A few bursts of fire

escaped from his mouth and scorched the ceiling of the library. Kur quickly let his head fall back down to face Thyra and Siguren. He was now at full capacity, full alertness, and fully annoyed.

The dragon reared back once more, ready to unleash a trumpeted inferno. In a crack and blast of combustion, Kur launched his wave of scorching fire and embers towards Thyra and Siguren, but Siguren had already flung his foot at the plate in the floor.

Just as the blaze of agony was about to get close enough to harm and burn them, Siguren keyed in the command to end the imaging sequence. Kur and his hurled flames were gone. All that reached Thyra and Siguren by the time the projection ceased, was the leading gust of hot air that had been set in motion by Kur.

Immediately after Kur's presence receded back into the emitters, the two Astraeans crumbled to the ground in exhausted relief. For some time, the two sat there without saying a word as they caught their breath, though much was communicated through relieved and fatigued expressions.

"I'm uh," Siguren finally began, still huffing. "I'm going to... put a note on that one," he continued, while stretching up to reach the terminal . "Extremely dangerous. Big. Hot. Dangerous. Dragon."

He slumped back to the ground and looked over to Thyra. She was just about done heaving for air and was planting her best *I-can't-believe-you-did-that* glance on Siguren.

"I know, I know," he said before chuckling.

Thyra's body language quickly transitioned into the hearty amusement that her burgeoning affection for Siguren demanded. She couldn't help but succumb to laughter.

"You better count yourself lucky," Thyra began, through interrupting chuckles. "I would've been extremely upset if we had died!"

Siguren shared in her unabashed laughter and collapsed onto his back in respite. While he was of course happy that Kur didn't kill them, he was even more pleased that Thyra wasn't mad at him.

"A dragon? In the middle of space? Really?" Thyra teasingly complained.

Siguren shrugged in false ignorance.

"What? I didn't think he'd be so..." Siguren searched feverishly for the right word. "Big and... real!"

Thyra was practically suffocating in laughter.

"Or, that his breath would be so bad!" Siguren added.

Thyra choked and gasped for air through her tickled heaves and howls.

"Yeah! I tried to tell you. I even showed you!" Thyra barely got out through silly anger.

"Well, I've learned my lesson, Mistress Librarian!" Siguren calmly, yet tauntingly admitted. "In the future, I'll leave the summoning of the beasts of annihilation to you!"

Thyra rolled onto her back. She couldn't take anymore and needed the support of the floor. She had passed beyond the hysterical laughter phase, into the breathless, closed-eyes, falling-tears stage, of silent and painful laughter. And Siguren was absolutely relishing every second.

* * *

Between the excitement of barely surviving sixty seconds with a dragon, the fatigue from the stress, and the wealth of stomach-busting laughter, the two new friends were worn out. But, the experience was a perfect catalyst to resume their increasingly intimate and personal conversation. Not long after they had dispensed with Kur, both Thyra and Siguren sat next to each other, both of them leaning back against the imaging terminal. They had the entirety of the library to themselves, and whether or not they knew it, the majority of the public areas of the Harbor. Most of the crowds had retired to the living areas for the remainder of the day.

"So, it seems like it's mostly a matter of energy storage and regeneration," observed Siguren, after a lull in their casual conversation.

"Yeah, that's pretty much the conclusion we've come to," Thyra concurred. "A good portion of the restricted area of the library is dedicated to ribbon energy capacitors for the imaging system to work."

"Well, I think the technology can be sized up or down as needed, but also with an improvement in efficiency and size," Siguren suggested.

"Good!" Thyra popped with eagerness. "How about we head to Imaging and Assembly to see if Hergie has some ideas on how to scale and improve the system?"

Siguren slapped the floor gently and jumped to his feet. He reached for Thyra and helped her up, intentionally pulling her close as she stood. Their faces were close enough to feel the breath of the other. Thyra's eyes raised slowly to meet his. She grinned and said plenty without uttering a syllable. Siguren's eyes and smile reciprocated a charming and silent flirtation as well. They just stood there, enjoying each other's face, each feature, each blemish, and the twitches of smiles and corners of eyes. Before they could enjoy much more than that, however, an engineer entered the library, preparing to resume the ongoing repairs.

Thyra and Siguren slowly parted from each other, both still smiling.

"Come on," Siguren winked. "Let's go see if Hergie's free."

Chapter X
A Force is Born

After Carthal, Heersan and Thyra filled Roson and the entire Caecusi leadership in on everything that was happening, they returned to Paige to communicate immediately with the Harbor. They thought about using some of the new personal transmission technologies being tested by the Harbor, but they were unsure of what unfriendly ears may be nearby.

After the three Astraeans were dropped back off at the Caecusi docks, they stomped heavily onto the pad that would take them back to the ship. Their feet were weighed down with the dread of having to relay how much steeper their uphill battle had become. The three of them didn't know what to say to each other. None of them spoke until they established a connection with the Harbor.

"We have good news," began Lannya, very plainly.

"And we have some very bad news," completed

Heersan, with disgust.

Rigella's expression didn't change as she turned to face her friends' communication display at a nearby terminal back at the harbor. She was the very definition of business and didn't hesitate as she replied.

"Well, give me the bad news first," she ordered.

Carthal had stepped into frame.

"Daebaugh's people have begun sending warnings out across the multiverse that the Astraeans will soon begin an offensive to take control of as much of the multiverse as possible."

Much like a stubborn warrior who has been wounded, Rigella's head rocked slightly to the side as her face hardened from a wave of adrenaline and anger.

Carthal, Heersan and Lannya stood patiently, waiting for Rigella's response.

"That makes sense from a strategic point of view," she admitted. "Get others to help defeat your enemy."

"That's a lot of 'others'," Carthal complained sarcastically. "They're telling everyone to prepare themselves and take preemptive action if possible."

Rigella shook her head to herself quickly. Her follow-up question only barely showed signs of optimism.

"What's the good news?"

"Well," Lannya began. "After we were finally able to convince the Caecusi that we are still their allies, and caught them up on everything, they did very reluctantly agree to allow us to use a portion of their planet as a safe area."

"Reluctantly." Rigella echoed in frustration. She then looked over her shoulder to Mamdod and Elcyd as she continued. "We're going to have to fight hard for every gain and practically rebuild all of the relationships we've ever had, in a fraction of the time we've ever had, for any advantage or assistance."

"And as might be expected," Heersan filled in, "they will not share with anyone that they are assisting us in any way. They will disavow any knowledge of helping us if questioned. For the safety of their own people, they have asked we respect that until we're able to combat Daebaugh's propaganda some."

Rigella stood up and rubbed her face violently. Her hands then fell to her hips as she began to consider their next move.

"We should have the beacons broadcast a secure message, Rigella. Especially the new ones that are further out," Elcyd urgently suggested, as he motioned to an engineer to come and wait for Rigella's confirmation.

"Yes," Rigella replied immediately. "Let's put a transmission on them explaining what has transpired between Mamdod, Akal and Daebaugh, and that any message threatening any kind of violence or plans to invade anyone, has been fabricated by those who attacked us recently and are entirely illegitimate."

After exchanging a few words with Elcyd, the engineer then ran off to make the adjustments to the beacons.

"We also need teams out in the multiverse communicating that same message," Rigella continued. "Diplomatic teams to actively combat Daebaugh's warnings, and let everyone know what's going on. We can hopefully get ahead of this before it's too late, and maybe gain some assistance as a result. Between that, and our reputation throughout the majority of the multiverse, hopefully we'll have some luck."

Rigella shifted her attention away from Elcyd and back to the communications display.

"Lannya, Carthal and Heersan," she continued.

"Will you three please resume your recon? We need to know where Daebaugh and his people are at, sooner rather than later."

"Of course," replied Heersan. "Everything here at Caecus seems to be wrapped up. It took longer than we had planned, but, we have a safe planet."

"Ok," replied Rigella. "Please be safe and provide any major updates as soon as you can."

"Roger that," Carthal affirmed. "We'll talk again soon."

With a quick nod, Rigella ended the transmission between Paige and the Harbor. She quickly leaned over to tap a few notes into a personal terminal, and then flipped back up towards Elcyd and Mamdod.

"Well, Daebaugh is going about this with an extremely strategic precision," Rigella continued. "We have to assume they have every advantage, have made every plan, and planned for every contingency. Our biggest concerns right now should be letting as many planets as possible know that the messages they're receiving are false, while simultaneously working to locate Daebaugh. Whenever that happens, it's probably going to come down to sheer numbers, and pure war."

"Speaking of numbers," Mamdod inquired. "What is the latest ADF progress?"

"Right, let me show you," Rigella said with enthusiasm. The pride she had for what she and her colleagues had come up with was evident as her eyebrows jumped up and down while using the nearby terminal to initiate the presentation projection. She enjoyed teamwork more than most other things. As she worked through her presentation, she gave quick kudos to various members of her team for proposing various suggestions.

"As has been discussed very prominently, the focus of this entire effort has been to always remember that the Astraeans are a peaceful and respectful race. But at the same time, we made no attempt to hide or suppress our unmatched knowledge of combat and warfare. With that awareness, and due in no small part to our immediate need for offensive capabilities, we developed our Astraean Defense Force with divisions centered on mostly traditional criteria, such as the type of environment a division would be fighting in. But, we also took into consideration things that are unique to Astraeans, such as the type of physical form a division may need to assume."

The presentation, with Thyra's active assistance, had already begun shuffling through images of various examples of military structures and units, throughout the multiverse. As Rigella spoke of pros and cons for each diagram, constructed from Thyra's analysis and discussions with various leaders, little notes in the margins popped up to call attention to specific areas of the three-dimensional presentation projection.

"With that said," Rigella continued, "We have three primary divisions in the ADF. We have a Guardian Division which is of course focused on groups of individual combatants. Our Ciconal Division is devoted to combat in seas, skies and atmospheres, and our Stellar Division is centered on combat in any given location's local or deep space. Each division is then further divided into groups assigned to a particular area of the multiverse, and then further divided into sections that are trained in various disciplines as traditional warfare, indigenous warfare for their assigned section of the multiverse, temporal warfare, inorganic warfare, and so on."

A very straight-forward visual accompanied the description, and once again, additional notes popped into and out of the margins as the presentation proceeded, to further outline the pros and cons of this approach.

"And while this is a military in every sense of the word, we have elected to have an element of democracy within the command chain of the ADF. Each Secondary Commander of the three divisions of the ADF have a single vote towards proposed decisions affecting the ADF as a whole. The Central Commander will have a vote that counts as two. Each Secondary Commander will have the final say over their division, with no Secondary Commander being able to override another. The Central Commander, however, can override the decisions of any Secondary Commander."

"We already have teams working to communicate the details of the formation, structure and responsibilities of the ADF, to all Astraeans, and have already begun a heavy recruitment campaign. As you might expect, the numbers are extremely promising. Willingness is high. Additionally, we are already coordinating with Hergie on making use of the new imaging and fabrication facility to provide the ADF with standardized ships, uniforms, weapons, tools, materials and vehicles. Finally, there are also plans in development to provide for cross-division and hybrid operations."

The room was quiet for a moment as Elcyd, Mamdod, a team of engineers, and a compliment of new ADF subordinates took in the presentation. There were a few quick and quiet side conversations while Mamdod and Elcyd stepped closer and reviewed the projection more closely.

"I think this is a very practical and well thought-out beginning," Elcyd finally announced.

"Thank you. We do, too." Rigella replied calmly and confidently. "While we work to finish the initial formation of the ADF, and then begin outfitting and training, I think we should work on getting those diplomatic teams out there to beat back Daebaugh's propaganda immediately. The extent of this fight with Daebaugh is potentially perpetual, and will have a drastic impact across the multiverse. We need to make our case and make this as public as possible."

Mamdod backed away from the projection and joined everyone else back at the table as he responded.

"I would think it best to make this diplomatic element something outside of the ADF as diplomacy by nature shouldn't be a militaristic device."

"We would be more than happy to incorporate that into the ADF if asked," Rigella replied respectfully, "But, I agree with you completely. Diplomacy should not be tarnished by being attributed with violence or warfare."

Elcyd looked around the room quickly to gauge impressions, but didn't hesitate long before speaking up.

"I am of the same mind. I don't think anyone here disagrees. Perhaps Mamdod and I can take that task and form the diplomatic team. We can advertise it and recruit for it similarly to how you're recruiting for the ADF. How does that sound?" Elcyd scanned the room once more.

"That's a wonderful plan," Rigella responded.

"Yes, we can take care of that," Mamdod obliged.

Elcyd tapped the table lightly with his knuckles.

"Good," he said, proud of how his people had come together so quickly and constructively in the wake of such horrific events. "We'll recruit the team, prepare them, and get them out there as quickly as possible to fight Daebaugh's propaganda machine."

Chapter XI
Claiming a Name

Azli walked towards Daebaugh but stopped slightly behind him. She was going to wait until he addressed her. She knew he probably heard someone approaching, but he made no immediate effort to see who it was. She took the opportunity to stop and dust her clothes to remove any specs or fuzz. It wasn't so much that she was worried about being presentable to Daebaugh, but that she was in no hurry to talk with him. While she waited for him, she tended to something she cared about much more. Her appearance. In fact, when it came to what *he* thought about her appearance, she couldn't have cared less.

She didn't really care for him at all. She didn't really care about anyone. Azli was just as tired of being subconsciously judged and held up to the perfection of the Astraeans, as Daebaugh was. She was just along for his ride until he gained control of the ribbon island, or until the

Astraeans were eliminated. Daebaugh's group just wanted to be free, or at least be what Daebaugh defined as being free. Azli, Daebaugh, and his followers didn't necessarily think that any particular species or individual universe was specifically judging them, but they knew the Astraeans probably did, and they just couldn't stand that.

Azli was on board entirely with the mission. She just hated her boss. She had seen and heard enough of Daebaugh while working for him, to not only have contempt for him, but to outright loathe him. She wasn't much better, and she knew that, but she had seen him kill at the drop of a hat for the most arbitrary of reasons. He stomped on life with zero hesitation. The more life there was, he felt, the more clutter, and confusion there was. The more life there was, the more sources for stress, and more obstacles to freedom there were, in Daebaugh's mind. His followers felt the same way, but that was due in large part to being *taught* to feel the same way.

Those who did Daebaugh's bidding also gained access to their previous lives, but that was where their similarities to Astraeans ended. A portion of the bonus of having billions of years to deceive and scheme, was using some of that time to engineer ways to subvert certain ribbon traffic. At all times, Daebaugh monitored ribbon activity, and could redirect certain spiritual travel to his location. He would then receive that spirit, and mold it how he wished. Those that arrived didn't know he had kidnapped their spirit. They knew nothing of the Astraeans until Daebaugh had cultivated them enough to receive and believe his lies.

It wasn't an open-ended and limitless technology he used to divert ribbon traffic, however. It took great planning and energy accumulation to activate his machinery, and have it plunder those certain souls he felt he could manipulate into believing in his cause. It took a methodical and sick mind to be so motivated and selective.

After brushing her sleeves and bending her neck to check her shoulders, Azli relaxed and leaned over to look at her pants and shoes. She was pleased. When she passed her own inspection, she punched out an impatient sigh that she hoped he would hear. He still showed no signs of caring who had approached. He tapped and zipped through dozens of reports at a time, sent to him from throughout the multiverse. Updates on the final damages to equipment and numbers of casualties, as a result of their attack on the Harbor, popped up and flew by. There were also succinct reports from around the multiverse on how successful their anti-Astraean sentiment was being received by various indigenous cultures.

"I don't know if any of this could be going any better, Daebaugh." Azli said with a dark enthusiasm, hoping she sounded interested enough for him to quit wasting her time. Her arms were bent out with her hands holding onto her hips as she spoke. She was ready for the next move. Ready for more work. Ready to be done.

With Azli's last syllable, Daebaugh poked the terminal he was giving his attention to, and finally looked over and glared at Azli.

"I'm tired of saying this," he said, slicing the air with unmistakably clear and concise pronunciation. "The name of Daebaugh does not exist anymore."

Azli opened her mouth with the inclination to take umbrage with his domineering tone, but stopped short with her mouth slightly opened, and visibly bit her tongue.

"Right," she eventually conceded, with just enough energy to make the word audible. "Einar."

"Einar Tyndur," he completed. "There is absolutely no reason to hide behind that powerless and pointless Daebaugh name. The life I got it from was as arbitrary as the ribbons themselves. That's what this is all about, Azli."

Her jutted-out hip and blank stare of disinterest wasn't what Einar wanted to see. He braced himself on a nearby table and slung a stack of star map modules into the floor as he vaulted over to Azli in two steps. He grabbed her throat, extended his arm and slammed her into the wall.

"Is there something about asking you to address me how I wish to be addressed that is troublesome for you?" Einar began to squeeze her throat as he posed his question. "Please tell me there is," he goaded, as his fingertips clamped tighter around her lower jaw. "Please give me an excuse," he began to utter, deeply and slowly, almost with a tone of depraved sexuality. "Give me an excuse to hurt you. I would love to hurt you."

Azli wasn't intimidated, though she felt her jaw pop with a hollow click just before it started to break. She was definitely not going to take this display from Einar. Before Einar could react, Azli whipped a leg hanging below her, around to the side of Einar's head. The shock of the blow made him drop her and caused him to stumble clumsily to the side. He used the momentum from stumbling to then spin around, while comforting his head as he locked eyes with her. Azli stood confidently, ready for anything else he'd like to try.

There was an unspoken understanding between

them that they reaffirmed right at that moment with emotionless eyes of derision. Like Azli, Einar had no true concern for her, or anyone else. Both Einar and Azli, and each of their comrades, were all means to their collective end. But Azli was slightly more than that to Einar. She provided a large flint and steel to his plan. Her contempt for her parents carried over to the Astraeans as a whole, and Einar counted on that, exploited it, and nurtured it.

* * *

Everyone in Einar's camp was their own king, and each king was another king's serf. They all lived to fight for the clichéd and ambiguous goal of anarchy. They wanted to answer to no one and to feel that their wants, dreams, and desires were equally important. They were united under one banner, and one goal. However, there was rarely any discussion between them all on what was to happen once they realized their single, shared goal. They were under no ideological illusion. Once the Astraeans were ripped from the multiverse's throne, and the throne was subsequently destroyed, they would all scatter like the wind. There was no allegiance. Allegiance to them was a fleeting necessity.

The Astraeans made Einar sick. He thought their assumed responsibility, based on an ambiguous and rambling message on the floor of the Harbor, should not have been assumed to begin with. That the Astraeans or Mamdod thought it was incumbent on them to be the caretaker of the multiverse and its inhabitants, was a revolting insult that constantly gnashed away at Einar's nerves. He didn't need guidance. He didn't need enlightenment or saving. He just wanted to experience the multiverse however it naturally came to him, without interference from anyone.

Einar saw the Astraeans as another example of yet another arbitrarily, self-appointed group of enforcers. A group of enforcers that imposed their will and made people fall in line. They were just like any other self-righteous group deciding what was best for everyone, Einar believed. Einar had seen it time and time again across the multiverse. Someone was always holding the carrot of a moral compass over their head to bend people to their will.

The semi-immortal group of Astraean enforcers that once exterminated, would no longer prevent these Einarians from realizing their absolute freedom. They would be free, and the multiverse would be free. It would be unencumbered to progress without outside influences. Morality would be a forgotten construct and minding your business would be the rule. The only law would be that there is no law.

The Einarians were every bit as intelligent and powerful as the Astraeans, in that they had, in addition to also having previous lives, comparable knowledge, technology, and mastery of all things involving warfare. Combined with the contempt for the Astraeans, and the ages and eons of planning, this made them a formidable force of destruction.

The Einarians understood their advantages and power, but they were also not in any way spontaneous or reckless. They worked hard to maintain order within their ranks and squashed dissent or mutiny as quickly as hints of such things crept up. They also constantly reminded themselves that their victory was never assured. Not until the majority of Astraeans were killed, and the Harbor was destroyed, would they begin thinking of such things.

Even with Akal's death, and the apparent assurance that Einar would gain stewardship of the ribbon island when the tree's leaves fell, they remained alert and defensive. They sought to slow and disrupt any attempts from the Astraeans to retaliate. The Einarian ribbon monitoring and manipulating technologies were reinforced and bolstered at about the same time the Astraeans were bringing their technology up to speed, and their primary hope of success rested primarily on their continued mastery of abusing the beauty and power of the ribbons.

These multiversal introverts, and ultimate deniers of authority, community, or concern for others, were mostly hand-picked and groomed by Einar. The moment Mamdod had established the rules for his game and set Akal and Einar on their ultimate journeys, Einar claimed a secluded part of the multiverse for his own, and immediately developed technology to block any transmission of information to or from his location, unless he allowed it. He walled himself in, figuratively and literally, simply wanting to be left alone, and answerable to no one.

While Einar contemplated ways to ensure he could forever be free of Mamdod, his brother, and the ribbons, the Astraeans came to find the Harbor and settled there, in that far removed place, both philosophically and physically. Where Mamdod had initially intended Akal and his brother to eventually discover the Harbor together, and use it as a base for acts of compassion and goodness throughout their lives and experiences in the multiverse, that plan was largely ruined by Einar's treachery. Instead, Elcyd found it first, and luckily, but unknowingly, used the Harbor very closely in the way it was intended, and found others to perform those acts of altruism with, as they arrived at the Harbor.

Einar originally only sought to be alone, but the evolution of the Astraeans pushed him to do what he saw as helping others avoid the platitudes of the Astraean philosophy. He came to understand that, from the start, he had everything he needed to defeat them. He would use each and every one of his lives to go and become trusted across a myriad of species, forests, cities, planets and universes. He would work to insert doubt and fear. He would contort and mangle peace and beauty, into unrecognizable ugliness. Where he found acceptance and consideration, he would instigate rejection.

It wasn't a matter of small efforts to disrupt utopian perfection. That didn't exist. He had to work hard to extrapolate, multiply and mutate the moderate flaws inherent across all life. He influenced creatures from throughout time and space to misinterpret and twist religious, political, and cultural texts. He inspired others to exaggerate or confuse legitimate concerns. He multiplied chaos so that the Astraeans would constantly be distracted by the repercussions. He sat the entire multiverse up, over billions of years, to evolve with an instinct of rejection and suspicion, and a cynical disregard for the type of selflessness that Astraeans tried to perpetuate in their travels.

Little by little, Einar also expanded on the technologies he learned about the Harbor having, as well as technologies he had been exposed to in his numerous lives. He screened and filtered ribbon data to aide him in stealing those almost-Astraean souls that he wanted on his side.

Unbeknownst to Mamdod and the Harbor, Einar

constantly violated a major function of the ribbons. He kidnapped souls. He stole souls, and redirected them away from what should have been their first journey to the ribbon island as Astraeans. Einar thought he and the souls he plucked from destiny were being saved from a disgustingly predictable fate that would be forced upon them. A fate, Einar believed, to be a contrived facade conceived by Mamdod as an arbitrary context to his game. But, thanks to eons of planning, malice, and passion, Einar had assembled and manipulated his huge force, and convinced them that the Astraeans were the enemy. He painted the Astraeans as a sentimental and blubbering mess of an enemy in love with their manufactured mission. The Einarians were told lies from the moment they arrived at his hidden and gnarled capital of diseased ideology. Initial arrivals of those souls he kidnapped, or the return of an Einarian after a regular death, all came to Einar's primary vessel. He called it the Dark Artery.

The Dark Artery was roughly equivalent to the square footage of the Harbor, not including the Harbor's outlying exterior docks, buildings, and piers. Unlike the Harbor, however, the Dark Artery wasn't stationary. It had engines for propulsion and was assembled mostly by Einar with materials and systems from throughout the multiverse.

Aesthetically, the Dark Artery was a surprisingly sleek, symmetrical, and pleasing enigma on the outside. Shaped more like a ship than a structure, the main operational section of the hull was long and flat, with each side extending out to a point. At each end, there were two curved sections that branched out from the sides and curved inwards.

Most of the resources accumulated by Einar and the Einarians were spent to construct or replenish the technology used to hide their presence from the Astraeans and the various information-gathering mechanisms at the Harbor. While the Dark Artery could be moved under its own propulsion, very little time and energy were spent gathering or replenishing fuel. Moving the ship was rare, and took place only under extreme situations.

It was also largely unnecessary to move the Dark Artery because of how far away it was from the Harbor. There were dozens of universes between the Dark Artery and the Harbor. And considering Einar had the advantage of simultaneously being hidden and monitoring the activities of the Harbor, there was no urgency. The Einarians were able to conduct their operations in complete anonymity and seclusion.

The interior of the Dark Artery was neither morbid, nor filthy. There was an impressive order and functionality to the layout and design. Surprising to some, there were considerable amounts of paintings, sculptures, and archaeological treasures throughout the Dark Artery. Einar enjoyed collecting reminders of the species he found to be worthy, or at the very least, equal.

The ship had interesting focal points in the form of common areas that ran the entire length of the ship, with narrow passages that led to additional common areas. Connected to the sides of the long common areas were a stifling amount of rooms. The entryways to each room were a smothering wealth of identical gates. The gates were in the shape of a thick metal grid that could be heard and seen through, but not passed through. Very rarely was there a solid door that traditionally secured access to extremely sensitive areas.

The intent behind Einar's design was driven by his desire for symmetry, order and flow. While it was indeed that, the repetitive and identical arrangement of the interior was confusing and hard to navigate for new Einarians. What overflowed with practicality, was barren in character or inspiration.

* * *

Azli sauntered slowly back over to Einar, daring him to attack her again, but he gave her no ground or took any. He smiled as she approached.

"What now?" She inquired. She had had enough of this altercation and was eager to get back to accelerating the Astraean decline.

Einar let his grin fade back to business and slithered back over to his data terminal. His eyes stayed locked on Azli as long as possible. Swishing through a few pictures on the display, he pulled a diagram back up that showed many of the concentrated Einarian strongholds throughout the multiverse.

"Have some of our resources that are closer to the Astraeans launch some attacks to distract and stall their progress. We'll keep our forces closer to the Dark Artery in a defensive posture for now."

Einar turned off his display and walked back over to Azli to make sure there was no misunderstanding his next comment.

"We just have to keep them busy until the leaves fall."

Azli nodded and rolled her hand over a few times to silently rush him through what she already knew.

In a split second, Einar let his human hand disintegrate to ribbon energy and then grabbed Azli by the throat again. He closed his eyes and smiled from the pleasure of squeezing her fleshy neck as he forced her to the ground. The assault with a portion of his ribbon energy was much more painful than his first. A combination of pain and Einar's ribbon energy, that had a disruptive effect on Azli's ribbon energy, prevented her from immediately defending herself.

"Do you have somewhere else to be?" Einar asked. His eyes were stretched to the maximum with repugnance. "Do not motion at me like I'm an annoying servant."

He stared at her and squeezed while pushing her further down to the floor. Azli made one attempt to fight back again, but he was ready.

Azli grabbed around Einar's neck and tried to swing a leg around again. But Einar had already dissolved his other arm to ribbon energy as well. With minimal effort or exertion, Einar met Azli's leg and broke it in a compound fracture. Azli unleashed a nauseating and pain-filled wail.

Einar loved it. He rapidly and repeatedly loosened and re-tightened his grip and played with the sound coming from her throat in a perverse and sadistic thrill.

He waited for her painful noise to extinguish, to the point she seemingly couldn't cry or scream any longer. His patience for her agony was unending. He enjoyed every second of the hell he had her in. His body tingled from the power and control.

After more time than was necessary, Einar resumed

his instructions, and assumed he now had her full, and respectful attention.

"Keep them on the defensive. Keep them fighting. Keep them away from here, and just keep killing them."

He gave her a few more moments of gruesome misery to ensure his orders sunk in, and then released her throat. Azli crumbled into a fetal position on the floor. Einar smiled at her pathetic display of weakness, and laughed as she cried while reaching for her throat and leg.

"Count yourself lucky that I didn't block your ability to rewind time as well. Go ahead. Reverse your injuries," he smugly dictated after turning to look out a window. "We're almost there," he continued, callously changing the subject. "Soon, we won't have to worry about someone else having the power. Soon, there will be no such thing as power. It will be the true definition of freedom."

Chapter XII
Production Preoccupation

The Harbor was bustling and humming more than ever. Merchant and vendor numbers seemed to double from where they were before the attack on the Harbor. There was a dissonant beauty to the shouting of various languages, and gestures of numerous combinations of body movements, made by the multi-threaded quilt that was the merchant corridor. Lights flashed, and electric signs fizzed and whirred, as they flickered out messages showing what was for sale.

Booths and stations, sometimes two and three stories high, teetered and tottered as their owners ran up and down to search their stock for requested items, locked in almost-forgotten trunks and cabinets. When opened, their lids and doors creaked like the booths themselves, when their owners stomped, shook, and traversed the boards and platforms. And while the technology of the Astraeans was available to Astraean and non-Astraean merchants alike, many of them sourced their booth materials on their own, and manually built their booths for the pride shared by any craftsman. They took great care with their creativity, ingenuity, and abilities, to customize and maintain their booths themselves.

In addition to the traditional wares being sold in the merchant corridors, new booths started to pop up. These flashy and exciting newcomers offered weapons and items that had been recently created or modified as a result of the new fabrication facilities, for the arming and equipping of the ADF. New weapons, defensive tools, vehicle modifications, and countless other new items, started to make their way into the hands of the masses. And at one point, early before ship production started in earnest, and while the area was still being secured, one could look up to the new imaging and fabrication facilities from almost any area of the merchant corridors, and see new ships emerging from their massive output windows. While the shadow cast upon areas of the harbor by the new vessels was a source of pride and justified defense for many, it was an ominous and detracting burden for a few others.

* * *

While the production of new ADF resources cast a figurative and literal shadow upon various areas of the Harbor, Rigella cast her own shadow on the fabrication facilities. While not quite distracted, she was however heavily preoccupied with concern for making sure this newly added militaristic element of Astraean culture didn't mutate past its original scope. She took the largest portion of responsibility for the formation of the ADF, and how the

Astraeans adapted to it. Great care was taken to continuously inject her concern into all planning, meetings, and actions, so that the focus would remain steady and clear.

Rigella looked down and out onto the fabrication facilities as she ran scenario after scenario through her head on how the new ADF might respond in future battles. She stared intently without blinking. Her eyes were stretched wide, her ears were flexed and her breathing was deep and slow as she stroked her lips. In her mind, she watched as hypothetical wars were waged. She evaluated a plethora of response times, response tactics, defensive maneuvers, attack patterns, and effectiveness of weapons against the same type of weapon, or against different weapons, as well as troop formations and strategies. Everything she could imagine.

It's the type of obsessive thinking every military commander has done in some form or another since war was war, and since death brought the destruction of some and fortune of others. While the grace, honor, and integrity incorporated in war had been refined by others to an art form, war and causing death was a science. Any successful military leader knew that regardless of motive or intentions, it must be treated as a science. One must be able to devastate and kill more efficiently and more completely than the opposition.

Rigella obviously knew, just like others before her, that war and killing is what most creatures try to avoid at all costs, but when faced with the possibility of being the ones who are killed and devastated, especially in an unprovoked context, you have to set your objections aside. You have to set your morals aside. You must become better at that which you despise most. Rigella had no passion for destruction, but she had passion for the preservation and protection of the lives of those she loved, and her people as a whole. The two outlooks might even be considered by some as being equivalent. Regardless, she was good at her passion.

As she rubbed her lips and ran through strategies, she simultaneously recalled the memories of lifetime after lifetime that had been involved in combat of any and every kind. The amount of possibilities and scenarios, and then the branches of possibilities from those, and so on, would be absolutely unfathomable to a non-Astraean. And beyond the real and native species, Rigella contemplated their fictional creations from their literature, their technologies, artificial lifeforms, and anything else that may have transpired in entire histories of cultures that may have militaristic benefit. The mathematics of all of that, and similar types of Astraean thinking, could be displayed and explained, but could hardly be experienced or understood by any other type of being, or single-life creature.

The Kematairliur species. Universe 102. Evolved with ultraviolet saliva due to the proximity of their sun. Can be ejected far distances. Causes rapid and deep burns to skin of enemies. Their natural adversaries, the Perisai-Baja, evolved skin that became impervious to the saliva.

Thoughts like those, one every millisecond or less, sped through Rigella's mind. While one hand played with her lips absentmindedly, she used the other hand to type notes into a nearby terminal without looking. The notes were feedback for Hergie and his team on how she may want various equipment modified, prototypes created, or corrections to previous designs.

Only when an engineering advisor knocked and walked through the door without waiting for a response, was Rigella's concentration broken.

"Central Commander Rigella, we have an important bit of information for you," the advisor raced through excitedly.

"Since before your tournament, we've had a few dozen engineers going back through a few eons worth of ribbon data. After repeatedly cross-referencing the data manually and then using triangulation, trilateration, and multilateration by way of our ribbon technology, we believe we have identified an area that Daebaugh might be based. On my way here, I also stopped and told Mamdod and Elcyd of our findings."

Rigella, who along with the other Astraeans hadn't yet learned of the name Daebaugh had begun to go by, shoved the input terminal away and raced over to the engineering advisor.

Before he finished speaking, the advisor had already logged into a data terminal and brought up a three-dimensional projection of the multiverse.

"You see, for a multitude of reasons over time, we have been unable to receive data or track ribbon activity at various locations throughout the multiverse, but they were always only temporary issues. After a particular period of time, whatever anomalies were prohibiting data from being received from the ribbons in a particular area, eventually resolved themselves. Whether it was an issue with the ribbon, or something happening in the local space at a location, something involving indigenous cultures, etc., it was always temporary. Now, we have always known this happens and made note of it, but we have never thought to see if any of these lapses in data perpetuate for extended amounts of time over a great period of time. Well, we've done that now. We have reason to believe that someone, possibly Daebaugh, has been able to obscure his location from us, and is doing so every time he has moved, or while he is moving."

Rigella's attention dialed in sharply as her eyes shot up from the projection, to the advisor.

"Moved or moving? Are you able to determine which?"

"We should be able to, but we need to do more work," the advisor replied, eagerly.

"Well, that is very valuable information," Rigella slowly said with sincere appreciation. "What did Mamdod and Elcyd have to say?"

"They would like to have that area investigated in as many ways as possible, as soon as possible, but of course, they deferred to you on how we act first."

Rigella started walking around the projection of the multiverse and focused on the darkened paths that alluded to the areas where there was no data. Silently, she looked to see if there was any noticeable pattern to the paths. She then once again, began recalling knowledge of cultures and histories, searching her mind for any meaningful correlation. While still focusing on the display, she posed a question.

"Have you been able to determine when this data block originated, and from which point?"

"Yes, and no," the advisor replied quickly. "The block seems to have begun shortly after Mamdod's game started. It's within a few hundred million years, but when compared to the age of the multiverse, it was indeed just shortly after. We hope to dial that in a bit more."

"Understood," Rigella acknowledged. "And the origination point?"

"We don't have that information just yet," admitted the advisor. "But, we're hoping our new ribbon cartographer will be able to assist with that."

The advisor stepped back to reveal members of his team, and in the front of the group was an extremely meek and soft face of a young Astraean.

"Rigella, this is Dawel." The advisor was beaming with excitement as he introduced him. "He was just promoted to lead ribbon cartographer for this initiative. He should be able to assist us with knowing which end of that path to begin searching first."

"Well, the quicker the better," Rigella said as she shook Dawel's hand and grasped his shoulder. "Regardless of where we start, it's going to be a huge undertaking, and we need absolutely every second spent on this, spent as efficiently as possible. I have every bit of confidence in you, my advisors, and our engineers. And remember, please don't ever think of doing this work for me, but for us, and for our people."

Dawel smiled quickly, but with timid reservation as he ducked slightly into his shoulders and nodded.

"Thank you Rigella. I'm looking forward to getting to work. We will find Daebaugh."

"We will," echoed Rigella. She increased her volume as she addressed Dawel and the other engineers in the room. "We will find him, and we will defeat him. Thank you for all that you do. Ok. Let's get back to it."

As the bulk of the team started to shuffle out of the office with Dawel, the advisor remained to have a last word with Rigella.

"Thank you for those words. We will do you proud."

"No, let's all do each other proud," Rigella reciprocated with equality and respect. The advisor nodded and followed his team out of Rigella's strategy room.

As the door closed behind the advisor, Rigella bent down and slowly traced the blank paths in the holographic projection once more with her eyes. She took her time. She followed each branch of emptiness and then retraced it. Over and over. Additional cultures and histories began to soak her mind once more. Her thoughts inevitably came back to the new vessels and weapons being fabricated, and after tapping a nearby terminal to close the projection of the multiverse, she returned to the window overlooking the new facilities, and her necessary obsession with death.

* * *

Though the actual, new fabrication buildings could only be seen from a few areas of the Harbor, the sounds of machinery and flashes of ribbon technologies permeated the air. These wondrous and automated appliances of manufacturing were assembling some of the most ingenious creations Astraeans have ever made. Their work could be heard and or seen from almost anywhere. A protective barrier was being built to protect the work from Daebaugh and any of his allies, but not before the imaginations of many Astraeans were filled with the fun fodder of curiosity and intrigue.

Those actually working inside the new imaging and

fabrication facilities had the best show. The atmosphere was alive and exhilarating with a musical score orchestrated with hundreds of sounds, each belonging to a different robotic mechanism or ribbon panel. It was warm and inviting. An outsider looking in would be made to feel that the Astraeans stopped just short of giving a name to every piece of machinery.

Instead of the typical dank and grungy pits of industry around the multiverse, these facilities, much like Hergie's facility, were a proud part of the Harbor. The Astraeans took great care to incorporate the new facilities, in aesthetics, and in practicality. They kept them clean, well lit, and maintained. The Astraeans enjoyed respecting and tending to their artificial and mechanical creations as much as they enjoyed doing the same for the natural creations of the multiverse. No non-ribbon material was wasted. All leftover bits were recycled, repurposed, or incorporated into other projects in other ways.

Their respect for industry, and the responsibilities that came with it, was evident in the technology rolling off the line in the new facilities as well. The minute the last bolt, panel, or window was installed on a ship, for example, there would be a crew there to celebrate that particular vessel's last bit of assembly, by washing it, or treating it with a cleaner appropriate for the material that particular ship was made of. Following that, would come a buff and polish, coinciding with the installation of name and designation insignia.

No worker in the new fabrication facilities grew tired of, or bored with their work. A key part of Astraean craftsmanship, was that it was by no means a passive process.

They, of course, had the ability to automate virtually any process via ribbon technology, but, they worked hand-in-hand with that technology. They never desired to simply set it and forget it. They did much of the assembly on their own while the ribbon mechanisms were usually reserved for fabrication or handling of large items. This approach allowed for the Astraeans to take ownership and responsibility, not only of their facilities and technology, but what they created. They made sure to never be too far removed from anything they might ever be associated with.

Newly designed ships with advanced ribbon interfaces, allowing, among other things, ships to quickly enter and exit ribbons, kept facility workers' eyes opened wide with fascination. New vehicles with exotic propulsion systems made workers dream of their next chunk of time off to take such vehicles for a spin on the planets they were meant to function on. Weapons configured in different shapes, and with different projectiles, instilled in the workers, a sense of reverence and hope about the future of the Astraeans. Though it was death and deception that brought them to this point, it was a good time to be an Astraean.

Chapter XIII
Ontelbar

Whether they knew it or not, Lannya, Heersan, and Carthal were riding on one of the primary inspirations for much of the newly designed ADF fleet. With Hergie's assistance, Akal had originally designed her to take as much advantage of the ribbons as possible, while affording him and his passengers many tools, comforts, and options. Paige was an original. She served countless purposes and served them well. She kept her cargo, both alive and inanimate, safe, and was still doing so as she carried Lannya, Heersan, and Carthal to the Ontelbar Suburb.

After leaving Caecus, and after coordinating with the Harbor, they had decided that they needed to gather as much information as quickly as possible. Be it raw data, information from first-hand sources, telemetry, or insight gathered from their own reconnaissance, they had to rapidly collect actionable intelligence. They could think of few better options to obtain such data, than by enlisting the help of the Ontelbar.

Each minute was a leaf off of the ribbon island tree. Each minute brought the multiverse close to a ribbon island controlled by Daebaugh, and the uncertainty of what that would entail was something each of them had no desire to leave to chance. The three Astraeans were hoping that their destination would not only be time well spent, but highly lucrative in information.

The Ontelbar Suburb was an immense field of millions of asteroids that, due to its size, was within close proximity to numerous universal and galactic ribbon intersections. The indigenous Ontelbar are long-time and close friends to the Astraeans. Highly intelligent and known for innocent, yet corny humor, the Ontelbar are one of the few non-Astraean races who can see the ribbons with their regular vision. Their two pairs of huge front-facing eyes, set close together, sloped back to the sides of their heads, which provides for a highly developed sense of quadnocular, and peripheral vision. A single Ontelbar eye is approximately the circumference of a human torso, and is easily the single largest feature of an Ontelbar. They can see practically all of the electromagnetic spectrum.

The Ontelbar are known not only for their senses of vision and humor, but also for their temperament. They are an incredibly kind and inquisitive race and are renowned for being extremely passionate astronomers. Indeed, many Ontelbar can be found at the Harbor in astronomical and ribbon cartographer positions.

The Ontelbar live exclusively on the exterior of their asteroids, in modest, but highly functional and practical homes, constructed from asteroid material that they mine. But also, taking advantage of their compact frames and pointed snouts, they burrow out simple tunnel systems to allow them to get from one area of their asteroid to the other, more quickly. The tunnel systems are only used for travel. The Ontelbar do not hunt, dwell, or otherwise live inside the tunnel systems they create.

Since each Ontelbar family depends on the integrity of their family's asteroid to live safely, the entire species has long-since understood the notion that they not mine asteroid material carelessly. Their structures are built taller than wider, to conserve available asteroid surface area, and their tunnel systems normally consist of only a few paths, to cross the greatest lengths of their asteroid.

The Ontelbar have two appendages, and are bipedal, but traverse the tunnels faster than they would if they were walking, by falling to their side and rolling from one end of a tunnel to the other. Whenever they need to manipulate a tool or item, again, they roll to their back, or lean, and use their two appendages that most closely resemble short and stubby legs. They are an incredibly durable and stocky creature, whose bodies are protected by a hairless, thick and very firm skin.

While it was rare to find more than one Ontelbar family per asteroid, made up of five to six members on average, their entire race was highly communicative via a wireless transmission system using a method similar to radio waves. Despite their proximity, each asteroid was kept safe from colliding with another, via their massive, inherent and repellent magnetic fields.

Flying a vessel into the Suburb not specifically

built by the Ontelbar for the Ontelbar Suburb, could be extremely tricky. Though the asteroids were safe from each other, pilots of non-Ontelbar craft had to use an intricate and confusing system to simultaneously track dozens of transponders at a time. Each asteroid had its own transponder to assist visitors in such situations. Even the oldest and most experienced Astraean pilots of countless spacecraft had a terribly difficult time. It was no small feat making their craft dance between the asteroids and act artificially as a repelling magnet in its own right, in the sea of asteroids.

In Rigella's absence, arguably the best pilot of the original trio, Carthal was trusted to navigate through the outermost asteroids of the Suburb as they made their way to the Ontelbar Municipal Cluster.

Paige's numerous thrusters, from all around the ship, popped and burped as Carthal, with one hand, glided across a keypad of numerous buttons corresponding to each thruster. Delicately nudging the ship in various directions, his other hand was reserved for steering.

Carthal sang to himself softly while navigating the asteroids. The melody, articulation, length and spacing of notes was heavily influenced by how drastically he had to maneuver the ship at any given moment. Lannya and Heersan stood by quietly with moderately fearful eyes.

"I caaan't staaaaaaand flying in all of thiiiiiis," Carthal serenaded. "Caaaan't staaand it. Can't.. OOOH! Gah, that was a big one. Get awaayyyy... Get awaygetawayGET-AWAY! AH!"

Carthal instinctively ducked as if trying to avoid a punch as he continued singing while dodging another close call.

"WhewWHERE did that one come frommmm? Where diiiid you come from, you mean 'oleANDBIG 'OLE boy.. Get, get, get outta heeeerrreee! Get, get, gettie get!"

With absolutely no other movement, Lannya moved only her lips to calmly make an observation. Her gaze was locked on the field of asteroids ahead.

"Ok, the Municipal Cluster is over there on your 2 o'clock high."

"Ah, goodiegoodgood. Yes, yes. Leettt's get over there, let's get therrre," Carthal replied musically.

Heersan looked to Lannya and rolled his eyes. While Lannya had her attention focused on the Municipal Cluster's dock, she saw Heersan out of her peripheral vision and grinned widely.

The Municipal Cluster's dock grew nearer as Carthal approached it slowly. Paige's thrusters fired less and less as Carthal dialed her in. Small taps of the main steering gave Paige a few nudges of forward propulsion. Carthal's approach was perfect.

As the ship slid into the dock, Heersan bobbed his head up, down and around to take stock of the Municipal Cluster. This area of the Suburb consisted of a large group of asteroids that were attached to each other manually by numerous, long and thick metal cables. Having this group of asteroids physically connected to one another was simply a matter of convenience to the Ontelbar so that they could easily visit the various municipal asteroids in one general area rather than having them floating separately in random, scattered areas throughout the Suburb. Rather than having to track down a dozen different asteroids throughout the entire Suburb, the Ontelbar, or visitors, only needed to locate the entire single cluster.

Paige slid into place along the Municipal Cluster dock perfectly on the first attempt and required no additional thruster pulses. As the ship came to a final stop, Carthal looked up to see the mooring lines already being secured by some Ontelbar dockworkers.

"Yeaaaahhhh!!!" Carthal sang, in a final fermata of success.

Heersan rolled his eyes at Lannya again, and this time, it was seen by Lannya. Lannya couldn't help but chuckle as she slapped Carthal on his shoulder and congratulated him.

"Nicely done!" Lannya offered. "Looks like you'll be taking more pilot duty!"

"Hey, when you need it perfect, just let me know!" Carthal advised, while stretching out his imaginary suspenders.

"Ha!" Heersan blurted. "Perfect like that torpedo capacitor inventory that was off by 60?"

"Hey, you can't blame me for that!" Carthal let his imaginary suspenders snap as his hands started playfully pointing and accusing. "I didn't know Lannya had cleaned out that area under the fighter!"

"Yeah, yeah, and I'm the newbie around here! You know Paige better than I do, right?" Lannya replied with a wink and a smirk. She then slapped them both on the back to silently suggest they head out to talk with the Ontelbar.

The majority of the asteroids of the Ontelbar Suburb were large, but not so large that their occupants were immune to occasional balance issues. From time to time, when an asteroid grew close enough to another, the magnetic repellent effect would cause visitors to lose their balance or stumble. Carthal experienced this almost as soon as his feet hit the asteroid. He stumbled and scrambled forward while trying to catch his balance. He failed. Heersan and Lannya chuckled and hopped off the gangplank while an Ontelbar Gazer rolled onto his side and helped Carthal up with his feet. Gazers, the more senior and experienced astronomers of the Ontelbar, were the leaders of the Ontelbar culture and government.

"Thanks, friend!" Carthal bellowed. "I forgot how fun the Suburb was," Carthal huffed humorously.

By the time Carthal had come to his feet, Heersan and Lannya had approached.

"Yes, thank you," Lannya echoed. "Our friend's mouth and feet are always a few steps behind his brain."

"I'm sure that makes for some extremely interesting eating!" Having amused himself with his statement, the Gazer's mouth dropped as he spun his head back and forth looking for some affirmation from the visiting Astraeans.

Though Lannya probably wouldn't have laughed anyway, she was distracted and temporarily terrified by a quickly approaching asteroid.

"Hit the deck!" she shouted. But as soon as she said it, and before she dropped down, the miles-wide asteroid which had been hurtling towards the Municipal Cluster was gently repelled by the magnetic properties of the asteroid they were on. Heersan jokingly dusted Lannya's clothes off as she relaxed her posture.

"Please forgive us," Heersan requested of the Gazer, while chuckling and still dusting Lannya off. "None of us have been around Ontelbar in some time!"

The Astraeans were somewhat reserved and cautious, unaware if the Ontelbar had received the same malicious and false message the Caecusi had. Carthal couldn't think of a better time to bring it up.

"I'm curious, Gazer," Carthal began softly. "Have your people recently received a message warning you to be leery of Astraeans? And, saying that we're planning unprovoked attacks across the multiverse?"

The Gazer blinked numerous times very frequently as if silently responding in the affirmative as Carthal posed his question.

"We did indeed," replied the Gazer. "We assumed it must have been erroneous, or a bad joke of some kind. My fellow Gazers and I quickly contacted the Harbor to confirm, even though we had come to the conclusion on our own that it was false, given our large amount of accurate and widespread data on the goings-on in the multiverse."

The three Astraeans looked at each other in reassured incredulity. They were pleased to know that at least one race would seek to confirm such news, while still recuperating from the skepticism they were met with from the Caecusi.

Lannya replied to the Gazer with appreciative enthusiasm.

"Thank you very much for confirming that message. We've already started to run into problems with those who didn't, and were actually hoping we could talk with your leadership and submit a request for assistance."

"Ah! I see!" The Gazer replied sincerely and with excitement. In a display of pride and welcoming, he rolled backwards, and jumped up after making a complete rotation. "I am Gazer Orn! I would be thrilled to see, if I can help you see, what you have to see, in order to see what you need to see, using one of my four eyes that can see as well as anyone would want to see, or could ever possibly hope to see!"

Again, Orn's mouth dropped wide open in a stuck pose of satisfaction with his silly speech, while waiting for a reaction from the Astraeans. Carthal couldn't pass up the opportunity to try and oblige him.

"That is absolutely heavenly and truly lovely that you would be so voluntarily neighborly by philanthropically offering your time and perspicacity!" Carthal's mouth dropped in a similar manner to the Gazer's while waiting for a reaction.

The Gazer erupted in a prolonged machine-gun rip of honks, abundantly showing approval of Carthal's response. As the Gazer's guffaw finally wound down, Orn was finally able to speak once again.

"Yes my friends, yes!" Orn obliged after jumping and clapping his feet together. "We will do all we can to assist. Please follow me to the Control Spire to touch base with other members of the Ontelbar leadership and discuss your needs. I only need to make a quick detour to the Municipal Observation Spire to record this cycle's information."

"This cycle's information?" Heersan reiterated, hoping for clarification.

"That's correct," Orn confirmed as they began walking. The Astraeans' strides were short and slow to accommodate the short legs of the compressed stature of the Ontelbar. "We are constantly peering into the depths of this universe and recording data. We are aware of there being many other universes, but we stay quite busy with what we observe from our observatories in our Suburb here. There is so much to see with all of your ribbon traffic, and we take great pride in working to uphold our reputation as being extremely passionate about, and knowledgeable of, astronomical phenomena! It also makes sense that, as a result, our race has developed a biological means of recycling and living off of the energy we exert when using our eyes to observe!"

"You live off of and recycle your own body's energy?" Lannya's stride increased slightly to walk side-by-side with Orn as she sought confirmation. "That's remarkable!"

"Yes, we are very fortunate in that regard," Orn agreed stoically. "Especially considering we have no means of traveling outside our Suburb for any other means of sustenance!"

Lannya looked to Heersan and Carthal to see if they were sharing in her amazement. They indeed were. They all were extremely impressed with the efficiency of the Ontelbar and awareness of their limitations, while at the same time, appreciative of their gifts."

Orn, along with the Astraeans, continued walking for a short time while bringing each other up to speed on the happenings of Ontelbar life, but also while catching Orn up on what had transpired at the Harbor between the Astraeans and Daebaugh. It was made very clear to Orn how dire the Astraean situation was and how badly and quickly they needed to fill information gaps.

After a few more center of gravity stumbles, Lannya, Heersan, Carthal and Orn crossed the suspended bridge between two of the Municipal Cluster's asteroids, onto the Observation Spire.

"Ok, Astraeans," Orn announced. "Here we are at the Municipal Cluster's Observation Spire. We have observation spires throughout the Suburb, but this is by far our largest and most intricate one. If you would, please allow me a moment to collect this cycle's data from our team and I will return in a moment."

The Astraeans were awestruck as Orn fell to his side and rolled over to a control post, manned by other Ontelbar who were classifying and sorting data. The Observation Spire ahead of them was flooded on the surface with countless telescopes of various shapes and configurations. At the center of the asteroid were the largest and tallest telescopes. Thousands of feet in height, they cast a beautifully inspiring shadow down upon the smaller telescopes around them. At various points along the way to the top, these gargantuan telescopes articulated, to help them observe any area of space the operator wanted to. On the outside of the inner telescope bases were tracks made of a metal that looked similar to brass. Along the tracks, telescopes could be rolled by the operator to maneuver to different areas of the asteroid. These tracks with telescopes continued out to the edges of the asteroid.

In exchange for bits of information the Ontelbar obtained from their observations, they were able to trade for materials that were not native to their asteroid community. Over the years, the Ontelbar had traded for various materials to improve and extend their telescopes. And not only were their own eyes extremely impressive in their vision capabilities, but these telescopes of immense power increased their ability to observe their universe, exponentially.

Within a few moments, after the Astraeans had taken just enough time to appreciate all of the telescopes, Orn rolled back over, popped up and rejoined his new friends.

"This is one of the most impressive sights I've ever seen, Orn!" Heersan's neck was bent back as far as it could go while straining his vision to the top of the highest telescopes. Carthal and Lannya were similarly amazed as their heads twisted and peered through the crowds of telescopes.

"That is very kind of you, friend." Orn replied quickly and sincerely. "We take great pride in our work, and the gift of being able to observe and witness what we do."

"That work is why we have visited, Orn." Heersan forced himself to break his attention from the telescopes. His mouth melted and his tone sank as he continued. "We were hoping to review any records you might be able to provide us access to. We're trying to track any possible movements through this area of your universe of those that attacked us at the Harbor."

Displaying a rare lack of joy, Orn's face also dropped and his voice became weak and somber.

"We were so very sad to learn of that senseless terror that your people were subjected to," Orn offered solemnly. His large eyes glistened with empathy and true kindness. "Yes. We will assist you in any way we can. I will clear it with the rest of the Gazers. Have no fear of that. Some of our people work at the Harbor, so we consider it an attack on our people as much as you do. How can we help?"

The three Astraeans closed in slightly more on Orn in restrained enthusiasm.

"Thank you, so very much." Lannya offered with clasped hands.

Heersan came to his knees beside Orn and placed his hand on his back as Carthal also thanked him.

The mood of Orn's eyes lifted slightly in acknowledgment of their appreciation. "Many of the Gazers had already spoken recently about reaching out to the Harbor again, to offer our help. Where should we start?"

"Perfect," Heersan replied, looking to Carthal and Lannya to begin their brainstorming session. "If possible, we were hoping to review your older ribbon traffic data to look for any anomalies or patterns that may correspond with some of the information the Harbor has collected."

Lannya was already nodding in agreement with Heersan before she added to the conversation.

"Right. The Harbor has identified some areas of interest that could potentially lead to identifying where Daebaugh and his people are based, or at least some of their main travel routes."

Orn blinked as he stared and assimilated the Astraeans' needs while Carthal continued.

"The older data will be more essential because of gaps in how we monitored and tracked ribbon information before we were attacked. But by filling in those gaps with your information, and correlating your more recent observations with the information the Harbor has obtained with the new processes, we're hoping we can pinpoint a location sooner rather than later."

"Were you also hoping to set up some form of real-time monitoring, or do you only need to review past data?" Orn's voice had lifted back to a more neutral tone, slightly enhanced by the opportunity to have his people do what they do best, in order to help their Astraean friends.

"If you can spare your people, time and equipment," Lannya immediately replied. Her face elongated with hope. "That would be an extremely appreciated bonus!"

Orn once again rolled backwards and hopped back up to his feet.

"We would be glad to! And we will do it exceptionally!"

"Thank you again, so very much!" Heersan offered. He then turned to Carthal and Lannya specifically. "Let's have some of us stay with Orn to collect the old data, and one of us can go back to Paige and update the Harbor on our progress. This is too sensitive to trust to the new personal communicators."

"Yeah, that sounds good," Lannya obliged. "If you two want to work with Orn, I'll go message the Harbor and then come back and help finish up here."

"Ok, that will work," Carthal confirmed. "We'll see you in a bit."

Chapter XIV
A Glimpse of Things to Come

Lannya involuntarily skipped and lurched with the ebb and flow of the asteroid as she returned to Paige. With each step, she found herself thinking of Akal. But rather than pain or regret, she was trying to put herself in his shoes to rhetorically and silently ask him what he would do in their situation. She wondered if he would approve of their choices, or think they were wasting time. Inside her heart and mind, she spoke to him.

I hope we're all doing you proud, she sighed, mentally.

After completing her thought, the sea of asteroids shifted. Almost deliberately, they seemed to congregate and clump together, which left an unobstructed view, far into space. Lannya then saw it. Without obstruction or difficulty, Lannya's vision pierced straight to the nearest Ontelbar Suburb star. There were such an incredible amount of asteroids, Lannya didn't understand how it was possible. But she quickly forgot about caring how it was possible. The warmth of the nearby star sheltered her face from the silence, and surrounding silhouettes of other asteroids. Whatever the source, or reason she had received the gift of the starlight, she was thankful for it, and offered her silent appreciation, once more, from her heart, to the multiverse, and just in case, to Akal. Almost as quickly as it appeared, the clear path to the star was quickly flooded with asteroids once more. The shadow moved back in across Lannya's face.

Lannya rubbed her face casually, trying not to give away to the stars that she was checking for tears. She found none. She found only a warm smile as she resumed walking and hopped across Paige's gangplank. She ran up the stairs and through the hatch. After identifying herself, she let out a soft and smooth command.

"Paige. Open an encrypted communications channel with the Harbor."

The display flashed up immediately with a view of a field of ribbon energy. Within just the time it takes to gasp for air, extra bright flashes from the screen signaled the communication channel going through the extra layers of security and encryption that had been added to the Harbor's security measures. After the last quick flash, the display focused in on the Helper Desk. A larger portion of the Helper Desk had been rededicated to receiving incoming transmissions from outside the Harbor, to expedite assistance to those doing work specifically related to combating Daebaugh's efforts.

Upon recognizing Lannya, a Helper swiftly addressed Lannya and grinned widely when he saw her.

"Lannya! I am very glad to see you," the Helper greeted. "I trust you are well and safe. How can I help?"

"Hello, Muvooi. Not doing too bad," Lannya offered. "I hope you're doing well. Can you patch me through to Elcyd, Mamdod or Rigella? I just need to give them an update."

"Right away," Muvooi obliged cheerfully. He looked away and consulted other feeds and schedules. "It looks like Mamdod and Elcyd are unavailable. They're in the new fabrication facilities looking over some of the new equipment designs, but Rigella should be available. I'll connect you to her office now, if you like."

"That will be fine, thank you." Lannya gathered her thoughts and prepared for Rigella to pop up on the display.

Instead of Rigella, however, the newly promoted, lead ribbon cartographer appeared. He was surrounded by a dozen projected images of various sections of the multiverse. When Lannya appeared on his end, he casually stepped through the holographs and greeted her.

"Lannya! Good to see you!"

"Oh, hi there," Lannya replied, pausing shortly before remembering his name. "Dawel. I was hoping to get in touch with Rigella. Is she available?"

"I'm afraid not," Dawel quickly replied. "She stepped out just a bit ago to meet up with Mamdod and Elcyd over at the new fabrication facilities."

"Ah, right," Lannya huffed, remembering what the Helper had said. It made sense to Lannya that Rigella would be reviewing the equipment with them.

"Do you want me to have the Helper Desk try to reach out to them there, or, relay a message to Rigella when she returns?" Dawel tapped onto a command console nearby and brought up a few additional holographs of different multiverse imagery. He began to multi-task and examine them while waiting for Lannya to reply.

"Well, it's not extremely urgent, in that we don't need any input on how to proceed just yet. We were mostly just wanting to give them an update. Yeah, if you wouldn't mind," Lannya accepted gratefully. "Will you please just let Rigella know, and Mamdod and Elcyd if you can, that Heersan, Carthal and I have had a great meeting with the Ontelbar and that we'll be here for a bit reviewing their past observation data and making arrangements for real-time monitoring of this area, going forward."

"Yes," Dawel obliged swiftly. "I'll just be here reviewing these charts and should be here until at least Rigella returns."

"Wonderful, thank you very much. I'm off to meet back up with Carthal and Heersan. After we've reviewed some data and set up monitoring here, we'll probably start scouting some areas and will report in afterwards." Lannya started to collect a few items around her as she made preparations to end the communication and return to her friends.

"Understood," Dawel affirmed with an official and dry tone to his voice. "If they're not back before too long, I'll just head over and find them to tell them."

"Ok, thank you Dawel."

"My pleasure, Lannya. Talk with you again soon."

The display went dead as the communication ended. Lannya's pockets bulged from numerous portable data storage sticks. She didn't remember what type of computing systems or storage interfaces the Ontelbar had, so she grabbed a few different types. Some were filled with data. Some filled with programs. Others were blank so they could capture information that the Ontelbar shared with them. After taking a last glimpse around the command deck, Lannya headed back through the hatch and down the ladder and stairs, to meet back up with Carthal and Heersan.

Upon returning back to the Observation Spire, Lannya found Carthal and Heersan already bent over a table overflowing with astronomical data. Spilling over the sides were old charts and maps, from the early days of Ontelbar observations, as well as two-dimensional displays on data terminals, and holographic projections on small bases from more recent times, as their technology had advanced.

A team of Ontelbar had swarmed around the table. Some pointed and argued over a region on one chart, while others gestured at a different region on a projection. Heersan and Carthal had already learned to anticipate the movements of the assisting Ontelbar as they reviewed the data on the table and held conversations at the same time. They would bend their knees or bring their legs closer to the table as various Ontelbar collapsed and rolled around to other parts of the table. The tangled group of Ontelbar and Lannya's friends was a slippery bowl of spaghetti as they reviewed the data. No one was wasting time. It was all hustling business, yet Lannya couldn't help but smile and giggle at the busy scene before her.

When Lannya joined them at the table, the shadows of the surrounding telescopes flickered across the table as Heersan lifted his head up.

"Ah, Lannya, you're back. Good!"

"What did the Harbor have to say?" Carthal asked, through a muffling palm that held his chin. His eyes were still fixated on the data as he asked.

"Well," Lannya sighed, as she placed her hands on her hips, preparing mentally to begin assisting with the data review. "Elcyd, Rigella and Mamdod were inspecting some of the new equipment at the new fabrication facilities, but I was able to get an update to Dawel."

"Oh, the newly promoted cartographer guy?" Carthal sought to clarify. His focus still on the table.

"Right," Lannya confirmed. "He said he'd pass along our message."

"Ok, well, we've got a great start here," Heersan informed with an impressed humility. He shuffled and organized some of the papers and holographs nearest to him. "Orn has graciously asked a group of the finest Gazers to join us. All of the data on the table here was probably all brought out before you even got back to Paige. It's remarkable how quickly they got it to us. They're highly organized and know where all of their records are, but as you can see, we've already made a mess and have been reviewing it pretty heavily."

The commotion of the Ontelbar rolling all around the table, grabbing charts or pointing and poking at holographs as they discussed the issues with each other, continued, as Carthal finally raised his head and brought Lannya up to speed.

"Ok, so, Orn told us that the Ontelbar have a bunch of automated, low priority telescope arrays on many of their observation asteroids. Right now, they just have them dedicated to observing low impact, and rarely changing astronomical phenomena. He's going to let us change their monitored coordinates, indefinitely, to some of the locations the Harbor identified. Right now, we're reviewing their data to try and weed out some of the areas that are least likely to be Daebaugh's location."

"Perfect!" Lannya exclaimed, amazed and grateful. "That's going to allow us to narrow the gap of advantages pretty significantly."

"Exactly," Heersan agreed. "We'll have places to look, and we'll have eyes on a lot of places. Whether we find them, catch them traveling, or both, this will provide a huge boon to our ability to combat them, and force them to slow their operations down and be more careful."

"You'll have to keep up the pressure," Orn advised.

The three Astraeans nodded.

"Slowing them down is one thing," Orn continued. "But you'll eventually need to bring the fight to them, right?"

"Yes, that is definitely the plan." Lannya reciprocated.

"But getting information before launching an offensive is extremely wise," Orn said solemnly, recognizing their strategy.

"Yep." Carthal popped, as he bent back over to bury his head in another pile of charts and holographs of star systems.

"That's why we're here," added Heersan. "Thank you, Orn."

Orn performed another roll back, and hopped to his feet in acknowledgment.

* * *

For the next six hours, the Astraeans and Ontelbar

Gazers flipped through chart after chart, projections, diagrams and drawings. There were additional teams of Gazers brought in to cycle in and out of the planetariums they had along the perimeter of the main Observation Spire, to review, in larger scale, some of the areas they had concerns about. Data was being calculated, pondered over, and tabled or disregarded, in a fraction of the time most other races would take to do the same amount of work. The mathematics, physics, and astronomy being used, were tremendously advanced. The Astraeans were able to keep up for a long while, but after a time, had to mostly sit back and watch. There were of course Astraeans that would easily keep up and continue assisting, but the work the Ontelbar were doing was not what the three visiting Astraeans were experts in. Lannya, Carthal and Heersan soon turned to discussing how they would proceed, depending on what else the Ontelbar may uncover.

"Well, the Harbor's going to be busy for a while," Lannya correctly joked, while talking alone with Heersan and Carthal.

"You can say that again. It looks like they're about done analyzing their older information," added Heersan. "The data they've already compiled for us to take back to the Harbor is astounding."

"Yeah, when they started talking in their native language because it was faster for them, and started ignoring me..." Carthal chuckled. "I knew it was time to just step back and let 'em do their thing."

As Carthal, Heersan and Lannya continued small talk about the places the Ontelbar data would possibly suggest investigating, they saw Orn emerge from the crowd of Gazers and come rolling towards them. As he reached them, he vaulted to his feet. He was short of breath and extremely excited.

"Friends! I have just heard back from my contacts with the Quazlopian Mining Federation! They had commissioned our services using our largest and most powerful telescopes, but after asking them, they have agreed to temporarily suspend the contract, for a slightly reduced cost for our services, in the name of our efforts to assist you!"

There was a hesitance shared between the three Astraeans. They had only small amounts of knowledge about the Quazlopian Mining Federation, and what knowledge they had gave them cause for concern.

"I'm not sure I understand," Lannya muttered flatly, unable to hide her confusion. "You just... contacted them and asked if you could halt their contract, and they agreed?"

"Well, they asked why I was making the request..." answered Orn, unsure of the reason for Lannya's restrained reaction to his news.

"And what reason did you give them?" Heersan questioned sharply. His voice had raised not out of anger, but out of concern.

Orn's large eyes sloped up and in towards the center of his bulbous body as he began to understand.

"I told them that our Astraean friends were in desperate need for information to protect their people," Orn explained sheepishly.

"Orn!" Carthal's arms shout out from his side in helpless anger. "We were needing to keep what we're doing here extremely quiet! Wasn't it abundantly clear that we're engaged in a multiversal confrontation? The result of which will likely have a drastic impact on everyone in it?" Carthal stepped back and began to retrace circles in his steps as he ran his hands through his hair in frustration.

Lannya and Heersan continued the conversation more calmly.

"Why did you tell them we were here?" Lannya almost whispered, as she dropped slowly to one knee and addressed Orn respectfully.

"We don't know who we can trust," added Heersan. "We thought that was understood." Heersan completed his thoughts with a sigh. His eyes sagged with the beginning stages of fear of what this might mean for their efforts against Daebaugh.

"When did you reach out to them and ask if they would agree to place their contract on hold?" Heersan inquired. "I'm curious how long our intentions have been circulating among their people."

"I contacted them just after we developed the plan," admitted Orn, meekly. His short and stubby body began to slump over in regret and shame. "It was just as Lannya went back to your ship to communicate with the Harbor."

The Astraeans made their disapproval obvious as Carthal slapped a nearby wall. Heersan cursed and Lannya let her head drop.

"They've had that knowledge for the past almost eight hours, then," Heersan darkly approximated.

"I just didn't consider that they may betray you, or our business with them," Orn offered softly. "I'm... I'm sorry my friends."

Carthal had finished walking off his frustration and actively rejoined the group. Lannya stood back up and turned to Heersan and Carthal, silently curious as to how they should proceed.

"I don't know what to do," Carthal admitted first.

"I guess one of us, along with Orn," Heersan quickly spoke up, "could maybe reach back out to the Quazlopian Miners to try and establish some kind of rushed diplomatic agreement with them."

Lannya wasn't sure of that approach.

"Would that be worth it? There's no guarantee they would hold to any agreement. And even if they do agree, they might have already passed along our location hours ago."

Carthal spoke up after calming down. He had focused on what their next move should be.

"I'm with Lannya. I don't think that would do any good. None of us know enough about the Miners to invest in that kind of move. And the bit of information we do have doesn't really make me confident that a gesture like that would be received well, or enforced at all."

Orn, quiet during the Astraean's exchange rolled backwards and popped to his feet. This time, not out of enthusiasm, but after having an epiphany.

"Friends! What if I were to contact them again and give them misinformation. Perhaps you have changed your plans and moved on?"

"That might work, Orn. It's quick and has a good a chance at working as anything else, I guess" Carthal this time, lowered himself to one knee and continued to address Orn. "And I'm sorry for snapping at you previously. You didn't deserve that. You and your people have been nothing but generous and helpful."

"Thank you for that apology, Carthal," Orn graciously accepted. "I understand. Please think nothing of it."

Carthal patted Orn on the side affectionately as Orn addressed the entire group of Astraeans.

"If you like, Heersan and Lannya, I'll reach back out to the Quazlopian Miners and tell them..."

Orn's voice began to trail off as his attention was distracted by movement far in the distance. His large eye sockets flexed and contorted as he walked past the Astraeans to peer deep into the background space behind them. Carthal, Heersan and Lannya couldn't even see what had caught Orn's attention yet, but Orn's highly developed Ontelbar vision had no trouble.

"Friends," Orn began. His attention was unwavering and his focus was like a laser. "There's a large vessel approaching very quickly. I've not seen anything like it before. It's pushing our asteroids out of the way with some kind of shield or energy field. Within the protective bubble it's creating, are numerous smaller ships of some kind accompanying it."

"We need to get that data to Paige and get to the Harbor!" Heersan shouted.

"Orn, the Miners sold us out to Daebaugh," Lannya rapidly began to spit out. "Our being here puts your people in danger. Do anything and everything you can to protect yourselves. We will leave and try to get you some sort of reinforcements as soon as possible."

Before Orn could acknowledge, a dozen of the smaller craft accompanying the larger vessel had flown ahead through the small bit of remaining asteroid field that had yet to be parted by the larger ship. The wave of scout ships dropped down and unleashed an unforgiving strafing run consisting of extremely wide and sustained pulses of energy, instantly damaging numerous structures in the Municipal Cluster, including many of the telescopes on the Observation Spire.

"Yes, go!" Orn shouted. "Keep that information safe! I'm sorry for this!"

Carthal made sure Orn caught his eye as he began to back away to prepare to run to Paige.

"No one person needs to apologize for the evil of others, Orn. Thank you for your help. Take care of your people and we will try to contact you soon."

Orn just barely bowed in appreciation before collapsing to his side to rapidly roll back to his people.

While Lannya, Carthal and Heersan were in an all-out sprint back to Paige, their arms full of rolled up charts, stacks of maps and various types of data modules falling from pockets in their shirts and pants, the strafing runs were beginning to become more frequent and more sustained. The energy pulses from the attacking fighters seemed to not have a particular target. Structures of all types were being attacked, as well as telescopes, and groups of Ontelbar. The attacks could be seen to be taking place on any and every asteroid. No one was safe and nothing was being spared. It seemed that the attackers were out to wreak as much havoc and destruction as possible, on as many locations and targets.

As the Astraeans finished racing back to Paige, after dodging strafing runs by taking refuge numerous times behind objects and structures, Orn and the other Gazers were starting to coordinate a response. The ship that cleared the path for the bulk of the attacking craft had reached the Municipal Cluster. From countless asteroids all around, horrified Ontelbar watched as various hangar doors began opening on the intruding ship, which had unleashed dozens and dozens of additional waves of attacking fighters.

Just when these enigmatic killers seemed to come to their full potential, and their total numbers were beginning to cause the most chaos and death, the asteroids began to move again, but this time, they were moving by the hands of the Ontelbar.

Using the communications system that linked every inhabited asteroid in the Ontelbar Suburb, Orn advised all Ontelbar to take immediate shelter in their tunnels and to make preparations for what happened next. Rolling onto his back to free up his feet, Orn flipped switches and turned knobs on the communication station on the Observation Spire to open a channel with the Defense Spire.

"Defenders, this is Gazer Orn requesting immediate activation of all, I repeat, all defensive belts. Emergency activation code Orn..."

Orn then conveyed an audible series of grinding sounds, which have no lingual interpretation. It was more advanced than any mathematically-based encryption. Immediately after Orn finished his code sequence, the Defenders replied.

"Compliance! Emergency activation of all defensive belts initiated."

The asteroids quickly seemed to come to a rest from their random trajectories. Very rapidly, the asteroids began to move along calculated paths to form dotted circles of various shape. Using a system of propulsion and magnetic influence, the Ontelbar Defenders began having the asteroids spin. The asteroids spun slowly at first, but then rapidly picked up speed. The inhabiting Ontelbar were sheltered safely below each asteroid's surface.

But the intruding attackers outside in Ontelbar space were not safe. The spinning asteroid rings, ranging in size from the small craft to planet-size, caught the attacking ships in their kinetic rings of destruction. The attacking fighters had no way to adequately anticipate how the defensive belts would behave or interact with each other. The bulk of the strafing runs were interrupted as the fighters scrambled to dodge the belts and escape. Most were unsuccessful and were destroyed shortly after the defensive belts were activated. This came at a cost to the Ontelbar, however. While most Ontelbar were safe below the surface of their asteroids, many of their structures were destroyed in the process of being members of the defensive rings.

Within minutes, the majority of the attackers had been destroyed by the defensive rings. The highly effective, blunt power of the spinning rings, combined with the coordination and control from the Defenders, answered the attack decisively. Those who hadn't already been destroyed were those who began to flee very shortly after the defensive rings were initiated. However, the ring system extended throughout the Suburb, and by the time the fleeing attackers reached the outer layers of the Suburb, the Defenders had reorganized the rings at that location to be closer in proximity. None of the fighters escaped the Suburb's rings. Only by being protected by its large energy field was the large host ship able to escape.

Chapter XV
A Proposal

Lannya, Heersan and Carthal had only barely made it onto Paige by the time the attacking forces had unleashed their full numbers. They had no intention of engaging any of the fighters. It would have been absolutely futile. Instead, Carthal violently jerked Paige away from the Municipal Cluster docks, ripping the mooring lines away from the rocky bollards. There was no confidence of any kind in Carthal's mind. He was almost completely consumed by fear and the realization that they wouldn't survive this attack. Only almost consumed. He had enough fortitude to devote the proper attention to their escape.

It was enough. Between Carthal's piloting, and Heersan and Lannya picking off tailing fighters with Paige's guns, they were able to make it to a ribbon intersection and disappear. Once it was clear they had made it to the ribbons and were no longer being pursued, the three Astraeans only then took a break for what seemed like their first breaths in many minutes. There was no pleasure in their escape, or pride taken in their escape. If anything, they shared the stink of shame. The piles of maps, and unfurled charts rolled around on the floor where they had been thrown down by the three Astraeans on their return to Paige. The various data modules slid here and there as Paige changed course. The data had to necessarily be protected, but they were weighed down by the shame of not only having to escape, but the shame of having to abandon their friends. Astraeans didn't abandon friends. Luckily, the Ontelbar defensive rings were formidable, and did what they were intended to do.

Mixed with their shame, and regret for leaving the Ontelbar on their own, there was also a feeling of hopelessness. Just as the Astraeans felt that they were beginning to regroup and carry out a feasible plan to answer Daebaugh, they were humiliated and slapped in the face with the betrayal of the Quazlopian Mining Federation. The Astraeans were not guaranteed any friends. They never were. They should not have expected any. They should have learned to be more careful. Without saying a word, Carthal, Heersan, and Lannya exchanged glances with each other, reciprocating the proverbial disgust on each of their faces. They knew better than to not better protect their movements and actions. They also knew better than to not make it clear how sensitive their situation was when they spoke with Orn. They knew it was their fault, and placed no blame on the Ontelbar.

After taking only a few seconds to catch her breath

after their escape, Lannya stumbled over to a nearby command terminal. She flipped up the collapsible display and keyed in a sequence that attempted to initiate a communications channel with the Ontelbar Suburb. The attempt timed out. The repetitive, electronic gongs finally stopped as the communication attempt was ignored, or unable to be answered. Still panting, Lannya initiated another attempt as she looked helplessly to Carthal and Heersan. Carthal joined her at the command terminal and tapped a few commands to confirm the signal being sent had the best chance of being received.

GooonnngTEE! GooonnngTEE! GooonnngTEE! The call to the Ontelbar was still going unanswered, and with each pulse, the three Astraeans' shame and disgust with themselves, grew. They had no clue as to the fate of the Ontelbar, and were losing hope. Their cowardice had caused the deaths of so many innocent and wise creatures.

Tttssshshshhhhhhhhhhhhshshhhhhhhh, the static of the previously black display hissed. The gong tones from their attempted call stopped. They were replaced by rips and punches of white noise. And then, a picture. It was a wounded Gazer, surrounded by a few other Gazers. Behind the Ontelbar, the Astraeans could see some of the Municipal Cluster's structures burning, but they could also see the surface of the asteroid was no longer receiving any fire from any attackers. The asteroids in the sky behind them were also no longer grouped together or spinning. The fight was over.

"Has the attack ended?" Lannya heaved with a dry throat. "What is your status?"

The Ontelbar were weak and also out of breath.

Each eye on every Ontelbar was bloodshot and fatigued. Many of the tough creatures had collapsed to the ground to rest, or because they had run out of strength to stand. But, the Ontelbar nearest to the camera answered Lannya, after having to take a moment to compose himself.

"Yes, yes, Astraean," the Ontelbar answered through labored breathing. "We have destroyed all of the fighters. Everything but the host ship, which escaped not long after you left..."

Carthal bent further into the frame.

"Do you have many wounded? How can we assist? Please tell Orn..."

"I can see from where I am," interrupted the Ontelbar Gazer, "there appear to be a few dead Ontelbar, with approximately twice that wounded, but that is just here in the courtyard of the Municipal Cluster. What were your other questions?"

"How can we assist?" Carthal repeated. "Is Orn nearby?"

"I believe Orn is one of the dead I can see from my position," the Gazer shot out with a cold thud.

Carthal took his time to close his eyes as he slumped away from the terminal. He slid down a wall of the command deck and held his face. Heersan shuffled into frame to address the Ontelbar.

"I can't tell you how sorry we are for bringing this upon your people," Heersan offered. "We will send help and supplies back as soon as possible.

"That would be appreciated," the Gazer replied sincerely. Disappointment in the Astraeans and the sadness over the lost Ontelbar however, was chiseled into his eyes.

The connection ended and the screen cleared.

The three Astraeans weighed down the spots where they stood or sat without moving or saying anything for the majority of the ride to the Harbor. After a dozen minutes that felt like hundreds of hours, Lannya couldn't take it anymore. The thought in her head repeated over and over again to the point that it gave her a headache. She had to share it.

"I can't believe we left them like that," she whispered. Her disappointment in their group stained each sound and syllable.

All three of them felt the same way. At that moment, they felt that the tracking and observation data provided by the Ontelbar wasn't worth leaving their friends to fend for themselves. It was just a matter of time until someone said something. They were stunned and shocked at how they behaved. At the same time, however, they obsessed over scenario after scenario that they could have followed rather than the one they acted out. What if they had stayed and fought? What if they had taken shelter with the Ontelbar in their tunnels? What if they had delayed getting the data to the Harbor, or if the information was lost to begin with? They were obviously aware that any other option would have probably resulted in their deaths, but none of them had an answer as to why they just didn't try anything else but fleeing.

"I don't understand it," Heersan mumbled just loud enough for the others to hear. Carthal and Lannya looked to Heersan, hoping he'd expand. "I don't know that much about the Quazlopian Miners, but what I do know doesn't paint them as the type to sell us out like that."

Lannya agreed as she added on.

"I've only ever known them to be space cowboys. They don't get into bounties or political stuff."

Carthal, in a rare show of quiet reserve, had nothing to add. He only rubbed his chin while thinking of Orn. Lannya walked over to Carthal and slid down the wall to meet him. She placed her hand on his knee and patted it lightly a few times.

"Well, we'll definitely be able to dig deeper when we get to the Harbor," Heersan huffed through a fatigued breath.

Showing no overt regard for Lannya's hand on his knee, Carthal leaned to his side and stood up. Without looking Heersan or Lannya in the eye, he finally spoke up.

"I'll go see what Paige can pull up on the Miners." Carthal rushed to get the sentence out. His voice was distant, saying just enough to be left alone as he took the stairs down and away from the command deck.

"He could have just used that terminal right there," Lannya observed, subliminally recognizing Carthal's need to be alone.

Heersan understood completely.

"Let's just leave him alone for now," Heersan requested. "I'm sure he thinks Orn was his fault, but he's going to have to realize on his own, we really didn't have any other option."

"At least that's what we'll have to try and convince ourselves of," Lannya replied, already injecting an abundance of doubt in her own statement.

There was no sign of Carthal, and no further discussion between Heersan and Lannya for the remainder of the ride to the Harbor.

* * *

The silence continued through the Harbor beacons, the docking procedure, and systems shut-down. Only when Heersan and Lannya emerged from the command deck hatch and walked down the stairs did they meet back up with Carthal who had exited from a different area of the ship. Carthal made no attempt to follow closely with Lannya, or Heersan for that matter, and showed no affection to him. The three still had said nothing to each other in hours, and Heersan's concern for Carthal began to show on his face.

Carthal took the lead on the gangplank and landed back on the Harbor docks, first. When Heersan twitched to say something to Carthal, he paused and looked at Lannya first, to weigh her silent opinion on if he should say anything. Lannya shrugged in response, and her eyes widened without having any better of an indication than he had. Heersan decided it was indeed not time yet, and let Carthal disappear into the crowd. As Heersan and Lannya lost sight of Carthal, they gained a sight of Rigella, jogging up to them. She shot her hands up in the air to call their attention to her, and smiled widely at seeing her old friends for the first time in what seemed like years.

Rigella got to Lannya first and scooped her up into a rapid hug before pushing her away and grabbing her by the shoulders to inspect her for any signs of wear.

"I'm so, so very glad you're here and safe!" Rigella shouted, full of legitimate joy and exasperation. She let go of Lannya and hopped over to Heersan and wrapped him up in her arms this time. She repeated the shoulder push on Heersan so she could look him over as well.

"What's going on with Carthal?" Rigella asked, slightly annoyed that she had one more hug to deploy, but couldn't. "He went right by me without saying a word."

"He's taking the attack at Ontelbar pretty hard," Lannya explained. Heersan added more.

"Orn, the Ontelbar Gazer that was helping us, died during the attack."

Rigella let her hands fall off of where she had propped them on her waist. She took a deep long breath, sighed and looked to Heersan, then Lannya, and back to Heersan.

"None of you need to carry that baggage." Rigella suggested to her friends, almost ordering. Her intentions however, were noble. "There was no other viable option. I know that, we knew it here at the Harbor, and the Ontelbar knew it. We needed that information. They had a significant defense mechanism that functioned the way it was supposed to, and you three escaped. Don't take on guilt or a burden that you don't need to."

Rigella's voice was confident, yet warm and wise. She was not in ADF Central Commander mode, but rather, complete and nothing-but-friend, mode. Heersan and Lannya shuffled their feet and let their eyes wander around the floor of the docs, then back up and around the exterior of the Harbor. Heersan and Lannya finally looked back to Rigella. She put a hand on each of their shoulders and bent her neck to stare directly into their eyes. Her head shifted back and forth to meet their eye level.

"You guys hear me? It wasn't your fault," Rigella reinforced as she squeezed their shoulders. "If anything, I dropped the ball. I should have sent some ships with you, or been able to reinforce you more quickly. You did the right thing by making that data, and getting it here, the priority."

"No," Lannya responded. "You couldn't have done anything. By the time we would have reached out to the Harbor, the Ontelbar would have taken care of the attackers anyway, and any forces you would have dispatched would have left the Harbor weakened by whatever amount. No, it wasn't your fault either."

As they started to come around and see things more objectively, both Heersan and Lannya returned a squeeze to Rigella's arms in appreciation for her compassion. To Rigella, this was once again another example of needing to either share all blame, or abandon it and share none, while understanding that over-analyzing hindsight serves no constructive purpose, and wastes time.

"Let's go find Carthal," Rigella suggested. "He doesn't need to be alone right now."

Heersan's eyes fell into Rigella's with a deep appreciation. He had missed being able to rely on Rigella's strength and focus since Akal died, and after she had to stay behind to form the ADF. He slowly bowed his head at Rigella. Lannya fell in beside the two old friends as they left to look for Carthal.

There were of course easier and quicker means to locate Carthal. By way of a number of ribbon-related methods or the Helper Desk, they could have found him quickly, but there was an unspoken understanding that while they needed to find Carthal, they wanted him to have a bit of time to himself. It also allowed Heersan and Lannya to wind down from their recent travels and attack on Ontelbar, while catching up a bit with Rigella. The quiet times were rare, for everyone, and they all needed the momentary soft cushion of quiet around their hearts and minds.

None of the discussion between the three consisted of anything related to the events on Ontelbar, Daebaugh's attack on the Harbor, or any of the subsequent preparations the Astraeans had made. As they strolled through the crowd, around the Harbor, through the lobby and in and out of various corridors, they all took solace in telling old jokes and rehashing old fights and laughs. They were doing what most races across the multiverse do in the middle of hard times. They were looking back, replacing bad feelings with good feelings, and for a time, they enjoyed the lie they told themselves that bad things can't be all that bad, and even if they can be, that they won't last.

Heersan, Rigella, and Lannya walked around enough places of the Harbor, and took long enough doing it, to the point they lost track of time. They hadn't really done any searching for Carthal, but it wasn't an intentional neglect or disregard for him. They were simply doing what Carthal was doing. Getting away from it all for a bit. Carthal needed to be left alone, Rigella needed to spend time with her old friends, with Lannya and Heersan simply wanting to wander. They were all doing what they needed at that moment. They were being refueled by the concentrated reminders of what truly matters.

After walking around the Harbor for over an hour, Heersan, Lannya, and Rigella finally came to a rest in a random corner of the lobby. Whether it was their feet that were tired or their lips that were dry from talking, something prompted them to stop. Each one breathed in deeply and sighed through a smile in the satisfaction that only friendship can provide. They shared glances with each other, conveying an empathy for the stress, pain and fear they all shared without ever bringing those topics up specifically. They were in it together. It being specifically however each one of them needed it to be defined. They were in it together and would be together through it. Regardless of their individual definition, it was all bundled together in the form of hope. With each other, and with their fellow Astraeans as a whole, there was hope.

The glances of hope stayed on their faces for some time. Through continued silence, pivoting back and forth on their feet, or looking around the lobby, their faces held onto the hope. They held on to that unspoken and sometimes unjustified strength until the absolute very last second. They knew someone had to bring reality back into the mix, though, whether it was resuming their efforts to defeat Daebaugh, or to find Carthal, they knew it was just a matter of time before someone said something.

Before anyone had to speak, however, Heersan's concentration broke. His face morphed from their shared masks of hope to a mischievous and loving glance. His body turned slightly to match the angle of his stare. Curious as to what had caught his attention, Rigella and Lannya followed Heersan's eyeline until they saw him. It was Carthal.

They were unsure of how long he had been there, but there he was. With his back leaning against the rails, Carthal was sitting on the top step of the staircase attached to the landing of the floor that led to the library. He looked relaxed, as they had also come to be while wandering and talking. He looked unburdened with a slight smile as he cast his playful stare down into the throbbing mass circulating throughout the lobby.

Carthal hadn't seen his three friends yet, and Heersan took advantage of that. Without saying a word, Heersan winked at Lannya and Rigella as he smoothly slipped away from their group, thanking them with squeezes to their arms for sharing the walk with him. As Heersan crouched into the crowd and sheltered himself as best he could to sneak up on Carthal, Rigella and Lannya only had to turn slightly and watch the fun unfold.

Heersan's tongue tip escaped from the confines of his mouth only slightly as he weaved in and out of groups of Astraeans. Over there he would hide behind a column for a moment, and then here, he would slide up next to a group and pretend to be talking whenever Carthal's eyes grew near. At one point, Heersan even bellied up to the Helper Desk and pretended to ask a question. After a great deal of stealthy shuffling and scooting, Heersan finally reached the base of the staircase and could no longer hide from Carthal.

Carthal was still sitting up against the rails. His eyes would float around to scan the crowd and then back to his lap where he was picking at his fingertips. As he lifted his head up to scan the crowd again, he saw Heersan down at the base of the stairs. They stared at each other for a second until Heersan let his head fall slightly to one side. Heersan's face let an empathetic yet admiring smirk escape from the corner of his mouth.

Heersan, no longer attempting to hide himself from Carthal in the peppered lobby of the Harbor, began to plod up the stairs to Carthal. He took his time and matched the weariness on Carthal's face with his steps. Carthal showed no signs at all of being bothered by being found by Heersan as he spun his body around to face forward on the steps. The only notification of being disturbed was a forced inhale that Carthal took his time with taking. It was his last gulp of escape. As his nose shoved the breath out, reality was once again front and center. Heersan's arrival softened the blow as he sat down next to Carthal. There wasn't immediately any spoken greeting or embrace of any kind. They simply sat next to each other, facing forward, looking down the stairs into the lobby.

The two of them eventually took turns looking over at the other. Still nothing was said, but Heersan finally turned and pulled Carthal's head over gently and kissed him on the temple. Carthal smiled as Heersan kissed his head. The smile came from knowing that Heersan was there to sit with him and keep him company for as long as Carthal needed him to, but Carthal was finally ready to talk and plunge headlong, and completely back into reality. When Heersan released his head, Carthal came back up and looked at Heersan.

"I miss Akal," Carthal lamented. His eyes returned to aimlessly scanning the crowd.

"Mmm hmm, I do too." Heersan returned softly, bobbing his head in agreement.

"And I've been sitting here thinking about everything else I miss," Carthal continued. "Everything was so much more..." Carthal's voice slowly ground to a halt as he didn't know how to finish his thought or do it justice. "Joyful! Everything was so much more joyful," Carthal finished, satisfied he had chosen the right word, but aggravated at the same time by his realization. "This war with Daebaugh has ripped the joy from us. We can't just live as part of the multiverse and help people anymore. We've had to completely change what we are, and change our focus. I absolutely can't stand that. We have to be on the defensive while developing an offensive, when having a military used to be the farthest thing from our minds."

"Well, look what not being prepared got us," Heersan fairly proposed.

"I know, I know," Carthal recognized. His dry reply coated the cold air. "A bunch of dead Astraeans, and dead friends."

Heersan turned to look at Carthal and saw his eyes were heavy with tears still being just barely held back by the dam under his eyes. Heersan let Carthal be alone with his tears, appreciating that countless races who cry, don't like to be watched while they cry. Instead, Heersan looked back to the crowd and simply sat next to Carthal and placed one of his hands on his knee.

"Orn was just trying to help us," Carthal continued. His voice was still strong despite the emotion. "Without a thought of wanting something from us in return, he helped us, and I jumped down his throat."

Heersan squeezed Carthal's knee slightly, just to let Carthal know he was there, listening, as Carthal took the opportunity to release some of his grief.

"Please don't hold onto that pain for too long, Carthal," Heersan pleaded. "You apologized to him just before the attack. He knew you didn't mean it."

"That's part of it though!" Carthal erupted. "This evil with Daebaugh is making us do things that we never would have done before. Feel things we didn't need to feel before, and say things we wish we could have taken back the moment we said them."

Heersan squeezed Carthal's knee again and sighed in reciprocity. He knew Carthal wasn't mad at him. Carthal, along with Heersan and all other Astraeans, were angry with the situation. They were angry they were having to evolve. They were having to evolve their philosophy into a result that had not yet been cemented. Not only were they angry at the evil Daebaugh had brought to them, but they were also angry at the uncertainty of what the Astraean philosophy would eventually settle into.

As with anyone comforting a loved one, friend, or family member, Heersan slung old thoughts and ideas around in his mind, trying to uncover or discover something he could do or say that would bring some relief to Carthal. The frustration and futility of searching for something plagued his mind. There wasn't any feasible prescription Heersan could issue whether by act or speech that could bring solace to his timeless love of a billion forms. But then, like the biggest and brightest star from the entire multiverse, the king of all ideas, in a family of a billion, billion ideas, finally surfaced from the depths of Heersan's soul.

"Let's get married," Heersan blurted unceremoniously.

Carthal spun his body around on the step, leaned back and stretched his face in the complete shock of Heersan's random and modest proposal. Motionless, his face and body remained stunned as Carthal tried to reboot his completely surprised mind.

After a few odd chuckles of confusion, Carthal was finally able to speak again.

"What?"

Another few puzzled chuckles.

"Who, where, when, why?" He humorously questioned, still having not much of a clue as to what Heersan was implying.

Heersan's face conveyed a sense of complete confidence and understanding of the details he was about to share.

"Us, here, now, because I love you." Heersan said quickly and easily.

Carthal still sat, humorously paralyzed, blown away.

"After billions of years, forms and memories with you," Carthal almost whispered, almost completely at peace, and more than humbled, "I have never been more surprised by anyone or anything."

Heersan smiled, humorously pleased with himself, but also due to being thoroughly confident in, and excited by his suggestion.

"Yeah," Heersan affirmed. "I want to marry you. And we should have an official, full, true, Astraean wedding. What better way to remind us of who we are, but most importantly, what we are to each other?"

Not realizing it was possible, Carthal's body and face expanded to even greater proportions. He had never been more in love with Heersan. He had never been more humbled by Heersan. His pain and fears had never been more tended to by Heersan. Carthal was beyond tears of happiness. With Heersan's help, Carthal had reclaimed his joy.

"I can't even remember how long it's been since there has been a full Astraean wedding," Carthal said, while blankly staring into the steps, trying to remember. "They take forever!"

Heersan laughed heartily and replied at the same time.

"Ha ha! I know! If you're up for it, let's see if we can make it happen," Heersan suggested.

Carthal answered by grabbing for Heersan's head, and kissing him on his temple.

Chapter XVI
Fruits of Their Labor

Heersan and Carthal stood up, stretched, and scampered down the stairs to meet back up with Rigella and Lannya who had been patiently waiting. Their faces were giddy and silly as they descended. Rigella and Lannya looked to each other, slyly suspicious of the mischievous demeanor the two were approaching with.

"So," Rigella wondered, her lips forming a long, exaggerated tunnel. "You two alright?"

"Yeah," Lannya added, looking at Heersan and Carthal with a penetrating, yet light side glance. "What have you two been talking about?"

"Well," Carthal replied, glancing to Heersan and then back to Lannya. "We're going to get married."

Lannya's head snapped back to look them straight on.

"What!?" she exclaimed, completely taken by

surprise. It was the last thing she had expected to hear.

"Yeah, that's what I said when Heersan asked!" Carthal blurted with excitement.

"That's," Lannya said, looking for words, shaking her head in silly amazement. "That's absolutely perfect! Ha ha!" She hopped over and hugged them both.

As they hugged, Heersan looked over Lannya's shoulder to Rigella. She looked confused. She was confused, not from misunderstanding, but from a standpoint of timing and what her priorities were. She didn't react immediately at all, and thought carefully on how to reply to her two oldest friends.

"Just your two usual forms? A quick little quaint wedding?" Rigella proposed for clarification.

Lannya, unsure of where the conversation was headed, released Carthal and Heersan from her hug and allowed the engaged couple to focus on Rigella's question.

"No," Carthal responded. "We want to have a full Astraean wedding."

"The works." Heersan added.

"You know those take forever, right?" Rigella questioned, slightly annoyed.

Heersan's face quickly and noticeably returned Rigella's attitude, not understanding where it was coming from.

"Yeah," Heersan replied sharply. "We're Astraeans. Time is something we're pretty comfortable with. What's the problem?" Heersan took a step towards Rigella.

Rigella had grown even more upset.

"The point is, is that we don't have a lot of time left!" Rigella shouted back, standing her ground and daring

Heersan to take another step.

"What are you talking about? We have all the time in the..." Carthal attempted.

"In the what?" Rigella interrupted. "Once that last leaf falls, on the ribbon island tree, we will be out of time, Carthal." She repeated herself for emphasis. "Out. Of. Time!"

Lannya attempted to diffuse the argument.

"Rigella, they're just wanting to get married. Surely there's..."

"Stay out of this, Lannya!" Rigella shouted with confident authority. "They're obviously not aware of what's going on. They don't understand what we've been doing. What I've been doing. I've been stuck here trying to create and run a military to save us, while they've been out..."

Carthal was done with Rigella's diatribe.

"While we've been out abandoning allies and letting them die? Can you hear yourself? Are you really wanting to go down this road with us and accuse us of something? It hasn't been fun or an adventure. It's been full of pain and death!"

Carthal took a step, but then a few more, to pass Heersan and get as close to Rigella's face as he could.

"You need to make sure you know exactly what you're saying before you open your mouth again!" Carthal let the last syllable reverberate around Rigella's face, shouting it as loud as he could. Nearby Astraeans stopped and peered into the argument.

Rigella held her ground firmly and made no concession with her face. She did however not immediately speak again. Carthal and Rigella's eyes were locked.

Heersan spoke next, calmly. His tone was soft, but easily heard.

"Stop. Stop. Both of you. This isn't you. This isn't us. Stop."

Carthal and Rigella were both extremely tense and wound up. They were angry for a million reasons, but at that moment, each was at the top of the other's list. Neither of them moved nor spoke. Their eyes were still locked, waiting for something else to react to. But whether from fatigue, or Heersan's request, their violent readiness finally began to melt. Their faces released, extremely slowly. Their muscles relaxed as the two straightened back up and no longer leaned in towards each other.

Heersan broke the silence again.

"Carthal and I were just talking about this, Rigella. This mess with Daebaugh is turning us into something that we haven't been before. It's too early to tell if it's good or bad, but the Astraeans are changing. We're becoming a people we haven't needed to be before. We need to be aware of that, and try to hold on to who we are."

Rigella let her head drop the moment Heersan finished speaking and let her head roll from side to side slowly, trying to let some stress leak from her soul. She then looked back up at Carthal and took a small step back. Looking over to the distracted Astraeans who had stopped at the raised voices, she lifted up her hands in a simultaneous sign of apology and reassurance that all we well.

"You're absolutely right, Heersan," Rigella acknowledged quietly, looking over Carthal's shoulder. She then looked back to Carthal.

"I'm sorry, Carthal." She offered, while bringing her

hands up with palms out in a sincere display of submission. "I'm sorry. You're right, too. No one has escaped the stress or pain of all of this. I was wrong to get anywhere near implying that was the case."

Rigella then took a step to the side to address Lannya specifically.

"And Lannya, you didn't deserve that at all. I'm sorry for telling you to stay out of it. Sure, you haven't run around with us as long, but I trust you and appreciate you just as much as I do these other two crazies."

Lannya who had receded back to let the argument unfold, stood with her weight mostly on one leg, and allowed a small yet genuine smile appear. She nodded in recognition of, and thanks for Lannya's sentiment. Heersan turned to Lannya and watched as Carthal came over and put his arm around Lannya to bring her back to the group. Carthal showed in his eyes, an affectionate gratitude for Lannya, and noticeable introspection on Akal. Lannya recognized his affection for their old friend, and winked at him for it. All four of them grabbed for each other's shoulders. Despite having been separated recently, they were always a cohesive unit, and would now be an even stronger and united group.

Rigella resumed the initial discussion with enthusiasm. With what Rigella said, and her friends reactions, there was no hidden resentment or implication that anyone was running from reality. They all knew what they needed to do as an Astraean people. But at that moment, Rigella knew what needed to happen for their group, and its newly engaged pair.

"Ok. Let's go talk with Elcyd and see about getting

an Astraean wedding planned," Rigella offered, followed by a gigantic smile.

"There we go!" Carthal shouted, not only out of being excited about his engagement, but also thrilled that some of the joy that defined Astraeans had returned to their group.

"At some point" Rigella said, hinting at a detour before or after. "Can I show you what I've been up to?"

Everyone looked around the group and found nothing but smiles. Lannya walked to Rigella to stir up the group's momentum. She slapped her on the back and pushed slightly to get her and the group moving.

"Of course!" Lannya bellowed. "I can't wait to see!"

* * *

The original Trio and Lannya walked through the Harbor together, lighter in mood and lighter in foot. There had been a much-needed injection of hope after their resolved altercation and each of them were able to focus on what was important and what needed to be done. The two didn't need to be mutually exclusive. They could address both simultaneously.

The four made their way to the engineering section, looking to meet up with Elcyd and Mamdod, but had no luck finding them. Dawel, however, was there speaking with some of the engineers.

"Rigella? Heersan and Carthal, also! It's so very nice to see you! I'm so glad you're here and safe! I'm not sure I've met you yet," Dawel kindly admitted, reaching to Lannya for a handshake. "I'm Dawel."

"Hi there," Lannya replied, while warmly shaking his hand.

"Thank you. Yes, we're back safely and very glad to be," Heersan replied respectfully. "Thank you for passing along our message. We were in over our heads on that visit, unfortunately."

"Yes, thank you, Dawel," Rigella echoed. "We'll be making sure things like that don't happen again."

"Right," replied Dawel. "I'm just glad you're safe."

"Have you seen Mamdod or Elcyd recently?" Rigella inquired.

"No, I'm afraid I haven't," Dawel replied regretfully. "I've been here for hours working with the engineers."

"No trouble," Rigella responded, as she walked up to a command terminal.

After a few taps on the screen, Rigella saw that Mamdod and Elcyd were at the new fabrication facilities.

"Ah ok, perfect. Two birds with one stone." Rigella observed. "We can talk to them about the news and I can show you some stuff!"

"What news? Anything I can assist with? Would it be alright if I came along?" Dawel inquired innocently. "I'd love to take a break from the dark!" Dawel playfully poked. He then rolled his eyes at the always-dimly lit areas of engineering, due to all of the bright ribbon charts, screens, and data terminals.

"Well, not just yet," Rigella lightly denied. "I'll give you a personal tour of the new fabrication facilities when we're ready to deploy what we've been working on, which isn't too far away. We just needed to see Elcyd and Mamdod anyway about something unrelated."

"Ok, sure, I understand," acknowledged Dawel. "I'd prefer to wrap up some of these charts we've been working on today, anyway. The historical Ontelbar data will help tremendously."

"Perfect. Thank you Dawel," Rigella offered, as they began to backtrack out of Engineering.

After making the long trek out of engineering, up to the lobby, and hiking to the other side of the Harbor, the group traversed through the merchant corridors and then crossed the bridge to the new fabrication facility. Rigella's adrenaline was pumping with excitement to reveal some of the work that had been done, and at the same time, excited for Heersan and Carthal to reveal their news to Elcyd.

When they crossed the bridge, Heersan, Carthal and Lannya took a moment to bend their heads back and pour their vision onto the intimidating size of the new fabrication facilities. The new area hadn't yet been completed when they took off for their scouting missions. The three of them were stupefied by the finished construction. Nothing like this had been built since Mamdod initially created the Harbor. With his guidance and with the practical planning of the engineers, the new facility was the very definition of a compliment to the original Harbor, as well as the smaller additions constructed over time.

Much like the Harbor, it was surrounded by docks at the outermost section, followed by a large exposed walk that wrapped around the main structure. The structure itself began at the bottom with an extremely large base. Its diameter was extreme, and it was incredibly tall. The top of the bottom section rounded off to a flat roof, where the second section sat, noticeably, but only slightly, smaller than the first. The entire fabrication facility continued upwards in a similar fashion, for a total of nine sections, each section smaller than the one below it. The facility was constructed so that each section would be dedicated to constructing items appropriate for its size. The largest section at the bottom would craft the largest vessels, for example, where the smallest section at the top of the structure might generate weapons, equipment and clothing.

"This is spectacular, Rigella!" Lannya exclaimed.

"Ha! And you haven't even seen the inside yet!" Rigella proudly retorted.

"Aren't you worried about secrecy or containment of what's going on here? I mean, this whole operation is just, kind of... all out in the open." Heersan posed logically.

"Yes, definitely. That's why we control who can see it." Rigella snapped back playfully and enigmatically.

"Well," Carthal began through a chuckle. "I don't see a drawbridge or anything."

"That's right," Rigella answered, mischievously delaying an explanation. "You wouldn't."

Lannya crossed her arms and smiled, and then punched out a playful command.

"Alright, Rigella, spill it!"

"Ha! Alright, ok!" Rigella stepped over to a terminal to demonstrate.

"Just a bit ago, when we were in engineering and ran into Dawel, while looking for Mamdod and Elcyd?"

Carthal, Heersan and Lannya all comically gestured for her to hurry up with her story.

"Well," Rigella continued. "In addition to using one of the terminals there, to locate Mamdod and Elcyd, I also took the opportunity to quickly give you three access to the new facilities.

The three were disappointed in the speed of the progression of Rigella's explanation.

"What do you mean?" Carthal prompted. "We didn't pass through any kind of security or access point."

"Watch," Rigella whispered. Her grin stretched across her face. "And now," Rigella said as she tapped the nearby terminal. "I am removing your access."

As she completed her command, Heersan, Carthal and Lannya watched as an only barely-visible, but enormous curtain of sorts sprung up before them, and encompassed the fabrication facilities. It visually cut the new area off from the Harbor and vice versa. Without the proper access, a person could not pass through or otherwise see through the protective curtain. And if one were to somehow lose access while inside the protected area, they would be ejected back to a public access area of the Harbor within ten seconds, which prompted Rigella to end the demonstration.

"Before you get kicked out, let me restore your access." Her fingers flew across the command terminal keypad as she continued. "And... there we are!"

Her three friends spun around and around, watching as the curtain quickly rolled up into itself.

"Wow!" Carthal hollered. "That was awesome! How does that all work?"

"It was a pretty simple bit of work for Mamdod, actually," Rigella replied, humble enough to immediately give credit where it was due. "He came to us one day and suggested that we use the ribbons to control who has access to the new facilities, whether by physical access, or by sight."

Heersan, Rigella and Carthal were totally enthralled while Rigella explained this new invention.

"He developed a way for the technology that already exists here at the Harbor to create and operate this ribbon curtain, and then developed a bit of new ribbon technology that uses ribbon energy but works independently of the main ribbons, to identify those who attempt to pass through the curtain, and restrict sight and access. The reason for the system being independent of the main ribbons is for added security and control."

"That is remarkable," Heersan offered, making no attempt to hide how impressed he was.

"It is pretty amazing," Rigella agreed. "And actually, the best part about it, is that the new facilities are not so much a secret as they are protected. The majority of the Harbor knows what is here, and mostly how this curtain system works. They know the facilities are here and how we protect it, but we don't allow what we're making, the methods, or the quantity, to be public knowledge."

"I like that," Carthal concurred.

"Yes," added Lannya. "Sharing what needs to be shared and protecting what can't be."

Rigella nodded and sighed in relief that her friends had a good reaction to their work.

"Alright, come on!" Rigella resumed. "Let's go inside so I can show you the *really* fun stuff!"

The fabrication facility docks were just as busy, if not more so, than the docs of the central Harbor. Each level of the fabrication facilities had multiple entry and exit points. The largest section was ejecting multiple ships and vessels of various styles and purpose. They would then be temporarily steered and held at piers that extended far out into observable space.

Heersan, Carthal and Lannya stood and watched in silent awe of the ingenuity and speed at which their Astraean kin worked. The first few levels of the new facilities were being dedicated primarily to vessels. Large, capital ships were being made in the bottom level, with medium ships in the second, and personal ships and fighters in the third.

The middle sections were kicking out various craft and vehicles for atmospheric travel or navigating terrain on planets. These were being loaded into larger cargo ships, which would then be docked at the new facility's piers, or whisked off to a different section of the Harbor. The top levels had a similar situation with cargo ships loading up with equipment and weapons. The variety was almost unimaginable. There were various things being generated for species from across the multiverse.

"Alright, enough drooling!" Rigella jokingly blurted. "Let's go in for a closer look."

* * *

After crossing the threshold into the entryway of the bottom fabrication facility, Rigella stayed back while Lannya, Carthal and Heersan shuffled a few more steps in until they came to a stop as well. Rigella didn't have to say a word at first. As she crept up behind them after they had stopped, she could see her three friends wearing dropped jaws. She didn't think their faces could show more astonishment than when they first saw the outside of the facilities. She was wrong.

For an Astraean to be stunned into silence and overwhelming emotion, it takes something beyond extraordinary. It takes something close to the miracle of existence and colossal feats of creation. This was one of those times. What Rigella, Mamdod, Elcyd, and Hergie conceived of, for this structure to outfit the ADF with, was nothing short of supreme and paramount on a multiversal scale. Where most Astraeans were humbled at the site of Hergie's original fabrication factory, this new fabrication facility eclipsed it both in size and function, multiple times, and almost frighteningly.

But there was nothing frightening about the new facility aesthetically, however. The walls and floors were made of the same bright materials, and the floors separating each progressively smaller level above, were clear. It was a beautiful and harmonious sight.

The group took their time to linger and meander around what they saw as Rigella led them around the expansive floor. Their eyes floated here and there, and landed on the walls, the machinery, and the vessels. They watched as Harbor fabricators, Astraean and non-Astraean alike, worked side by side to manufacture tremendous portions of ships. Heersan, Carthal and Lannya's heads pivoted up and down, around, and to the side, as they watched the processes unfold before them. The three of them were the very definition of dumbstruck. Until then, none of them had considered that Astraeans were possible of things on this scale.

After billions of years' worth of experiences between billions of Astraean lives, nothing like this had ever been dreamed of, or attempted. But as much as their eyes and heads bobbled aimlessly, the majority of their attention kept being stolen by gigantic islands of machinery ahead of them. After walking through a modest staging and storage pass-through between the first and smallest room of the lower facility structure, and the innermost and largest room, Lannya, Heersan, and Carthal had their eyesight blanketed and blinded by the largest single opus of construction any of them had ever seen.

"Before you," Rigella began firmly, staunchly proud of and satisfied with the accomplishments of her team, and the rest of the Astraeans, "emerges the last few hundred meters of a representative from the largest group of vessels we are creating for the Astraean Defense Force. It is a Markarian-Class Capital Station. At 32,100 meters in total length, the Markarian-Class Capital Stations, also unofficially being referred to by many as thirty-two-ones, or mini Harbors, are built to remain largely stationary in space, one per universe, and give support to all other subordinate Astraean vessels in that particular universe. The Markarian-Class Capital Stations are intended to be, as much as possible, and as one of their pet names suggests, a mini-Harbor, with the same capabilities, protections, support, and resources as the actual Harbor. They are, as you can see, absolutely massive, however, and take an almost incalculable amount of time and resources to fabricate, despite our ribbon technologies. Because of that, we are building these extremely slowly, a few at a time, and deploying them to a few key universes. This one that has just been completed is the first, and will be the only one for a time. We have named it, Triangulum. The Astraean Defense Ship (A.D.S), Triangulum."

Heersan, Carthal and Lannya made no effort to look at Rigella as she spoke. They hadn't moved from where they were when they first caught site of the Triangulum. It wasn't only the largest thing the Astraeans as a whole had ever created, Heersan, Carthal and Lannya were all trying to think of something larger created by any of the various races they had previously lived as. They were unable to think of anything.

Heersan, still frozen in place with inundated vision, forced himself to speak.

"Rigella..." He whispered, alarmed, and almost fearful.

Rigella walked over to hear him better as he continued.

"This... this..." he stammered, unable to find the words at first. "This... is too much!" He whispered, but huffed into her face as he turned his head finally.

"It might be," Rigella surprisingly confirmed. Lannya and Carthal were listening but still unable to break their attention away from the Triangulum. "It might be. But Heersan," she resumed, quietly and restrained. "There is not a single soul, aware of this ship that is not also aware of the possibilities and the implications. For a large portion of the time you've been away, I, along with Mamdod, Elcyd and Thyra, sat and poured through volume after volume, memory after memory of military strategy, history, and tactics. We argued, proposed and conceded points from countless directions. I beg you friends, to trust me when I say that we are all keenly aware of what this ship has the potential for."

Heersan looked back to the ship as Carthal and Lannya finally looked over to Rigella. She then spoke to them.

"Our philosophy in the creation of our military was driven by the primary motivator of ensuring our race's survival, which was closely tied in with helping to ensure the protection of non-Astraeans, a primary tenet of our existence already. It was decided that if we were setting out to build a military, then we needed to create an effective and decisive one. The operational elements of our fleet will accordingly be directed, coordinated and supported by the Markarian-Class Capital Stations as they continue to be constructed and deployed."

"Yeah," Rigella offered with a smooth and realistic lilt. "I am extremely glad we, as a people, have developed a military." Rigella's voice trailed off as she looked back to the Triangulum. "I just..." she continued, locked in focus, back on the ship, "I just... we're just... trying to take it all in."

Another block of silence followed. The Triangulum had almost cleared the exit window in a side of the fabrication facility, and the touring Astraeans looked down the length of the ship that reached into space to the point that they couldn't make out the end of it.

"How are you able to hide such an immense ship from those outside that security barrier?" Carthal asked, having no clue as to how it was possible.

"Oh, that extends along the length of the new fabrication facilities' docks. It begins way out past some of the beacons, approaches the harbor, wraps around the new fabrication facilities, and then travels back out into space.

"Ah, I see," Heersan said with little fanfare.

Rigella was not frustrated or in any way bothered by her friends' hesitance, and she allowed them to continue absorbing and pondering. To the contrary, she wished for nothing more than their approval, in the least, and at the most, perhaps a shared bit of excitement and enthusiasm for their improved capabilities to defend themselves and counter Daebaugh. That was it. Rigella was excited that they had a chance to defeat him, from her point of view, with the strides made with the ADF.

Heersan at last cracked his own statue of shock and shifted his weight. He then scratched his head, ran his hands down his face, breathed in quickly and shoved out a sigh.

"I've been going back and forth on how I feel, and the words I want to say, Rigella," Heersan's mouth raced before taking a slight, final pause. "If this direction is what you, Mamdod and Elcyd have come up with, then I'm on board. For better or worse. Win or lose. I've never had a reason to doubt you or Elcyd, and I won't create one now."

Rigella's head and eyes rolled backwards in relief before she snapped them back down and lurched at Heersan to hug him. She squeezed tightly, but quickly, to let go and look at Lannya and Carthal for their reactions. Lannya just smiled with some of the enthusiasm Rigella had been looking for. Carthal answered in his own way.

"I'm all for it, as long as they have good food on these things," Carthal blurted out, pointing his thumb in the direction of the Triangulum.

Rigella stepped over to Lannya and Carthal and gave them their own hugs.

"Thank you. Thank you. All three of you," Rigella gushed heartily. I had no idea how you would react, and how you did was an extremely big burden lifted from my back. All through our discussions, I kept trying to consider what you would think."

"I know I've known you the least in comparison to Heersan and Carthal," Lannya began. "But I've had nothing but complete confidence in you for some time. You always have our people's best interests at heart."

Rigella's eyes softened as she swallowed to make room for more gratitude. Lannya continued.

"This thing? It's a tool. It's just one of all the other tools you've been coming up with here. They're the things we need to defeat Daebaugh."

"Exactly. That's how we were looking at it," Rigella responded. Her hands were clasped together, thanking Lannya silently as she spoke. "We just wanted to give our people the best shot possible, and have the ability to defend ourselves in the future, and defend others, after this mess with Daebaugh is taken care of."

The four friends took a moment to survey each other to see if there were any additional thoughts or comments on the path of the ADF, or the Triangulum. Nothing else was said immediately, and there was an understanding in everyone's eyes of hope, and progress towards a victory over Daebaugh. Rigella took the opportunity to press on.

"You mentioned other tools, Lannya?" Rigella asked rhetorically. A mischievous crack crept up the side of her mouth. "Come look at some of the others!"

Chapter XVII
Capable Classes

Rigella skipped a few steps back to the front of the group and scooped her hand around to the side, motioning for them to follow. As Carthal, Heersan and Lannya fell in behind her, Heersan kept his eyes on the Triangulum. The last bit of it slid from the interior of the lower fabrication facility, completely out into space, to be sent to the end of the new facility's holding docks. As Heersan's eyes lingered, he considered under what circumstances he would see it again.

He eventually relented and relaxed, and turned to focus on their next destination. Rigella, Lannya, Carthal, and finally Heersan, hopped onto a platform which rapidly thrust them up to the second level. As the platform raced up, they were able to see dozens of other vessels, which were in turn blocking dozens and dozens more behind them. Rigella stood at the front of the platform, ready to be the first to leap off, and bounced up and down on the balls of her feet.

"Now here is where we start to get into the heart of our fleet," she said with a humble pride. "Our fleet is primarily classified by, and split into size classes. After the size classes, we have secondary designations for a vessel's means of propulsion. There are six primary size designations and seven secondary designations. We went back and forth on how we wanted to order our fleet and how to label it, and it was actually Hergie that suggested we use some of the terms used on Earth since Paige and her design were a heavy influence in his suggestions and ideas for the fleet."

Heersan had already been looking at the ships immediately before them and had started accumulating questions.

"So, obviously, these aren't as large as the Triangulum." His head tilted and rotated while inspecting the ships, as they sat next to each other in a ribbon dry dock of sorts "Which are these?"

"Yes," resumed Rigella. "These are the second largest vessels in our fleet. The Carina-Class Capital Carriers. These beauties are 5,650 meters in length and are home to 4500 fighter drones. Three decks of 1500 fighters each. And while the carriers themselves are a bit sluggish, they do have a good amount more maneuverability than the capital stations. But, since they're still pretty slow, they also have significant shielding and defensive armaments."

"So, what kind of engines or, uh, secondary designation do these have?" Carthal asked, hoping to confirm he understood Rigella's comments on designations.

"Ah ok, right," Rigella said as she spun around.

"Yeah, all of these that you can see from here, on this level, are all Carina-Class-NRE Capital Carriers. The NRE stands for non-ribbon energy. These are made to navigate in environments consisting of energy that are not ribbon-based. That's an extremely broad category on its own, of course. But, any further classification beyond that isn't officially categorized and will only be relevant to the crew for a particular ship. The other secondary designations in addition to NRE are: A for air, L for land or ground-based, O for oceanic or fluid, T for temporal and of course, S for space, and RE for ribbon energy."

Rigella scanned the faces of her friends and thought an extra bit of explaining would help.

"In other words, all of the ships of this size," she continued, as she gestured towards the Carina-Class ships before them, "are all Carina-Class. The secondary designation after the class, or any class, tells you what type of environment they're outfitted for. There are hybrids of course, and new hybrids will be developed as we go."

"Sure, sure" Heersan said softly while rubbing his chin, beginning to give in slightly to the justifiable excitement for the tremendous work Rigella and her team had done. "What are the other size classifications?" His blossoming interest was beginning to show.

"Well, we've already seen the first Markarian-Class Capital Station. Here again," Rigella continued as she pivoted to gesture at the ships nearest them once more, "are the Carina-Class Capital Carriers."

Before continuing, Rigella leaned and stretched, trying to see if she could see the next class from their position.

"N... Nope," she grunted. "Well, far down behind this row of carriers, we're making some Scuti-Class Battleships. At 1,708 meters, we've designed these to have the best balance between offensive and defensive capabilities in our fleet, in addition to improved handling as far as our larger ships go. After the Scuti-Class, we have the Cephei, Centauri, and Persei classes. Those are 1,435 meters, 1,070 meters, and 790 meters respectively. Our heavy cruisers, regular cruisers and frigates."

For the next few hours, the Trio and Lannya meandered and questioned, answered and laughed. They continued refilling their goblets of friendship while dawdling in and out of rows and rows of ships, and ascending through more and more floors of the fabrication facilities. Carthal, Heersan, and Lannya made sure to ask all the questions they could think of while Rigella was sure to answer them thoroughly. Rigella wanted to make sure they knew she and her team had taken as many considerations into account as possible when they designed their vessels and equipment, while the others wanted Rigella to know they appreciated it. Along with asking all they could to learn about all of the new designs, they were genuinely appreciative and interested. It was as if the time they had spent apart had never taken place.

Rigella's tour finally found its way to the top-most level of the new fabrication facilities. By the time they had ascended to the top, Carthal, Heersan, and Lannya had caught up completely. Not only were they up to speed with the ADF's ships, but also with the weapons, vehicles, ribbon manipulating devices, wearable technology, ribbon interacting devices, tools, and countless other advances and advantages. As their conversations finally began to include moments of pause and silence, the group found themselves in the middle of the floor of the top-most and smallest level of the fabrication facilities. They all looked down through the clear floor, until either equipment or distance prevented them from seeing any further. The smell in the air resembled newly created or unwrapped plastic. The sound around them consisted of thousands of individual, but similar sounds made from the automated fabrication machines throughout the facility. Everything was bright, clean and could intoxicate one with excitement.

In one of the breaks in conversation, while the group was looking down through the other levels, a familiar pair approached.

"What'cha looking at?" one of the pair wondered, poorly disguising his voice.

Carthal jumped a few feet to the side and jerked his body to face the person that startled him. It was Elcyd.

Elcyd grinned with satisfaction. He had intended to scare someone.

Heersan and Rigella began to chuckle, never really making an effort to hold it in. Lannya's huge smile gave her away as enjoying it also.

"Ha!" Elcyd trumpeted. "I'm sorry. I just had to!"

"Alright. Ok. I'll add that to the list. Watch out! Just when you least expect it!"

Elcyd was laughing more now as he held his palms up in surrender.

"Ok, fine, fine." He acknowledged. His voice was still breaking from chuckling. "I'm up for it."

As Carthal glared at Elcyd teasingly, Rigella

changed the subject.

"We were looking for you and Mamdod, actually. We have some things to talk about regarding the Ontelbar, and some, um, other news." Rigella cut her eyes towards Carthal and Heersan, prompting Mamdod to oblige his curiosity.

"News?" Mamdod echoed innocently. "What would that be?"

"Well," Carthal replied. "Heersan and I are going to get married."

Mamdod chuckle-scoffed in glad surprise.

"Ha! Congratulations! That is positively wonderful!" Mamdod clapped once and then held his hands. He was so pleased to hear something not related to military planning. "When did this get decided? When and where will it take place?"

Heersan looked to Carthal before turning back to Mamdod with a smile.

"We were hoping to have a full Astraean wedding, as soon as possible," he answered.

Mamdod looked to Elcyd. Mamdod's face was still reflecting excitement, but had stretched to include shock at the conditions.

"A full wedding? All the lives, with all available races and forms?" Elcyd looked back to Mamdod, as if to communicate something silently. There was a noticeable unknown understanding of some kind between them.

Heersan initially interpreted the silent glances from Mamdod to Elcyd as disapproval, and Heersan let them know as much.

"Look, don't give us any grief about it not being the

right time, or not appropriate right now due to what we're dealing with and such." Heersan outlined, firmly. His voice had raised slightly after already running into objections from Rigella. He wasn't in the mood to have to justify his and Carthal's decision again, much less to fellow Astraeans.

"No, no, that's not it at all," Elcyd replied. His hands were up, teasingly attempting to disarm Heersan. "It's actually very interesting you two have decided to do this, and do it now. I also think it's perfect." Elcyd then whipped his eyes over to Mamdod. He accompanied his glance with a playful smirk before continuing. "I think it's perfect, and, a perfect time."

Heersan squinted and turned his head a pinch. He was unable to decipher Elcyd's enigmatic tease.

Chapter XVIII
Extending the Offer

Lannya repeatedly hammered Heersan and Carthal on their shoulders.

"I'm so excited for you two!" Her voice was the lightest and happiest it had been since she met up with the Trio.

Elcyd chuckled and wrangled the group in.

"Ha! Yes, we will make this happen for you both," Elcyd confirmed. His face turned less jubilant as he looked quickly to Mamdod. "But, before we get into the planning for that," he prefaced with a quick and serious tone. "We need to talk about our plan to reinforce and protect the Ontelbar Suburb. They've already provided us with some great information, but we still need the help of their observational abilities, but even if we didn't, we need to help them."

"And we have the means to help them," Rigella

added.

"Definitely," agreed Mamdod.

Carthal was the next to respond. He quickly and appropriately put the conversation about his and Heersan's wedding on hiatus.

"Oh, good. Yes, thanks Elcyd. I'll do whatever I can to help them." His interlaced fingers slid back and forth on each other. He was anxious to help, but focused.

"Rigella," Elcyd began to pose respectfully. "Mamdod and I had some ideas, but what have you been thinking in terms of assisting the Ontelbar?" Elcyd referenced a portable terminal to review his notes and take new notes as Rigella spoke.

"Well, as we said, we're in a position to help, and I think we should help extremely soon, rather than later," Rigella answered confidently. She then tapped a nearby screen to bring up a diagram of the ADF's currently available numbers.

She reviewed it quickly and completed some math silently before continuing.

"Ok. Let's do something along these lines," she began while tapping the screen to select ships. "Let's send them a Carina-Class-S Capital Carrier along with its fighters, two Scuti-Class-S Battleships, and four Persei-Class-S Frigates, each with 500 ribbon infantry."

"If there aren't any major concerns," Rigella continued, her focus shifting directly to Elcyd and Mamdod, "let's reach out to the Ontelbar and see if that arrangement will work for them. Also, be sure to make them aware that if they agree to any of the ribbon infantry, that they will have complete control over those forces while they are boots down on their asteroids."

Rigella then took turns looking from the terminal as she tapped the display to close the diagram, back to Heersan and Carthal.

"The ribbon infantry is one of our biggest new advantages," Rigella beamed. "And we owe this one entirely to Thyra. She's been working, with a bit of help from her friend Siguren, to duplicate the library's imaging system, but then also made the technology portable. We're outfitting most of our vessels with those systems. For our ships that are large enough, they can carry a compliment of ribbon infantry. And while any lost infantry can be replaced by their host ship, they can only be done so extremely slowly, and at a great temporary hit to the vessel's energy stores. We're working to make that entire technology more efficient, but right now it is just practical enough to be deployed to our ships."

"Well done, Thyra and Siguren!" Heersan whispered in slow astonishment. "To be able to reduce some of the risk to Astraeans by using virtual soldiers? Well done!"

"Thank you, Heersan," she replied softly. "I hope the technology serves us well and only continues to improve. We'll be working to make sure that happens."

Rigella smiled at Thyra and Siguren. She was extremely impressed and very grateful for the work they had done. Rigella then turned back to Mamdod and Elcyd.

"What do you think of that plan friends? What did you have in mind?"

Mamdod, who had crossed his arms and leaned back slightly while listening and assimilating Rigella's plan, nodded rapidly and made no sound. His eyes flickered back and forth, seemingly trying to consider hypothetical scenarios and contingencies.

Elcyd looked at Mamdod and allowed him to continue pondering as he replied.

"Well, the only relevant difference," Elcyd started, "is that our plan had fewer ships, and more infantry. We were concerned about the safety of our ships in the dense asteroids of the Suburb."

Rigella heard Elcyd's comments and began to pace slowly. Her head pointed up and stared out through the see-through ceiling of the top level of the fabrication facility.

"Yes," she mumbled. "They are dense. And the fact is, we don't have the time to mess with avoiding or dodging them."

She strolled and pondered more.

"Let's start with this. Reach out to the Ontelbar and propose my plan and numbers to them. Let them know about our concerns with the safety of our ships. Ask for assistance with the asteroids, and if they want to make any substantial changes to the amount of ships or infantry, reach out to me. If they don't want to make any drastic changes, there's no need to contact me. Just make sure the deployment is properly recorded with the senior commanders in charge of the involved ships and units reporting to me once the arrangement is confirmed. Remember. We are at the disposal of the Ontelbar. Give them as much leeway as you can, and adapt to any realistic changes they may propose as best you can."

"Great. Mamdod and I will do that," Elcyd obliged, as he tapped commands into a nearby terminal to begin communicating with the proper ADF personnel.

Rigella then turned to her friends.

"Carthal, Lannya and Heersan... Any thoughts or concerns?"

"I don't believe so," Lannya quickly provided. "I'm with Mamdod and Elcyd on the asteroid proximity topic. So, as long as we check in on that and ask what they think about the rest of it, we should be set."

Carthal and Heersan nodded to concur with Lannya but then flipped an open palm and shook their heads, having nothing else to add.

"Ok, thank you. Let's make that happen," Rigella politely ordered. "Also, while we touch base with the Ontelbar on reinforcements and support, let's work with them on looking further into the Quazlopian Mining Federation and get some details on why they gave us up to Daebaugh."

"Right, we need to do that," agreed Elcyd. "We've only ever barely had any interactions with them and don't have a relationship of any significance with them."

"Ok. Well, everyone has their price, I guess," Rigella snapped bitterly as she shrugged with contempt. "But sadly, the consequences of blind greed are never revealed until it's too late. They probably have no clue who they're helping."

"That's probably extremely accurate, Ri," Heersan agreed. "If they don't know who they're helping, then they don't know what is at stake."

"Then we need to help them understand," Carthal shot out in frustration.

"Yes. Elcyd, let's finalize the arrangements for sending the Ontelbar reinforcements and protection, and work with them to dig up all info we can on the Miners."

Rigella inhaled quickly and shot the breath out just as fast, having made up her mind on a plan they were all confident in.

"Heersan, Carthal and Lannya," Rigella continued. "Depending on the initial information we obtain about the Miners, would you three be willing to meet with them?"

Carthal quickly replied.

"Yes, definitely."

"Well hold on," Lannya inserted. "Depending on the information we get." Lannya was looking directly at Carthal who was noticeably angry and emotional over the attack on the Suburb.

Heersan reiterated Lannya's reminder towards Carthal.

"Yes, only when we've learned what we need to learn and decided meeting with them is even a viable and worthwhile move."

"Hey," Carthal threw out quickly, feeling slightly ganged up on. "I know. I get it. We'll be careful."

Lannya and Heersan looked back to Rigella. Their eyebrows floated and small grins appeared, to silently communicate that they would have to work to keep Carthal's justified emotions in check if they were to meet with the Quazlopian Mining Federation.

* * *

While Rigella remained behind to continue talking with Heersan, Carthal and Lannya, Mamdod and Elcyd took their leave to prepare to contact the Ontelbar. On their way to discuss some of the particulars and logistics of their first deployment of ADF resources, they expressed concerns with each other.

"I didn't feel strongly enough about it to express it until now," Elcyd began. "But I'm slightly uncomfortable with the idea of putting control of any of our extremely green venture with a military, into the hands of someone outside of the Harbor."

Mamdod responded without hesitation.

"Oh, I agree completely, but I felt that the need to reinforce and protect the Ontelbar needed to be done. Putting control of our forces in their hands isn't ideal, but I think it is just slightly, the best way to handle it. It not only restores a bit of good will after they were attacked moments after our people arrived, but instills some trust in our allies, and confidence in their unequaled knowledge of the Suburb, as well as the surrounding space."

Elcyd took Mamdod's words in carefully. His thoughts were similar.

"The truth is," Mamdod replied. "We simply don't have the luxury of debating some of these details, or dragging out a potential diplomatic issue between ourselves."

"That's definitely true," Elcyd emphasized.

Upon reaching some of Rigella's subordinates, Mamdod and Elcyd relayed the plan to them and fleshed out some of the details. They needed to quickly consider time estimates on how quickly they could be ready for deployment while taking into consideration such things as ship and crew readiness, and systems status. While there were already hundreds of ships available, which were perfectly constructed due to the ribbon systems in the new fabrication facilities, there hadn't been too many shake-down cruises. They were fortunate to have had any at all. But everyone and everything was green, and Mamdod and

Elcyd were concerned.

"So, you think we can have the ships and crew ready that Rigella wants to go to Ontelbar ready by when?" Mamdod pointed his eyebrow at the ADF Readiness Officer, suggesting he make sure he figure conservatively, and give a realistic estimate.

"I'm pretty confident we can have everything ready to be underway within four Harbor days," the Readiness Officer supplied.

"Four Harbor days," Elcyd repeated as he looked at and checked with Mamdod.

"Can you decrease that time at all?" Mamdod asked with respectful curiosity. "We need to have these forces in place before we can take some of our next steps."

The ADF Readiness Officer grimaced with doubt, but took to a portable terminal to check some calculations.

"Well," he started while still calculating. "I don't want to put any of our crews at risk in any way, and I know you don't either." The officer looked up to catch eyes with Mamdod and Elcyd as he spoke his assumption. "I just don't want to short-change our people when it comes to supplies, weapons or defensive systems."

The Readiness Officer continued tapping out calculations but quickly gave up to cut to the heart of the situation.

"Let me speak with some of the other Readiness Officers about any ideas they may have to cut that time down some and I'll get back to you. Will that work?"

"Of course," Elcyd responded with sincere gratitude. "The safety of our people is the top concern."

"We only want to see what's possible. Nothing

more," Mamdod clarified calmly. Mamdod bowed his head only enough to be noticeable. He was sure to make it clear that they had no unrealistic expectations of the Readiness Officer or his team.

"Understood. Let me start checking," the officer genuinely conceded.

The officer then turned and started motioning for some of his fellow officers to his side as they started making their way to an extremely tall and vibrant display of a list of ships, vessels, systems and crew. The display was split into hundreds of rows and columns outlining the various elements of the ADF and their readiness level.

Mamdod and Elcyd resumed their private conversation while letting the Readiness Officers get to work.

"While they do that," Mamdod began to suggest. "We can go ahead and reach out to the Ontelbar and confirm the plan with them."

Elcyd's face lit up as things began to come together.

"Good. Right. And depending on what they say, there should be time to modify the deployment specifics. It sounds like we'll have at least two days or so."

"Alright," Mamdod nodded, settling their next move. "Let's go talk to the Ontelbar."

Elcyd and Mamdod began to make their way back to Elcyd's office. They could have returned more quickly by the elevators, but they purposely took the long way which included numerous sets of stairs and corridors that lent themselves perfectly to hushed discussion and whispered suggestions. The plan, while fairly solidified, still had an element of fluidity to it. They needed and took every available second to iron out details between them, and to try and anticipate any challenges or blunders.

They eventually reached Elcyd's office and without flinching, hesitating, or missing a beat in their discussion, both of them shot through his office door's threshold. They were frantically ironing out details without wasting a second as they dropped miscellaneous items off on a pitiful wooden table next to the door. It was a pitiful table that had seen too many years, but it was an important table. It held the most necessary items of the day as Elcyd came in and slapped various things onto it, and protected them until he left and picked the items back up. It was a good table, full of as much pitiful but important character as an item such as the table might have. It was one of Elcyd's favorite items in his office.

The door slid down and sealed behind them. Mamdod finally allowed their discussion to lapse as he tapped on his portable terminal.

"Hello," Mamdod began urgently, immediately after a connection was established with an ADF office. "Elcyd and I were up there a little while ago discussing some deployment preparations with one of your Readiness Officers. Do you know if he has made any progress on the matter we asked him to check into?"

The face looking back at Mamdod was one he hadn't encountered before.

"Ah, hello Mamdod! Let me ask the officer working on that for you."

"Great," Mamdod whipped back gratefully.

While Mamdod was checking on an update from the ADF Readiness Officers, Elcyd was already initiating a highly encrypted communications channel with the Ontelbar Suburb, using some of the Harbor's new developments. Previously, any Astraean could open a communications link with any location in time or space that had the capabilities, but many of those abilities, including long-distance communications with non-Astraean races and equipment, had been restricted somewhat in light of the need for more secure transmissions.

"Yes, hello engineering. Please initiate a temporary, but securely randomized communications ribbon with the Ontelbar Suburb. I will interface with the ribbon scanner now for identification."

Mamdod continued to wait for the Readiness Officers while Elcyd inserted his hand into the scanner.

The engineer receiving Elcyd's call could be seen to be looking away from his call with Elcyd. He referenced an immense set of displays on his end, cross-checking biological and temporal signatures, and confirming his spiritual markings matched up with the known and recorded experiences of Elcyd's soul. He checked out.

"Everything looks great, Elcyd. Thank you," the engineer respectfully obliged. "One moment while we create the temporary secure ribbon."

Elcyd took the opportunity to glance at Mamdod and see if he'd made any progress with the Readiness Officers.

"Anything?"

Mamdod shook his head. But just as he was about to speak, the ADF Officer came back into frame. He was slightly out of breath. He had raced to get back as quickly as possible out of respect for Mamdod.

"My apologies, Mamdod. I was interrupted on my way back to the terminal. I was told by the Readiness Officer heading up this particular Ontelbar relief, that he could have the time decreased from four to three days. He doesn't want to sacrifice any systems or weapons, so he's going to pull some workers from other areas and projects to get everything done in three days."

"A full day?" Mamdod confirmed with an impressed increase in volume. "That's great. A full day will definitely help. Please tell your colleagues that they are doing amazing work and that we appreciate their efforts, immensely."

A wide and unrestrained smile shot across the ADF Officer's face before he replied.

"I will! I will tell them. Thank you, Mamdod, for your kind words!"

"Oh, not at all," Mamdod replied. "Take care friend."

Mamdod tapped his portable terminal to close his communications session, and flicked the tablet onto the table with the rest of the items they had thrown down as they entered the room. He then approached Elcyd.

"Well, that will help," Elcyd whispered, waiting for the engineer to finish establishing the secure ribbon with the Ontelbar Suburb. "I was hoping to cut it down by two days, but one will be fine. I'm extremely proud of our people and their accomplishments, especially their most recent achievements."

Mamdod's face immediately started nodding broadly and quickly in sincere agreement. The engineer began to address Elcyd once more.

"Ok, Elcyd," the engineer resumed. "The secure

ribbon signal has been established and is en route to the Suburb. They will receive the ribbon transmission in 5... 4... 3..." The engineer didn't speak the last two numbers, as to avoid any potential over-talking as the communications link was established. At the end of five seconds, an audio and visual link was established and once again, Elcyd looked into his portable terminal as Mamdod watched nearby.

"My friends and Gazers," Elcyd began, as he quickly scanned the cavernous room from one of the buildings in the Ontelbar Municipal Cluster. "I wanted to reach out as soon as we had some specific information on the assistance we were hoping to provide if that is something you were still interested in. And before we address that, please let me once again express my sincere apologies and regret at the tragedy the Miners brought upon your people. We have every intention of helping you avoid such violence again."

There was a stoic silence on the other end of Elcyd's transmission, and the faces of the Ontelbar wore fatigued frowns. There were no overt displays of gratitude or excitement. The blood of their people still reflected brightly on the surfaces of their asteroids.

"We are glad to hear of this news, Elcyd," a Gazer replied flatly. "Please forgive us however if we are already weary of this conflict."

"I completely understand," Elcyd provided. His voice was solid and strong. He wanted the Ontelbar to know he was doing everything he could to empathize. "We cannot adequately make up for your loss. We just want, at this time, to do everything we're capable of doing, to help your people now, as well as provide some protection. Also, if we can somehow resume our joint efforts on monitoring the area around the Suburb, it will not only help us in locating Daebaugh, but it will help improve our collective ability to prevent future attacks as well."

"What details do you have on this support you will provide?" The Gazer asked, with no mood for delay, and little concern for the needs of the Astraeans.

"Right. In three days or less," Elcyd began. "We are prepared to dispatch to you one of our carriers, and its 4500 fighters, along with two battleships, and four frigates, each with 500 ribbon infantry."

"Ribbon infantry?" The Gazer repeated, as his four eyes tilted inward in confusion.

"Yes, they are a type of virtual army." Elcyd explained succinctly. "They can fight, die and be regenerated after a time, using ribbon energy."

"Ah, that is quite a technology." The Gazer blurted with the bare minimum of awe.

Elcyd watched as a different Gazer approached the transmission.

"Too bad we can't regenerate the lives we've already lost!" The interrupting Gazer shouted. "And not only that, but you have the audacity to ask us to continue helping you?"

The Gazer that Elcyd was originally speaking with, turned and rolled towards the upset Ontelbar. He spoke to him words that Elcyd couldn't hear. Elcyd let his head droop slightly in regret for the needless deaths the Ontelbar had sustained. After a moment, he lifted his head up and saw the original Gazer he was speaking with return to the transmission terminal.

Elcyd wet his lips, uncomfortable and at a loss at

what to say. He stuck with facts and information. The Gazer looked at him with eyes hardened with sadness, but had not yet been ignited with anger.

"While our ships, fighters and infantry are deployed in the Suburb," Elcyd continued softly, "they will be under strict orders to obey your command. They are at your disposal. We will have officers and crew there to advise and provide information, but your people will have the last call on their actions.

"We will be ready for their arrival," the Gazer responded. "Thank you."

Elcyd wet his lips again and nodded.

"Of course."

Chapter XIX
Threadbare

Elcyd watched the transmission with the Gazer terminate, and then turned to Mamdod. They were both thinking the same thing.

"We can't let things like that happen to our friends again," Mamdod summarized painfully.

Elcyd knew that and Mamdod knew he knew it. It had been said a few times already, but he just had to say it again. And at the same time, Elcyd knew he didn't make that comment because Mamdod wasn't aware, they just both understood that something, somewhere, needed to hear one of them recognize it once more.

Elcyd forced out a sigh of disappointment and began fumbling with some items on his desk in a frustrated itch.

While Elcyd picked up miscellaneous and insignificant items laying around his office, Mamdod took a moment to let his mind play out the daydreaming it had begun. For the first time since Mamdod arrived at the Harbor, and through all of the interactions with Elcyd and meetings in his office, he had never paid much attention to Elcyd's charming and cluttered quarters.

Elcyd's office was a cramped but abundantly customized and personalized room high in the main Harbor complex, only a few floors down from the cavernous upper dome. It wasn't a special or significant office, but it had been Elcyd's work nook for ages. One of hundreds of humble offices that wrapped around that interior level of the Harbor, this one was his.

Along the clean, but worn and stomped garnet carpet, which had been replaced half as many times as a human blinks in their lifetime, were piles of papers, and broken, but reparable, portable terminals from various ages of the Harbor's past. Also on Elcyd's office carpet, was a deeply faded and almost threadbare area where Elcyd often stood and contemplated most of his worries, hopes, and ideas.

Obnoxiously sizzling and malfunctioning holograph displays leaned against a fraction of the books and collections of indigenous texts, which had been stuffed and stowed into the compartments on the walls. Mamdod broke from his daydreaming briefly to chuckle, as he wondered if Thyra knew that Elcyd had all these materials strewn about. Elcyd was too busy flipping through a stack of paper to hear Mamdod's laugh.

The sizes and configurations of the various items were wildly different from one to the next, as they had been accumulated from countless locations and times. Bits of glowing material the size of marbles floated in the air, high above their heads. These were just other forms of data storage utilized by one of the millions of races of the multiverse.

The office was plainly square in design, with four walls, and a tall ceiling, approximately five times Elcyd's height. One wall had a door, but the remainder of that wall, and the whole of the others, except for one, were packed with shelves, cabinets, cupboards, hooks, and hangers that crawled up to the ceiling. The many shelves and cabinets were mostly constructed from a mixture of salvaged wood, but many others were custom made by Elcyd using materials and designs from all over the multiverse. Some were made of ribbon energy to accommodate the uniquely shaped artifact decorating them.

There was no room for any significant seating, however, there was one lonely, but comfortable, stool behind Elcyd's desk. A simple, solid blue cushion with gold seams, sewn by an obvious amateur, rested on top of the stool. The fourth wall of Elcyd's office was translucent up to about ten feet, like many of the walls and floors of the Harbor, and curved out slightly at the top towards the center of the Harbor, to structurally reflect the beginnings of the upper dome. This allowed Elcyd to look up, down and around through various parts of the main Harbor structure. Above ten feet, however, the wall returned to more sagging shelves, and overflowing cabinets.

Right as Mamdod felt he had taken in, and devoted a good deal of appreciation for, the character in Elcyd's office, Elcyd stepped to the worn area of his carpet at the foot of the windowed wall and looked out into the interior of the Harbor. He then thought out loud.

"I know Rigella already asked them," Elcyd said softly, almost to himself. "But, we'll need to make sure that Heersan, Carthal and Lannya speak with the Ontelbar before they talk with the Miners. The Ontelbar deserve a respectful, in-person, and hands-on approach when talking about resuming our monitoring agreement. I don't want us to drop our relief forces on their doorstep and just leave without a good conversation."

"Oh, I definitely agree," offered Mamdod. "I don't see why that should be an issue. We could have just spoken with the Ontelbar if they were going to attend tomorrow, but, they obviously have other things to tend to."

"Right, the Multiverse Assembly," Elcyd said, after almost forgetting about it. He turned around towards a stand holding a portable terminal. He flipped on the single light sconce hanging crooked from one of his shelves, and then began to tap some notes. "That reminds me. I had a few things I needed to add to my speech for tomorrow."

"It's such a shame you've had to keep this Assembly under wraps," Mamdod sympathized. "The Astraeans have never had to do that before, right?"

"That's right," Elcyd sighed while still tapping notes. "The Assemblies are normally a massively exciting, energetic, and positive experience, but we needed to keep the specific date for this one known only to our guests and a select few Astraeans. Even though the dates and times have been fairly fluid in the past, we still didn't believe it was safe to announce it. There are still just too many unknowns."

"Well," Mamdod began, trying to see an upside. "I guess a good thing about the secrecy is that Heersan and Carthal will be surprised."

Elcyd smiled affectionately at the thought of his friends getting married. His head was still down while he tapped away at his terminal. His smile started to slide wickedly to a particular side due to the extra bit of secrecy in the planning for the wedding that Carthal and Heersan were unaware of.

* * *

Mamdod, Elcyd, and Rigella had masterfully taken advantage of the situation handed to them. Using the need to deploy their forces to Ontelbar as a legitimate guise, they had successfully distracted Carthal and Heersan by having them assist in the deployment preparations. The work the two were doing to prepare to talk with the Ontelbar when the relief forces deploy, as well as their plan to meet with the Quazlopian Mining Federation, only helped hide them from the work being done to prepare for the Assembly, and in turn, their surprise wedding ceremony.

Ships, cosmic zeppelins, ribbon flashes, lightspeed gates, temporal jumpgates, and a host of other travel methods, began bringing thousands of citizens from across the multiverse to the Harbor. While some of the visitors didn't think the recent events and timing were quite appropriate for an Astraean wedding, many welcomed the surprise wedding ceremony as a bonus to the Assembly and genuinely looked forward to it. Most were of the same mind. Now, more than ever, was a perfect time to have one.

The Astraeans who were in the know about the Assembly were helping to blend the incognito arrivals in with the typical, day-to-day traffic. And while the huge influx of visiting vessels would normally be noticed, they also were blended perfectly into the busy docks, piers and ports around the Harbor. Some were even temporarily hidden inside the security barrier used to shield the new fabrication facilities. To anyone not aware of what was happening, the increased activity could very easily go unnoticed due to the hard work of the Astraeans and Harbor officials.

Special teams of Helpers and engineers shuffled around the Harbor to covertly greet and meet arriving dignitaries, presidents, tribal leaders, kings, emperors and just as many similar types of representatives of different species, cultures, languages and meaning. These trusted allies had been caught up on the situation with the attack on the Harbor, if they weren't already aware, as well as the circumstances surrounding Mamdod, Daebaugh and Akal.

They had arrived at the Harbor for the ages-old Multiverse Assembly that took place periodically for members of the multiverse to come together to discuss issues facing their cultures, planets and star systems. They shared philosophies and technologies, where appropriate, and primarily worked to cultivate respect and friendships. It was an entirely constructive, yet sometimes emotional event, depending on what may be happening locally to a particular species.

It wasn't always perfectly devoid of stress or drama-free, however. Considering not all species in the multiverse were aware of the Astraeans, or because of evolving diplomatic situations, the Assembly membership very often had additions or drop-outs in membership. Sometimes conflicts arose between the Astraeans, their allies, and those who left the Assembly. There had luckily however, never been a significant or violent repercussion.

This time around was very different. There were no

exciting and inviting announcements or advertisements for it, weeks leading up to the event, like there normally were. The visiting allies were met and escorted to private quarters, or remained on their vessels while waiting for the Assembly to start. It was initially suggested the Assembly be canceled or postponed indefinitely, but it was finally agreed to, after countless encrypted and back-channel communications, that an Assembly was not only encouraged, but absolutely necessary.

A window for the visiting Assembly members had been established so that everything could be coordinated very specifically, and safely. A few hours after Carthal, Heersan and Lannya returned from Ontelbar, the Assembly members began arriving. By the time Mamdod and Elcyd had arrived at Elcyd's office, most of the Assembly had arrived and were waiting for the Assembly the following day. The announcement that the Assembly was not only taking place, but beginning very shortly, would be made within mere minutes of when it was scheduled to take place. That time had almost come.

Elcyd finished up his notes on his terminal and turned to Mamdod.

"Alright. Let's go touch base with Rigella," Elcyd suggested. "I'm all set here and ready for tomorrow."

"Great," Mamdod replied quickly. He then took a deep breath and held onto it for a bit.

"What is it?" Elcyd asked. His head tilted and his eyebrows folded in with curiosity.

"Well, honestly," Mamdod started. "I'm a little nervous about the Assembly. This will be the first time I've ever spoken at one. After an eternity of practically causing them to exist to begin with, I never even knew they were taking place."

Elcyd's breath skipped gently with empathetic laughter. Recognizing Mamdod's need to stay a bit longer and talk through his hesitation to speak at the Assembly, Elcyd took the opportunity to do some additional straightening up in his office. He grabbed a stack of books from his desk and heaved them up onto a shelf. Afterwards, he poked an antiquated button, framed by a warped and bent wooden plate, made of a different grain than its host bookcase shelf was made of. It wasn't intended to be hidden, but had become deeply recessed from millennia of being pressed, slapped and mashed.

When he pressed it, a narrow and somewhat circular staircase made of ribbon energy popped into place, out from the shelves and cupboards, leading up to the top of his office. He grabbed a few handfuls of trinkets and artifacts he had been studying and began to scale the steps. As he ascended, he blew a few thin clouds of the glowing and floating bits of information out of his way, and replied to Mamdod.

"I can see how that may be daunting," Elcyd said through more skipping laughter. He looked down after reaching his intended height, to measure how intimidated Mamdod was. Elcyd then started placing his handfuls of items into their respective pockets in an ancient shadowbox.

Mamdod huffed a sigh through puffed lips and rolled his eyes up at Elcyd who wasn't helping.

"No, ok," Elcyd chuckled, succumbing to Mamdod's need for advice as he came back down the stairs. He pressed the button and the stairs slid away into barely noticeable ribbon energy emitters.

"Mamdod," Elcyd resumed with a compassionate sincerity. "Every single one of our allies knows the situation. We've caught them up on what's happened with you and your return. I highly doubt you can expect any more anger or judgment over your innocent game that you started at the dawn of the multiverse, than what you received from us when you first arrived."

Mamdod's lips deflated as his nervous sigh ran out of air.

"I've said this a million times," Elcyd continued. "Daebaugh and his actions are not on you. You cannot be expected to predict or prevent all evil."

Mamdod's jaw quivered, not for long or drastically, but enough for Elcyd to notice. Mamdod then went and tried out Elcyd's worn spot on the carpet. He had to take a moment, but eventually replied.

"Well, regardless, I do and will always feel somewhat responsible," Mamdod said with a rhetorical loneliness.

Elcyd glanced around his office, satisfied with its half cluttered, half orderly state, and waved for Mamdod to give himself a break, and to have him follow him out.

"I know. All you can do is focus on moving forward. Tell us whatever you want about how you feel, but focus mostly on moving forward. Our plans for protecting our people and our allies. Our future. Don't worry. You'll say what needs to be said, for the audience, and yourself."

Mamdod was thankful for Elcyd's words. Mamdod began nodding as he looked out the window into the interior of the Harbor once more, and then back at Elcyd.

"Alright," Mamdod said, inspired, and temporarily relieved. "Let's go."

Chapter XX
Strength in Numbers

After Mamdod and Elcyd met back up with Rigella to confirm the various plans for the Assembly, Ontelbar relief, and wedding, they and the majority of the Astraean leadership retired to rest. Everyone needed it, and much of the Harbor followed suit, though many were unaware of why an unexplained calm had been unfurled upon the Harbor. Much of the commerce and general business had drastically slowed down and the largest remaining concentration of activity was coming out of the new fabrication facilities. Their work was essentially unending.

When the forces being deployed to the Ontelbar Suburb were approximately a day out from being ready, the corridors, docks and lobbies of the Harbor started to fill once more. There was a sense of rejuvenation and pride that had been absent for some time. The very rare decrease in business and activity had seemingly been what a great many of the Astraeans had needed. It was an unspoken holiday. A chance to rest and remember. A time to wind down and let their hair down.

To the majority of Astraeans, there was only a knowledge that they were preparing a military, and preparing a fleet of some kind. Many of the particulars and specifics decided after Rigella won the tournament, were being kept secret by Astraean leadership, not to mention the physical barrier between the new fabrication facilities and the rest of the Harbor. However, just before the announcement for the start of the Assembly was made, excitement got the better of some Astraeans. Rumors and excitement began to trickle down and spread. Soon after, the time had come for the Harbor-wide announcement.

"Fellow Astraeans and friends!" A senior Helper began. "It is my honor to announce that the next Multiverse Assembly will begin in one hour! For reasons related to the safety of our people and the visiting Assembly members, the awareness of this Assembly has been held in secret for as long as possible by senior Astraeans and ADF Officers. You are welcome to calmly make your way to the upper dome for the Assembly, where a great deal of important information will be revealed. If you have any questions or concerns prior to the start of the Assembly, please feel free to engage a Helper, senior engineer or ADF Readiness Officer."

Carthal, Lannya, and Heersan, who were on Paige working on some equipment under the main mast, stopped their work to finish listening to the announcement.

"An Assembly?" Carthal said with aggravation from being kept in the dark. "Those are always announced long in advance. They're doing it now?"

He was as confused as any other Astraean that wasn't previously aware, only because the secrecy was such a precedent. The reasoning quickly sunk in and made sense to him.

"Well, I can see why they handled it like that," Carthal realized.

"Yeah," Lannya grunted as she returned to rotating a fluxspanner. "I'm just glad we're having one."

"Just in time, too," Carthal added. "We're going to head out to Ontelbar tomorrow, right?"

"That's what I was thinking," Heersan confirmed. "Arrive with the Ontelbar relief, or maybe just before?"

"Sure, that sounds good," Lannya said as she tossed some tools into a drawer. "Want to head over to the Assembly?"

Heersan grunted and hunkered down on the bolt he was working on. He then grabbed a rag and wiped his hands. "Yeah, let's go."

After Lannya, Carthal, and Heersan finished up their work and secured Paige, they saw other Astraeans filing out from the docks and piers towards the Harbor. They mixed in with everyone else and headed towards the lobby to then make their way to the upper dome. The crowds were thick and progress to the upper dome was sluggish. Assemblies usually attracted the majority of the Astraeans present at the Harbor, but there was previously far more notice and preparation. Everyone was cramming in to get up there in time.

When Carthal, Heersan, and Lannya arrived at the entrance to the interior of the upper dome, they saw what they had grown accustomed to seeing for the Multiverse

Assemblies. It had been a while however since the last one. They took place at random intervals when the majority of the Assembly membership thought one was warranted.

The entire expanse of the dome interior walls had been covered in small booths that were usually folded into and concealed within the walls—thousands of booths, large enough only to seat three or four human-sized representatives from any given location in the multiverse. The few large holes in the dome that normally served for ribbons to come in and terminate for ship entries and departures, became huge windows into the alluring beauty of the space surrounding the Harbor. Down on the floor of the upper dome were concentric rings of thousands of additional booths. These rings of booths were all of the same height on the floor of the dome, except for the few, innermost rings, which were raised slightly higher.

In those interior rings, special guests and speakers would queue up to visit the center ring where they would make presentations and speak to the Assembly. All of the normal vessel docking mechanisms and ribbon transport paths had been temporarily moved or redirected outside the dome to accommodate the event.

Lannya, Carthal, and Heersan slowly shuffled in behind those in front of them. They looked up far into the heights of the inside of the dome and saw fellow Astraeans starting to take their seats. The staircases leading to the various tiers of booths were mostly stagnant, full of those waiting for others to take their seats. The booths in the rings had been largely occupied.

Only when Carthal and Heersan finally claimed seats in one of the lower levels of booths on the wall of the dome, did they notice that they had lost Lannya along the way.

"Where'd Lannya go?" Carthal questioned in complete confusion.

"Uhh," Heersan said while looking around in all directions. "I have no idea. She must have peeled off at some point.

"She may have said something to us," added Carthal, "but I guess we missed it. It's pretty loud in here."

Carthal was right. The volume inside had grown significantly. Despite the holes in the dome for the ribbons to enter and exit, the acoustics inside were incredibly live in that they held and reverberated much of the sound from the thousands of conversations taking place.

Shortly after sitting down however, they noticed that the staircases began to flow more freely. Less and less people occupied them. From their vantage point, they could see through the clear floors of the booths above them, and see that most of them had been filled. Looking down, they saw the booths on the floor were filled as well. Though they couldn't make out everyone from their seat, Carthal and Heersan noticed that people began to congregate in the interior, raised rings as well.

Heersan leaned towards Carthal and slightly shouted so he could hear him.

"It looks like we're about ready to start!"

"Good!" Carthal shouted back while resting his head on his folded arms, which were in turn resting on the rail of the booth.

A few seconds later, the siren to announce the arrival or departure of an extremely large vessel sounded, to let everyone know the Assembly was about to begin. Every being inside the dome that had a sense of hearing similar in sensitivity to a human, which were many, grabbed their variously placed ears, to rapidly shield themselves from the excruciating sound. It was normally only heard by dome engineers that wore ear protection, if they were in the form of a hearing species at the time.

The sustained and bass bellow with overtones that sounded like a saw blade cutting through stone sounded again. The stairs were clear. The booths were filled. Any meandering or loitering conversationalists returned to their seats and sat down.

Carthal and Heersan could see movement down below inside the slightly raised, interior circle. It was still too difficult to make out who it was, but they soon found out.

"Hello my fellow Astraeans, and our treasured friends and allies," Elcyd began. His voice swelled with amplification and enveloped the entire dome as he continued.

"Welcome to our 47,792,276th Multiverse Assembly! This Assembly, for the first time since they began, had to be arranged, coordinated and kept, in secret, due to the recent attack and subsequent threats from Daebaugh. These threats are now public knowledge to all Astraeans and all those who call the Astraeans friends and allies. For understandable strategic reasons, we had to keep the health and state of our people, as well as our plans to regroup and react, secure. Going forward, we will never again seek to hide from anyone or anything. We are prepared for the threat, and we will be ready for what comes next! We have gathered here, once more, as we have for hundreds of millions of years, to discuss the things that matter. The good things. To discuss the matters that are affecting us all, and yes, to also discuss how we will persevere, and triumph, over anyone that wishes to bring us harm. Again, welcome to the Multiverse Assembly!"

The massive gathering of Astraeans, and the tens of thousands of representatives of only a portion of their allies, erupted in an immediate and solid applause that quickly became balled up in some form of unrecognizable mesh of sound. Accompanying the applause, was an ovation. Both lasting for many minutes. Once it finally died down, Elcyd continued.

"That was a very, much-appreciated reception. We Astraeans have had a hard time recently, but so have some of you. Our allies. This conflict is starting to seep into the daily goings-on of many universes, galaxies and systems. Allegiances are forming and diplomatic relations are changing throughout the multiverse, constantly. You, and many of our other friends who weren't able to make it to this Assembly have our continued loyalty and support. We will always be there for you if and when you need anything of us. We renew our pledge to assist with the overall prosperity and peace of the multiverse. And now, not only can we assist as individuals or small groups, but we have recently developed a defense force to help us with our mission. The Astraean Defense Force. This force is made up of hyper-formidable vessels, weapons, and supporting technologies. For more information on this, let me please introduce Rigella, the first Central Commander of our new Astraean Defense Force!"

A welcoming applause once again caused the volume in the dome to soar to impressive levels. The Astraeans and guests in the rings of booths closest to the center platform watched Rigella stand up. She stood slowly, not from being timid but out of appreciation for the moment. The moment that the Astraeans more or less announced that they had grown beyond being a mostly passive peacekeeping force. The moment they accepted, answered, and assumed the role that was forced upon them. It was a role that if they had to take it, they were going to embrace it. They were going to own it and see it through to its conclusion as masterfully and efficiently as they could. That's what Astraeans did. Rigella wore those thoughts on her face and emitted that philosophy to anyone who could see her, no matter the distance.

After reaching the center of the platform, a broadcast disc of ribbon energy lit up under her as it had under Elcyd as he spoke, previously. As Rigella stepped onto the broadcast disc, a barely noticeable beam of ribbon energy shot up around her, amplifying her voice throughout the dome, and projecting her image onto three-dimensional projections in the higher and further-out areas of the dome. As she began to speak, the applause came to a conclusion once more.

"Thank you, Elcyd. Thank you. And thank each and every one of my fellow Astraeans and our allies, for being here today, and for joining us at this special Assembly. As Elcyd alluded to, this isn't just an Assembly, and it is in no way tarnished because we had to keep it secret for a time. The Astraean philosophy, our friendships with all of you, and our collective ways of life, are in no way diminished because of that, or because of the attack on us and what may happen as a result. This is, on the contrary, possibly one of, and arguably, the most important Assembly that has ever taken place. Today, we want to formally announce to you that accompanying our promises, commitment and abilities as Astraeans, will be our Astraean Defense Force. The Astraean Defense Force, or ADF, is an absolutely unrivaled offensively equipped, defensively minded, and overall, unparalleled, expert military. This force will ensure that we are absolutely prepared to answer the threats from any type of enemy, of any means."

Throughout Rigella's initial comments, a few Astraeans and friends could be heard cheering and shouting here and there. But her next statement brought everyone to their feet for an extended amount of time. "Not only will the Astraeans be prepared my friends, but, as always, whenever you need us, we will be there for you, and this time, we will be there with the Astraean Defense Force!"

The cheering and applause sprung forth once again and mutated into something more ravenously excited than anything that had taken place during this particular Assembly, so far. As soon as Rigella finished her last sentence, the applause coincided with towering, three-dimensional projections being beamed into the center and spacious area of the dome. The first holograph, reduced in scale to fit inside the dome, was the Carina-Class Capital Carrier. Below the image of the carrier were a few sentences featuring some of the most prominent, but least sensitive, aspects of the ship. The noise from the reception to the first image did the Carina-Class justice.

Following the Carina-Class holograph and data,

were images of, and public information for, the Scuti-Class ships, the Cephei-Class ships, and the remainder of the fleet. Following the presentation for the fleet, was information on some of the vehicles, equipment, technology, weapons, as well as drones and ribbon elements in the ADF. Though an impressive display, it was far from comprehensive. All tactical information, or otherwise general information that could in anyway be exploited by Daebaugh or other enemies, was not revealed.

As the presentation progressed, the interruptions in-between new images and information became less and less. It wasn't for apathy or boredom. The Astraeans and of course, the allies that weren't involved with the development of the ADF, were simply in awe of what had been developed. The air within the artificial atmosphere of the Harbor was thick with wonder and the weight of responsibility. This was no pep rally or irresponsible display of reckless war machines. There was no feeling of an assured victory over Daebaugh. After all, the clock was already ticking. It was simply a justified reaction to what had been prepared to answer Daebaugh's actions.

Rigella's presentation eventually came to a close after being delayed by frequent interruptions of applause. Much to Rigella's relief, the light overview of elements of the ADF, new vessels and technologies, were received very warmly. She and the few senior Astraeans in the know were concerned how the Assembly would react to the secrecy, but there were no obvious signs of anger or dissent. She wanted to make sure her fellow Astraeans, and the Astraean allies knew that there would never be any attempt or desire to take advantage of that trust. As Rigella began to wrap up her closing statements, she wanted to make that clear.

"There it is, my friends. A bit of information on the ADF and some of the tools at our disposal. This presentation was in no way an exhaustive outline or description. By nature of military strategy, we did indeed have to continue keeping some information secure. But know this, fellow Astraeans and allies. The awareness of our reaction to Daebaugh's threat will eventually spread. It will eventually spread and make it into the ears and minds of our fellow allies, as well as our enemies. They should, at a minimum, be extremely concerned about having to face the Astraeans in a post-Daebaugh multiverse. We will never be caught off guard again, and we will always be ready. Friends, your faith in our collective Astraean Defense Force will never be misplaced, and any trust you may provide will never be taken advantage of. Thank you for allowing me the privilege of serving as the first Central Commander of the Astraean Defense Force, and for your time in letting me share some of our accomplishments with you."

The reaction to Rigella as she finished her comments was different than what had taken place up until then. There wasn't an attempt to be as raucous and penetrating with their applause and noise. There was however, a consistent and dignified round of applause. There was a respect to it. In showing restraint, the crowd gave Rigella and the ADF the biggest compliment they could receive. As the crowd continued clapping, Rigella stepped off the broadcast disc and shook the hands of her immediate subordinates. She then reached for Elcyd and gave him a long and strong hug. After Mamdod also received a respectful and meaningful hug, he then stepped up onto the lit broadcast disc.

The crowd was extremely interested in hearing what Mamdod had to say. Most of the Astraeans had only heard his initial comments when he first returned, immediately after Daebaugh's attack. Between now and then, he had been incredibly busy with lending where he could with the development of the ADF, but mainly with ribbon technologies and intelligence research, regarding anything that may be related to Daebaugh.

The applause as Mamdod stepped onto the disc was a soft and succinct one of respect. The Astraean allies knew even less about Mamdod than those who hadn't been working with him. They knew the primary facts involving his age, as well as Akal and Daebaugh, but that was mostly it. Very quickly, the crowd's curiosity outweighed their desire to welcome Mamdod and the applause faded. Mamdod looked to the disc below his feet which was once again beaming up a very faint beam of ribbon energy, ready to amplify anything he said, and to project his image.

"It is very humbling to address you today. Here at this, my very first Assembly." Mamdod cleared his throat while calmly soaking in the dome interior view and continued.

"I'm not sure what information any of you might have about me, and I'm sure our allies have less information than the Astraeans, so if you would, please oblige me while I attempt to get everyone on the same page. My name is Mamdod. I am an extremely old resident of the multi-verse that, up until recently, was by my own hand, confined to the ribbon island. You see, my memory eventually extinguishes the further I think back, but I evolved, in a way, on the ribbon island. I matured through the ages and developed an understanding of the ribbons. I respected them. I used them to learn. But surprisingly, I grew tired of my existence in that form. I was simply fatigued from directing the multiverse's citizens to their next ribbon destination, or explaining their options to them. So, I developed a game after asking the multiverse for offspring. This game would decide who would succeed me as ribbon guide. These offspring, or the closest thing to offspring, were created of the ribbons. Their names were Akal and Daebaugh. To skip to the relevant bits for the sake of this speech, the fact is that Daebaugh betrayed Akal and me by contorting and manipulating the rules of this game so that he didn't have to play fairly. So that he could become the ribbon guide and master of the ribbon island. During the attack on the Harbor, his brother, Akal was killed, which set off a timer that will eventually end in Daebaugh assuming the role of ribbon guide. This mostly brings us up to where we are now. We hope to destroy Daebaugh and prevent him from corrupting the ribbons and disrupting what they are, where they go, and what they do."

"The fact is my friends, that I made a mistake," Mamdod continued. "I left too much to chance. While I didn't know at that early stage of the universe that betrayal and corruption of that magnitude could take place, I should not have left so much to chance by blocking my memory during the game. Hindsight is a blessed burden, and I learned never to be so naive again."

The crowd was absolutely silent. Tens of thousands of Astraeans and friends were absolutely enthralled by Mamdod's admissions and humility. His admissions were faults that brought with them, an ensuing equality.

Mamdod shuffled his feet as if he were getting a better footing. His feet planted a little firmer, and he stood a bit more erect.

"And I am sorry, friends. I am sorry for the amount of death that has come to the Astraeans and some of our friends already. But let me say this. I will never say that I am sorry again. I will never say that I am sorry again, because I won't have to. I won't fail you again. I will never make the same mistake again. I am no god, nor am I any more powerful than any of you, but I will continue digging deep to search time and my soul for absolutely anything and everything I can muster to help defeat Daebaugh, and to protect our families and friends."

The eruption this time was the wildest of all so far, and the wave of sound that flooded the dome blistered Mamdod's face. He was taken completely by surprise and instinctively leaned back, but then had to step backwards off of the broadcasting disc. He looked back to Elcyd and Rigella with a gaping smile of surprise and gratitude. Elcyd nodded at him to respectfully acknowledge Mamdod's concern they had discussed while they were in his office. Mamdod had said exactly what he needed to, for his fellow Astraeans and their allies, but most importantly, for himself.

Chapter XXI
Secret Traditions

Carthal and Heersan looked at each other as they clapped along with every other being in the dome. Their mouths were gaping with grins of pride. Mamdod's existence, significance, and future since his departure from the island, had been largely nebulous to the majority of the Astraean community. The Astraeans were unsure of what he was capable of lending to their needs and most of their allies had only barely heard of him until recently.

That was no longer the case. He was needed and he was valuable. His ancient life was no longer broken into billions of pieces, shared a fraction at a time with those who had died. He was the oldest resident in time's neighborhood. The oldest citizen of the multiverse. People were as eager to learn from him as he was hungry to learn about everyone else. He was significant and wiser by far, than he ever was while on the ribbon island. And the intricacies of his knowledge and experience with the ribbons were only beginning to unfold.

Mamdod remained in the spot that he stepped back to, gazing up and around at his friends and fellow citizens of the multiverse, as they continued to clap. Only when the guests nearest to him and senior Astraean officials began approaching him to hug him, shake his hand, or pat him on the back, was his appreciation for the crowd disrupted.

For ages and epochs, Astraeans proceeded through their experiences with no answers to their most important questions. There were of course still lingering questions about the origins of the multiverse and what transpired between its start and Mamdod's awareness coming to fruition, but regardless, their oldest and most specific questions had been answered. In the time since Mamdod showed up at the Harbor, they knew more about Mamdod, how the Harbor got there, and how they came to be a species and race, consisting of all species and races. More than ever, the Astraeans felt united and empowered, under not just Mamdod's banner, but the banner held and waved by the entirety of the Astraeans as a whole. The fact that Mamdod was keenly aware that he was one of many holding that banner, made their realization that much more meaningful and powerful.

The applause from Mamdod's reception trickled down, but only after the crowd had become completely depleted of energy. They shouted and clapped, stomped and banged. Onlookers from high above looked down as it seemed he was approached by every person seated in the booths encircling the center platform. The energy was palpable. The thoughts of failure, death, destruction, and obliteration of the Astraeans and their allies, which had permeated the minds of so many recently, were for a moment, dissolved. For a moment, the essence and power of those terrible thoughts were reclaimed, restructured, and then used to mold substantiated hope, purpose and renovated strength.

It didn't stop there, however. Just as each person and being inside the dome at that moment thought that the energy levels had reached their climax of positivity, there was an extra item on the agenda. Another item kept in secret. Something else being kept secret from most Astraeans. Carthal and Heersan were two of the Astraeans that were in the dark as to what was about to happen.

When it seemed like the tens of thousands of Astraeans and guests had finished catching up and talking with each other after all of the presentations, Rigella approached the broadcasting disc once more.

"Friends," Rigella began, and then paused, waiting for the ambient sound to die down once more.

"Friends! Friends. Please take your seats one final time," she requested.

The sounds of shuffling legs and seats unfolding rippled through the dome. While waiting for the crowd to sit again, Rigella looked around to those nearest her. Many were puzzled. Their heads tilted with concern and curiosity.

"Please forgive us friends and allies, for we have one final thing to take care of during this Assembly. Many of you knew, or now know about, my ages-old friend, Akal. We traveled together for eons, along with our friends Heersan and Carthal. They are with us here today."

Carthal and Heersan's heads jerked to face each

other in suspicious shock. They initially had no clue as to why Lannya split off from them, but ideas were starting to creep in. Like being called out to make a speech and being completely unprepared, they both were swallowed by an awkward uneasiness. Their faces then relaxed slightly as they silently started to develop an inclination of what this was about.

"Carthal and Heersan," Rigella continued, "are amazing Astraeans. I personally have never known more loyal beings. To their friends, yes, but especially, to each other. They love us all, but by an unrivaled amount, love each other more than anything. They have experienced an extraordinary amount together. They have no memory of how they met, or what form or species they were in when they met. I can easily say that I am completely at a loss when trying to think of another love that immense, old, or true. And given the uncertainty that has transpired in the multiverse, these two friends of mine made it known recently that they wanted to marry. Not just marry, but have an Astraean wedding. We had to tell some white lies and hide some things to make it happen, but I'm here to tell you my friends, that after some incredibly amazing efforts, we Astraeans and ancient allies are here to help you realize your request. For the first time, in more years of the multiverse than I can remember, today, we are having an Astraean wedding. Your Astraean wedding."

As Rigella's last syllable escaped her lips, jarring metallic thuds popped and smacked along and around the outside of the dome. Something had unlocked, and was beginning to shift. Some small portions of the crowd, unaware of what was taking place, screamed at the vibrations and movement they began to witness and feel through their booths. The fearful noises died down quickly however from realizing what was happening, or by being informed by those that knew what was going on.

Slight seams began to appear and separate in the dome walls, revealing that the dome's hemisphere was made up of dozens of smaller sections that, when necessary, could open up and spread outwards like the petals of a flower. Very deliberately, these massive and substantial individual pieces of the dome opened up, exposing the interior of the dome to the vastness of the multiverse's outer space.

As the dome opened up, the Astraeans and their friends were given an extremely rare and unparalleled view of not only the surrounding Harbor, but the space around it. While the dome continued transforming, Rigella made a request of her friends.

"Please, Carthal and Heersan, please come join me down at the center ring!"

After the request was made, the fresh round of urging ruckus from the crowd caused Heersan to shake his head in amazement while wearing a large, embarrassed smile. He looked over at Carthal. He was just as stunned and surprised as Heersan was. After kneeing open the door to their booth, Carthal gestured for Heersan to exit. He did, and Carthal followed.

Slowly but surely, they made their way down, flight after flight of stairs. The stairs that ran along the interior of the dome were always there, but new, temporary ribbon stairs had been generated into place, between the now-separated sections of dome. Fellow Astraeans, citizens of the multiverse, and allies greeted, saluted, patted and slapped

Heersan and Carthal on their way down.

As they descended, an equally triumphant and charming march began to play. Musicians from around the multiverse had gathered around the outermost circle on the floor of the dome and began to play instruments of various types and configurations. After a short and powerful introduction, the music collapsed in volume, but then began to build again, as Carthal and Heersan made their way to the floor. This piece of venerable music, simply titled, "Astraean Wedding March," was an ancient and highly revered melody, known throughout the multiverse to Astraeans and non-Astraeans, alike.

It had been played far more often, long ago, when Astraeans were newer and smaller in number. Astraean weddings were fairly common in the early ages of the multiverse, but after many millions of years, they grew less and less common as Astraeans gained more lives, and as the logistics and coordination to properly stage an Astraean wedding increased. They hadn't taken place in so long, many Astraeans hadn't lived their last life and become an Astraean until long after the last wedding.

Many were in agreement, however. It was long overdue, and was a perfect time to stage one of the most extraordinary and uniquely Astraean events. An Astraean wedding celebrated not only the love shared between the pair of souls getting married, but the love they shared across many of the countless forms, genders, races, and species the two soulmates experienced.

As Heersan and Carthal reached the bottom of the stairs, the wedding march had swelled to an intoxicating and commanding volume. The previously unmatched volume of the crowd could only barely be heard. Banners, streamers, and confetti fell, flew, and blew through almost every imaginable cubic inch of air.

When the two engaged old souls breached the outer ring and began making their final few hundred steps to the center ring, the ends of the dome sections that were now pointed straight up into space, began erupting bursts of artificial ribbon energy. These bursts of energy launched out and exploded high above the Harbor, and were then attracted to and absorbed by the actual ribbons nearby. When each cloud of particles from the dome tips reached the actual ribbons, a bright flash would begin at the end of the respective ribbon web closest to the Harbor, and then ripple out into the abyss of the multiverse until they could no longer be seen by the naked eye. They were an announcement. A beacon of sorts, to the multiverse, that two of its own were in love, and were getting married.

The march had reached an energetic and cosmic crescendo. The timbre and tone coming from the large ensemble of musicians couldn't be defined as tonal or atonal. Dissonant or melodic didn't apply either. Powerful and passionate were the best terms to describe it. The final climax of the march coincided with Carthal's and Heersan's arrival at the center ring as the bursts of artificial energy from the dome sections increased in speed. The bright ribbon web flashes were becoming almost constant from the increased stimulation from the domes.

The music drove and pushed, and seemingly covered all sounds and genres from every intelligent culture in the multiverse. It was raw and rough. It was smooth and serene as well. The sound in their ears began to become muffled from the extreme volume. But then, in a split second of cosmic percussion, the march ripped the silent skies of space to its conclusion. The tens of thousands of Astraeans, friends and allies, were left for a moment, only with the diminishing reverberations of the completed march, and the shock waves of previously flashing ribbon webs.

After the sound was silenced, and the bursts of energy stopped, the interior of the Harbor, still with bloomed petals of dome sections, had become almost pitch-black with darkness, save the quietly confident and sufficient lights from the salted stars of outer space. It was very still and calm. The exact opposite of just moments before.

Rigella slowly stepped up to her pair of friends and joined their hands. She then leaned in slightly further and kissed Carthal on his cheek. Then, Heersan on his. Carthal bent his head back just slightly with amusement, being surprised by Rigella's rare display of affection towards them. Heersan allowed a grin to form. When Carthal and Heersan caught sight of Lannya, sitting one row back from the front row on the center platform, they squinted their eyes in false disapproval for her involvement in the surprise. Rigella then stepped back onto the broadcasting disc.

"We have not had an Astraean wedding in some time," Rigella began. "The amount of time since the last one is so great that it is almost as if there had never been any to begin with. To the large majority of us here, this is the first Astraean wedding they have ever witnessed, or at least, the first they've witnessed in as many years as times their hearts have beaten. To some, in a way, this could be thought of as the first Astraean wedding. The first wedding of a new Astraean culture. A redefined culture. But also, a culture that is remembering, and at the same time, learning, of their greatness. This wedding today, between you, two of my oldest friends, is a new beginning for you both of course, but for all Astraeans, and all of our friends. Know that and cherish that. Together, with you both, we all celebrate love, time and timeless love."

Rigella took a breath and motioned for Heersan and Carthal to drop their hands and step back away from each other slightly.

"Friends and allies," she continued. "We ask you now to assist us in uniting our friends in marriage. Please do what your ancestors did long ago for our oldest Astraean ancestors. Please bless this couple, my friends, as we witness their love through the ages."

Rigella quickly stepped off of the broadcasting disc and made a gesture to cue someone that couldn't be seen from their position. Immediately after making the gesture, the tops of the extended dome sections once again fired another burst of artificial ribbon energy into the skies. This time, instead of absorbing the energy and rippling light into the distance, the ribbon webs from all directions flashed brightly and then united into a tangled, but concentrated ball above the center of the Harbor. As soon as the ribbons joined into the ball, it then poured a large, wide and wavy beam of ribbon energy downwards, enveloping both Carthal and Heersan.

As soon as they were enveloped, their forms changed. They no longer appeared as Carthal and Heersan. Their souls reflected the forms of their last regular lives and then started cycling backwards. Slowly at first, and then rapidly. The speed at which their souls were remembering their past lives increased quickly but soon reached a constant speed and stayed there.

Shortly after this backwards cycling began, their changing forms stopped abruptly. Heersan and Carthal's souls had paused on one of the times they existed together as the same race in the same time from their regular lives. They loved each other then as well. Heersan and Carthal smiled quickly, recalling briefly their love from those lifetimes. As they did, the outer rim of the booth where the representatives of that race sat, lit up. The representatives then pressed a button in their booth that had also lit up, which fired shots from the tips of the dome sections once more. After these bursts were fired, they stimulated the ribbon webs as a whole, which engulfed the entire area in a microsecond of blinding light. This light not only traveled out into the immeasurable distance of space, but also down through the tangled ball and ribbon beam that encompassed Heersan and Carthal. Once that culture "blessed" Carthal and Heersan, the backwards cycling of their past lives resumed.

This happened not once, or 142,008 times, but over a million times.

Over a million.

Heersan and Carthal who had lived hundreds of millions of lives shared love for each other in over a million different individual lifetimes. Many of them were of the same culture, but from different times.

The upper Harbor dome had become a bewitching hemisphere of beauty and wonder as the faces of each Astraean and guest reflected the bright flash as each blessing came and went. As each blessing struck down and around

Carthal and Heersan, the crowd exploded into cheers. The music during the blessing ceremony helped mold the magic of the moment. Unlike the Astraean Wedding March, the blessing ceremony music was very calm and restful, but still soulfully penetrating and timeless. A low and calming drone sustained the ancient and primordial significance of the ceremony, while higher-registered instruments shifted their pitches frequently enough to sustain the span between the times Heersan and Carthal's past lives matched.

The music kept the passionate excitement alive in the hearts of all who were witnessing the event. The constant flashes from the ribbons down onto Heersan and Carthal kept each eye watered with emotion. The moment was the epitome of irreplaceable. This wedding was a supreme example of what Astraeans were about. There wasn't a soul, brain, heart or body there, that was in anyway impressed or pleased with itself or otherwise under any impression of superiority over anything or anyone. They had all come together as one, gargantuan display of humility, and love.

And though there was no witness to the wedding that was missing out on any of the sights or sounds, and even though there was no viewing angle better than another, there was one person whose viewpoint, both physical and mental, might have been coveted by the rest of the audience. Mamdod had slid out from the small group on the center platform, slipped through the rings of booths, and then climbed slowly but surely up along the dome wall stairs, and then to the top of one of the dome sections. After ascending to the extreme point of the dome section, very near where this tip was shooting its energy bursts, Mamdod then fingered and towed to scale the last few feet up to the mechanism firing the bursts. He then crawled out to the edge of the base supporting the mechanism, whipped his legs around and let his feet dangle free. With perhaps the best seat in the house, Mamdod felt closer to the ribbons than he did during any given chopped up memory, which was an intense sensation. He felt, oddly he thought, so proud of the ribbons, or blessed by them. He couldn't decide which. It wasn't a sense of sentimentality or anything else that could possibly be construed as reductive. It was a thankfulness and an empowerment. Though he was almost as old as time itself, he was still awestruck by the ribbons.

But there wasn't really any other option except to be humbled and passionate about the experience, and about what everyone was lending to. What was taking place inside that center platform was the ultimate example of what was glorious about the multiverse. Hours and hours ago, Heersan and Carthal had long flipped past their usual male human forms. They had flipped past female human forms. Kestrellian forms and Ontelbar forms. They flipped through races without gender and cultures with two dozen genders. Plants and animals, stars and planets, (condensed in scale by the encompassing ribbon). There were just too many to consider one being more important than another. They all glazed together and were indistinguishable, but at the same time, stood out and were equally revered by all that witnessed the event.

Not long after the blessings had begun, both Heersan and Carthal began showing signs of their emotions through their various lives. Regardless of the form they were in, most were very often decorated with glistening eyes, filled with, emptying, or refilling with, tears of joy. Nothing quite matched the display of true love like this. Almost every eye in the dome shared in those tears of joy, because honestly, anything with any amount of goodness in their being can never run out of appreciation for true love.

Ironically, the Astraeans, as well as their allies, seemingly lost track of time during the blessings. It was simply so overwhelming, no one really felt overwhelmed. Everyone was lost in what they were witnessing, they felt as if they had fallen out of time. That was essentially the case at the Harbor anyway, but even so, existence everywhere else seemed to come to a halt for Heersan and Carthal. Concerns for the speed at which it was taking place, or when it would be done, just didn't pollute their enjoyment of the moment. Right then, they all just lived in, and for the moment.

The amount of lives that were cycled through, between their soulmate matches, went by so inconceivably fast that the majority of the blessing ceremony seemed to consist just of matches and bright ribbon strikes. None of the onlookers experienced any mental or physical fatigue. Each of them were sustained by the honor of being a part of Heersan and Carthal's wedding.

The blessings did finally cease, however. What seemed like an undefinable amount of time was finally defined once the backwards cycling of their past lives stopped when their first soulmate matching was reached. The ribbon webs, concentrated ribbon mass above, and the beam enveloping Heersan and Carthal, flashed one last time and stayed lit.

The music that had recently reached a serene ending started back up with a new melodic push to accompany what was the final step of the blessings. This final blessing upon their souls, and their love for each other in spiritual form, was given by the ribbons themselves. The trumpeting and triumphant fanfare shouted at the stars as the ribbon beam began to recede up to the focused center of ribbon energy above. As it rose, it revealed Carthal and Heersan's first and oldest forms. That of pure, spiritual energy. There were not two separate forms of energy, however. There was only one. The combined energy of their married souls had been united.

The further the beam receded, up to the ball, and then out into the ribbon webs, the light emitted from Carthal and Heersan's souls grew larger and brighter. When the ribbons had returned to their normal distance, placement and brightness, Carthal and Heersan's souls popped in one final explosion of bright light, harmlessly blinding all within the dome for a moment. Once the light faded and every one's vision returned, down below, low in the center ring of booths on the floor, stood Heersan and Carthal in the forms they usually assumed.

They were married. Their souls and millions of lives had been joined by the love they already shared, millions of times before. But now also, by their friends and allies, and finally, by the multiverse itself.

The culmination of the numerous blessings, capped by such a display from the ribbons and multiverse, was immediately followed by another eruption of applause and admiration. Heersan and Carthal walked over to Rigella and sandwiched her face between their lips. She rolled her eyes while silently giving them a pass for so sloppily, but playfully, kissing her on the cheeks.

Afterwards, it was just like the ending of any other similar ceremony of union, from any given location in the multiverse. Family and friends gathered, greeted, hugged and kissed the newlyweds. Only, this took a much longer time. The group of family and friends was enormous in comparison. Not all Astraeans or allies waited their turn to congratulate Heersan and Carthal right at that moment, but while some did, Mamdod, Elcyd, Lannya, and Rigella took the opportunity to relax one last time and discuss what came next.

Chapter XXII
Comes with the Territory

Elcyd, Mamdod, Lannya and Rigella stood around a bit, waiting for Carthal and Heersan, but it was clear they were going to be a while. There was no shortage of people waiting to speak with them, and there didn't seem to be any unfinished preparations for the Ontelbar relief deployment happening the following day. As much as they hated to take away from the moment, though, everyone but Carthal and Heersan couldn't help but shift their minds towards those less peaceful matters.

The initial conversation after the wedding ceremony was sparse but sincere. Mamdod had rejoined Elcyd, Lannya and Rigella shortly before the end of the blessings. Mamdod was very quiet and reflective on what he had seen while high above. Lannya and Elcyd traded a few short but appreciative comments which quickly led to a noticeably upset Lannya.

"Lannya?" Elcyd attempted softly. "Is everything

ok?"

She swallowed.

"I just wish Akal was here to see them," she said clearly, showing no weakness in her voice.

Elcyd retreated slightly, knowing he had no suitable words for her. Instead he placed his hand on her back as Mamdod looked over at Lannya as well. He wished Akal was there, too. Lannya looked back at Mamdod with a face shimmering with wetness. They didn't need to say anything.

Looking back to Carthal and Heersan, Rigella added sorrowfully, "He would have absolutely loved this."

Rigella then stepped towards Lannya and put her hand on her shoulder. "We'd be honored to share whatever amount of pain you'd like to, Lannya."

The silence that followed signaled the end of the conversation about Akal. They all missed him, and the pain from his death not only remained, but stayed at the horizon of their collective vision. His death was one of many symbols that kept their focus trained on never allowing anything like that to happen again.

As the silence perpetuated, Rigella, Lannya, and Mamdod continued to look on at Heersan and Carthal being congratulated and embraced. Here and there, they would allow a smile to escape in admiration of their friends. Elcyd however, was distracted. His thoughts were hijacked more and more by the Ontelbar relief preparations, plans for Ontelbar monitoring, and the subsequent plans to pursue Daebaugh after that. After a few prolonged minutes of unbroken silence, Mamdod looked to Rigella and Lannya, and then Elcyd.

"What's on your mind, Elcyd?" Mamdod asked casually.

"Nothing. I'm just..." Elcyd's head shook slightly and quickly while absentmindedly fiddling with his lip. "I'm just thinking about tomorrow."

Rigella was listening and turned to him.

"The ADF will assist the Ontelbar brilliantly." She spoke softly but with a fortified sense of assurance. Rigella left no doubt in her statement.

"I know, I know," Elcyd replied honestly. His eyes still stared deadly ahead as he continued running through their preparedness in his head. "I'll be back in a minute," he spit out, as his eyes centered. "I want to go look through some of my notes."

He snapped himself erect, pulling himself off the edge of the booth he was leaning on. Before Rigella, Lannya, or Mamdod could inquire or probe further, Elcyd launched himself off the platform and settled into a brisk walk through the rest of the rings. Within moments, he was lost in the darkness of the outermost areas of the dome. The previously extended sections of the dome walls began folding down to their usual positions.

Elcyd slapped open a pair of doors that led from the upper dome to a perimeter service hallway. He walked briskly, though calmly. He just felt the overwhelming need to review his data, the historical Ontelbar data which was an immense help, the ADF plan, the numbers, and the timelines. The Astraeans were about to take another step that they hadn't ever taken before, and before their forces deployed to Ontelbar tomorrow, he just needed to run through everything again.

He hopped into the first elevator he came across and considered going to his office, but decided instead to go to engineering. There he could review not only his own notes, but ribbon data, ribbon systems, and fleet deployment preparedness information, as well.

"Engineering," he quickly blurted at the elevator. After an initial sound that resembled a quick expulsion of air, the elevator was off.

Floor after floor within only a few seconds, whizzed by, visible through the clear elevator doors. The speed of the elevator made it appear the various floors were being smeared on the doors. Offices, the library, small fabrication offices, the lobby, infrastructure, and others. At last, engineering finally arrived.

Elcyd began to step off before the elevator doors had even opened. He was on his way to the primary review center with the largest and most display screens. He was craving information, and wanted to review it all before he had any part in putting any of his people in harm's way when they deployed. Again, more brisk walking. His rapid but consistent gait allowed him a steady rhythm to internally hammer away thoughts to.

Ok, the carrier, the battleships, he rambled through his head. *Oh, I need to confirm the fighter numbers, ah, and the infantry. If we already have... deploy that many... we'll be left with...*

His thoughts remained uninterrupted and his attention didn't falter for the whole time he sped deeper and deeper into engineering, closer to the primary review center.

Engineering, as usual, was dark because of all the

displays in every room, in every nook, alcove and on every wall. Only periodic sconces, powered and lit by ribbon energy, brushed Elcyd's face with a spectral light as he walked by. That, and the flashing and changing data from the various displays.

It was quiet. Which was an extremely rare event. The veins and passages of engineering are always teaming with engineers, Harbor officials, Helpers, and more recently, ADF Officers. But it was extremely quiet now. All of engineering was still apparently in the upper dome for the aftermath of the wedding, or at least making their way back. It was empty, and Elcyd relished the emptiness, not because he didn't want to be bothered by anyone, but because he wanted to get to his information as quickly as possible.

As he approached the primary review center, he started to feel his adrenaline spike. Like an addict needing a fix, he just wanted to check over their deployment plans, one final time.

He took the last turn in the corridors and heaved a hefty breath in anticipation of finally reaching his destination. But something made his ears rise. Just before reaching the low, but wide archway leading to the primary review center, he began to hear broken chunks of speech that quickly ran together and formed understandable sentences. If it wasn't for what Elcyd immediately heard, he would have walked right in, disturbed the person speaking, and possibly missed what was being said. Instead, he stopped dead in his tracks and had to whip his momentum backwards to prevent himself from breaching the archway.

The unidentified voice addressed an unknown

listener in an agitated whisper.

"I haven't been able to uncover specifics, yet. The ADF leadership has the info locked down pretty tight. But they're deploying some kind of fleet tomorrow!"

Elcyd's thoughts raced by in a millisecond.

They? Who's this person referring to a they? If they're not part of they, then they're not part of us!

Elcyd's paranoia and fear combusted, which consumed his thoughts as he slipped up against a wall. He couldn't believe someone had already infiltrated the Harbor. *How long ago? Who else? What do they know? The Astraeans must have the answers.*

He first had to identify the person. Elcyd deduced, given the sound quality of the person's voice that they weren't facing in his direction. He took the opportunity to flip around, putting his stomach on the wall. He then slid over enough to where he could bend his head to barely look around the framing of the archway's threshold.

Elcyd saw the mysterious backstabber. A cold wave of mixed anger and surprise flooded Elcyd's veins, but that initial feeling was the only time he afforded those emotions any of his time. He had to act.

He was furious, but disciplined. Elcyd walked towards his target like a newly personified statue. His rigid frame coursed with violent intentions. The plan was already in his head. Being silent wasn't part of it. For his immediate plan, silence wasn't necessary.

"I know they're sending some kind of ground forces as well," this apparent traitor continued, "but I have no way to confirm whether or not it will be enough. If they have..."

Mid-sentence, he stopped speaking into the

transmission chip embedded into his palm, and began to turn slowly towards Elcyd.

"In the middle of engineering, Dawel? Really?" Elcyd lilted. The condescension was spread thick on his question.

"Shouldn't you still be at the after-party?" Dawel returned with an uninterested sarcasm.

With the last syllable of his question still on his lips, Dawel lurched for a weapon. He fired off multiple groups of energy bolts at Elcyd while also sprinting for another exit.

It didn't matter though, Elcyd had already activated his newly developed personal ribbon mail, similar in appearance to armors of various cultures throughout the history of the multiverse, but made out of ribbon energy. Strong and light, it didn't impede movement at all. It only complimented its wearer. Though Elcyd was struck by the energy bolts, he was unharmed. The personal ribbon mail absorbed the bolts. Before Elcyd took off after Dawel, he jumped to a command terminal.

"Defense alert level 1," Elcyd said clearly to the terminal. "Secure all engineering entrances, exits, and ribbon interfaces. Scramble and repeatedly encrypt all command information and commands at random intervals until released by voice command by Mamdod, Rigella or myself. Each random interval should be no longer than two minutes each. Send alert status to Rigella, Mamdod, engineering staff, and ADF Harbor Sentinels. Append note. Traitor cornered in engineering. Identified as Dawel. Attempting to apprehend. Please send assistance."

The terminal, already displaying a diagram of engineering, reflected the secured entrances and exits, as well as a command confirmation regarding command control. These security measures were part of the newly developed technologies and safeguards. Dawel's role, security access and system permissions prevented him from being privy to most of the new sensitive ADF data and developments, to include tactical planning and intelligence operations. Regardless, a mole sharing mere bits of data or hints at activity can sometimes be just as damaging.

Once Elcyd saw the confirmation of his commands, he sprinted off to find Dawel. The corridors in engineering are numerous, but from the primary review center, there were only a few initial paths one could take towards the entrances and exits. Elcyd also knew the Harbor better than anyone, save possibly Mamdod now that he had his memory back. Elcyd took off, confident that one way or another, Dawel would not escape.

Elcyd jogged, lightly and quietly as possible, in the center of the corridors where it was almost completely dark. The darkness was only barely diluted by the ambient light from the ribbon sconces and engineering displays. Though he was initially worried about the plan, and then struck with paranoia and fear at uncovering a mole, Elcyd was calm and confident.

He jogged slowly, pausing here and there to carefully examine corridor junctions, or to peer inside rooms that would make for effective hiding places. Looking for any sign of Dawel's path, Elcyd was hunting. And he was hunting in his domain. His home. His workplace. His everything. It was just a matter of time before Elcyd found his prey.

Though no help had yet arrived, probably due to grouping and coordinating, Elcyd assumed, he wasn't too incredibly concerned. Room after room, corridor after corridor, Elcyd hadn't come across any signs of Dawel's whereabouts. Until, out of darkness, came the sound of some form of electric feedback. Stopping to remain still while listening, Elcyd was able to hear that it was some form of voice transmission that was horribly harsh and choppy.

Elcyd then realized, *that's Dawel's transmission chip!*

Elcyd pushed off from the wall he had come to rest on and stalked the sound around corners and down corridors, which was then followed by a new scratch of sound. This new sound was what seemed like someone trying to crush a small piece of machinery. Dawel was trying to damage the voice transceiver in his palm. After a few additional hops, Elcyd had found Dawel.

As he stepped up to confront him, Dawel who had been distracted, turned to meet Elcyd's advance, but he had acted too slowly. Elcyd held a small ribbon cube in his hand. These cubes, a new development issued to senior Helpers, ADF Sentinels, and some Harbor officials, could slightly manipulate various physical forces and phenomena at the behest of the one holding the cube. While still holding the cube, Elcyd jerked his wrist and pushed his palm holding the cube in Dawel's direction. With the might of what appeared to be many hundreds of pounds of force, Dawel was slammed back up against a wall. With another flick of Elcyd's hand, he lifted his hand holding the cube up, and then slammed it down. The temporarily manipulated air around Dawel, controlled by the cube, slammed Dawel down flat against the ground with a violent smash. While still alive, Dawel was however pinned and completely at Elcyd's mercy.

Elcyd took a few steps towards Dawel and bent down at his knees. He leaned forward and to the side so that Dawel could look into his eyes.

"I don't know how long you've been doing what you're doing, or who you're involved with, but it stops, today," Elcyd calmly informed Dawel.

Dawel made no immediate statement in reply, nor flashed any signs of psychotic maladjustment. Dawel merely grunted under the pressure from the momentary force applied by the contained hunk of ribbon energy, controlled by the ribbon cube in Elcyd's hand.

As Elcyd examined Dawel more closely under the strain of the ribbon cube, a secure door near them clicked and unlocked. The ribbon barrier slid out of the way.

Mamdod rushed through the door first and slid to a stop just shy of Elcyd and Dawel. He breathed rapidly in the fearful awareness of the Astraeans possibly being infiltrated and the subsequent implications. Following closely behind Mamdod was Rigella, with a full complement of ADF Harbor Sentinels, as well as a few high-level engineers. As Rigella and the ADF Sentinels reached the scene of the apprehension, she quickly issued orders with a decisive might.

"Engineers, please confirm and ensure the security protocols Elcyd initiated are functioning as intended," Rigella began. "Sentinels, use the ADF-restricted corridors and ribbon transports to take Dawel to the new holding chambers for processing and questioning."

Being sure to make eye contact with everyone in the

vicinity, she issued a final command.

"Unless you or Mamdod feel differently," she said, beginning with a glance to Elcyd, "this should be considered an ADF-managed security event." She then looked to the engineers and Sentinels. "Until you hear differently from me, this incident should remain known only to those with clearances equal to that of myself, Mamdod, Elcyd, and the Sentinels. Understood?"

Rigella then returned the acknowledging salute given to her by the Sentinels. Looking to Mamdod and Elcyd, she saw no hesitation in their agreement on her appraisal of how Dawel was to be handled, or who should manage the situation. Rigella never showed any signs of not accepting input from her closest friends or, as dictated in the rules and laws establishing the ADF, the Harbor leadership. This incident was no different.

As the Sentinels started to restrain Dawel and prepare him for removal from engineering, Elcyd pressed on the ribbon cube in a particular way with his palm, releasing Dawel from its pressure. And to the surprise of Mamdod, Elcyd and Rigella, through the door sprinted Lannya, Heersan and Carthal. Their faces were covered in confusion and concern.

"Lannya? And you two? What are you doing here" Rigella asked the newlyweds, almost with an annoyed tone.

"We felt the alert," Heersan replied.

"Oh, right," Rigella remembered. "We recently gave them Sentinel-level clearance," she reminded everyone.

"Good to see you, too," Carthal added, flatly.

"Well, no, it's just... you shouldn't need to be worried with this right now. You just got married," Rigella explained.

"We just wanted to get married. Not leave the fight," Carthal clarified strongly and respectfully.

Rigella nodded as she, Mamdod, and Elcyd looked at each other and then turned towards Heersan, Carthal and Lannya, to silently welcome them over. They knew deep down that they never intended to exclude the married couple, or that Heersan and Carthal had any intentions of not remaining involved. They just maintained a relaxing illusion, if only for a few minutes, that their friends may be able to relax and have a normal peace, regardless of how short.

Carthal, Heersan and Lannya walked over and joined their friends as the doors slammed shut behind Dawel and his escorts.

"Ok," Elcyd said, resuming the business at hand. "I wasn't able to find out who he was talking with, or exactly what he knows, but Dawel was telling them about the deployment tomorrow."

"Well, it was probably the Quazlopian Miners he was talking with, right?" Lannya posed rhetorically to the group. "What did he say?" Lannya correctly assumed that the group needed whatever details Elcyd had.

"Just that we were deploying a fleet of some kind and that there may be ground troops involved," clarified Elcyd. "I did hear him say specifically that he didn't have all the details or exact numbers because we had the information locked down."

"Just rumors? No fleet specifics or deployment location?" Rigella questioned in exasperation, with the hope of relief.

Elcyd shrugged with doubt, unaware of how much information was shared.

"Well, he knew we were at Ontelbar recently because he's the one Lannya spoke with while we were there. So seeing that he, rather than the Miners, has been tipping off Daebaugh, and if he knew we're planning to reinforce Ontelbar," Heersan began, "then Daebaugh might also know that we've asked them to monitor the area for us."

"We need to get that relief fleet to the Suburb as soon as possible," Carthal hotly interjected, with memories of Orn still fresh in his mind.

"That's what we're going to do," Rigella decided, more so than agreed. "I'll have the Readiness Officers report on their status and what's left for them to do. Depending on what they say, I will tell them to leave for Ontelbar immediately."

Carthal tensed up before sighing heavily through his nose, hoping the Ontelbar could get the help they needed before it was too late.

"Secondly," continued Rigella. "We need to extract as much information as possible from Dawel, as quickly as possible."

The entire group offered no immediate reply as Rigella's eyes shook with burning anger.

"We will set the precedent on how traitors are dealt with," Rigella added. "We have never had to deal with such things before, but now that we have to, let us make it perfectly clear how we handle deception and betrayal."

She let her words soak into every one's ears so that there was no doubt as to how she felt.

"I'm going to check in with my Readiness Officers,"

Rigella began to conclude. "I'll leave it up to Elcyd, but if the rest of you want to start questioning Dawel, I'll join you afterwards."

She waited a quick moment for any comments, and then snapped around and marched out of engineering.

After Rigella had taken her leave, Mamdod felt compelled to address the rest of the group.

"I would just like to say that I agree, absolutely, with what Rigella just said. But please, friends," Mamdod implored, with the most staunch and ominous tone he had yet used. "Please, let us not take steps we cannot return from, or commit actions that tarnish our souls, with our methods or deeds. We are newly threatened, and newly responding, with a new military. We must proceed now, with more discriminating concern than ever before."

There was no ambiguity in Mamdod's words, and they were all clearly understood by all those around him. The group knew to what Mamdod was referring. They had to be careful on how they underwent Dawel's questioning. No one was under the impression that they, or Rigella, given her passionate anger before she left engineering, had any intention of crossing the line of ethics when questioning their prisoner. They had a keen understanding of the ethical implications, as well as a keen respect for Rigella and her methods. Never before was a reminder of what the Astraeans were, and what they were not, unequivocally critical.

Chapter XXIII
Detention

The room that they took Dawel to was recently altered to be a holding room for those detained by the ADF Harbor Sentinels. There were dozens of physical restraints made of numerous materials connected to the floor, the walls, and draped from various locations on the ceiling. In contrast to the elegance of the majority of the Harbor, this was an absolutely practical room. There was no old or romantic appearance to it. It was meant to accommodate detainees of various species and sizes, and needed to minimize as many strengths that any particular species may have, and maximize their weaknesses.

In addition to the variety of physical restraints, there were numerous nozzles sticking out of recessed paths in the floor, ceiling, and walls. These nozzles slid along the paths as programmed, and shot beams of ribbon energy to their matching receiver at the other side of the room, in the floor, or in the ceiling. These beams were to be used in conjunction with physical restraints, and would prevent any spiritual manipulation of the detainees' forms or their abilities, and disabled their ability to call upon the ribbons in any way to change their form, that is, if the detainee was an Astraean, or had any Astraean-like abilities.

The final feature of the room was not a feature at all. There was no visible exit, entry, window, hole, or other break in the wall. There was seemingly no way to enter or leave the room. Unbeknownst to a detainee, however, was an unseen and constantly moving ribbon pad on the floor of the room. Just outside the wall of the enclosed room was a linked ribbon pad. Those who wished, or more appropriately, those who were able to leave or enter the room, stood on the pad outside of the room, at which point they would be shifted by the ribbon pad from outside the room to the interior of the room, or, vice versa.

This is where Dawel was being held.

While sitting precariously on a conventional metal stool, his feet, slightly off the floor, were restrained by stiff rubber cuffs wrapped around his ankles, which were molded onto imposingly thick chains. The chains were then pulled tight and secured to some of the various connectors on the floor, causing his legs to be stretched out from him, and spread far apart. His hands and arms were restrained in much the same way. His wrists were also in cuffs, attached to chains, and in turn, attached to the walls. His arms were stretched out tightly behind, and away from him. He was forced by the restraints and chains to sit on the stool, and lean back slightly, so that he would not have the full capacity of his strength or center of gravity as he might have if he were standing.

It wasn't entirely necessary to have his hands and feet pierced by ribbon beams, given that he was in a human form, but they were, just for good measure. They didn't cause any pain. The most important ribbon restraints were thick beams that pierced and passed from the ceiling to the floor, through the center of his chest and down through the top of his head. Again, while not necessary at the moment, the ribbon restraints were precautions only to scramble any possible manipulation of ribbon energy he may try to muster.

Along the shadowed edges of the room, stood a perimeter of ADF Harbor Sentinels. Each Sentinel presented an identical ribbon rifle, capable of firing bolts of ribbon energy. The rifles were also capable of generating physical, and electrical projectiles, toggled by the operator, and generated by the primary ribbon energy magazine. Given the type of target, the Sentinel could quickly change the type of projectile needed, as well as toggling a safety, and the rate of fire.

Every Sentinel also carried a sidearm, but the type of sidearm varied wildly from one Sentinel to another. The sidearm was left to that particular Sentinel's discretion, after a mild approval process by their superior. The idea was that no Sentinel would ever be unprepared for any type of combat.

The outward appearance of the Sentinels was clean and sharp. Their uniforms, a combination of mostly dark blue with lighter blue seams and accents, were simple and comfortable. They were made from an artificial ribbon energy that could change in size and configuration as the Sentinel needed, if a change in the uniform's shape was required. The uniform could not adapt to any and all forms however. Only some of the more common forms were provided for in their construction, with new forms being accommodated in the uniform's options, from time to time. And seeing that the uniforms were made from an artificial ribbon energy, the entire uniform emitted a very slight, but visible glow. This in no way added to the effectiveness of the uniform, but was simply a byproduct of the material.

Atop each Sentinel's head, rested an inconspicuous helmet. Made from similar materials as the uniforms, but more firm, these helmets also covered the eyes of the Sentinels with a darkened and attached visual display. While the Sentinels wore these helmets, their eyes would revert to a state of ribbon energy so that they could securely interact with the display, which was in turn linked to ADF-specific areas of engineering, as well as mobile ADF Operations if away from the Harbor, or usually, ADF Operations based at the Harbor. The display provided any and all information accessible by a Sentinel, and allowed them to interact with each other, silently if need-be. When wearing the helmets, those looking at the Sentinel could see a faint hint of the brightly glowing ribbon energy of their eyes. When not wearing the helmet, their eyes would return to whatever state their form would normally have.

The Harbor Sentinels had quickly gained a reputation of being beyond lethal, but extremely humble and respectful. At no point had a Sentinel ever acted in a way to make any civilian Astraean doubt their strength, intelligence, integrity, or honor. The majority of the initial

Sentinel force had been formed out of the initial wave of eager and willing ADF recruits. They had been tested and trained, and then trained and tested again, in numerous rounds of review and examination. These Sentinels were the absolute last line of Harbor defense.

The individual Sentinel's awards and decorations were worn in a compact and symmetrical location at the center, top section of the Sentinel's back. This was to instill a sense of unity in purpose, anonymity, and humility to the Sentinels when interacting with each other, or while on duty, as well as convey a sense of being a single, powerful unit to onlookers. Only when a Sentinel had come off duty, or left a conversation, did their individual achievements become noticeable and appropriate for conversation when the viewing of their backs was no longer a conscious concern. When in a combat zone or combat readiness posture, the uniforms worn by Sentinels differed in some ways, but most noticeably, their awards, rank and other distinguishing insignia were left off, in lieu of personally identifying information being available to each Sentinel through their secure visual displays. The only other distinguishing feature on their normal dress, were small, golden hash marks above their decorations, indicating how long they had served as a Sentinel.

These capable and respected Sentinels are what Dawel saw surrounding him as he would lift or move his head the slight amount he was able. It was an intimidating sight to Dawel, and would be to anyone. Their glowing eyes behind their black display visors were especially chilling. Though any onlooker could make some fairly safe assumptions as to what Dawel might have been feeling or thinking, Dawel however, showed no outward signs of fear, discomfort, or intimidation. As he assessed his surroundings, he was calm, and quiet.

Without any indication it was about to happen and with no accompanying sound, the room flashed and was consumed entirely by light, but only for a moment. The light then retracted rapidly into the temporarily lit ribbon pad on the floor. On top of it, stood Elcyd, Mamdod, Lannya, Carthal and Heersan.

Dawel strained to raise his head up as much as he could, against the force of the ribbon restraint running through his head. He managed to do so just enough to identify who had just appeared. A side of his mouth twitched slightly. He had wondered how much longer it would take for them to arrive.

Heersan, Carthal, and Lannya stayed where they arrived for the moment. Elcyd took the lead in moving closer to Dawel with Mamdod following, but at a distance.

"Dawel, our cherished ribbon cartographer prodigy," Elcyd let drip with sarcastic disappointment.

Dawel looked up at Elcyd. His eyes were relaxed and cold.

Elcyd looked back quickly to Mamdod and the others to see if they had any comments before continuing. They stood quietly, and motionless.

"We're going to find out who you were talking to," Elcyd continued. "But, it doesn't really matter, because I heard what you said. You don't even know anything."

Dawel let loose a hearty chuckle.

"You don't know what I know," Dawel continued through a muffled chuckle.

The ribbon restraint running through his head affected his speech slightly. After swallowing and attempting to adjust his jaw, he resumed.

"You all only know of your perfection, beautiful things, and your piety. You're all always too pleased with yourselves to notice that other things go on around you. You're too busy worshiping the concept of fire to realize you're burning."

Mamdod's eyes met Elcyd's as he turned around. They exchanged glances of total confusion.

"The Astraeans are part of all of those, as you say, other things, Dawel," Carthal began with a purposeful emphasis on *other things*, before being interrupted by louder, mocking laughter from Dawel. "We notice and respect everything, because without all those differences, we are nothing."

Heersan slowly walked up to Dawel with crossed arms, for no other reason but that he needed to see him up close.

"Oblivious to oblivion," Dawel added. No longer smirking, grinning or chuckling, he had returned to his initial state. His eyes looked up, coldly, at nothing, but continued to speak.

"Oblivious to oblivion. Perpetuating the unfounded hope of purpose. Shining light where none should exist."

Heersan looked around the room at his friends, with no idea of any kind as to what Dawel was referring to.

An hour or so passed, mainly consisting of silence, or short exchanges between the Astraeans in the room. They were all at a loss on how to interpret what Dawel had said up to that point, but Elcyd had plenty of other questions.

Before he could immediately ask more, however, the room was again engulfed in light by the ribbon pad activating.

Rigella had arrived.

Dawel strained to lift his head up once more, and after seeing Rigella, exclaimed, "Ah! Now we can really get started!"

Lannya stepped over to Rigella, leaned in and softly brought her up to speed.

"Elcyd's the only one that's spoken to him," she whispered, while keeping her eye on Dawel. "He's been saying we're oblivious to others and that we shine light where we shouldn't. We don't know what he knows. That kind of stuff."

Rigella looked at Lannya, pulled her head back and dipped her eyebrows in the shared confusion in the room. She then lightly patted Lannya on the back to thank her for filling her in on what she had missed.

Rigella locked her hands behind her and walked over to Dawel's feet. She looked at Elcyd and lifted her head, silently saying she'd like to give the questioning a try.

"You don't need to pretend or lie, Dawel," Rigella began. "We know you were talking with the Quazlopian Miners."

Dawel then laughed at Rigella for the first time. It was a substantial and sane-sounding laugh. Not maniacal or exaggerated. It was simply confident and arrogant. There was no fear in his voice or his demeanor.

"Now you've just confirmed you really have no idea what's going on," Dawel exclaimed with amusement.

Rigella's head tilted. Her eyes flicked across the room to Elcyd and Mamdod in an attempt to see if they showed any signs of knowing what he was talking about.

Elcyd, who had been rubbing his chin while trying to decipher the enigmatic statements, accusations and denials, whipped his head up with an epiphany. He looked to Mamdod, Rigella, and then back to Dawel. He leaned down slightly and asked his next question.

"You work for Daebaugh, don't you?"

"DO NOT CALL HIM DAEBAUGH!" Dawel shouted aggressively, with a dark hate none of them had yet heard come from him. It wasn't just aggression or hate, it was an obvious and personal defense of Daebaugh and his cause.

Elcyd jumped back, only out of surprised instinct and reflex. He wasn't expecting such a reaction. Rigella stood in place, steadfast, as Dawel tested all of the restraints with the most force he had exerted up until then.

"He rejects and abhors that name assigned to him by the multiverse, by the ribbons, by the Astraeans," Dawel continued, in a disgusted and agitated growl.

"His name is Einar. And we are his Einarians," Dawel began to proudly perform. "We will no longer hide in the shadows, and we will no longer be your inferiors. No longer will anyone in the multiverse be your inferiors. You and your ivory towers will burn, blister, bake and boil!"

Dawel spit as he strained to get out every last syllable for his contempt for the Astraeans. He was not going to breathe again until he got it all out.

As Dawel continued grunting and testing his restraints to no avail, Rigella walked over to Carthal, Heersan, and Lannya and then motioned for Elcyd and Mamdod to join them. As they approached, Lannya pressed a button on the wall, which dropped a thin dome of ribbon energy over Dawel. The small dome was visible from the outside, but not from the inside. Dawel couldn't see it. It served to block the sound between each side of the barrier.

"I suspected he could have been talking with Daeba..., I mean, Einar," Elcyd began, flippantly correcting the name to Einar. "I suspected he could have been talking with Einar, but I didn't think we could have been infiltrated so easily."

"Well, it makes sense," Rigella replied. "We know that Einar has been plotting ever since Mamdod sent him and Akal into the multiverse, so he's had plenty of time to plan and infiltrate. Having a spy is almost a forgone conclusion."

"We must assume there are others," Lannya proposed. "Even if there aren't, we must develop a way to confirm that."

"I agree," Heersan concurred.

"Let's see what other info we can get out of him," suggested Carthal.

"Speaking of which," Mamdod jumped in with. "Doesn't he seem to be offering up some of this info pretty easily?"

There was no disagreement.

"I'm not comfortable with that," Mamdod concluded.

"Well, as long as we're not presented with an immediate need to stop, I would suggest we keep talking to him, to see how much he'll keep talking," Elcyd proposed.

"I think so, too," replied Rigella. "Let's get whatever we can, while we can. We can sort it, decipher it, and assimilate it all, later."

The group traded nods and had no other comments. Lannya pressed the button to lift the sound barrier dome away from Dawel.

"Alright, good!" Dawel shouted as the group of Astraeans gathered around him. "When is the fun really going to start?"

"What fun, you mumbling peon?" Rigella immediately snapped back.

"The questions! The torture, of course!" Dawel whispered back with a gritty rasp.

Rigella leaned over and stabbed a stare into his eyes that he wouldn't forget.

"Listen to me, and listen to me like you've never listened before," she began with brutal reality. "You will not be tortured. We have no need to torture. We do however, have plenty of methods to steal the information from you. Take it. Tear it. To extract the information we need, from you. In a way, it's even more fun for us, because we don't have to waste our time to retrieve it. We don't have to wait for you to grow weak from pain and fatigue. And you don't get to feel like you protected the information or held out. We can just take it from you, whenever we like. You have absolutely no say in the matter. You're just a worthless, nameless, slab of data."

Dawel started laughing, seemingly not bothered by anything Rigella said.

"Oh! That was scary! I love it!" Dawel replied, now beginning to sound slightly deranged.

Rigella joined him with similar-sounding laughter in an attempt to mock him.

Dawel quit laughing as he stared at her with an almost tangible annoyance.

"We haven't even asked you any real questions yet, have we?" Rigella asked, reinforcing her statement about not needing his cooperation.

"We just wanted to see what you'd give up immediately," Rigella continued. "Oh well, we can fire up our extraction tools."

Chapter XXIV
Sunset

The room flashed quickly once again. A new Sentinel had arrived. He marched rapidly over to Rigella and handed her a display pad before stepping back to attention. Rigella zoomed through the message.

"Something wrong, Commander?" Dawel asked, with a twisted tune.

Rigella looked up. Her eyes zipped back and forth as she calculated her next action.

"Sentinels," she called, addressing the Sentinels that were standing guard. "The half of you closest to me, come with us. The rest of you, remain here and guard Dawel until further notice. Everyone else, out."

While everyone in the room stepped onto the ribbon pad, save half of the Sentinels present, Rigella waited for everyone else, and remained cool and collected during the entire interruption. After Rigella finished watching the ribbon pad fill up, she turned a last time to Dawel and found him slipping her a grotesque grin, spawned from the excitement of what he thought would be another one-sided attack on the Harbor.

But instead of joining everyone on the pad, she took a step back towards Dawel.

"Rigella?" Carthal asked in confusion.

She took a slow second to plant herself in place and then smiled back at Dawel. Her own dark mind that had recently been obsessing with as many ways to efficiently kill as possible, was now taking the time to reciprocate the obscene and sadistic silence from Dawel. Rigella was a warrior. She was a Central Commander of semi-immortal warriors that fought more wars and battles than there were molecules of anything. She not only took the poor attempt at intimidation from Dawel, but welcomed it, and with a quick twist of demented thrill, she was flooded with the thirst to outdo him.

It was enough to give him pause. Not only was he momentarily caught off guard by such a sadistic glance from Rigella, but it was the fact that, despite the urgent message from the Sentinel, she had time to sit and stare. She had time because she was confident.

"We're ready this time," she whispered to Dawel. Each syllable slipped off each other like old grease draining from a pan.

She never took her eyes off of him as she walked backwards to the ribbon pad. The Sentinels and her friends parted slightly to make room for her. Her hateful and bleak sneer remained unmolested and undiminished.

Then, with a quick flash, Rigella and the rest exited,

and found themselves standing outside the room. Rigella stepped out from the group and turned to address her friends and the Sentinels, in an impressively rapid return to her typical personality. Those who knew her best tried their best to refrain from exchanging mildly concerned glances with the others over Rigella's abrupt shift in disposition.

"I was just handed a message saying that our outer beacons have detected a sizable radar blob headed straight for the Harbor," Rigella informed calmly.

"He was just rambling and stalling!" Heersan realized.

"It would seem so," Elcyd agreed.

"Let's get to the control center and try to identify who and what is approaching," Rigella stated with authority. "Depending on what we find, we may need the convoy slated for Ontelbar to remain here until this threat is addressed. We were anticipating another attack on Ontelbar, but it looks like the fight is coming here, first."

Carthal began to step forward but stopped out of respect for his friend's position and orders. He did however have to say something.

Rigella, we committed and promised to send..." Carthal attempted before Rigella stepped back in.

"I know, Carthal, I know," she said with a firm understanding. "My priority right now, is the absolute safety of the Harbor and our people. I'm sure you have to appreciate that."

Rigella let her statement stand alone for a moment. She was definitely issuing a command to the Sentinels, but it was also partially a rhetorical statement for Carthal. She was respectfully suggesting to her friend that he step back and look at the situation objectively. Carthal offered no additional retort or argument, though he visibly wanted to.

"We will not go back on our word or abandon the Ontelbar. I just need to confirm what we're dealing with, and then we'll go from there," she reassured, and reiterated to Carthal. His chest, previously heaving with indignation, began to subside a bit. He nodded in hesitant acknowledgment at Rigella.

"Ok," Rigella finalized. "Let's go."

* * *

Rigella, Mamdod, Elcyd, Carthal, Heersan and Lannya, together with the group of Sentinels, all quickly made their way from Dawel's holding room. They rushed and trampled up a dozen flights of stairs, from the bottom of one of the outermost sections of the Harbor, up to the first available exit.

There were no means of quicker ribbon transport, or any automated transit up through the depths of this far-removed section of the Harbor, which was by design, and due to recent necessity. Movement within the detention building had intentionally been designed to be slow. Aside from the ribbon pad immediately outside the primary holding room, there was no other ribbon technology inside the structure. Not until someone left the building and crossed a bridge, would they reach a section of docks that eventually connected to the main Harbor complex.

The group slammed the door of the exit open. As soon as they stepped through the threshold, Rigella began jogging. Everyone else joined in. They weren't sprinting and they weren't panicking, nor did Rigella wish to incite panic. Rigella just didn't want to waste any time getting to the control center.

They arrived at the bridge soon enough, and began to cross. As they jogged along, Carthal looked over the side and could see that the general activity along the docks had become more fluid and orderly. It looked as if everyone was moving with purpose. He wasn't sure what announcements, if any, had been made to the general population, but from what he could see, it looked as though there was a sense of urgency in the crowd below. The amount of personal ships of various origins zipping by seemed to increase as they ran.

When they finished crossing, Rigella ran over to a nearby terminal. With the tap of a few commands, a newly installed, compact imaging panel slid up from a storage compartment in the section of docks they were at. The imaging panel popped out, and quickly threaded together a temporary transport out of ribbon energy. The Astraeans, except for Rigella, filed into the first one. The panel then created another one that the accompanying Sentinels entered. After Rigella confirmed they were all in a transport, she tapped a last command to stow and secure the imaging panel back into that section of dock's storage compartment. Rigella then jumped into the first transport, and off they went.

The two transports sped along and above the path that had recently been sectioned off in the center of the various streets and docks of the Harbor. While transports flew the twenty or so feet above the path, the lines designating the path below lit up in a bright orange to make those in the vicinity know to be aware of vehicles overhead.

The ride to the control center in the main Harbor

structure was quiet. Everyone was contemplating and planning. Some, were just waiting. Looking out through the transport windows, the Astraeans and Sentinels took in the sights and sounds of everything they held dear and all, whether they knew it or not, shared thoughts of nothing being more precious to them than their friends and allies.

As they approached the main Harbor structure, the transports joined up with a recently established ADF service ribbon that flowed into an upper area of the building, just below the upper dome. When the transports came to a rest, Rigella was the first to exit. She walked to the nearest terminal and waited for her friends and Sentinels to exit. Once everyone had gotten out, she tapped a command to produce another ribbon imaging panel which then reincorporated the temporary transports, bit by bit, back into the ribbon panel. Once the energy from the transports had been reincorporated, the imaging panel folded down and disappeared into the floor. Without saying a word, Rigella then took the group's lead and led them to the control center.

The control center was pulsating and flowing with perfectly coordinated activity. Engineers, ADF intelligence, senior ADF Officers, and Sentinels. Everyone was ready to evaluate the possible threat. The oldest son of the multiverse, Mamdod, was focused. The first Astraean to arrive at the Harbor, Elcyd, no longer doubted their preparations. Rigella, the Central Commander of the Astraean Defense Force, had every confidence in the ADF, and the work put into its creation by so many. Lannya, the wife to Akal, a murdered ribbon prince, was resolute and eager to shift the balance in this war. And two of the most renowned

Astraeans, Carthal and Heersan, were renewed and fortified by their recent marriage. Neither of them ever felt stronger or more capable.

Rigella first needed to make an important announcement to those in the control center. She did so after initiating a broadcast module from the nearest terminal.

"ADF and Harbor personnel, this is Central Commander, Rigella," she announced with clear authority. "Be aware that former ribbon cartographer Dawel is being held at this time on suspicions of espionage. Effective immediately, he has been stripped of any and all privileges and access that his former position carried with it. Please inform your subordinates, where appropriate, through our chain of command. If any of my direct reports present have any questions, please pose them to me after we have addressed this most recent radar contact."

Rigella made her way straight for the ADF Deputy Radar Commander-in-charge, who had already begun making his way to her, as well.

"What's the latest on these contacts?" Rigella asked of the Deputy Radar Commander.

"The blob hasn't breached the outer perimeter beacon just yet," he answered swiftly. "It's still reporting the contact, but the integrity of the contact, while clean, is frequently changing. What we thought might have been a pip of only a few large contacts, seems to be numerous smaller ones, flying in close proximity."

Rigella took a moment to look at a radar display.

"Whatever this is, seems to be approaching at a steady clip," she observed.

"We believe so, yes," the Deputy confirmed. "We've also detected that there are some similarities between the ambient energies given off by these contacts, and that of the ship we destroyed when Dae..., excuse me, Einar, attacked."

"Thank you, Deputy," Rigella acknowledged. "Please resume your monitoring of the contact and report any changes."

"Yes, Commander," the Deputy responded.

Rigella turned to her friends.

"It seems Einar is indeed wanting to pay us another visit," she began.

"Possibly," Elcyd added curiously. "But why not make any attempt to jam our radar?"

"They must not have known about our new technologies, or about the radar, at least," considered Heersan.

"Or," Carthal proposed, "they knew about it, or found out too late, and couldn't come up with a way to counter it in time."

Mamdod then externalized a very comforting thought.

"Then they probably also don't think we have any realistic means to meet them in battle, if that's what they're coming for."

"Hmm, yes," Lannya hummed in affirmation. "Elcyd said he heard Dawel say just that we have some forces ready for deployment. No numbers or details."

"He must have been in engineering during the whole presentation before the wedding," Rigella assumed.

Rigella caught Mamdod allowing a smile to creep up.

"It sounds like Dawel was acting alone. They have no idea what they're flying into," Lannya surmised with a reserved chuckle. "Surely if anyone in here was in on it, we'd be in a much different situation."

It was an unspoken feeling of relief as they all seemed hopeful that they had the advantage.

"Regardless, we need to be careful with our sensitive information and discussions until we can do a thorough security review of our personnel after this is over," Rigella clarified. Everyone nodded quickly and heartily in agreement. She then gestured for the Harbor Defense Deputy-in charge to approach.

"Make a Harbor-wide announcement," she began to order, "that all civilian Astraeans should return to their residences in preparation for a possible attack, and specifically say that ADF leadership is confident that the threat will be met, and dealt with, successfully."

Some of the group looked up or back to Rigella. Their expressions were unsure of Rigella's certainty with her claims.

"I am confident, and I will not have our people experience any more of the fear they felt when Einar attacked us the first time."

There was no argument. They were only concerned at the presumption of superiority over the mostly unknown force that was approaching.

Rigella continued with her orders for the Defense Deputy.

"Once this suspicious contact breaches the outer beacon perimeter, initiate the protection barriers between all other interior beacons, and temporarily suspend all ribbon arrivals and departures, as well as any atmospheric flight in and around the Harbor. Immediately afterwards, activate the new ribbon shield, and ready all Harbor turrets and defenses."

"Yes, Commander," the Defense Deputy replied.

"Finally," Rigella began to add. "Have the Ciconal and Stellar Secondary Commanders, on my order, have each and every vessel we have sufficiently crewed and equipped, put on alert. Confirm that all information we have on these contacts is current and shared with them, and updated at their requested frequency. Tell them to take all necessary measures to prepare for a defense of the Harbor, while maintaining their hidden status behind our security barrier, for as long as possible."

"Yes, Commander, right away," the Defense Deputy obliged once more.

Once the Defense Deputy turned to take care of his orders, Rigella turned her attention back to her friends.

Mamdod bent down slowly and back up in a stretch. Carthal took a visibly large breath and was extremely slow with the exhale.

"Good, good," Elcyd said softly, feeling as if they were ready.

"I would rather have an element of offensive surprise, and send some of our forces out to meet them," offered Rigella to her friends, "but there wasn't enough time, so I'll gladly take the element of defensive surprise."

There was a bit of confidence floating throughout the room, but mostly, the room was filled by the encouragement of knowing they were far more prepared than they ever had been before, for anyone, or anything. There was a peace in their awareness and preparation, that some may consider as being more powerful than an unwanted result of any given situation. After Einar's original attack, the Astraeans deserved to have a little confidence this time.

Where knowledge of war and battle lived in the minds of each individual life, across the millions of lives experienced by each Astraean, it had always been far removed from the overarching Astraean consciousness. War was always something that happened to a *single* species on a *single* planet, where people lost *single* lives. Death had since come to the Astraean existence when Einar attacked, but they were now equipped to hopefully prevent it from happening again.

The room was quiet and vigilant. The radar continued being monitored while quiet conversations between various Harbor and ADF staff took place. Rigella had begun walking throughout the control center, answering questions, giving and confirming orders, and checking on the status of the Harbor defenses and fleet.

Breaking the silence, came an update on the contact from a Harbor radar official.

"The approaching radar mass has breached the outer beacon. Bearing and velocity remain unchanged."

A different voice then made an announcement on a defensive change.

"Beacon protection barriers activated. Until further notice, all ribbon arrivals and departures, have been halted, as well as Harbor atmospheric flight."

The room then slowly began to light up in a dull blue as the Harbor's ribbon shield powered into place. As the shield formed and congealed, the initial wave of light from its activation, subsided.

"Ribbon shield activated. All Harbor defenses, online," a final and different voice declared over the control center's communications.

Rigella then spoke to the room.

"Alright, ADF and fellow Astraeans. Here comes a test that we are now prepared to take. Report all changes to the approaching contacts and maintain communications silence unless related to this, or any new, threats."

The control center immediately dropped to a hush of nothing, and became the quietest it had been since Rigella had arrived. Only the slight hum of equipment and displays could be heard, just under the radar sounds and ADF communications.

"Radar contact is changing," a radar analyst began to report calmly. "The larger mass has dissolved into multiple smaller blips, Commander."

"Well, they must really want to get here. They're trying to dodge the beacons," Mamdod proposed quietly to Elcyd.

"When the larger blips started breaking into multiple contacts, Commander," continued the ADF radar analyst, "the total contacts numbered eight-six-zero. Eight hundred and sixty. Total contacts reported after passing the initial beacon protection barrier is eight-two-two. Eight hundred and twenty-two, Commander."

"Thank you. Continue monitoring and report changes in contacts," requested Rigella. She then stepped back and continued watching the various displays with Carthal, Heersan and Lannya.

"The barriers are working. That's great," Lannya

offered.

"Yes," Rigella confirmed reservedly while maintaining sight on the primary radar display. "But if any of their pilots or leaders are worth anything, they'll adapt and quickly learn to dodge them."

"Contacts have breached the next beacon protection barriers. Total contacts have been reduced by two."

Carthal looked at Heersan and shrugged, disappointed that the approaching forces did in fact seem to learn and adapt.

Over the next hour, very few voices were heard. That was mostly reserved for the occasional updates on the approaching radar contacts. As they approached and met each subsequent beacon protection barrier, the total contacts remained predominantly the same. A few more contacts were eliminated, however. But the barriers were largely seen as doing their job, especially for their first test. Each contact eliminated was one less attacker an Astraean had to risk their life fighting against.

By the time the contacts reached the last beacon barrier, the total number of contacts had been reduced to 798. Rigella, as well as the rest of the room were glad to have had the total number reduced, though they wished it could have been reduced more. Despite that, their mood and concentration remained positive and reserved.

At last, the group of contacts avoided the defenses of the last beacon barrier and lost no additional numbers. Without warning, the entire mass of invading vessels came to a dead stop. A radar analyst immediately reported it.

"Commander, all radar contacts have stopped just inside the inner beacon," he said with a hint of slightly heightened alarm.

The Defense Deputy-in-charge leaned in to address Rigella.

"Should we attack, Commander?" The Deputy asked nervously.

"No," Rigella answered immediately. "Tell our ships to stay on alert, but do not have them reveal their location or attack until I order it, if I order it. Understood?"

"Yes, Commander," the Deputy replied submissively.

Rigella then addressed the room as a whole.

"We will not jump into this headfirst like we are newly born amateurs just now learning of the multiverse," Rigella appropriately dictated. "We are Astraeans, and we will act as Astra..."

"Commander," interrupted a communications analyst. "We are receiving a request for communications from the lead contact."

Rigella looked at Elcyd, Mamdod and her friends quickly, not out of hesitation or to seek their input, but to silently tell them to prepare for whatever may happen in the next few moments.

"Accept the request," ordered Rigella.

"Yes, Commander. Channel established."

The massive primary display in the control center immediately flooded the room with extremely bright video that revealed the unexpected image of Azli, sitting in the command chair of the lead ship in what was apparently an Einarian attack fleet. Without instruction, the Defense Deputy assigned a magnified video feed of the attacking force as a whole, to a display on one side of the primary display. On the other side, a listing of ships and their configurations starting being outlined as the Harbor scanned them. Most of ships listed were small to medium fighters, hosted by their fewer, larger ships. The larger ships must have deployed the smaller ships at the outer beacon so as not to lose whole squadrons of the attacking force, in the event one of the larger ships was unable to escape the beacon protection barriers.

Rigella let her eyes slightly move to the left and right to size up what they were dealing with. Once she felt she had a good handle on the data, she looked back to the center display.

Azli sat on the edge of her chair, supporting herself slightly with one hand on the respective side of her chair. She looked fresh and eager. She was confident and ready to pounce. Rigella took the opportunity to speak first.

"Did you have any trouble on your way in?" Rigella asked flippantly, referring to the losses Azli's ships sustained at the outer beacons.

"We brought more than enough," Azli replied with an unaffected boredom. "Cute little protection net you have there," she added, referring to the beacon barriers.

The sight and sound of Azli was ripping Lannya's soul apart with teeth of rotten regret. Heersan gently grabbed and held her wrist as he saw the pain in Lannya's face. Lannya wanted to scream at Azli, but the tons of mangled thoughts in her head made a scramble of everything. She wouldn't know where to start. Instead, each thing she wanted to say was kept inside her heart and mind, and acted as individual pounds of salt on the open wound of her beloved and hated daughter.

"Enough for what, Azli?" Mamdod asked with

feigned ignorance.

"Ah, Mamdod!" she replied. Her face sprang to forced and exaggerated life. "We assumed you would be out and about. But here? You couldn't find something more, tropical, than the Harbor to spend your twilight years?"

"You're quite mistaken," Mamdod began to reply. "These are far from my or any of our twili..."

Azli shot out of her chair with a furious hate.

"SILENCE! THIS WILL BE YOUR, AND THE ASTRAEANS' FINAL SUNSET!" she screamed, with everything her throat could provide.

She wanted everyone to hear.

She wanted to hear nothing and no one else as she screamed.

Everyone would hear her.

No one would doubt her.

"YOUR END!" she added, sucking in a gulp of air between words.

Rigella took advantage of Azli's dramatic loss in composure to quickly tap a command into a terminal with as little movement as possible.

Prepare to attack at my command, she transmitted silently to her subordinates' terminals in the room.

Elcyd calmly posed the next question, without taking Azli's inflammatory bait.

"You've already killed Akal. Mamdod told us what happens next. Why are you here?"

Azli looked up and closed her eyes. She took a slow, deep breath and looked back to them.

"To kill the rest of you," she answered.

The control center began to stir a bit. She had

successfully injected a slight amount of doubt into the air. But Rigella wasn't having any of it.

"Isn't Einar going to be joining us?" Rigella asked, deliberately goading Azli on even more.

"Ah, ha! You know his new name!" Azli blasted in between condescending laughter. "So, you've discovered our friend, Dawel, I take it."

She began to walk back to her chair.

"It doesn't matter," Azli added as she sat back down. "He did his job, perfectly. He kept us apprised of your repairs and reconstruction from our first attack. You pacifist simpletons apparently thought we would just sit and wait while the leaves fell at the ribbon island. Are you kidding? How pompous!"

After a few more laughs, she had one final comment for them.

"No, no," she continued quietly. "We're thorough. We're going to kill you all, so that we can dispose of all of your bodies and souls in time for the party we're going to throw for Einar, and for freedom, on the roof of the Harbor!"

Quickly and softly, the communications channel went dead, just before a radar analyst erupted with an announcement.

"Radar contacts have resumed course at triple their original speed, straight for the Harbor," the analyst said.

"Well, hate to tell you, Azli, but Dawel was a terrible spy," Rigella quipped to her nearby friends. She then spun back around to her command console.

"When Azli's ships are in range of our long distance turrets, begin firing at will." Rigella ordered, with a strength that can only come from the throat of an Astraean. She was thriving on the readiness of her people, the ADF, and everyone involved in the defense of the Harbor. She was thriving on the excitement because she and every other Astraean had earned the excitement over being sufficiently prepared this time, for yet another, unprovoked attack.

"Tell our fleet to stay hidden behind the security curtain for as long as possible while positioning to flank Azli's ships," Rigella continued. "Once the turrets begin firing, deactivate the fabrication facility's security curtain and have the fleet engage and begin firing at will also. The Einarians will be soundly outmatched. They will have already been surprised by our new, extended range defense turrets as well. Overwhelm them, Astraeans. Best them. Defeat them."

Everyone snapped to it, performing their bits and pieces that led to the entire, well-orchestrated whole of the defense of the Harbor. Rigella scanned the room quickly to assess their performance. She smiled with pride as she then focused fiercely on some nearby peripheral displays where one was monitoring a video feed of the Einarian approach.

The ships advanced without resistance. If they had received better intelligence, she might have thought it suspicious, but they didn't. Azli thought the Harbor was low hanging fruit that would require little effort. She was about to learn whether or not she had assumed accurately.

It was almost time. Carthal, Heersan, Lannya, Elcyd, and Mamdod stood and sat in various positions of anxious anticipation and provided information or advice to any nearby engineers or ADF Officers that needed their assistance. The ADF Officers and engineers spoke only in succinct chunks of relevant defense communications between themselves. They all knew the plan, and were coordinating with all ADF forces. Everyone was ready. They were ready to execute. Rigella tapped a console and moved the video feed of the Einarian approach to the main, center display. Just as she did, it began.

The Harbor began to rumble with the relentless turret blasts, cycling and repeating, over and over. Just before the first volley of turret blasts reached Azli's ships, those in the control center saw the Astraean Defense Force's fleet reveal itself. Never before had their own fleet been seen like this before.

It was one of the most impressive sights the billion year-old beings had ever seen.

By this point, all turrets at all ranges were firing. The Astraean fleet, led by the stupefying Triangulum, was also firing. The smaller ships and their tens of thousands of fighters were all on the offensive as they started to engage. It took almost no time for Azli's forces to react.

"Commander, the Einarians have broken their formation. They seem to be trying to retreat," advised the Defense Deputy.

Rigella made no gesture, change in posture or exclamation. She had locked her mind down from everything except for the mission at hand. Elimination. Extermination. Merciless destruction.

"Order the Triangulum to remain at its current position just outside the inner-most beacon," Rigella's new set of orders began. She continued with her orders after referencing their list of currently activated vessels.

"Designate our carriers, battleships, cruisers and

frigates that have names beginning with Q through Z, as defense group A, and have them assume a protective posture around the Harbor. Have the remainder of our forces designated as attack group A and have them pursue the Einarians. If there are any Einarian forces remaining by the second to last beacon, have our forces request additional orders. Provide me with all updates as they're available from the attack group," instructed Rigella.

As Rigella gave her last order, Lannya jumped up out of her seat. Her face was drenched and crumbling with a frenzied paranoia. She looked at her friends, begging for help from someone on what to say, but nothing came. She didn't have to say anything though. They all knew what she was thinking. Before anyone could say anything, she started to sprint out of the room.

"Lannya! Wait!" Carthal shouted. He looked to Heersan and then Rigella.

"I can't go," Rigella said softly, unable and unwilling to leave before the entire Einarian threat was addressed. Everyone knew that Rigella couldn't leave. Heersan, however, had already stood up.

"You two go," Rigella suggested to her friends. "Keep her safe."

Before Lannya had even made it out of the room, Heersan and Carthal were already sprinting to try and catch up.

Lannya was flying across the floor, through corridors, and down steps. She had to get to Azli to at least try to talk to her. Any other plans were in the back of her mind, but they were there.

Carthal and Heersan were able to keep Lannya in

their sight for most of the time they were chasing after Lannya, and they knew where she was going. She was headed for Paige's secure dock. When Carthal saw her take a particular hall, he knew a quicker way that he hoped would allow them to catch up with her before she could leave on her own.

"Heersan, let's cut through the lobby to the spiral staircase under the Helper Desk," suggested Carthal, through spaced and huffed speech as they ran.

"Right!" Heersan confirmed.

They lost sight of Lannya, but they weren't worried. They split off from her and raced into the rarely barren lobby, and then through the Helper Desk, to the staircase in the middle. As they hit the stairs, they both leaned back slightly and put their feet up on the rails to quickly slide down the tall length of steps. When they reached the bottom, they came out at a corridor that led to a wide, side door that opened to a section of secure docks where Paige was moored. In an all-out sprint now, Carthal and Heersan saw Paige and reached her gangplank with no sign of Lannya. After another second, they crossed and climbed through a hatch, and then made their way to Paige's command deck.

Carthal and Heersan had used up every spare ounce of energy they had. While they waited for Lannya, they gladly collapsed onto the deck and rolled into walls in exhaustion. They clamored for air, breathing heavily from the sprint. Long before they had caught their breath, they heard a pair of panicked footsteps rapidly clawing up the stairs to the command deck.

Lannya, not as out of breath, came launching through the main hatch and saw her exhausted pair of friends. More annoyed than angry, she laughed as she addressed them.

"You two are getting out of shape," she jokingly observed.

"We're not," Carthal began before needing more air, "letting you go alone."

"This is something I need to do," Lannya quickly retorted. "I need to do this for me, and for Akal. This isn't a ride you two should be on."

Heersan, having mostly recovered now, reached over to a command terminal and quickly locked out Lannya's authorization codes. She jumped towards the terminal when she realized what he was doing, but it was too late.

"Let me go after her!" Lannya screamed through furious tears.

"You're not going without us!" Heersan shouted back. He wasn't going to back down. Lannya had long since passed beyond feeling like an outsider to their group, and Lannya felt the same way. Even if she didn't want to admit it, she loved them, and they loved her, and they were not going to let her go alone, just as they wouldn't have let Akal do something like this on his own.

Lannya's tears thinned, and her face relaxed in the realization that if she didn't agree, then her chances of catching up to Azli would decrease by the second. She looked up and gave in.

"Alright," she said through a broken inhale. "Let's go."

Heersan nodded and quickly tapped Lannya's code back into Paige's list of authorized operators.

"Paige, bypass systems check and perform emergency

departure procedure," Heersan commanded.

"After clearing the Harbor, Paige," Carthal began to add, "establish a link with the ADF control center radar to confirm position of the Einarian lead ship target as identified by the ADF and pursue at full speed."

Lannya affectionately squeezed Heersan's arm and reached to help Carthal up to his tired feet.

"Thank you," Lannya offered to both of them, sincerely and delicately.

Heersan smiled at her like she had been his sister for his soul's entire existence.

* * *

Paige, improved and modified, chased after Azli at full ribbon speed, to make up for the head start the fight had in front of them.

"What are you wanting to do if we catch up with her?" Carthal wondered.

Lannya looked around the deck, and out to the blurs of space.

"I don't know," she shouted so that she could be heard.

Heersan glimpsed to Paige's radar which up until then had been clear.

"We're starting to catch up to some of them," he said, as he looked up to Carthal and then Lannya.

"Do you see Azli's ship yet?" Lannya asked with a thick anxiety.

"No, not yet," Heersan replied.

The silence passed in a tangible tenseness as they sailed deeper and deeper into the battle.

"There she is!" Carthal shouted. "Paige! Lock onto

your radar target OTJ-9 and move to intercept!"

Carthal and Heersan moved to the command deck rail, waiting for Paige to close in on Azli's ship. While they waited, Lannya slipped quietly over to a command terminal.

Her friends didn't notice. Paige grew closer and closer to Azli's ship as they trained their sight on the ship and the surrounding battle. Carthal assisted his fellow Astraeans by firing shots at some of Einar's remaining forces from one of Paige's deck guns. Heersan remained focused on Paige's approach and shield condition. Just before they both started to leave the command deck to go below and prepare for intercepting Azli and to board her ship, they began to lose feeling of their forms.

Lannya had activated the command deck ribbon pad. Before they could react, Lannya used the ribbon pad to send Carthal and Heersan to an ADF carrier adjacent to Paige. She then used the terminal to remove their command authorizations so they couldn't immediately plot a return.

"Lannya!" Carthal shouted after they landed. His anger however, was snuffed out quickly in the vast black vacuum of multispace.

Heersan pounded the carrier's nearest terminal, and rushed to open a public communications channel with Paige.

"Lannya!" he began. "Don't do this! We'll do it together! If anything happens to you..."

Lannya interrupted with a stubborn finality. She had decided on her plan the moment she sprinted from the Harbor control center.

"I told you," she started, with a grated and pained voice. "I need to do this on my own."

Heersan and Carthal could do nothing but helplessly watch as Lannya disappeared into a spec, indistinguishable from the countless other specs in the blackness. Lannya was on a path she craved being on more than anything else at that moment, so, despite their best efforts, Heersan and Carthal stepped away from the carrier's terminal and stopped fighting her wishes.

After Lannya had long been lost in the expansive sea of distant multispace, Carthal and Heersan reluctantly let go of their sight on the spot Rigella flew away towards, and disappeared into. They examined their surroundings and identified the carrier they were on so they could make themselves known and assist with the remaining fight around them. The two pivoted reluctantly to locate a member of the carrier's crew, but Heersan couldn't help but look back one final time to see if Lannya had indeed disappeared from sight. Seeing no change on the horizon, he turned back and joined back up with Carthal.

Chapter XXV
Universe CG

There weren't really any meaningful options left for Azli. She and the remnants of her forces were entirely on the defensive. Azli was in absolute survival mode. She knew it and the Astraeans knew it.

Many of Einar's secrets were beginning to be unraveled. The biggest one being that he even existed, in the capacity that he existed. Mamdod had solved that, despite being the reason it was a secret to begin with. The Astraean technologies were modernized and improved. Some of the Einarian technologies had been matched, their power had been equaled, or in some very significant ways, they had been surpassed. The ADF was nothing short of a miraculously timed boon to their effort. There was only one primary piece of information remaining for the Astraeans to obtain. Einar's location. And as Lannya temporarily claimed Page as her own and continued after

Azli, she had every intention of getting Einar's location, one way or another.

Keep on running, Lannya thought. *I'll be ready for you when you stop.*

She leaned over Paige's top rail and attempted to squeeze it in anticipation. Her palms creaked from the friction. The recent advancements in tracking and radar technologies were already proving their worth. Previously, souls traveling in ribbon energy could not be tracked reliably, but now Lannya was able to follow Azli easily and accurately. Lannya's chest throbbed with adrenaline. She didn't know how the impending confrontation would end, but she was craving it. She was consumed with absolute lust for the fight.

She squeezed the rail again and then punched a command into the nearest command terminal, opening a one-way communications current with Azli.

"I'll track you all over this multiverse, Azli, and I'll be ready for you wherever you stop!"

As soon as she finished her threat to Azli, Lannya closed the communications ribbon and launched a flux torpedo directly for Azli's ship. Almost immediately, the torpedo flawlessly tracked and disintegrated Azli's ship, forcing Azli to continue her escape in spiritual form only. As Lannya instinctively ducked to avoid the incoming debris, despite being protected by Paige's shields, she launched another torpedo. This time, Lannya fired a ribbon cage which again tracked successfully, and enveloped Azli's soul in a cocoon of sorts, that blocked her ability to send communications of her own, or manipulate her form while inside the ribbon at that moment.

Now, I just have to wait you out, daughter. I'm ready when you are, Lannya thought calmly.

She didn't squeeze the rail this time. She stepped back from the rail and stood at ease. She took as deep a breath as she could. Not from confidence or arrogance, but to calm herself down. One hand held the other. As Lannya's eyes glazed over, transfixed on the blur of Azli's spirit racing through the ribbons ahead of Paige, she steadied herself like a boulder in the smallest of creeks. Every ounce of her body's mass felt like the weight of the largest planet. She was centering and collecting herself. Like the racing rapids flying by a stone that splits them, her past lives raced through and around her mind and soul. She was ready to call upon any of them to combat Azli. But she looked beyond Azli to find even more focus. Her goal was not to defeat Azli. Her goal was to get information to lead her to Einar. Azli was just another unearthed and rough rock in the stream.

Azli made an odd turn, and then another strange turn. She went to obscure ribbon intersections and started to arbitrarily make changes in her path, or she would double-back on herself. She was trying to lose Lannya.

It wasn't happening. Paige had no issue keeping up, and Lannya stood expressionless on the top of the command deck as she waited for Azli to quit wasting her time. But the thought finally broke the cold composure of Lannya's stoic skin. She smirked at the thought of having her time wasted. She had plenty of time.

But she didn't, really. They only had a few more months until the leaves finished falling at the ribbon island. Her smirk didn't last long. Lannya stepped for the terminal as she began to think of what she could do to force the issue of making Azli stop, but before she could think of what to do, Azli took another sharp turn onto a ribbon with no additional branches or intersections. The realization of where Azli was headed shot Lannya with a cold wave of fear. The confidence and focus she had just spent so much time accumulating and collecting, were eroded.

This was the narrow, long and mostly avoided ribbon to Universe CG. One of the oldest universes, it was also the absolute largest universe. And for good reason.

Universe CG is like most other universes in the sense that within it, there are stars, planets, black holes, and so on. But, Universe CG is the only known universe that contains intelligent beings made up of the various astronomical phenomena. There is a level of sentience at the galactic level. Universe CG, (or cognizant galaxies), contains races of intelligent, galactic beings, made up of entire star systems.

The Astraeans have had very little interaction with Universe CG because of the sheer scale and implications of interacting with the intelligence of CG. Just like any other universe, the galaxies in CG have life, and disturbing the natural progression of an intelligent galaxy would affect the life and progression of practically countless lifeforms and events. Because of this, Astraeans have always had an immeasurable amount of respect for CG and left it largely alone.

That's where Azli was headed.

Lannya absolutely did not want to confront Azli there. The thought of causing any harm to millions of planets, their histories, and the trillions and trillions of inhabitants, made her eyes water out of fear and panic. As she began spamming Paige's nearest console with hasty commands, the fear wasn't from a possible fight with Azli, but only for concern for those living in CG.

Attempting to attack a spirit while it was inside a ribbon was mostly worthless. The currents made it extremely hard for the attacker to aim, and the potential for souls to dodge and weave increased the difficulty exponentially. But now that Lannya saw where Azli was headed, she had to try.

First, she tried conventional weapons of various types with various payloads. They shot out of Paige's hull one after the other. Dozens, hundreds at a time shot out and exploded at various types, depending on the technology, or tracked for a while before exploding without finding their target. Many exploded out ahead of Paige, but many were too close and violently shook the ship.

Next, Lannya tried ribbon energy fluxes of various types to disturb Azli's path, or the energy ahead of her. These weren't successful either. They either didn't find their target once again, or Azli was able to play slalom with the attacks and weave in and out of their disturbances.

Finally, Lannya tried launching many forms of space charges. These are similar to depth charges used in the seas of Earth to damage submarines. Again, these were easily avoided. Lannya was attempting to more accurately anticipate Azli's speed adjustments and navigation of the ribbon, but Azli was too slippery.

She was out of time. They were within seconds of crossing the threshold into Universe CG.

"Paige, cease all attacks! Come to an emergency stop at 1 on my reverse count. 5, 4, 3, 2, 1!"

By "3" Paige had already crossed into the outermost universe membrane of Universe CG. At "1" Paige went from full soul ribbon speed to zero.

Lannya had prepared by climbing to the top rail of the command deck. When Paige stopped, Lannya was slung forward through space, and like the most serene, yet predatory bird, Lannya dove majestically into the bit of remaining ribbon. With only a sip of time to think before shooting out from the end of the ribbon, Lannya could no longer could think about Einar being the end goal of this chase. She had to unleash everything on Azli. She had to have no remorse or compassion for any inhabitants of Universe CG. Only then could she defeat Azli and rewind time to reverse the destruction they were about to cause. This was not going to be a fight just between mother and daughter. This was senseless devastation, for absolutely no reason but for Azli's perpetual hate for her parents, and her unqualified belief that they had abandoned her. These hateful blinders that Azli wore, clouded her soul with Einar's contorted lies of promised freedom.

Lannya emerged from the ribbon. Her initial core essence first emerged not as her human Lannya form, but as the beginnings of a spiral galaxy that rapidly and exponentially grew and swirled into an intoxicating wreath of bright life and energy. Her CG form sprouted branches brought together by the sinew of cosmic debris, then quickly stars, and subsequent nebulae. These branches were many and of various lengths and patterns, made of black holes, comets, asteroid belts and planets. As Lannya's galactic form seemed to finish assuming its final size, a particularly long and delicate branch could be seen to circle around and hurl a wealth of entire solar systems at the galactic entity that Azli had assumed. This first, initial attack took what non-Astraean humans would interpret as hundreds of millions of years. To the majority of civilizations that came and went down below on the planets of Lannya's galaxy, this galactic attack was never noticed.

Azli most closely resembled the form of an E-Zero elliptical galaxy. It was large and broad and emitted a predominantly dull and malicious red color. From Lannya's point of view, Azli's dense and bumpy galaxy throbbed in beefy irritation. Azli shot forth billions of miles worth of asteroid belt rings to meet Lannya's attack. Over the course of a billion Earth years, these asteroid rings chewed up and neutralized Lannya's barrage of stars and planets.

The amount of galactic materials slung, thrown and flung between Azli and Lannya increased. The fight escalated quickly with Lannya showing less and less regard for what she was using as weapons. Much to the ignorance of the inhabitants, creatures, and histories of millions of planets, they were merely ants on rocks being thrown in a war between galactic gods. Their accomplishments and struggles meant nothing. They were nothing. They were merely bullets in a cosmic rifle.

Within only minutes on the galactic time scale, black holes had feasted hundreds of times over, and thousands of stars had been made to prematurely go nova in a form of timed delay throughout the attack. Millions of planets became worthless projectiles being spit here and there at the opponent.

Just as the fight between Azli and Lannya began to hit its stride, other cognizant galaxies started to take notice and show interest. Instantly recognized as outsiders causing alien destruction to their universe, the indigenous galaxies teamed up and began attacking Azli and Lannya.

Some galaxies seemed to collide or team up and use their collective black holes to suck up portions of Azli's and Lannya's galaxies. From throughout Universe CG, the galaxies seemed to jump and launch themselves at Azli and Lannya with their walls of black holes causing hunks of the trespassers to disappear like pitch black fly traps.

Other indigenous defenders would form funnels from their various planetary, asteroid, and meteor debris to concentrate the light from millions of their stars into various areas of Azli and Lannya, to either blind various parts of their galaxies, or to burn them. Some of the defending galaxies could also be seen grabbing onto other entire galaxies, and using them as something akin to cosmic shuriken, and throwing them at Azli and Lannya, hoping to substantially harm and disable entire portions of their galaxies.

While Azli and Lannya had both become more defensive, they were still carrying on their attacks on each other, though drastically reduced. Azli, however, was having a harder time maintaining her attack on Lannya. Lannya was more coordinated and calm. Where she would dodge attacks or return volleys of planets or asteroid belts and slip in a few attacks on Azli in between, Azli was unable to return attacks as often. Lannya began to move in closer to Azli.

When it seemed that enough distance had been closed to warrant hand-to-hand, or, galaxy-to-galaxy combat, Azli visibly began to retreat. Her galactic form began to condense and shrink. Lannya repulsed attacks from the indigenous galaxies but continued to press in on Azli. Lannya matched her movement for movement and watched her intently.

Lannya didn't know what to expect or what Azli had planned. When Azli's galactic form had condensed to roughly the size of a small solar system, Lannya saw Azli abandon her galactic form. Lannya watched as Azli's soul vaulted to a mangled ribbon and shot down to the surface of a nearby planet. Lannya immediately did the same and followed her.

They both arrived within eyesight of each other on the surface of the planet. Azli was weak, but was crawling quickly along the ground in an attempt to hide behind some nearby brush. Between having to evade Lannya in the ribbon, and from not being as coordinated during her attacks and defenses in galactic form, she was absolutely exhausted. Lannya stomped quickly towards her.

Lannya approached Azli without fanfare and stood over her. She had complete control of the situation.

Azli collapsed on her back, into the dark green clay of the planet and looked over her mother's shoulder into the unobstructed and star-filled night sky. She gasped for air in her human form. And while her vision from her galactic form was quickly diminishing to her human sight, she could still see some of the last moments of their previous fight coming to a close. Because of the remaining galactic inertia, a planet slammed into another, high above them in space, and obliterated each other to dust and sand. Azli then focused on Lannya.

"That was fun," Azli said flatly. Her throat was

dry, and her voice was accordingly low. She huffed a raspy chuckle and summoned a ribbon.

Lannya gave her a look as if being offended she'd so stupidly try to call a ribbon. In the millisecond it took for the ribbon to appear, she had already thrown a ribbon scrambling device at Azli which attached to her boot. She then followed it up with a ribbon energy restraint device. Azli wasn't changing forms or going anywhere.

"You lost," Lannya spit out quickly with as much intentional condescension as possible.

Through her heavy breathing, Azli's chin dropped and her eyes narrowed with hate.

"Please," Azli hatefully pleaded. "Don't waste my time. I'm not going to give you or tell you anything. The Astraeans have judged the multiverse long enough!"

Lannya allowed herself to feel for the first time since before the chase began. Her eyes instantly blurred from tears. Her throat hardened and her soul flushed with helplessness. She had defeated Azli in combat, but failed at winning her heart back.

"Everything I am as an Astraean is dying. I have no idea why you think of us as judges. Whoever has made you think that has enslaved you, and you don't even realize it."

"Shut up! I say, you say... It doesn't matter!" Azli shouted and spitted. "Shut up! Enough!"

Lannya's tears stopped, though her face was still glistening. She wouldn't allow any more to fall for Azli's benefit.

"I would have done anything to get you back." Lannya's voice cracked as she forced her voice to extract the sounds from her sadness. "I would let these worlds burn and die in abysmal horror if it meant I could have my daughter back."

The inertia of their previous battle high in space had not yet come to a halt. Additional planets could be seen colliding into each other. Stars combined into fiery explosions and waves of light. The planet Azli and Lannya were on was heading for a collision of its own. The planet they were careening towards was growing close, and claiming more and more of the space visible from the surface.

"You were the only thing I've ever given my complete heart to, before I even saw your face," Lannya continued. Her eyes had begun releasing the pain. "I never cared about who was in charge of the ribbon island, or what they did, I just wanted the love of my daughter."

Lannya fell to her knees, oblivious to, or emotionless about the approaching collision. Consumed by apathy towards the fate of this galaxy and its inhabitants, her regret for her part in the failures between her and Akal, and now the failure to win back her daughter's love, Lannya felt nothing. She let her mind and soul drift to blackness.

Azli started to struggle inside her restraint, the small amount that she could.

She began to speak, but the restraint also heavily muffled sounds coming from within it.

Lannya's despair was not interrupted.

If the planet they were on collided with the other, and caused their deaths or unconsciousness, neither of them would be able to rewind time and reverse the eons of destruction they had caused. But only one of them even had the ability to do that. In the chaos, both Lannya and

Azli had forgotten that the ability for Astraeans to rewind time had been severed. Everything Lannya had feared at the outset of the fight with Azli was about to come true.

Lannya's eyes continued burning a hole into the green clay of the planet's surface while Azli began to squirm more in hopes of catching Lannya's attention. Azli licked her lips and swallowed in hopes of strengthening her voice just enough for Lannya to hear her. Very faintly, with fear pushing Azli's voice beyond pain, a bit of sound finally began to escape the ribbon restraint.

"Mom," could finally be heard from outside the restraint, though Lannya was still unaffected. Her preoccupation with her losses and failures was still too strong. Azli's voice began to find more and more strength as the fear inside her grew more powerful. The fear, however, was evolving. What began as a personal fear was beginning to transition into a compassionate fear shared by her mother. She didn't want all the beings of this universe to suffer the permanent fate she had brought upon them.

Azli was now screaming as loudly as she could from inside the restraint. Her voice started to be overcome with shrill and indistinguishable overtones of panic. Her restraint began to show more signs of movement as Azli slung herself back and forth against the soft cocoon that she was enveloped in. But even though it was soft, she dislocated her shoulder from how violently she was struggling inside to get her mother's attention.

Lannya's obsessive nothingness wavered slightly and began to let the outside world in. Just as the planet they were on collided with the other, Lannya's focus shifted to Azli. Lannya was no longer oblivious to Azli, but she was still temporarily oblivious to the mammoth plumes of debris the planetary collision was shooting into the sky. There were only seconds until they became affected by the collision and the threat of being destroyed.

"MOM!" Lannya finally heard Azli scream in terror. There was no mistaking what was said or how it was said. This was a scream of fear, apology, regret and love, all kneaded into one dough of desperate concession.

"Rewind it, rewind it!" Azli begged, with her shouting being scraped with scratches of sorrow.

With a slapping sting, the recollection that Einar had blocked the Astraeans from rewinding time penetrated both of their minds. But the sting quickly subsided for Lannya. She wouldn't have even if she was able.

Lannya looked over her shoulder. Her face drooped in meaningless finality. Instead of staring the impending obliteration down until it reached them, however, she whipped back around and scrambled on her hands and knees over to Azli and shouted to her.

"If you want it rewound, you'll have to do it!"

The ground was breaking, and cracking, and falling away into the surrounding gravitational maelstrom. Swirls of dirt, rock, and fire danced around the mother and her daughter. The waves and avalanches of churning material grew closer and closer.

Lannya's fingers then flew through a combination code on the outer border of the restraint, followed by the same thing with the ribbon scrambling device. Azli was free.

The time had almost passed.

"Let it hit," Lannya shouted at Azli. "Let it come."

Her face was empty and beaten down.

Just as the harbinger of ruination from the planetary collision was upon them, both Lannya and Azli were wrapped in ribbon energy. Through the barely transparent ribbon walls, they watched as their galactic fight rewound through time. The histories of the innumerable planets involved in their war took place again. Heroes were anointed and evil menaces were once more destroyed in the lifespan of whole cultures and civilizations. The unaware creatures and beings of Universe CG were allowed to live again and experience the wonders of existence. Civilizations came and went, technologies were created and neglected. Belief was believed, disavowed, and then believed again. Thought was forgotten, and then remembered.

Lannya wrenched the rail of Paige's top command deck. She was back on the ship before the fight. Out ahead of her was a motionless and undisturbed ribbon, just before she crossed the threshold into Universe CG. It instantly bubbled to the top of her head that she hadn't rewound time, and that Azli must have. She stretched her neck to examine the ribbon out in front of Paige once more in search of Azli's whereabouts. Instinctively, she then spun around. Azli stood there before her, but not for long. Even weaker now, Azli crumbled to the cold steel decking, catching herself at the last minute as her palms slapped down to the ground. Tears fell from her face and reflected shimmers of light as they struck the floor. She raised her head slowly and locked aching eyes with her mother.

Lannya wasn't emotional. In fact, her face was noticeably less oppressed, and depressed. She looked upon Azli for the first time that she could remember, as a daughter, rather than an enemy. After walking over to a navigation terminal, Lannya keyed in a command. The navigation terminal read, Destination: Harbor.

As Paige came about and started off for the Harbor at a moderate speed, Lannya returned to Azli and met her on the floor of the command deck. She sat silently and looked her daughter over for wounds. Next, she didn't really understand why, but she began looking her clothes over for wear and tear. When she came across a cut in one of Azli's sleeves, she reached up and felt the frayed split with her fingertips, thinking of a thousand ways to mend it. Finally, she looked up to Azli's face which was wrinkled in curious affection.

Lannya reached up and slid her cupped hand down across Azli's cheek. Lannya's hand then found its way to Azli's arm as she helped her come to her feet. And at that exact moment, Lannya didn't know exactly what would happen once they reached the Harbor, but for now, she simply guided Azli to the top deck and placed her hand on the rail. Lannya and her daughter stared quietly, and peacefully, out into the waves of the ribbon racing along beneath them.

Epilogue

Lannya played the sound over and over again in her head. She couldn't recall any other previous time when Azli called her "mom." It was the only thing in her heart and mind at that moment. Her daughter sat next to her while Paige sped on, and while she listened on. She listened on to the repeated track of being called "mom," in her mind.

Occasionally, a hysteria of unknowns would try to break through and steal Lannya's concentration. The countless hypothetical scenarios of what may happen with Azli when they got back to the Harbor were ardently demanding attention, but Lannya kept them at bay for a long while. She kept those thoughts, and the burdens of life, space and time, at bay. At that moment, she just wanted to be a mom, and sit next to her daughter.

She had gotten what she wished for. Lannya's dream had come true. But the sweat of consequences quickly began to accumulate on her brow as those scenarios of reality beat on her mental door, louder and harder.

Lannya answered her brain's bullying by looking at Azli and smiling. Azli didn't see her. She was resting up against a support column, and wrapped in a blanket with her eyes closed. She was as weary of existence as Lannya was at the moment, it seemed. She was just resting.

Lannya's smile was a present to herself.

Shortly after they got underway, Lannya typed and sent a brief, encrypted message to the ADF Harbor Sentinels. She wanted to apprise them of the situation, but had no desire to get into a lengthy conversation with anyone:

> *Returning to Harbor under no duress, with Azli. Have reason to believe she will surrender. Request to be met by Rigella and Harbor Sentinels on our arrival. Proper security measures have been taken.*

When she sent the message, Lannya included with it, a ribbon watermark for the Harbor to confirm the legitimacy and authenticity of the message. The particular watermark used, also indicated that the message should be taken at face value, with no hidden codes or messages to indicate anything other than what was transmitted.

While still smiling at the image of a restful daughter in front of her, Lannya started to let curiosity over how her message was received, encroach deeper and deeper into her thoughts.

Upon noticing the flashing proximity light indicating they were approaching the Harbor's outermost beacon, her smile loosened. Lannya also noticed next to the beacon proximity light, a pending transmission light. She was sure the Harbor wanted to discuss her message in detail as soon as possible, but she knew plenty of opportunity for discussion would come. She let her eyes blur while she watched both of the flickering lights flash at different intervals, to the point their rhythms matched up, just to quickly fall back out of sync.

Lannya had tuned out Paige's beacon announcements, but the sound must have disturbed Azli. She began to stir.

Lannya forced a blink and gestured for Azli to stay seated if she wished. She then stood up and approached one of Paige's rails to watch Paige begin her automated docking procedures, but Lannya was quickly confused. Paige wasn't automatically steering to the lower dome's secure docks. Someone at the Harbor had modified Paige's course. Instead of the lower dome, Paige was headed for one of the most exposed and accessible piers out in front of the main Harbor complex. Paige then randomly announced that the weapons systems had gone offline and that the tactical fighter bay had been secured.

"Well, that's interesting," Lannya muttered with a smooth concern.

Azli joined her mother at the rail, still exhausted, and still wrapped in her blanket.

After sailing over the last structure that poses the final obstruction of the view of the main set of docks and piers, a startling sight popped into their view.

As Paige slid down the last bit of ribbon to the pier she would be moored at, Azli and Lannya saw it. The entire defense group that had stayed behind, had taken a hybrid defensive-offensive posture, flanking the upper Harbor dome, and facing Paige as she arrived. Part of the attack group had returned, and had fallen into formation as well, with the remaining, smaller portion of the attack group proceeding on to Ontelbar, to make good on the Astraeans' promise of relief and protection. In the immediate space between Paige and the larger ADF ships, were squadron after squadron of fighter drones.

Below on the docks, was a sizable combination of ribbon infantry, ADF Harbor Sentinels, and ADF Guardian infantry. The turrets on the roof of the upper dome that had a clear line of sight, also had their barrels trained on the arriving ship. As Paige came to a rest, Lannya could just make out the harsh postures of Rigella, Elcyd, Mamdod, Carthal and Heersan, grouped together in front of the massive ADF representation.

Lannya started to have second thoughts about not checking the message attached to the flashing light as she looked at it again. It must have been a request for more information, or someone wanting to let Lannya know what precautions would be taken when they returned. It was too late now. It didn't matter what the message said.

Azli looked to Lannya and waited for her to look back. She soon did. Azli was intimidated by what she saw, and Lannya could tell. There was no sense of malice or anger in Azli's face, and she wasn't afraid. She was just once again surprised, this time by the imposing proximity of the display of Astraean power. Azli was ready to face what was ahead of her. She was ready when she decided to rewind time in Universe CG. Her heart had released most of its hate, and that made her precarious future slightly less unnerving.

Thank you for buying *Games of Astraeus*! I truly do hope you were able to find something to enjoy.